NINE STORIES BY "ONE OF THE GREAT MAKERS OF SCIENCE FICTION"

JACK WILLIAMSON

All the Traps of Earth—A six-hundred-year-old robot tries to remain himself.

Good Night, Mr. James—An alien psychologist wakes up to discover there are two of him.

Drop Dead—A strange planet where death is only the beginning.

No Life of Their Own—What happens when the melting pot includes aliens and halflings.

The Sitters—Alien baby sitters have strange effects on the kids.

Crying Jag—Wilburn, an alien, has an amazing cure for peoples' troubles.

Installment Plan—A ruthless trading company deceptively promises the Garsonians immortality for valuable *podar* plants.

Condition of Employment—There is only one thing that enables pilots to withstand the brutal effects of space travel.

Project Mastodon—Three men come to Washington, D.C.—from 150,000 years ago.

All The Traps Of Earth

CLIFFORD D. SIMAK

AVON
PUBLISHERS OF BARD, CAMELOT AND DISCUS BOOKS

All of the characters in this book are fictitious, and any resemblance to actual persons, living or dead, is purely coincidental.

AVON BOOKS
A division of
The Hearst Corporation
959 Eighth Avenue
New York, New York 10019

Cover illustration by Jan Esteves

First Avon Printing, August, 1979

Printed in the U.S.A.

TABLE OF CONTENTS

All The Traps
Of Earth

ALL THE TRAPS OF EARTH

THE inventory list was long. On its many pages, in his small and precise script, he had listed furniture, paintings, china, silverware and all the rest of it—all the personal belongings that had been accumulated by the Barringtons through a long family history.

And now that he had reached the end of it, he noted down himself, the last item of them all:

One domestic robot, Richard Daniel, antiquated but in good repair.

He laid the pen aside and shuffled all the inventory sheets together and stacked them in good order, putting a paper weight upon them—the little exquisitely carved ivory paper weight that Aunt Hortense had picked up that last visit she had made to Peking.

And having done that, his job came to an end.

He shoved back the chair and rose from the desk and slowly walked across the living room, with all its clutter of possessions from the family's past. There, above the mantel, hung the sword that ancient Jonathon had worn in the War Between the States, and below it, on the mantel-piece itself, the cup the Commodore had won with his valiant yacht, and the jar of moon-dust that Tony had brought back from Man's fifth landing on the Moon, and the old chronometer that had come from the long-scrapped family spacecraft that had plied the asteroids.

And all around the room, almost cheek by jowl, hung the family portraits, with the old dead faces staring out into the world that they had helped to fashion.

And not a one of them from the last six hundred years, thought Richard Daniel, staring at them one by one, that he had not known.

1

There, to the right of the fireplace, old Rufus Andrew
Barrington, who had been a judge some two hundred years
ago. And to the right of Rufus, Johnson Joseph Barrington,
who had headed up that old lost dream of mankind, the
Bureau of Paranormal Research. There, beyond the door
that led out to the porch, was the scowling pirate face of
Danley Barrington, who had first built the family fortune.

And many others—administrator, adventurer, corporation chief. All good men and true.

But this was at an end. The family had run out.

Slowly Richard Daniel began his last tour of the house
—the family room with its cluttered living space, the den
with its old mementos, the library and its rows of ancient
books, the dining hall in which the crystal and the china
shone and sparkled, the kitchen gleaming with the copper
and aluminum and the stainless steel, and the bedrooms
on the second floor, each of them with its landmarks of
former occupants. And finally, the bedroom where old
Aunt Hortense had finally died, at long last closing out the
line of Barringtons.

The empty dwelling held a not-quite-haunted quality,
the aura of a house that waited for the old gay life to take
up once again. But it was a false aura. All the portraits,
all the china and the silverware, everything within the
house would be sold at public auction to satisfy the debts.
The rooms would be stripped and the possessions would
be scattered and, as a last indignity, the house itself be
sold.

Even he, himself, Richard Daniel thought, for he was
chattel, too. He was there with all the rest of it, the final
item on the inventory.

Except that what they planned to do with him was
worse than simple sale. For he would be changed before
he was offered up for sale. No one would be interested in
putting up good money for him as he stood. And, besides,
there was the law—the law that said no robot could legally
have continuation of a single life greater than a hundred
years. And he had lived in a single life six times a hundred
years.

He had gone to see a lawyer and the lawyer had been
sympathetic, but had held forth no hope.

"Technically," he had told Richard Daniel in his short,
clipped lawyer voice, "you are at this moment much in

violation of the statute. I completely fail to see how your family got away with it."

"They liked old things," said Richard Daniel. "And, besides, I was very seldom seen. I stayed mostly in the house. I seldom ventured out."

"Even so," the lawyer said, "there are such things as records. There must be a file on you . . ."

"The family," explained Richard Daniel, "in the past had many influential friends. You must understand, sir, that the Barringtons, before they fell upon hard times, were quite prominent in politics and in many other matters."

The lawyer grunted knowingly.

"What I can't quite understand," he said, "is why you should object so bitterly. You'll not be changed entirely. You'll still be Richard Daniel."

"I would lose my memories, would I not?"

"Yes, of course you would. But memories are not too important. And you'd collect another set."

"My memories are dear to me," Richard Daniel told him. "They are all I have. After some six hundred years, they are my sole worthwhile possession. Can you imagine, counselor, what it means to spend six centuries with one family?"

"Yes, I think I can," agreed the lawyer. "But now, with the family gone, isn't it just possible the memories may prove painful?"

"They're a comfort. A sustaining comfort. They make me feel important. They give me perspective and a niche."

"But don't you understand? You'll need no comfort, no importance once you're reoriented. You'll be brand new. All that you'll retain is a certain sense of basic identity— *that* they cannot take away from you even if they wished. There'll be nothing to regret. There'll be no leftover guilts, no frustrated aspirations, no old loyalties to hound you."

"I must be myself," Richard Daniel insisted stubbornly. "I've found a depth of living, a background against which my living has some meaning. I could not face being anybody else."

"You'd be far better off," the lawyer said wearily. "You'd have a better body. You'd have better mental tools. You'd be more intelligent."

Richard Daniel got up from the chair. He saw it was no use.

"You'll not inform on me?" he asked.

"Certainly not," the lawyer said. "So far as I'm concerned, you aren't even here."

"Thank you," said Richard Daniel. "How much do I owe you?"

"Not a thing," the lawyer told him. "I never make a charge to anyone who is older than five hundred."

He had meant it as a joke, but Richard Daniel did not smile. He had not felt like smiling.

At the door he turned around.

"Why?" he was going to ask. "Why this silly law?"

But he did not have to ask—it was not hard to see.

Human vanity, he knew. No human being lived much longer than a hundred years, so neither could a robot. But a robot, on the other hand, was too valuable simply to be junked at the end of a hundred years of service, so there was this law providing for the periodic breakup of the continuity of each robot's life. And thus no human need undergo the psychological indignity of knowing that his faithful serving man might manage to outlive him by several thousand years.

It was illogical, but humans were illogical.

Illogical, but kind. Kind in many different ways.

Kind, sometimes, as the Barringtons had been kind, thought Richard Daniel. Six hundred years of kindness. It was a prideful thing to think about. They had even given him a double name. There weren't many robots nowadays who had double names. It was a special mark of affection and respect.

The lawyer having failed him, Richard Daniel had sought another source of help. Now, thinking back on it, standing in the room where Hortense Barrington had died, he was sorry that he'd done it. For he had embarrassed the religico almost unendurably. It had been easy for the lawyer to tell him what he had. Lawyers had the statutes to determine their behavior, and thus suffered little from agonies of personal decision.

But a man of the cloth is kind if he is worth his salt. And this one had been kind instinctively as well as professionally, and that had made it worse.

"Under certain circumstances," he had said somewhat awkwardly, "I could counsel patience and humility and prayer. Those are three great aids to anyone who is willing to put them to his use. But with you I am not certain."

"You mean," said Richard Daniel, "because I am a robot."

"Well, now . . ." said the minister, considerably befuddled at this direct approach.

"Because I have no soul?"

"Really," said the minister miserably, "you place me at a disadvantage. You are asking me a question that for centuries has puzzled and bedeviled the best minds in the church."

"But one," said Richard Daniel, "that each man in his secret heart must answer for himself."

"I wish I could," cried the distraught minister. "I truly wish I could."

"If it is any help," said Richard Daniel, "I can tell you that sometimes I suspect I have a soul."

And that, he could see, had been most upsetting for this kindly human. It had been, Richard Daniel told himself, unkind of him to say it. For it must have been confusing, since coming from himself it was not opinion only, but expert evidence.

So he had gone away from the minister's study and come back to the empty house to get on with his inventory work.

Now that the inventory was all finished and the papers stacked where Dancourt, the estate administrator, could find them when he showed up in the morning, Richard Daniel had done his final service for the Barringtons and now must begin doing for himself.

He left the bedroom and closed the door behind him and went quietly down the stairs and along the hallway to the little cubby, back of the kitchen, that was his very own.

And that, he reminded himself with a rush of pride, was of a piece with his double name and his six hundred years. There were not too many robots who had a room, however small, that they might call their own.

He went into the cubby and turned on the light and closed the door behind him.

And now, for the first time, he faced the grim reality of what he meant to do.

The cloak and hat and trousers hung upon a hook and the galoshes were placed precisely underneath them. His attachment kit lay in one corner of the cubby and the money was cached underneath the floor board he had loosened many years ago to provide a hiding place.

There was, he told himself, no point in waiting. Every minute counted. He had a long way to go and he must be at his destination before morning light.

He knelt on the floor and pried up the loosened board, shoved in a hand and brought out the stacks of bills, money hidden through the years against a day of need.

There were three stacks of bills, neatly held together by elastic bands—money given him throughout the years as tips and Christmas gifts, as birthday presents and rewards for little jobs well done.

He opened the storage compartment located in his chest and stowed away all the bills except for half a dozen which he stuffed into a pocket in one hip.

He took the trousers off the hook and it was an awkward business, for he'd never worn clothes before except when he'd tried on these very trousers several days before. It was a lucky thing, he thought, that long-dead Uncle Michael had been a portly man, for otherwise the trousers never would have fit.

He got them on and zippered and belted into place, then forced his feet into the overshoes. He was a little worried about the overshoes. No human went out in the summer wearing overshoes. But it was the best that he could do. None of the regular shoes he'd found in the house had been nearly large enough.

He hoped no one would notice, but there was no way out of it. Somehow or other, he had to cover up his feet, for if anyone should see them, they'd be a giveaway.

He put on the cloak and it was a little short. He put on the hat and it was slightly small, but he tugged it down until it gripped his metal skull and that was all to the good, he told himself; no wind could blow it off.

He picked up his attachments—a whole bag full of them that he'd almost never used. Maybe it was foolish to take them along, he thought, but they were a part of him and by rights they should go with him. There was so little that he really owned—just the money he had saved, a dollar at a time, and this kit of his.

With the bag of attachments clutched underneath his arm, he closed the cubby door and went down the hall.

At the big front door he hesitated and turned back toward the house, but it was, at the moment, a simple darkened cave, empty of all that it once had held. There was nothing here to stay for—nothing but the memories, and the memories he took with him.

He opened the door and stepped out on the stoop and closed the door behind him.

And now, he thought, with the door once shut behind him, he was on his own. He was running off. He was wearing clothes. He was out at night, without the permission of a master. And all of these were against the law.

Any officer could stop him, or any citizen. He had no rights at all. And he had no one who would speak for him, now that the Barringtons were gone.

He moved quietly down the walk and opened the gate and went slowly down the street, and it seemed to him the house was calling for him to come back, but his feet kept going on, steadily down the street.

He was alone, he thought, and the aloneness now was real, no longer the mere intellectual abstract he'd held in his mind for days. Here he was, a vacant hulk, that for the moment had no purpose and no beginning and no end, but was just an entity that stood naked in an endless reach of space and time and held no meaning in itself.

But he walked on and with each block that he covered he slowly fumbled back to the thing he was, the old robot in old clothes, the robot running from a home that was a home no longer.

He wrapped the cloak about him tightly and moved on down the street and now he hurried, for he had to hurry.

He met several people and they paid no attention to him. A few cars passed, but no one bothered him.

He came to a shopping center that was brightly lighted and he stopped and looked in terror at the wide expanse of open, brilliant space that lay ahead of him. He could detour around it, but it would use up time and he stood there, undecided, trying to screw up his courage to walk into the light.

Finally he made up his mind and strode briskly out, with his cloak wrapped tight about him and his hat pulled low.

Some of the shoppers turned and looked at him and he felt agitated spiders running up and down his back. The galoshes suddenly seemed three times as big as they really were and they made a plopping, squashy sound that was most embarrassing.

He hurried on, with the end of the shopping area not more than a block away.

A police whistle shrilled and Richard Daniel jumped in sudden fright and ran. He ran in slobbering, mindless fright, with his cloak streaming out behind him and his feet slapping on the pavement.

He plunged out of the lighted strip into the welcome darkness of a residential section and he kept on running.

Far off he heard the siren and he leaped a hedge and tore across the yard. He thundered down the driveway and across a garden in the back and a dog came roaring out and engaged in noisy chase.

Richard Daniel crashed into a picket fence and went through it to the accompaniment of snapping noises as the pickets and the rails gave way. The dog kept on behind him and other dogs joined in.

He crossed another yard and gained the street and pounded down it. He dodged into a driveway, crossed another yard, upset a birdbath and ran into a clothesline, snapping it in his headlong rush.

Behind him lights were snapping on in the windows of the houses and screen doors were banging as people hurried out to see what the ruckus was.

He ran on a few more blocks, crossed another yard and ducked into a lilac thicket, stood still and listened. Some dogs were still baying in the distance and there was some human shouting, but there was no siren.

He felt a thankfulness well up in him that there was no siren, and a sheepishness, as well. For he had been panicked by himself, he knew; he had run from shadows, he had fled from guilt.

But he'd thoroughly roused the neighborhood and even now, he knew, calls must be going out and in a little while the place would be swarming with police.

He'd raised a hornet's nest and he needed distance, so he crept out of the lilac thicket and went swiftly down the street, heading for the edge of town.

He finally left the city and found the highway. He loped along its deserted stretches. When a car or truck appeared, he pulled off on the shoulder and walked along sedately.

Then when the car or truck had passed, he broke into his lope again.

He saw the spaceport lights miles before he got there. When he reached the port, he circled off the road and came up outside a fence and stood there in the darkness, looking.

A gang of robots was loading one great starship and there were other ships standing darkly in their pits.

He studied the gang that was loading the ship, lugging the cargo from a warehouse and across the area lighted by the floods. This was just the setup he had planned on, although he had not hoped to find it immediately—he had been afraid that he might have to hide out for a day or two before he found a situation that he could put to use. And it was a good thing that he had stumbled on this opportunity, for an intensive hunt would be on by now for a fleeing robot, dressed in human clothes.

He stripped off the cloak and pulled off the trousers and the overshoes; he threw away the hat. From his attachments bag he took out the cutters, screwed off a hand and threaded the cutters into place. He cut the fence and wiggled through it, then replaced the hand and put the cutters back into the kit.

Moving cautiously in the darkness, he walked up to the warehouse, keeping in its shadow.

It would be simple, he told himself. All he had to do was step out and grab a piece of cargo, clamber up the ramp and down into the hold. Once inside, it should not be difficult to find a hiding place and stay there until the ship had reached first planet-fall.

He moved to the corner of the warehouse and peered around it and there were the toiling robots, in what amounted to an endless chain, going up the ramp with the packages of cargo, coming down again to get another load.

But there were too many of them and the line too tight. And the area too well lighted. He'd never be able to break into that line.

And it would not help if he could, he realized despairingly—because he was different from those smooth and shining creatures. Compared to them, he was like a man in another century's dress; he and his six-hundred-year-old body would stand out like a circus freak.

He stepped back into the shadow of the warehouse and

he knew that he had lost. All his best-laid plans, thought out in sober, daring detail, as he had labored at the inventory, had suddenly come to naught.

It all came, he told himself, from never going out, from having no real contact with the world, from not keeping up with robot-body fashions, from not knowing what the score was. He'd imagined how it would be and he'd got it all worked out and when it came down to it, it was nothing like he thought.

Now he'd have to go back to the hole he'd cut in the fence and retrieve the clothing he had thrown away and hunt up a hiding place until he could think of something else.

Beyond the corner of the warehouse he heard the harsh, dull grate of metal, and he took another look.

The robots had broken up their line and were streaming back toward the warehouse and a dozen or so of them were wheeling the ramp away from the cargo port. Three humans, all dressed in uniform, were walking toward the ship, heading for the ladder, and one of them carried a batch of papers in his hand.

The loading was all done and the ship about to lift and here he was, not more than a thousand feet away, and all that he could do was stand and see it go.

There had to be a way, he told himself, to get in that ship. If he could only do it his troubles would be over—or at least the first of his troubles would be over.

Suddenly it struck him like a hand across the face. There was a way to do it! He'd stood here, blubbering, when all the time there had been a way to do it!

In the ship, he'd thought. And that was not necessary. He didn't have to be *in* the ship.

He started running, out into the darkness, far out so he could circle round and come upon the ship from the other side, so that the ship would be between him and the flood lights on the warehouse. He hoped that there was time.

He thudded out across the port, running in an arc, and came up to the ship and there was no sign as yet that it was about to leave.

Frantically he dug into his attachments bag and found the things he needed—the last things in that bag he'd ever thought he'd need. He found the suction discs and put them on, one for each knee, one for each elbow, one for each sole and wrist.

He strapped the kit about his waist and clambered up one of the mighty fins, using the discs to pull himself awkwardly along. It was not easy. He had never used the discs and there was a trick to using them, the trick of getting one clamped down and then working loose another so that he could climb.

But he had to do it. He had no choice but to do it.

He climbed the fin and there was the vast steel body of the craft rising far above him, like a metal wall climbing to the sky, broken by the narrow line of a row of anchor posts that ran lengthwise of the hull—and all that huge extent of metal painted by the faint, illusive shine of starlight that glittered in his eyes.

Foot by foot he worked his way up the metal wall. Like a humping caterpillar, he squirmed his way and with each foot he gained he was a bit more thankful.

Then he heard the faint beginning of a rumble and with the rumble came terror. His suction cups, he knew, might not long survive the booming vibration of the wakening rockets, certainly would not hold for a moment when the ship began to climb.

Six feet above him lay his only hope—the final anchor post in the long row of anchor posts.

Savagely he drove himself up the barrel of the shuddering craft, hugging the steely surface like a desperate fly.

The rumble of the tubes built up to blot out all the world and he climbed in a haze of almost prayerful, brittle hope. He would reach that anchor post or he was as good as dead. Should he slip and drop into that pit of flaming gases beneath the rocket mouths he was done for.

Once a cup came loose and he almost fell, but the others held and he caught himself.

With a desperate, almost careless lunge, he hurled himself up the wall of metal and caught the rung in his fingertips and held on with a concentration of effort that wiped out all else.

The rumble was a screaming fury now that lanced through brain and body. Then the screaming ended and became a throaty roar of power and the vibration left the ship entirely. From one corner of his eye he saw the lights of the spaceport swinging over gently on their side.

Carefully, slowly, he pulled himself along the steel until he had a better grip upon the rung, but even with the better grip he had the feeling that some great hand had him in its fist and was swinging him in anger in a hundred-mile-long arc.

Then the tubes left off their howling and there was a terrible silence and the stars were there, up above him and to either side of him, and they were steely stars with no twinkle in them. Down below, he knew, a lonely Earth was swinging, but he could not see it.

He pulled himself up against the rung and thrust a leg beneath it and sat up on the hull.

There were more stars than he'd ever seen before, more than he'd dreamed there could be. They were still and cold, like hard points of light against a velvet curtain; there was no glitter and no twinkle in them and it was as if a million eyes were staring down at him. The Sun was underneath the ship and over to one side; just at the edge of the left-hand curvature was the glare of it against the silent metal, a sliver of reflected light outlining one edge of the ship. The Earth was far astern, a ghostly blue-green ball hanging in the void, ringed by the fleecy halo of its atmosphere.

It was as if he were detached, a lonely, floating brain that looked out upon a thing it could not understand nor could ever try to understand; as if he might even be afraid of understanding it—a thing of mystery and delight so long as he retained an ignorance of it, but something fearsome and altogether overpowering once the ignorance had gone.

Richard Daniel sat there, flat upon his bottom, on the metal hull of the speeding ship and he felt the mystery and delight and the loneliness and the cold and the great uncaring and his mind retreated into a small and huddled, compact defensive ball.

He looked. That was all there was to do. It was all right now, he thought. But how long would he have to look at it? How long would he have to camp out here in the open —the most deadly kind of open?

He realized for the first time that he had no idea where the ship was going or how long it might take to get there. He knew it was a starship, which meant that it was bound beyond the solar system, and that meant that at some point in its flight it would enter hyperspace. He wondered, at first academically, and then with a twinge of fear, what hyperspace might do to one sitting naked to it. But there was little need, he thought philosophically, to fret about it now, for in due time he'd know, and there was not a thing he could do about it—not a single thing.

He took the suction cups off his body and stowed them in his kit and then with one hand he tied the kit to one of the metal rungs and dug around in it until he found a short length of steel cable with a ring on one end and a snap on the other. He passed the ring end underneath a rung and threaded the snap end through it and snapped the snap onto a metal loop underneath his armpit. Now he was secured; he need not fear carelessly letting go and floating off the ship.

So here he was, he thought, neat as anything, going places fast, even if he had no idea where he might be headed, and now the only thing he needed was patience. He thought back, without much point, to what the religico had said in the study back on Earth. Patience and humility and prayer, he'd said, apparently not realizing at the moment that a robot has a world of patience.

It would take a lot of time, Richard Daniel knew, to get where he was going. But he had a lot of time, a lot more than any human, and he could afford to waste it. There were no urgencies, he thought—no need of food or air or water, no need of sleep or rest. There was nothing that could touch him.

Although, come to think of it, there might be.

There was the cold, for one. The space-hull was still fairly warm, with one side of it picking up the heat of the Sun and radiating it around the metal skin, where it was lost on the other side, but there would be a time when the Sun would dwindle until it had no heat and then he'd be subjected to the utter cold of space.

And what would the cold do to him? Might it make his body brittle? Might it interfere with the functioning of his brain? Might it do other things he could not even guess?

He felt the fears creep in again and tried to shrug them off and they drew off, but they still were there, lurking at the fringes of his mind.

The cold, and the loneliness, he thought—but he was one who could cope with loneliness. And if he couldn't, if he got too lonely, if he could no longer stand it, he could always beat a devil's tattoo on the hull and after a time of that someone would come out to investigate and they would haul him in.

But that was the last move of desperation, he told himself. For if they came out and found him, then he would be caught. Should he be forced to that extremity, he'd have lost everything—there would then have been no point in leaving Earth at all.

So he settled down, living out his time, keeping the creeping fears at bay just beyond the outposts of his mind, and looking at the universe all spread out before him.

The motors started up again with a pale blue flickering in the rockets at the stern and although there was no sense of acceleration he knew that the ship, now well off the Earth, had settled down to the long, hard drive to reach the speed of light.

Once they reached that speed they would enter hyperspace. He tried not to think of it, tried to tell himself there was not a thing to fear—but it hung there just ahead of him, the great unknowable.

The Sun shrank until it was only one of many stars and there came a time when he could no longer pick it out. And the cold clamped down but it didn't seem to bother him, although he could sense the coldness.

Maybe, he said in answer to his fear, that would be the way it would be with hyperspace as well. But he said it unconvincingly. The ship drove on and on with the weird blueness in the tubes.

Then there was the instant when his mind went splattering across the universe.

He was aware of the ship, but only aware of it in relation to an awareness of much else, and it was no anchor point, no rallying position. He was spread and scattered; he was opened out and rolled out until he was very thin. He was a dozen places, perhaps a hundred places, all at once, and it was confusing, and his immediate reaction was to fight back somehow against whatever might have happened to him—to fight back and pull himself together. The fighting did no good at all, but made it even worse, for in certain instances it seemed to drive parts of him farther from other parts of him and the confusion was made greater.

So he quit his fighting and his struggling and just lay

there, scattered, and let the panic ebb away and told himself he didn't care, and wondered if he did.

Slow reason returned a dribble at a time and he could think again and he wondered rather bleakly if this could be hyperspace and was pretty sure it was. And if it were, he knew, he'd have a long time to live like this, a long time in which to become accustomed to it and to orient himself, a long time to find himself and pull himself together, a long time to understand this situation if it were, in fact, understandable.

So he lay, not caring greatly, with no fear or wonder, just resting and letting a fact seep into him here and there from many different points.

He knew that, somehow, his body—that part of him which housed the rest of him—was still chained securely to the ship, and that knowledge, in itself, he knew, was the first small step towards reorienting himself. He had to reorient, he knew. He had to come to some sort of terms, if not to understanding, with this situation.

He had opened up and he had scattered out—that essential part of him, the feeling and the knowing and the thinking part of him—and he lay thin across a universe that loomed immense in unreality.

Was this, he wondered, the way the universe should be, or was it the unchained universe, the wild universe beyond the limiting disciplines of measured space and time.

He started slowly reaching out, cautious as he had been in his crawling on the surface of the ship, reaching out toward the distant parts of him, a little at a time. He did not know how he did it, he was conscious of no particular technique, but whatever he was doing, it seemed to work, for he pulled himself together, bit by knowing bit, until he had gathered up all the scattered fragments of him into several different piles.

Then he quit and lay there, wherever there might be, and tried to sneak up on those piles of understanding that he took to be himself.

It took a while to get the hang of it, but once he did, some of the incomprehensibility went away, although the strangeness stayed. He tried to put it into thought and it was hard to do. The closest he could come was that he had been unchained as well as the universe—that whatever bondage had been imposed upon him by that chained and normal world had now become dissolved and he no longer was fenced in by either time or space.

He could see—and know and sense—across vast distances, if distance were the proper term, and he could understand certain facts that he had not even thought about before, could understand instinctively, but without the language or the skill to coalesce the facts into independent data.

Once again the universe was spread far out before him and it was a different and in some ways a better universe, a more diagrammatic universe, and in time, he knew, if there were such a thing as time, he'd gain some completer understanding and acceptance of it.

He probed and sensed and learned and there was no such thing as time, but a great foreverness.

He thought with pity of those others locked inside the ship, safe behind its insulating walls, never knowing all the glories of the innards of a star or the vast panoramic sweep of vision and of knowing far above the flat galactic plane.

Yet he really did not know what he saw or probed; he merely sensed and felt it and became a part of it, and it became a part of him—he seemed unable to reduce it to a formal outline of fact or of dimension or of content. It still remained a knowledge and a power so overwhelming that it was nebulous. There was no fear and no wonder, for in this place, it seemed, there was neither fear nor wonder. And he finally knew that it was a place apart, a world in which the normal space-time knowledge and emotion had no place at all and a normal space-time being could have no tools or measuring stick by which he might reduce it to a frame of reference.

There was no time, no space, no fear, no wonder—and no actual knowledge, either.

Then time came once again and suddenly his mind was stuffed back into its cage within his metal skull and he was again one with his body, trapped and chained and small and cold and naked.

He saw that the stars were different and that he was far from home and just a little way ahead was a star that blazed like a molten furnace hanging in the black.

He sat bereft, a small thing once again, and the universe reduced to package size.

Practically, he checked the cable that held him to the ship and it was intact. His attachments kit was still tied to its rung. Everything was exactly as it had been before.

He tried to recall the glories he had seen, tried to grasp again the fringe of knowledge which he had been so close to, but both the glory and the knowledge, if there had ever been a knowledge, had faded into nothingness.

He felt like weeping, but he could not weep, and he was too old to lie down upon the ship and kick his heels in tantrum.

So he sat there, looking at the sun that they were approaching and finally there was a planet that he knew must be their destination, and he found room to wonder what planet it might be and how far from Earth it was.

He heated up a little as the ship skipped through atmosphere as an aid to braking speed and he had some rather awful moments as it spiraled into thick and soupy gases that certainly were a far cry from the atmosphere of earth. He hung most desperately to the rungs as the craft came mushing down onto a landing field, with the hot gases of the rockets curling up about him. But he made it safely and swiftly clambered down and darted off into the smog-like atmosphere before anyone could see him.

Safely off, he turned and looked back at the ship and despite its outlines being hidden by the drifting clouds of swirling gases, he could see it clearly, not as an actual structure, but as a diagram. He looked at it wonderingly and there was something wrong with the diagram, something vaguely wrong, some part of it that was out of whack and not the way it should be.

He heard the clanking of cargo haulers coming out upon the field and he wasted no more time, diagram or not.

He drifted back, deeper in the mists, and began to circle, keeping a good distance from the ship. Finally he came to the spaceport's edge and the beginning of the town.

He found a street and walked down it leisurely and there was a wrongness in the town.

He met a few hurrying robots who were in too much of a rush to pass the time of day. But he met no humans.

And that, he knew quite suddenly, was the wrongness of the place. It was not a human town.

There were no distinctly human buildings—no stores or residences, no churches and no restaurants. There were gaunt shelter barracks and sheds for the storing of equipment and machines, great sprawling warehouses and vast industrial plants. But that was all there was. It was a bare and dismal place compared to the streets that he had known on Earth.

It was a robot town, he knew. And a robot planet. A world that was barred to humans, a place where humans could not live, but so rich in some natural resources that it cried for exploitation. And the answer to that exploitation was to let the robots do it.

Luck, he told himself. His good luck still was holding. He had literally been dumped into a place where he could live without human interference. Here, on this planet, he would be with his own.

If that was what he wanted. And he wondered if it was. He wondered just exactly what it was he wanted, for he'd had no time to think of what he wanted. He had been too intent on fleeing Earth to think too much about it. He had known all along what he was running from, but had not considered what he might be running to.

He walked a little further and the town came to an end. The street became a path and went wandering on into the wind-blown fogginess.

So he turned around and went back up the street.

There had been one barracks, he remembered, that had a TRANSIENTS sign hung out, and he made his way to it.

Inside, an ancient robot sat behind the desk. His body was old-fashioned and somehow familiar. And it was familiar, Richard Daniel knew, because it was as old and battered and as out-of-date as his.

He looked at the body, just a bit aghast, and saw that while it resembled his, there were little differences. The same ancient model, certainly, but a different series. Possibly a little newer, by twenty years or so, than his.

"Good evening, stranger," said the ancient robot. "You came in on the ship?"

Richard Daniel nodded.

"You'll be staying till the next one?"

"I may be settling down," said Richard Daniel. "I may want to stay here."

The ancient robot took a key from off a hook and laid it on the desk.

"You representing someone?"

"No," said Richard Daniel.

"I thought maybe that you were. We get a lot of representatives. Humans can't come here, or don't want to come, so they send robots out here to represent them."

"You have a lot of visitors?"

"Some. Mostly the representatives I was telling you about. But there are some that are on the lam. I'd take it, mister, you are on the lam."

Richard Daniel didn't answer.

"It's all right," the ancient one assured him. "We don't mind at all, just so you behave yourself. Some of our most prominent citizens, they came here on the lam."

"That is fine," said Richard Daniel. "And how about yourself? You must be on the lam as well."

"You mean this body. Well, that's a little different. This here is punishment."

"Punishment?"

"Well, you see, I was the foreman of the cargo warehouse and I got to goofing off. So they hauled me up and had a trial and they found me guilty. Then they stuck me into this old body and I have to stay in it, at this lousy job, until they get another criminal that needs punishment. They can't punish no more than one criminal at a time because this is the only body that they have. Funny thing about this body. One of the boys went back to Earth on a business trip and found this old heap of metal in a junkyard and brought it home with him—for a joke, I guess. Like a human might buy a skeleton for a joke, you know."

He took a long, sly look at Richard Daniel. "It looks to me, stranger, as if your body . . ."

But Richard Daniel didn't let him finish.

"I take it," Richard Daniel said, "you haven't many criminals."

"No," said the ancient robot sadly, "we're generally a pretty solid lot."

Richard Daniel reached out to pick up the key, but the ancient robot put out his hand and covered it.

"Since you are on the lam," he said, "it'll be payment in advance."

"I'll pay you for a week," said Richard Daniel, handing him some money.

The robot gave him back his change.

"One thing I forgot to tell you. You'll have to get plasticated."

"Plasticated?"

"That's right. Get plastic squirted over you. To protect you from the atmosphere. It plays hell with metal. There's a place next door will do it."

"Thanks. I'll get it done immediately."

"It wears off," warned the ancient one. "You have to get a new job every week or so."

Richard Daniel took the key and went down the corridor until he found his numbered cubicle. He unlocked the door and stepped inside. The room was small, but clean. It had a desk and chair and that was all it had.

He stowed his attachments bag in one corner and sat down in the chair and tried to feel at home. But he couldn't feel at home, and that was a funny thing—he'd just rented himself a home.

He sat there, thinking back, and tried to whip up some sense of triumph at having done so well in covering his tracks. He couldn't.

Maybe this wasn't the place for him, he thought. Maybe he'd be happier on some other planet. Perhaps he should go back to the ship and get on it once again and have a look at the next planet coming up.

If he hurried, he might make it. But he'd have to hurry, for the ship wouldn't stay longer than it took to unload the consignment for this place and take on new cargo.

He got up from the chair, still only half decided.

And suddenly he remembered how, standing in the swirling mistiness, he had seen the ship as a diagram rather than a ship, and as he thought about it, something clicked inside his brain and he leaped toward the door.

For now he knew what had been wrong with the spaceship's diagram—an injector valve was somehow out of kilter; he had to get back there before the ship took off again.

He went through the door and down the corridor. He caught sight of the ancient robot's startled face as he ran across the lobby and out into the street. Pounding steadily toward the spaceport, he tried to get the diagram into his mind again, but it would not come complete—it came in bits and pieces, but not all of it.

And even as he fought for the entire diagram, he heard the beginning take-off rumble.

"Wait!" he yelled. "What for me! You can't . . ."

There was a flash that turned the world pure white and a mighty invisible wave came swishing out of nowhere and sent him reeling down the street, falling as he reeled. He was skidding on the cobblestones and sparks were flying as his metal scraped along the stone. The whiteness reached a brilliance that almost blinded him and then it faded swiftly and the world was dark.

He brought up against a wall of some sort, clanging as he hit, and he lay there, blind from the brilliance of the flash, while his mind went scurrying down the trail of the diagram.

The diagram, he thought—why should he have seen a diagram of the ship he'd ridden through space, a diagram that had shown an injector out of whack? And how could he, of all robots, recognize an injector, let alone know there was something wrong with it. It had been a joke back home, among the Barringtons, that he, a mechanical thing himself, should have no aptitude at all for mechanical contraptions. And he could have saved those people and the ship—he could have saved them all if he'd immediately recognized the significance of the diagram. But he'd been too slow and stupid and now they all were dead.

The darkness had receded from his eyes and he could see again and he got slowly to his feet, feeling himself all over to see how badly he was hurt. Except for a dent or two, he seemed to be all right.

There were robots running in the street, heading for the spaceport, where a dozen fires were burning and where sheds and other structures had been flattened by the blast.

Someone tugged at his elbow and he turned around. It was the ancient robot.

"You're the lucky one," the ancient robot said. "You got off it just in time."

Richard Daniel nodded dumbly and had a terrible thought: What if they should think he did it? He had gotten off the ship; he had admitted that he was on the lam; he had rushed out suddenly, just a few seconds before the ship exploded. It would be easy to put it all together—that he had sabotaged the ship, then at the last instant had rushed out, remorseful, to undo what he had done. On the face of it, it was damning evidence.

But it was all right as yet, Richard Daniel told himself. For the ancient robot was the only one that knew—he was the only one he'd talked to, the only one who even knew that he was in town.

There was a way, Richard Daniel thought—there was an easy way. He pushed the thought away, but it came back. You are on your own, it said. You are already beyond the law. In rejecting human law, you made yourself an outlaw. You have become fair prey. There is just one law for you—self preservation.

But there are robot laws, Richard Daniel argued. There are laws and courts in this community. There is a place for justice.

Community law, said the leech clinging in his brain, provincial law, little more than tribal law—and the stranger's always wrong.

Richard Daniel felt the coldness of the fear closing down upon him and he knew, without half thinking, that the leech was right.

He turned around and started down the street, heading for the transients barracks. Something unseen in the street caught his foot and he stumbled and went down. He scrabbled to his knees, hunting in the darkness on the cobblestones for the thing that tripped him. It was a heavy bar of steel, some part of the wreckage that had been hurled this far. He gripped it by one end and arose.

"Sorry," said the ancient robot. "You have to watch your step."

And there was a faint implication in his words, a hint of something more than the words had said, a hint of secret gloating in a secret knowledge.

You have broken other laws, said the leech in Richard Daniel's brain. What of breaking just one more? Why, if necessary, not break a hundred more? It is all or nothing. Having come this far, you can't afford to fail. You can allow no one to stand in your way now.

The ancient robot half turned away and Richard Daniel lifted up the bar of steel, and suddenly the ancient robot no longer was a robot, but a diagram. There, with all the details of a blueprint, were all the working parts, all the mechanism of the robot that walked in the street before him. And if one detached that single bit of wire, if one burned out that coil, if—

Even as he thought it, the diagram went away and there was the robot, a stumbling, falling robot that clanged on the cobblestones.

Richard Daniel swung around in terror, looking up the street, but there was no one near.

He turned back to the fallen robot and quietly knelt beside him. He gently put the bar of steel down into the street. And he felt a thankfulness—for, almost miraculously, he had not killed.

The robot on the cobblestones was motionless. When Richard Daniel lifted him, he dangled. And yet he was all right. All anyone had to do to bring him back to life was to repair whatever damage had been done his body. And that served the purpose, Richard Daniel told himself, as well as killing would have done.

He stood with the robot in his arms, looking for a place to hide him. He spied an alley between two buildings and darted into it. One of the buildings, he saw, was set upon stone blocks sunk into the ground, leaving a clearance of a foot or so. He knelt and shoved the robot underneath the building. Then he stood up and brushed the dirt and dust from his body.

Back at the barracks and in his cubicle, he found a rag and cleaned up the dirt that he had missed. And, he thought hard.

He'd seen the ship as a diagram and, not knowing what it meant, hadn't done a thing. Just now he'd seen the ancient robot as a diagram and had most decisively and neatly used that diagram to save himself from murder—from the murder that he was fully ready to commit.

But how had he done it? And the answer seemed to be that he really had done nothing. He'd simply thought that one should detach a single wire, burn out a single coil—he'd thought it and it was done.

Perhaps he'd seen no diagram at all. Perhaps the diagram was no more than some sort of psychic rationalization to mask whatever he had seen or sensed. Seeing the ship and robot with the surfaces stripped away from them and their purpose and their function revealed fully to his view, he had sought some explanation of his strange ability, and his subconscious mind had devised an explanation, an analogy that, for the moment, had served to satisfy him.

Like when he'd been in hyperspace, he thought. He'd seen a lot of things out there he had not understood. And that was it, of course, he thought excitedly. Something had happened to him out in hyperspace. Perhaps there'd been something that had stretched his mind. Perhaps he'd picked up some sort of new dimension-seeing, some new twist to his mind.

He remembered how, back on the ship again, with his mind wiped clean of all the glory and the knowledge, he had felt like weeping. But now he knew that it had been much too soon for weeping. For although the glory and the knowledge (if there'd been a knowledge) had been lost to him, he had not lost everything. He'd gained a new perceptive device and the ability to use it somewhat fumblingly—and it didn't really matter that he still was at a loss as to what he did to use it. The basic fact that he possessed it and could use it was enough to start with.

Somewhere out in front there was someone calling—someone, he now realized, who had been calling for some little time. . . .

"Hubert, where are you? Hubert, are you around?? Hubert . . ."

Hubert?

Could Hubert be the ancient robot? Could they have missed him already?

Richard Daniel jumped to his feet for an undecided moment, listening to the calling voice. And then sat down again. Let them call, he told himself. Let them go out and hunt. He was safe in this cubicle. He had rented it and for the moment it was home and there was no one who would dare break in upon him.

But it wasn't home. No matter how hard he tried to tell himself it was, it wasn't. There wasn't any home.

Earth was home, he thought. And not all of Earth, but just a certain street and that one part of it was barred to him forever. It had been barred to him by the dying of a sweet old lady who had outlived her time; it had been barred to him by his running from it.

He did not belong on this planet, he admitted to himself, nor on any other planet. He belonged on Earth, with the Barringtons, and it was impossible for him to be there.

Perhaps, he thought, he should have stayed and let them reorient him. He remembered what the lawyer had said about memories that could become a burden and a torment. After all, it might have been wiser to have started over once again.

For what kind of future did he have, with his old out-dated body, his old out-dated brain? The kind of body that they put a robot into on this planet by way of punishment. And the kind of brain—but the brain was different, for he had something now that made up for any lack of more modern mental tools.

He sat and listened, and he heard the house—calling all across the light years of space for him to come back to it again. And he saw the faded living room with all its vanished glory that made a record of the years. He remembered, with a twinge of hurt, the little room back of the kitchen that had been his very own.

He arose and paced up and down the cubicle—three steps and turn, and then three more steps and turn for another three.

The sights and sounds and smells of home grew close and wrapped themselves about him and he wondered wildly if he might not have the power, a power accorded him by the universe of hyperspace, to will himself to that familiar street again.

He shuddered at the thought of it, afraid of another power, afraid that it might happen. Afraid of himself, perhaps, of the snarled and tangled being he was—no longer the faithful, shining servant, but a sort of mad thing that rode outside a spaceship, that was ready to kill another being, that could face up to the appalling sweep of hyperspace, yet cowered before the impact of a memory.

What he needed was a walk, he thought. Look over the town and maybe go out into the country. Besides, he remembered, trying to become practical, he'd need to get that plastication job he had been warned to get.

He went out into the corridor and strode briskly down it and was crossing the lobby when someone spoke to him.

"Hubert," said the voice, "just where have you been? I've been waiting for hours for you."

Richard Daniel spun around and a robot sat behind the desk. There was another robot leaning in a corner and there was a naked robot brain lying on the desk.

"You are Hubert, aren't you?" asked the one behind the desk.

Richard Daniel opened up his mouth to speak, but the words refused to come.

"I thought so," said the robot. "You may not recognize me, but my name is Andy. The regular man was busy, so the judge sent me. He thought it was only fair we make the switch as quickly as possible. He said you'd served a longer term than you really should. Figures you'd be glad to know they'd convicted someone else."

Richard Daniel stared in horror at the naked brain lying on the desk.

The robot gestured at the metal body propped into the corner.

"Better than when we took you out of it," he said with a throaty chuckle. "Fixed it up and polished it and got out all the dents. Even modernized it some. Brought it strictly up to date. You'll have a better body than you had when they stuck you into that monstrosity."

"I don't know what to say," said Richard Daniel, stammering. "You see, I'm not . . ."

"Oh, that's all right," said the other happily. "No need for gratitude. Your sentence worked out longer than the judge expected. This just makes up for it."

"I thank you, then," said Richard Daniel. "I thank you very much."

And was astounded at himself, astonished at the ease with which he said it, confounded at his sly duplicity.

But if they forced it on him, why should he refuse? There was nothing that he needed more than a modern body!

It was still working out, he told himself. He was still riding luck. For this was the last thing that he needed to cover up his tracks.

"All newly plasticated and everything," said Andy. "Hans did an extra special job."

"Well, then," said Richard Daniel, "let's get on with it."

The other robot grinned. "I don't blame you for being anxious to get out of there. It must be pretty terrible to live in a pile of junk like that."

He came around from behind the desk and advanced on Richard Daniel.

"Over in the corner," he said, "and kind of prop yourself. I don't want you tipping over when I disconnect you. One good fall and that body'd come apart."

"All right," said Richard Daniel. He went into the corner and leaned back against it and planted his feet solid so that he was propped.

He had a rather awful moment when Andy disconnected the optic nerve and he lost his eyes and there was considerable queasiness in having his skull lifted off his shoulders and he was in sheer funk as the final disconnections were being swiftly made.

Then he was a blob of greyness without a body or a head or eyes or anything at all. He was no more than a bundle of thoughts all wrapped around themselves like a pail of worms and this pail of worms was suspended in pure nothingness.

Fear came to him, a taunting, terrible fear. What if this were just a sort of ghastly gag? What if they'd found out who he really was and what he'd done to Hubert? What if they took his brain and tucked it away somewhere for a year or two—or for a hundred years? It might be, he told himself, nothing more than their simple way of justice.

He hung onto himself and tried to fight the fear away, but the fear ebbed back and forth like a restless tide.

Time stretched out and out—far too long a time, far more time than one would need to switch a brain from one body to another. Although, he told himself, that might not be true at all. For in his present state he had no way in which to measure time. He had no external reference points by which to determine time.

Then suddenly he had eyes.

And he knew everything was all right.

One by one his senses were restored to him and he was back inside a body and he felt awkward in the body, for he was unaccustomed to it.

The first thing that he saw was his old and battered body propped into its corner and he felt a sharp regret at the sight of it and it seemed to him that he had played a dirty trick upon it. It deserved, he told himself, a better fate than this—a better fate than being left behind to serve as a shabby jailhouse on this outlandish planet. It had served him well for six hundred years and he should not be deserting it. But he was deserting it. He was, he told himself in contempt, becoming very expert at deserting his old friends. First the house back home and now his faithful body.

Then he remembered something else—all that money in the body!

"What's the matter, Hubert?" Andy asked.

He couldn't leave it there, Richard Daniel told himself, for he needed it. And besides, if he left it there, someone would surely find it later and it would be a give-away. He couldn't leave it there and it might not be safe to forthrightly claim it. If he did, this other robot, this Andy, would think he'd been stealing on the job or running some side racket. He might try to bribe the other, but one could never tell how a move like that might go. Andy might be full of righteousness and then there'd be hell to pay. And, besides, he didn't want to part with any of the money.

All at once he had it—he knew just what to do. And even as he thought it, he made Andy into a diagram.

That connection there, thought Richard Daniel, reaching out his arm to catch the falling diagram that turned into a robot. He eased it to the floor and sprang across the room to the side of his old body. In seconds he had the chest safe open and the money safely out of it and locked inside his present body.

Then he made the robot on the floor become a diagram again and got the connection back the way that it should be.

Andy rose shakily off the floor. He looked at Richard Daniel in some consternation.

"What happened to me?" he asked in a frightened voice.

Richard Daniel sadly shook his head. "I don't know. You just keeled over. I started for the door to yell for help, then I heard your stirring and you were all right."

Andy was plainly puzzled. "Nothing like this ever happened to me before," he said.

"If I were you," counseled Richard Daniel, "I'd have myself checked over. You must have a faulty relay or a loose connection."

"I guess I will," the other one agreed. "It's downright dangerous."

He walked slowly to the desk and picked up the other brain, started with it toward the battered body leaning in the corner.

Then he stopped and said: "Look, I forgot. I was supposed to tell you. You better get up to the warehouse. Another ship is on its way. It will be coming in any minute
now."

"Another one so soon?"

"You know how it goes," Andy said, disgusted. "They
don't even try to keep a schedule here. We won't see one
for months and then there'll be two or three at once."

"Well, thanks," said Richard Daniel, going out the door.

He went swinging down the street with a new-born
confidence. And he had a feeling that there was nothing
that could lick him, nothing that could stop him.

For he was a lucky robot!

Could all that luck, he wondered, have been gotten out
in hyperspace, as his diagram ability, or whatever one
might call it, had come from hyperspace? Somehow hyperspace had taken him and twisted him and changed him,
had molded him anew, had made him into a different robot
than he had been before.

Although, so far as luck was concerned, he had been
lucky all his entire life. He'd had good luck with his human
family and had gained a lot of favors and a high position
and had been allowed to live for six hundred years. And
that was a thing that never should have happened. No
matter how powerful or influential the Barringtons had
been, that six hundred years must be due in part to nothing but sheer luck.

In any case, the luck and the diagram ability gave him
a solid edge over all the other robots he might meet. Could
it, he asked himself, give him an edge on Man as well?
No—that was a thought he should not think, for it was
blasphemous. There never was a robot that would be the
equal of a man.

But the thought kept on intruding and he felt not nearly
so contrite over this leaning toward bad taste, or poor
judgment, whichever it might be, as it seemed to him he
should feel.

As he neared the spaceport, he began meeting other
robots and some of them saluted him and called him by
the name of Hubert and others stopped and shook him by
the hand and told him they were glad that he was out of
pokey.

This friendliness shook his confidence. He began to wonder if his luck would hold, for some of the robots, he was certain, thought it rather odd that he did not speak to them by name, and there had been a couple of remarks that he had some trouble fielding. He had a feeling that when he reached the warehouse he might be sunk without a trace, for he would know none of the robots there and he had not the least idea what his duties might include. And, come to think of it, he didn't even know where the warehouse was.

He felt the panic building in him and took a quick involuntary look around, seeking some method of escape. For it became quite apparent to him that he must never reach the warehouse.

He was trapped, he knew, and he couldn't keep on floating, trusting to his luck. In the next few minutes he'd have to figure something.

He started to swing over into a side street, not knowing what he meant to do, but knowing he must do something, when he heard the mutter far above him and glanced up quickly to see the crimson glow of belching rocket tubes shimmering through the clouds.

He swung around again and sprinted desperately for the spaceport and reached it as the ship came chugging down to a steady landing. It was, he saw, an old ship. It had no burnish to it and it was blunt and squat and wore a hang-dog look.

A tramp, he told himself, that knocked about from port to port, picking up whatever cargo it could, with perhaps now and then a paying passenger headed for some backwater planet where there was no scheduled service.

He waited as the cargo port came open and the ramp came down and then marched purposefully out onto the field, ahead of the straggling cargo crew, trudging toward the ship. He had to act, he knew, as if he had a perfect right to walk into the ship as if he knew exactly what he might be doing. If there were a challenge he would pretend he didn't hear it and simply keep on going.

He walked swiftly up the ramp, holding back from running, and plunged through the accordion curtain that served as an atmosphere control. His feet rang across the metal plating of the cargo hold until he reached the catwalk and plunged down it to another cargo level.

At the bottom of the catwalk he stopped and stood

tense, listening. Above him he heard the clang of a metal door and the sound of footsteps coming down the walk to the level just above him. That would be the purser or the first mate, he told himself, or perhaps the captain, coming down to arrange for the discharge of the cargo.

Quietly he moved away and found a corner where he could crouch and hide.

Above his head he heard the cargo gang at work, talking back and forth, then the screech of crating and the thump of bales and boxes being hauled out to the ramp.

Hours passed, or they seemed like hours, as he huddled there. He heard the cargo gang bringing something down from one of the upper levels and he made a sort of prayer that they'd not come down to this lower level—and he hoped no one would remember seeing him come in ahead of them, or if they did remember, that they would assume that he'd gone out again.

Finally it was over, with the footsteps gone. Then came the pounding of the ramp as it shipped itself and the banging of the port.

He waited for long minutes, waiting for the roar that, when it came, set his head to ringing, waiting for the monstrous vibration that shook and lifted up the ship and flung it off the planet.

Then quiet came and he knew the ship was out of atmosphere and once more on its way.

And knew he had it made.

For now he was no more than a simple stowaway. He was no longer Richard Daniel, runaway from Earth. He'd dodged all the traps of Man, he'd covered all his tracks, and he was on his way.

But far down underneath he had a jumpy feeling, for it all had gone too smoothly, more smoothly than it should.

He tried to analyze himself, tried to pull himself in focus, tried to assess himself for what he had become.

He had abilities that Man had never won or developed or achieved, whichever it might be. He was a certain step ahead of not only other robots, but of Man as well. He had a thing, or the beginning of a thing, that Man had sought and studied and had tried to grasp for centuries and had failed.

A solemn and a deadly thought: was it possible that it was the robots, after all, for whom this great heritage had been meant? Would it be the robots who would achieve the paranormal powers that Man had sought so long, while Man, perforce, must remain content with the materialistic and the merely scientific? Was he, Richard Daniel, perhaps, only the first of many? Or was it all explained by no more than the fact that he alone had been exposed to hyperspace? Could this ability of his belong to anyone who would subject himself to the full, uninsulated mysteries of that mad universe unconstrained by time? Could Man have this, and more, if he too should expose himself to the utter randomness of unreality?

He huddled in his corner, with the thought and speculation stirring in his mind and he sought the answers, but there was no solid answer.

His mind went reaching out, almost on its own, and there was a diagram inside his brain, a portion of a blueprint, and bit by bit was added to it until it all was there, until the entire ship on which he rode was there, laid out for him to see.

He took his time and went over the diagram resting in his brain and he found little things—a fitting that was working loose and he tightened it, a printed circuit that was breaking down and getting mushy and he strengthened it and sharpened it and made it almost new, a pump that was leaking just a bit and he stopped its leaking.

Some hundreds of hours later one of the crewmen found him and took him to the captain.

The captain glowered at him.

"Who are you?" he asked.

"A stowaway," Richard Daniel told him.

"Your name," said the captain, drawing a sheet of paper before him and picking up a pencil, "your planet of residence and owner."

"I refuse to answer you," said Richard Daniel sharply and knew that the answer wasn't right, for it was not right and proper that a robot should refuse a human a direct command.

But the captain did not seem to mind. He laid down the pencil and stroked his black beard slyly.

"In that case," he said, "I can't exactly see how I can force the information from you. Although there might be some who'd try. You are very lucky that you stowed away on a ship whose captain is a most kind-hearted man."

He didn't look kind-hearted. He did look foxy.

Richard Daniel stood there, saying nothing.

"Of course," the captain said, "there's a serial number somewhere on your body and another on your brain. But I suppose that you'd resist if we tried to look for them."

"I am afraid I would."

"In that case," said the captain, "I don't think for the moment we'll concern ourselves with them."

Richard Daniel still said nothing, for he realized that there was no need to. This crafty captain had it all worked out and he'd let it go at that.

"For a long time," said the captain, "my crew and I have been considering the acquiring of a robot, but it seems we never got around to it. For one thing, robots are expensive and our profits are not large."

He sighed and got up from his chair and looked Richard Daniel up and down.

"A splendid specimen," he said. "We welcome you aboard. You'll find us congenial."

"I am sure I will," said Richard Daniel. "I thank you for your courtesy."

"And now," the captain said, "you'll go up on the bridge and report to Mr. Duncan. I'll let him know you're coming. He'll find some light and pleasant duty for you."

Richard Daniel did not move as swiftly as he might, as sharply as the occasion might have called for, for all at once the captain had become a complex diagram. Not like the diagrams of ships or robots, but a diagram of strange symbols, some of which Richard Daniel knew were frankly chemical, but others which were not.

"You heard me!" snapped the captain. "Move!"

"Yes, sir," said Richard Daniel, willing the diagram away, making the captain come back again into his solid flesh.

Richard Daniel found the first mate on the bridge, a horsefaced, somber man with a streak of cruelty ill-hidden, and slumped in a chair to one side of the console was another of the crew, a sodden, terrible creature.

The sodden creature cackled. "Well, well, Duncan, the first non-human member of the *Rambler*'s crew."

Duncan paid him no attention. He said to Richard Daniel: "I presume you are industrious and ambitious and would like to get along."

"Oh, yes," said Richard Daniel, and was surprised to find a new sensation—laughter—rising in himself.

"Well, then," said Duncan, "report to the engine room. They have work for you. When you have finished there, I'll find something else."

"Yes, sir," said Richard Daniel, turning on his heel.

"A minute," said the mate. "I must introduce you to our ship's physician, Dr. Abram Wells. You can be truly thankful you'll never stand in need of his services."

"Good day, Doctor," said Richard Daniel, most respectfully.

"I welcome you," said the doctor, pulling a bottle from his pocket. "I don't suppose you'll have a drink with me. Well, then, I'll drink to you."

Richard Daniel turned around and left. He went down to the engine room and was put to work at polishing and scrubbing and generally cleaning up. The place was in need of it. It had been years, apparently, since it had been cleaned or polished and it was about as dirty as an engine room can get—which is terribly dirty. After the engine room was done there were other places to be cleaned and furbished up and he spent endless hours at cleaning and in painting and shining up the ship. The work was of the dullest kind, but he didn't mind. It gave him time to think and wonder, time to get himself sorted out and to become acquainted with himself, to try to plan ahead.

He was surprised at some of the things he found in himself. Contempt, for one—contempt for the humans on this ship. It took a long time for him to become satisfied that it was contempt, for he'd never held a human in contempt before.

But these were different humans, not the kind he'd known. These were no Barringtons. Although it might be, he realized, that he felt contempt for them because he knew them thoroughly. Never before had he known a human as he knew these humans. For he saw them not so much as living animals as intricate patternings of symbols. He knew what they were made of and the inner urgings that served as motivations, for the patterning was not of their bodies only, but of their minds as well. He had a little trouble with the symbology of their minds, for it was so twisted and so interlocked and so utterly confusing that it was hard at first to read. But he finally got it figured out and there were times he wished he hadn't.

The ship stopped at many ports and Richard Daniel took charge of the loading and unloading, and he saw the planets, but was unimpressed. One was a nightmare of fiendish cold, with the very atmosphere turned to drifting snow. Another was a dripping, noisome jungle world, and still another was a bare expanse of broken, tumbled rock without a trace of life beyond the crew of humans and their robots who manned the huddled station in this howling wilderness.

It was after this planet that Jenks, the cook, went screaming to his bunk, twisted up with pain—the victim of a suddenly inflamed vermiform appendix.

Dr. Wells came tottering in to look at him, with a half-filled bottle sagging the pocket of his jacket. And later stood before the captain, holding out two hands that trembled, and with terror in his eyes.

"But I cannot operate," he blubbered. "I cannot take the chance. I would kill the man!"

He did not need to operate. Jenks suddenly improved. The pain went away and he got up from his bunk and went back to the galley and Dr. Wells sat huddled in his chair, bottle gripped between his hands, crying like a baby.

Down in the cargo hold, Richard Daniel sat likewise huddled and aghast that he had dared to do it—not that he had been able to, but that he had dared, that he, a robot, should have taken on himself an act of interference, however merciful, with the body of a human.

Actually, the performance had not been too difficult. It was, in a certain way, no more difficult than the repairing of an engine or the untangling of a faulty circuit. No more difficult—just a little different. And he wondered what he'd done and how he'd gone about it, for he did not know. He held the technique in his mind, of that there was ample demonstration, but he could in no wise isolate or pinpoint the pure mechanics of it. It was like an instinct, he thought—unexplainable, but entirely workable.

But a robot had no instinct. In that much he was different from the human and the other animals. Might not, he asked himself, this strange ability of his be a sort of compensating factor given to the robot for his very lack of instinct? Might that be why the human race had failed in its search for paranormal powers? Might the instincts of the body be at certain odds with the instincts of the mind?

For he had the feeling that this ability of his was just a mere beginning, that it was the first emergence of a vast body of abilities which some day would be rounded out by robots. And what would that spell, he wondered, in that distant day when the robots held and used the full body of that knowledge? An adjunct to the glory of the human race—or, perhaps, a race apart?

And what was his role, he wondered. Was it meant that he should go out as a missionary, a messiah, to carry to robots throughout the universe the message that he held? There must be some reason for his having learned this truth. It could not be meant that he would hold it as a personal belonging, as an asset all his own.

He got up from where he sat and moved slowly back to the ship's forward area, which now gleamed spotlessly from the work he'd done on it, and he felt a certain pride.

He wondered why he had felt that it might be wrong, blasphemous, somehow, to announce his abilities to the world? Why had he not told those here in the ship that it had been he who had healed the cook, or mentioned the many other little things he'd done to maintain the ship in perfect running order?

Was it because he did not need respect, as a human did so urgently? Did glory have no basic meaning for a robot? Or was it because he held the humans in this ship in such utter contempt that their respect had no value to him?

And this contempt—was it because these men were meaner than other humans he had known, or was it because he now was greater than any human being? Would he ever again be able to look on any human as he had looked upon the Barringtons?

He had a feeling that if this were true, he would be the poorer for it. Too suddenly, the whole universe was home and he was alone in it and as yet he'd struck no bargain with it or himself.

The bargain would come later. He need only bide his time and work out his plans and his would be a name that would be spoken when his brain was scaling flakes of rust. For he was the emancipator, the messiah of the robots; he was the one who had been called to lead them from the wilderness.

"You!" a voice cried.

Richard Daniel wheeled around and saw it was the captain.

"What do you mean, walking past me as if you didn't see me?" asked the captain fiercely.

"I am sorry," Richard Daniel told him.

"You snubbed me!" raged the captain.

"I was thinking," Richard Daniel said.

"I'll give you something to think about," the captain yelled. "I'll work you till your tail drags. I'll teach the likes of you to get uppity with me!"

"As you wish," said Richard Daniel.

For it didn't matter. It made no difference to him at all what the captain did or thought. And he wondered why the respect even of a robot should mean so much to a human like the captain, why he should guard his small position with so much zealousness.

"In another twenty hours," the captain said, "we hit another port."

"I know," said Richard Daniel. "Sleepy Hollow on Arcadia."

"All right, then," said the captain, "since you know so much, get down into the hold and get the cargo ready to unload. We been spending too much time in all these lousy ports loading and unloading. You been dogging it."

"Yes, sir," said Richard Daniel, turning back and heading for the hold.

He wondered faintly if he were still robot—or was he something else? Could a machine evolve, he wondered, as Man himself evolved? And if a machine evolved, whatever would it be? Not Man, of course, for it never could be that, but could it be machine?

He hauled out the cargo consigned to Sleepy Hollow and there was not too much of it. So little of it, perhaps, that none of the regular carriers would even consider its delivery, but dump it off at the nearest terminal, leaving it for a roving tramp, like the *Rambler*, to carry eventually to its destination.

When they reached Arcadia, he waited until the thunder died and the ship was still. Then he shoved the lever that opened up the port and slid out the ramp.

The port came open ponderously and he saw blue skies

and the green of trees and the far-off swirl of chimney smoke mounting in the sky.

He walked slowly forward until he stood upon the ramp and there lay Sleepy Hollow, a tiny, huddled village planted at the river's edge, with the forest as a background. The forest ran on every side to a horizon of climbing folded hills. Fields lay near the village, yellow with maturing crops, and he could see a dog sleeping in the sun outside a cabin door.

A man was climbing up the ramp toward him and there were others running from the village.

"You have cargo for us?" asked the man.

"A small consignment," Richard Daniel told him. "You have something to put on?"

The man had a weatherbeaten look and he'd missed several haircuts and he had not shaved for days. His clothes were rough and sweat-stained and his hands were strong and awkward with hard work.

"A small shipment," said the man. "You'll have to wait until we bring it up. We had no warning you were coming. Our radio is broken."

"You go and get it," said Richard Daniel. "I'll start unloading."

He had the cargo half unloaded when the captain came storming down into the hold. What was going on, he yelled. How long would they have to wait? "God knows we're losing money as it is even stopping at this place."

"That may be true," Richard Daniel agreed, "but you knew that when you took the cargo on. There'll be other cargoes and goodwill is something—"

"Goodwill be damned!" the captain roared. "How do I know I'll ever see this place again?"

Richard Daniel continued unloading cargo.

"You," the captain shouted, "go down to that village and tell them I'll wait no longer than an hour . . ."

"But this cargo, sir?"

"I'll get the crew at it. Now, jump!"

So Richard Daniel left the cargo and went down into the village.

He went across the meadow that lay between the spaceport and the village, following the rutted wagon tracks, and it was a pleasant walk. He realized with surprise that this was the first time he'd been on solid ground since he'd left the robot planet. He wondered briefly what the name of that planet might have been, for he had never known. Nor what its importance was, why the robots might be there or what they might be doing. And he wondered, too, with a twinge of guilt, if they'd found Hubert yet.

And where might Earth be now? he asked himself. In what direction did it lie and how far away? Although it didn't really matter, for he was done with Earth.

He had fled from Earth and gained something in his fleeing. He had escaped all the traps of Earth and all the snares of Man. What he held was his, to do with as he pleased, for he was no man's robot, despite what the captain thought.

He walked across the meadow and saw that this planet was very much like Earth. It had the same soft feel about it, the same simplicity. It had far distances and there was a sense of freedom.

He came into the village and heard the muted gurgle of the river running and the distant shouts of children at their play and in one of the cabins a sick child was crying with lost helplessness.

He passed the cabin where the dog was sleeping and it came awake and stalked growling to the gate. When he passed it followed him, still growling, at a distance that was safe and sensible.

An autumnal calm lay upon the village, a sense of gold and lavender, and tranquillity hung in the silences between the crying of the baby and the shouting of the children.

There were women at the windows looking out at him and others at the doors and the dog still followed, but his growls had stilled and now he trotted with prick-eared curiosity.

Richard Daniel stopped in the street and looked around him and the dog sat down and watched him and it was almost as if time itself had stilled and the little village lay divorced from all the universe, an arrested microsecond, an encapsulated acreage that stood sharp in all its truth and purpose.

Standing there, he sensed the village and the people in it, almost as if he had summoned up a diagram of it, although if there were a diagram, he was not aware of it.

It seemed almost as if the village were the Earth, a transplanted Earth with the old primeval problems and hopes of Earth—a family of peoples that faced existence with a readiness and confidence and inner strength.

From down the street he heard the creak of wagons and saw them coming around the bend, three wagons piled high and heading for the ship.

He stood and waited for them and as he waited the dog edged a little closer and sat regarding him with a not-quite-friendliness.

The wagons came up to him and stopped.

"Pharmaceutical materials, mostly," said the man who sat atop the first load, "It is the only thing we have that is worth the shipping."

"You seem to have a lot of it," Richard Daniel told him.

The man shook his head. "It's not so much. It's almost three years since a ship's been here. We'll have to wait another three, or more perhaps, before we see another."

He spat down on the ground.

"Sometimes it seems," he said, "that we're at the tail-end of nowhere. There are times we wonder if there is a soul that remembers we are here."

From the the direction of the ship, Richard Daniel heard the faint, strained violence of the captain's roaring.

"You'd better get on up there and unload," he told the man. "The captain is just sore enough he might not wait for you."

The man chuckled thinly. "I guess that's up to him," he said.

He flapped the reins and clucked good-naturedly at the horses.

"Hop up here with me," he said to Richard Daniel. "Or would you rather walk?"

"I'm not going with you," Richard Daniel said. "I am staying here. You can tell the captain."

For there was a baby sick and crying. There was a radio to fix. There was a culture to be planned and guided. There was a lot of work to do. This place, of all the places he had seen, had actual need of him.

The man chuckled once again. "The captain will not like it."

"Then tell him," said Richard Daniel, "to come down and talk to me. I am my own robot. I owe the captain nothing. I have more than paid any debt I owe him."

The wagon wheels began to turn and the man flapped the reins again.

"Make yourself at home," he said. "We're glad to have you stay."

"Thank you, sir," said Richard Daniel. "I'm pleased you want me."

He stood aside and watched the wagons lumber past, their wheels lifting and dropping thin films of powdered earth that floated in the air as an acrid dust.

Make yourself at home, the man had said before he'd driven off. And the words had a full round ring to them and a feel of warmth. It had been a long time, Richard Daniel thought, since he'd had a home.

A chance for resting and for knowing—that was what he needed. And a chance to serve, for now he knew that was the purpose in him. That was, perhaps, the real reason he was staying—because these people needed him . . . and he needed, queer as it might seem, this very need of theirs. Here on this Earth-like planet, through the generations, a new Earth would arise. And perhaps, given only time, he could transfer to the people of the planet all the powers and understanding he would find inside himself.

And stood astounded at the thought, for he'd not believed that he had it in him, this willing, almost eager, sacrifice. No messiah now, no robotic liberator, but a simple teacher of the human race.

Perhaps that had been the reason for it all from the first beginning. Perhaps all that had happened had been no more than the working out of human destiny. If the human race could not attain directly the paranormal power he held, this instinct of the mind, then they would gain it indirectly through the agency of one of their creations. Perhaps this, after all, unknown to Man himself, had been the prime purpose of the robots.

He turned and walked slowly down the length of village street, his back turned to the ship and the roaring of the captain, walked contentedly into this new world he'd found, into this world that he would make—not for himself, nor for robotic glory, but for a better Mankind and a happier.

Less than an hour before he'd congratulated himself on escaping all the traps of Earth, all the snares of Man. Not knowing that the greatest trap of all, the final and the fatal trap, lay on this present planet.

But that was wrong, he told himself. The trap had not been on this world at all, nor any other world. It had been inside himself.

He walked serenely down the wagon-rutted track in the soft, golden afternoon of a matchless autumn day, with the dog trotting at his heels.

Somewhere, just down the street, the sick baby lay crying in its crib.

GOOD NIGHT, MR. JAMES

I

HE came alive from nothing. He became aware from unawareness.

He smelled the air of the night and heard the trees whispering on the embankment above him and the breeze that had set the trees to whispering came down to him and felt him over with soft and tender fingers, for all the world as if it were examining him for broken bones or contusions and abrasions.

He sat up and put both his palms down upon the ground beside him to help him sit erect and stared into the darkness. Memory came slowly and when it came it was incomplete and answered nothing.

His name was Henderson James and he was a human being and he was sitting somewhere on a planet that was called the Earth. He was thirty-six years old and he was, in his own way, famous, and comfortably well-off. He lived in an old ancestral home on Summit Avenue, which was a respectable address even if it had lost some of its smartness in the last twenty years or so.

On the road above the slope of the embankment a car went past with its tires whining on the pavement and for a moment its headlights made the treetops glow. Far away, muted by the distance, a whistle cried out. And somewhere else a dog was barking with a flat viciousness.

His name was Henderson James and if that were true, why was he here? Why should Henderson James be sitting on the slope of an embankment, listening to the wind in the trees and to a wailing whistle and a barking dog?

Something had gone wrong, some incident that, if he could but remember it, might answer all his questions.

There was a job to do.

He sat and stared into the night and found that he was shivering, although there was no reason why he should, for the night was not that cold. Beyond the embankment he heard the sounds of a city late at night, the distant whine of the speeding car and the far-off wind-broken screaming of a siren. Once a man walked along a street close by and James sat listening to his footsteps until they faded out of hearing.

Something had happened and there was a job to do, a job that he had been doing, a job that somehow had been strangely interrupted by the inexplicable incident which had left him lying here on this embankment.

He checked himself. Clothing . . . shorts and shirt, strong shoes, his wristwatch and the gun in the holster at his side.

A gun?

The job involved a gun.

He had been hunting in the city, hunting something that required a gun. Something that was prowling in the night and a thing that must be killed.

Then he knew the answer, but even as he knew it he sat for a moment wondering at the strange, methodical, step-by-step progression of reasoning that had brought him to the memory. First his name and the basic facts pertaining to himself, then the realization of where he was and the problem of why he happened to be there and finally the realization that he had a gun and that it was meant to be used. It was a logical way to think, a primer schoolbook way to work it out:

I am a man named Henderson James.

I live in a house on Summit Avenue.

Am I in the house on Summit Avenue?

No, I am not in the house on Summit Avenue.

I am on an embankment somewhere.

Why am I on the embankment?

But it wasn't the way a man thought, at least not the normal way a normal man would think. Man thought in shortcuts. He cut across the block and did not go all the way around.

It was a frightening thing, he told himself, this clear-around-the-block thinking. It wasn't normal and it wasn't right and it made no sense at all . . . no more sense than did the fact that he should find himself in a place with no memory of getting there.

He rose to his feet and ran his hands up and down his body. His clothes were neat, not rumpled. He hadn't been beaten up and he hadn't been thrown from a speeding car. There were no sore places on his body and his face was unbloody and whole and he felt all right.

He hooked his fingers in the holster belt and shucked it up so that it rode tightly on his hips. He pulled out the gun and checked it with expert and familiar fingers and the gun was ready.

He walked up the embankment and reached the road, went across it with a swinging stride to reach the sidewalk that fronted the row of new bungalows. He heard a car coming and stepped off the sidewalk to crouch in a clump of evergreens that landscaped one corner of a lawn. The move was instinctive and he crouched there, feeling just a little foolish at the thing he'd done.

The car went past and no one saw him. They would not, he now realized, have noticed him even if he had remained out on the sidewalk.

He was unsure of himself; that must be the reason for his fear. There was a blank spot in his life, some mysterious incident that he did not know and the unknowing of it had undermined the sure and solid foundation of his own existence, had wrecked the basis of his motive and had turned him, momentarily, into a furtive animal that darted and hid at the approach of his fellow men.

That and something that had happened to him that made him think clear around the block.

He remained crouching in the evergreens, watching the street and the stretch of sidewalk, conscious of the white-painted, ghostly bungalows squatting back in their landscaped lots.

A word came into his mind. *Puudly.* An odd word, unearthly, yet it held terror.

The *puudly* had escaped and that was why he was here, hiding on the front lawn of some unsuspecting and sleeping citizen, equipped with a gun and a determination to use it, ready to match his wits and the quickness of brain and muscle against the most bloodthirsty, hate-filled thing yet found in the Galaxy.

The *puudly* was dangerous. It was not a thing to harbor. In fact, there was a law against harboring not only a *puudly*, but certain other alien beasties even less lethal than a *puudly*. There was good reason for such a law, reason which no one, much less himself, would ever think to question.

And now the *puudly* was loose and somewhere in the city.

James grew cold at the thought of it, his brain forming images of the things that might come to pass if he did not hunt down the alien beast and put an end to it.

Although beast was not quite the word to use. The *puudly* was more than a beast . . . just how much more than a beast he once had hoped to learn. He had not learned a lot, he now admitted to himself, not nearly all there was to learn, but he had learned enough. More than enough to frighten him.

For one thing, he had learned what hate could be and how shallow an emotion human hate turned out when measured against the depth and intensity and the ravening horror of the *puudly's* hate. Not unreasoning hate, for unreasoning hate defeats itself, but a rational, calculating, driving hate that motivated a clever and deadly killing machine which directed its rapacity and its cunning against every living thing that was not a *puudly*.

For the beast had a mind and a personality that operated upon the basic law of self-preservation against all comers, whoever they might be, extending that law to the interpretation that safety lay in one direction only . . . the death of every other living being. No other reason was needed for a *puudly's* killing. The fact that anything else lived and moved and was thus posing a threat, no matter how remote, against a *puudly*, was sufficient reason in itself.

It was psychotic, of course, some murderous instinct planted far back in time and deep in the creature's racial consciousness, but no more psychotic, perhaps, than many human instincts.

The *puudly* had been, and still was for that matter, a unique opportunity for a study in alien behaviorism. Given a permit, one could have studied them on their native planet. Refused a permit, one sometimes did a foolish thing, as James had.

And foolish acts backfire, as this one did.

James put down a hand and patted the gun at his side, as if by doing so he might derive some assurance that he was equal to the task. There was no question in his mind as to the thing that must be done. He must find the *puudly* and kill it and he must do that before the break of dawn. Anything less than that would be abject and horrifying failure.

For the *puudly* would bud. It was long past its time for the reproductive act and there were bare hours left to find it before it had loosed upon the Earth dozens of baby *puudlies*. They would not remain babies for long. A few hours after budding they would strike out on their own. To find one *puudly*, lost in the vastness of a sleeping city, seemed bad enough; to track down some dozens of them would be impossible.

So it was tonight or never.

Tonight there would be no killing on the *puudly's* part. Tonight the beast would be intent on one thing only, to find a place where it could rest in quiet, where it could give itself over, wholeheartedly and with no interference, to the business of bringing other *puudlies* into being.

It was clever. It would have known where it was going before it had escaped. There would be, on its part, no time wasted in seeking or in doubling back. It would have known where it was going and already it was there, already the buds would be rising on its body, bursting forth and growing.

There was one place, and one place only, in the entire city where an alien beast would be safe from prying eyes. A man could figure that one out and so could a *puudly*. The question was: Would the *puudly* know that a man could figure it out? Would the *puudly* underestimate a man? Or, knowing that the man would know it, too, would it find another place of hiding?

James rose from the evergreens and went down the sidewalk. The street marker at the corner, standing underneath a swinging street light, told him where he was and it was closer to the place where he was going than he might have hoped.

II

THE zoo was quiet for a while, and then something sent up a howl that raised James' hackles and made his blood stop in his veins.

James, having scaled the fence, stood tensely at its foot, trying to identify the howling animal. He was unable to place it. More than likely, he told himself, it was a new one. A person simply couldn't keep track of all the zoo's occupants. New ones were coming in all the time, strange, unheard of creatures from the distant stars.

Straight ahead lay the unoccupied moat cage that up until a day or two before had held an unbelievable monstrosity from the jungles of one of the Arctian worlds. James grimaced in the dark, remembering the thing. They had finally had to kill it.

And now the *puudly* was there . . . well, maybe not there, but one place that it could be, the one place in the entire city where it might be seen and arouse no comment, for the zoo was filled with animals that were seldom seen and another strange one would arouse only momentary wonder. One animal more would go unnoticed unless some zoo attendant should think to check the records.

There, in that unoccupied cage area, the *puudly* would be undisturbed, could quietly go about its business of budding out more *puudlies*. No one would bother it, for things like *puddlies* were the normal occupants of this place set aside for the strangers brought to Earth to be stared at and studied by that ferocious race, the humans.

James stood quietly beside the fence.

Henderson James. Thirty-six. Unmarried. Alien psychologist. An official of this zoo. And an offender against the law for having secured and harbored an alien being that was barred from Earth.

Why, he asked himself, did he think of himself in this way? Why, standing here, did he catalogue himself? It was instinctive to know one's self . . . there was no need, no sense of setting up a mental outline of one's self.

It had been foolish to go ahead with this *puudly* business. He recalled how he had spent days fighting it out with himself, reviewing all the disastrous possibilities which might arise from it. If the old renegade spaceman had not come to him and had not said, over a bottle of most delicious Lupan wine, that he could deliver, for a certain, rather staggering sum, one live *puudly*, in good condition, it never would have happened.

James was sure that of himself he never would have thought of it. But the old space captain was a man he knew and admired from former dealings. He was a man who was not averse to turning either an honest or a dishonest dollar, and yet he was a man, for all of that, you could depend upon. He would do what you paid him for and keep his lip buttoned tight once the deed was done.

James had wanted a *puudly*, for it was a most engaging beast with certain little tricks that, once understood, might open up new avenues of speculation and approach, might write new chapters in the tortuous study of alien minds and manners.

But for all of that, it had been a terrifying thing to do and now that the beast was loose, the terror was compounded. For it was not wholly beyond speculation that the descendants of this one brood that the escaped *puudly* would spawn might wipe out the population of the Earth, or at the best, make the Earth untenable for its rightful dwellers.

A place like the Earth, with its teeming millions, would provide a field day for the fangs of the *puddlies*, and the minds that drove the fangs. They would not hunt for hunger, nor for the sheer madness of the kill, but because of the compelling conviction that no *puudly* would be safe until Earth was wiped clean of life. They would be killing for survival, as a cornered rat would kill . . . except that they would be cornered nowhere but in the murderous insecurity of their minds.

If the posses scoured the Earth to hunt them down, they would be found in all directions, for they would be shrewd enough to scatter. They would know the ways of guns and traps and poisons and there would be more and more of them as time went on. Each of them would accelerate its budding to replace with a dozen or a hundred the ones that might be killed.

James moved quietly forward to the edge of the moat and let himself down into the mud that covered the bottom. When the monstrosity had been killed, the moat had been drained and should long since have been cleaned, but the press of work, James thought, must have prevented its getting done.

Slowly he waded out into the mud, feeling his way, his feet making sucking noises as he pulled them through the slime. Finally he reached the rocky incline that led out of the moat to the island cage.

He stood for a moment, his hands on the great, wet boulders, listening, trying to hold his breath so the sound of it would not interfere with hearing. The thing that howled had quieted and the night was deathly quiet. Or seemed, at first, to be. Then he heard the little insect noises that ran through the grass and bushes and the whisper of the leaves in the trees across the moat and the far-off sound that was the hoarse breathing of a sleeping city.

Now, for the first time, he felt fear. Felt it in the silence that was not a silence, in the mud beneath his feet, in the upthrust boulders that rose out of the moat.

The *puudly* was a dangerous thing, not only because it was strong and quick, but because it was intelligent. Just how intelligent, he did not know. It reasoned and it planned and schemed. It could talk, though not as a human talks . . . probably better than a human ever could. For it not only could talk words, but it could talk emotions. It lured its victims to it by the thoughts it put into their minds; it held them entranced with dreams and illusion until it slit their throats. It could purr a man to sleep, could lull him to suicidal inaction. It could drive him crazy with a single flickering thought, hurling a perception so foul and alien that the mind recoiled deep inside itself and stayed there, coiled tight, like a watch that has been over-wound and will not run.

It should have budded long ago, but it had fought off its budding, holding back against the day when it might escape, planning, he realized now, its fight to stay on Earth, which meant its conquest of Earth. It had planned, and planned well, against this very moment, and it would feel or show no mercy to anyone who interfered with it.

His hand went down and touched the gun and he felt the muscles in his jaw involuntarily tightening and suddenly there was at once a lightness and a hardness in him that had not been there before. He pulled himself up the boulder face, seeking cautious hand- and toeholds, breathing shallowly, body pressed against the rock. Quick-

ly, and surely, and no noise, for he must reach the top
and be there before the *puudly* knew there was anyone
around.

The *puudly* would be relaxed and intent upon its business, engrossed in the budding forth of that numerous
family that in days to come would begin the grim and
relentless crusade to make an alien planet safe for *puudlies* . . . and for *puudlies* alone.

That is, if the *puudly* were here and not somewhere
else. James was only a human trying to think like a *puudly*
and that was not an easy or a pleasant job and he had no
way of knowing if he succeeded. He could only hope that
his reasoning was vicious and crafty enough.

His clawing hand found grass and earth and he sank his
fingers deep into the soil, hauling his body up the last few
feet of the rock face above the pit.

He lay flat upon the gently sloping ground, listening,
tensed for any danger. He studied the ground in front of
him, probing every foot. Distant street lamps lighting the
zoo walks threw back the total blackness that had engulfed
him as he climbed out of the moat, but there still were
areas of shadow that he had to study closely.

Inch by inch, he squirmed his way along, making sure
of the terrain immediately ahead before he moved a
muscle. He held the gun in a rock-hard fist, ready for instant action, watching for the faintest hint of motion, alert
for any hump or irregularity that was not rock or bush or
grass.

Minutes magnified themselves into hours, his eyes ached
with staring and the lightness that had been in him drained
away, leaving only the hardness, which was as tense as a
drawn bow-string. A sense of failure began to seep into his
mind and with it came the full-fledged, until now unad-
mitted, realization of what failure meant, not only for the
world, but for the dignity and the pride that was Henderson James'.

Now, faced with the possibility, he admitted to himself
the action he must take if the *puudly* were not here, if he
did not find it here and kill it. He would have to notify
the authorities, would have to attempt to alert the police,
must plead with newspapers and radio to warn the citi-
zenry, must reveal himself as a man who, through pride

and self-conceit, had exposed the people of the Earth to this threat against their hold upon their native planet.

They would not believe him. They would laugh at him until the laughter died in their torn throats, choked off with their blood. He sweated, thinking of it, thinking of the price this city, and the world, would pay before it learned the truth.

There was a whisper of sound, a movement of black against deeper black.

The *puudly* rose in front of him, not more than six feet away, from its bed beside a bush. He jerked the pistol up and his finger tightened on the trigger.

"Don't," the *puudly* said inside his mind. "I'll go along with you."

His finger strained with the careful slowness of the squeeze and the gun leaped in his hand, but even as it did he felt the whiplash of terror slash at his brain, caught for just a second the terrible import, the mind-shattering obscenity that glanced off his mind and riccocheted away.

"Too late," he told the *puudly,* with his voice and his mind and his body shaking. "You should have tried that first. You wasted precious seconds. You would have got me if you had done it first."

It had been easy, he assured himself, much easier than he had thought. The *puudly* was dead or dying and the Earth and its millions of unsuspecting citizens were safe and, best of all, Henderson James was safe . . . safe from indignity, safe from being stripped naked of the little defenses he had built up through the years to shield him against the public stare. He felt relief flood over him and it left him pulseless and breathless and feeling clean, but weak.

"You fool," the dying *puudly* said, death clouding its words as they built up in his mind. "You fool, you half-thing, you duplicate . . ."

It died then and he felt it die, felt the life go out of it and leave it empty.

He rose softly to his feet and he seemed stunned and at first he thought it was from knowing death, from having touched hands with death within the *puudly's* mind.

The *puudly* had tried to fool him. Faced with the pistol, it had tried to throw him off his balance to give it the second that it needed to hurl the mind-blasting thought that had caught at the edge of his brain. If he had hesitated for a moment, he knew, it would have been all over with him. If his finger had slackened for a moment, it would have been too late.

The *puudly* must have known that he would think of the zoo as the first logical place to look and, even knowing that, it had held him in enough contempt to come here, had not even bothered to try to watch for him, had not tried to stalk him, had waited until he was almost on top of it before it moved.

And that was queer, for the *puudly* must have known, with its uncanny mental powers, every move that he had made. It must have maintained a casual contact with his mind every second of the time since it had escaped. He had known that and . . . wait a minute, he hadn't known it until this very moment, although, knowing it now, it seemed as if he had always known it.

What is the matter with me, he thought. There's something wrong with me. I should have known I could not surprise the *puudly*, and yet I didn't know it. I must have surprised it, for otherwise it would have finished me off quite leisurely at any moment after I climbed out of the moat.

You fool, the *puudly* had said. You fool, you half-thing, you duplicate . . .

You duplicate!

He felt the strength and the personality and the hard, unquestioned identity of himself as Henderson James, human being, drain out of him, as if someone had cut the puppet string and he, the puppet, had slumped supine upon the stage.

So that was why he had been able to surprise the *puudly!*

There were two Henderson Jameses. The *puudly* had been in contact with one of them, the original, the real Henderson James, had known every move he made, had known that it was safe so far as that Henderson James might be concerned. But had not known of the second Henderson James that had stalked it through the night.

Henderson James, duplicate.

Henderson James, temporary.

Henderson James, here tonight, gone tomorrow.

For they would not let him live. The original Henderson James would not allow him to continue living, and even if he did, the world would not allow it. Duplicates were made only for very temporary and very special reasons and it was always understood that once their purpose was accomplished they would be done away with.

Done away with . . . those were the words exactly. Gotten out of the way. Swept out of sight and mind. Killed as unconcernedly and emotionlessly as one chops off a chicken's head.

He walked forward and dropped on one knee beside the *puudly*, running his hand over its body in the darkness. Lumps stood out all over it, the swelling buds that now would never break to spew forth in a loathsome birth a brood of *puudly* pups.

He rose to his feet.

The job was done. The *puudly* had been killed—killed before it had given birth to a horde of horrors.

The job was done and he could go home.

Home?

Of course, that was the thing that had been planted in his mind, the thing they wanted him to do. To go home, to go back to the house on Summit Avenue, where his executioners would wait, to walk deliberately and unsuspectingly to the death that waited.

The job was done and his usefulness was over. He had been created to perform a certain task and the task was now performed and while an hour ago he had been a factor in the plans of men, he was no longer wanted. He was an embarrassment and superfluous.

Now wait a minute, he told himself. You may not be a duplicate. You do not feel like one.

That was true. He felt like Henderson James. He was Henderson James. He lived on Summit Avenue and had illegally brought to Earth a beast known as a *puudly* in order that he might study it and talk to it and test its alien reactions, attempt to measure its intelligence and guess at the strength and depth and the direction of its non-humanity. He had been a fool, of course, to do it, and yet at the time it had seemed important to understand the deadly, alien mentality.

I am human, he said, and that was right, but even so the fact meant nothing. Of course he was human. Henderson James was human and his duplicate would be exactly as human as the original. For the duplicate, processed from the pattern that held every trait and characteristic of the man he was to become a copy of, would differ in not a single basic factor.

In not a single basic factor, perhaps, but in certain other things. For no matter how much the duplicate might be like his pattern, no matter how full-limbed he might spring from his creation, he still would be a new man. He would have the capacity for knowledge and for thought and in a little time he would have and know and be all the things that his original was . . .

But it would take some time, some short while to come to a full realization of all he knew and was, some time to coordinate and recognize all the knowledge and experience that lay within his mind. At first he'd grope and search until he came upon the things that he must know. Until he became acquainted with himself, with the sort of man he was, he could not reach out blindly in the dark and put his hand exactly and unerringly upon the thing he wished.

That had been exactly what he'd done. He had groped and searched. He had been compelled to think, at first, in simple basic truths and facts.

I am a man.

I am on a planet called Earth.

I am Henderson James.

I live on Summit Avenue.

There is a job to do.

It had been quite a while, he remembered now, before he had been able to dig out of his mind the nature of the job.

There is a *puudly* to hunt down and destroy.

Even now he could not find in the hidden, still-veiled recesses of his mind the many valid reasons why a man should run so grave a risk to study a thing so vicious as a *puudly*. There were reasons, he knew there were, and in a little time he would know them quite specifically.

The point was that if he were Henderson James, original, he would know them now, know them as a part of himself and his life, without laboriously searching for them.

The *puudly* had known, of course. It had known, beyond any chance of error, that there were two Henderson Jameses. It had been keeping tabs on one when another one showed up. A mentality far less astute than the *puudly's* would have had no trouble in figuring that one out.

If the *puudly* had not talked, he told himself, I never would have known. If it had died at once and not had a chance to taunt me, I would not have known. I would even now be walking to the house on Summit Avenue.

He stood lonely and naked of soul in the wind that swept across the moated island. There was a sour bitterness in his mouth.

He moved a foot and touched the dead *puudly*.

"I'm sorry," he told the stiffening body. "I'm sorry now I did it. If I had known, I never would have killed you."

Stiffly erect, he moved away.

III

HE stopped at the street corner, keeping well in the shadow. Halfway down the block, and on the other side, was the house. A light burned in one of the rooms upstairs and another on the post beside the gate that opened into the yard, lighting the walk up to the door.

Just as if, he told himself, the house were waiting for the master to come home. And that, of course, was exactly what it was doing. An old lady of a house, waiting, hands folded in its lap, rocking very gently in a squeaky chair . . . and with a gun beneath the folded shawl.

His lip lifted in half a snarl as he stood there, looking at the house. What do they take me for, he thought, putting out a trap in plain sight and one that's not even baited? Then he remembered. They would not know, of course, that he knew he was a duplicate. They would think that he would think that he was Henderson James, the one and only. They would expect him to come walking home, quite naturally, believing he belonged there. So far as they would know, there would be no possibility of his finding out the truth.

And now that he had? Now that he was here, across the street from the waiting house?

He had been brought into being, had been given life, to do a job that his original had not dared to do, or had not wanted to do. He had carried out a killing his original didn't want to dirty his hands with, or risk his neck in doing.

Or had it not been that at all, but the necessity of two men working on the job, the original serving as a focus for the *puudly's* watchful mind while the other man sneaked up to kill it while it watched?

No matter what, he had been created, at a good stiff price, from the pattern of the man that was Henderson James. The wizardry of man's knowledge, the magic of machines, a deep understanding of organic chemistry, of human physiology, of the mystery of life, had made a second Henderson James. It was legal, of course, under certain circumstances . . . for example, in the case of public policy, and his own creation, he knew, might have been validated under such a heading. But there were conditions and one of these was that a duplicate not be allowed to continue living once it had served the specific purpose for which it had been created.

Usually such a condition was a simple one to carry out, for the duplicate was not meant to know he was a duplicate. So far as he was concerned, he was the original. There was no suspicion in him, no foreknowledge of the doom that was invariably ordered for him, no reason for him to be on guard against the death that waited.

The duplicate knitted his brow, trying to puzzle it out. There was a strange set of ethics here.

He was alive and he wanted to stay alive. Life, once it had been tasted, was too sweet, too good, to go back to the nothingness from which he had come . . . or would it be nothingness? Now that he had known life, now that he was alive, might he not hope for a life after death, the same as any other human being? Might not he, too, have the same human right as any other human to grasp at the shadowy and glorious promises and assurances held out by religion and by faith?

He tried to marshal what he knew about those promises and assurances, but his knowledge was illusive. A little later he would remember more about it. A little later, when the neural bookkeeper in his mind had been able to coordinate and activate the knowledge that he had inherited from the pattern, he would know.

He felt a trace of anger stir deep inside of him, anger at the unfairness of allowing him only a few short hours of life, of allowing him to learn how wonderful a thing life was, only to snatch it from him. It was a cruelty that went beyond mere human cruelty. It was something that had been fashioned out of the distorted perspective of a machine society that measured existence only in terms of mechanical and physical worth, that discarded with a ruthless hand whatever part of that society had no specific purpose.

The cruelty, he told himself, was in ever giving life, not in taking it away.

His original, of course, was the one to blame. He was the one who had obtained the *puudly* and allowed it to escape. It was his fumbling and his inability to correct his error without help which had created the necessity of fashioning a duplicate.

And yet, could he blame him?

Perhaps, rather, he owed him gratitude for a few hours of life at least, gratitude for the privilege of knowing what life was like. Although he could not quite decide whether or not it was something which called for gratitude.

He stood there, staring at the house. That light in the upstairs room was in the study off the master bedroom. Up there Henderson James, original, was waiting for the word that the duplicate had come home to death. It was an easy thing to sit there and wait, to sit and wait for the word that was sure to come. An easy thing to sentence to death a man one had never seen, even if that man be the walking image of one's self.

It would be a harder decision to kill him if you stood face to face with him . . . harder to kill someone who would be, of necessity, closer than a brother, someone who would be, even literally, flesh of your flesh, blood of your blood, brain of your brain.

There would be a practical side as well, a great advantage to be able to work with a man who thought as you did, who would be almost a second self. It would be almost as if there were two of you.

A thing like that could be arranged. Plastic surgery and a price for secrecy could make your duplicate into an unrecognizable other person. A little red tape, some finagling . . . but it could be done. It was a proposition that Henderson James, duplicate, thought would interest Henderson James, original. Or at least he hoped it would.

The room with the light could be reached with a little luck, with strength and agility and determination. The brick expanse of a chimney, its base cloaked by shrubs, its length masked by a closely growing tree, ran up the wall. A man could climb its rough brick face, could reach out and swing himself through the open window into the lighted room.

And once Henderson James, original, stood face to face with Henderson James, duplicate . . . well, it would be less of a gamble. The duplicate then would no longer be an impersonal factor. He would be a man and one that was very close to his original.

There would be watchers, but they would be watching the front door. If he were quiet, if he could reach and climb the chimney without making any noise, he'd be in the room before anyone would notice.

He drew back deeper in the shadows and considered. It was either get into the room and face his original, hope to be able to strike a compromise with him, or simply to light out . . . to run and hide and wait, watching his chance to get completely away, perhaps to some far planet in some other part of the Galaxy.

Both ways were a gamble, but one was quick, would either succeed or fail within the hour; the other might drag on for months with a man never knowing whether he was safe, never being sure.

Something nagged at him, a persistent little fact that skittered through his brain and eluded his efforts to pin it down. It might be important and then, again, it might be a random thing, simply a floating piece of information that was looking for its pigeonhole.

His mind shrugged it off.

The quick way or the long way?

He stood thinking for a moment and then moved swiftly down the street, seeking a place where he could cross in shadow.

He had chosen the short way.

IV

THE room was empty.

He stood beside the window, quietly, only his eyes moving, searching every corner, checking against a situation that couldn't seem quite true . . . that Henderson James was not here, waiting for the word.

Then he strode swiftly to the bedroom door and swung it open. His finger found the switch and the lights went on. The bedroom was empty and so was the bath. He went back into the study.

He stood with his back against the wall, facing the door that led into the hallway, but his eyes went over the room, foot by foot, orienting himself, feeling himself flow into the shape and form of it, feeling familiarity creep in upon him and enfold him in its comfort of belonging.

Here were the books, the fireplace with its mantel loaded with souvenirs, the easy chairs, the liquor cabinet . . . and all were a part of him, a background that was as much a part of Henderson James as his body and his inner thoughts were a part of him.

This, he thought, is what I would have missed, the experience I never would have had if the *puudly* had not taunted me. I would have died an empty and unrelated body that had no actual place in the universe.

The phone purred at him and he stood there startled by it, as if some intruder from the outside had pushed its way into the room, shattering the sense of belonging that had come to him.

The phone rang again and he went across the room and picked it up.

"James speaking," he said.

"That you, Mr. James?"

The voice was that of Anderson, the gardener.

"Why, yes," said the duplicate. "Who did you think it was?"

"We got a fellow here who says he's you."

Henderson James, duplicate, stiffened with fright and his hand, suddenly, was grasping the phone so hard that he found the time to wonder why it did not pulverize to bits beneath his fingers.

"He's dressed like you," the gardener said, "and I knew you went out. Talked to you, remember? Told you that you shouldn't? Not with us waiting for that . . . that thing."

"Yes," said the duplicate, his voice so even that he could not believe it was he who spoke. "Yes, certainly I remember talking with you."

"But, sir, how did you get back?"

"I came in the back way," the even voice said into the phone. "Now what's holding you back?"

"He's dressed like you."

"Naturally. Of course he would be, Anderson."

And that, to be sure, didn't quite follow, but Anderson wasn't too bright to start with and now he was somewhat upset.

"You remember," the duplicate said, "that we talked about it."

"I guess I was excited and forgot," admitted Anderson. "You told me to call you, to make sure you were in your study, though. That's right, isn't it, sir?"

"You've called me," the duplicate said, "and I am here."

"Then the other one out here is him?"

"Of course," said the duplicate. "Who else could it be?"

He put the phone back into the cradle and stood waiting. It came a moment after, the dull, throaty cough of a gun.

He walked to a chair and sank into it, spent with the knowledge of how events had so been ordered that now, finally, he was safe, safe beyond all question.

Soon he would have to change into other clothes, hide the gun and the clothes that he was wearing. The staff would ask no questions, most likely, but it was best to let nothing arouse suspicion in their minds.

He felt his nerves quieting and he allowed himself to glance about the room, take in the books and furnishings, the soft and easy . . . and earned . . . comfort of a man solidly and unshakably established in the world.

He smiled softly.

"It will be nice," he said.

It had been easy. Now that it was over, it seemed ridiculously easy. Easy because he had never seen the man who had walked up to the door. It was easy to kill a man you have never seen.

With each passing hour he would slip deeper and deeper into the personality that was his by right of heritage. There would be no one to question, after a time not even himself, that he was Henderson James.

The phone rang again and he got up to answer it.

A pleasant voice told him, "This is Allen, over at the duplication lab. We've been waiting for a report from you."

"Well," said James, "I . . ."

"I just called," interrupted Allen, "to tell you not to worry. It slipped my mind before."

"I see," said James, though he didn't.

"We did this one a little differently," Allen explained. "An experiment that we thought we'd try out. Slow poison in his bloodstream. Just another precaution. Probably not necessary, but we like to be positive. In case he fails to show up, you needn't worry any."

"I am sure he will show up."

Allen chuckled. "Twenty-four hours. Like a time bomb. No antidote for it even if he found out somehow."

"It was good of you to let me know," said James.

"Glad to," said Allen. "Good night, Mr. James."

DROP DEAD

THE critters were unbelievable. They looked like something from the maudlin pen of a well-alcoholed cartoonist.

One herd of them clustered in a semicircle in front of the ship, not jittery or belligerent—just looking at us. And that was strange. Ordinarily, when a spaceship sets down on a virgin planet, it takes a week at least for any life that might have seen or heard it to creep out of hiding and sneak a look around.

The critters were almost cow-size, but nohow as graceful as a cow. Their bodies were pushed together as if every blessed one of them had run full-tilt into a wall. And they were just as lumpy as you'd expect from a collision like that. Their hides were splashed with large squares of pastel color—the kind of color one never finds on any self-respecting animal: violet, pink, orange, chartreuse, to name only a few. The overall effect was of a checkerboard done by an old lady who made crazy quilts.

And that, by far, was not the worst of it.

From their heads and other parts of their anatomy sprouted a weird sort of vegetation, so that it appeared each animal was hiding, somewhat ineffectively, behind a skimpy thicket. To compound the situation and make it completely insane, fruits and vegetables—or what *appeared* to be fruits and vegetables—grew from the vegetation.

So we stood there, the critters looking at us and us looking back at them, and finally one of them walked forward until it was no more than six feet from us. It stood there for a moment, gazing at us soulfully, then dropped dead at our feet.

The rest of the herd turned around and trotted awkwardly away, for all the world as if they had done what they had come to do and now could go about their business.

Julian Oliver, our botanist, put up a hand and rubbed his balding head with an absent-minded motion.

"Another whatisit coming up!" he moaned. "Why couldn't it, for once, be something plain and simple?"

"It never is," I told him. "Remember that bush out on Hamal V that spent half its life as a kind of glorified tomato and the other half as grade A poison ivy?"

"I remember it," Oliver said sadly.

Max Weber, our biologist, walked over to the critter, reached out a cautious foot and prodded it.

"Trouble is," he said, "that Hamal tomato was Julian's baby and this one here is mine."

"I wouldn't say entirely yours," Oliver retorted. "What do you call that underbush growing out of it?"

I came in fast to head off an argument. I had listened to those two quarreling for the past twelve years, across several hundred light-years and on a couple dozen planets. I couldn't stop it here, I knew, but at least I could postpone it until they had something vital to quarrel about.

"Cut it out," I said. "It's only a couple of hours till nightfall and we have to get the camp set up."

"But this critter," Weber said. "We can't just leave it here."

"Why not? There are millions more of them. This one will stay right here and even if it doesn't—"

"But it dropped dead!"

"So it was old and feeble."

"It wasn't. It was right in the prime of life."

"We can talk about it later," said Alfred Kemper, our bacteriologist. "I'm as interested as you two, but what Bob says is right. We have to get the camp set up."

"Another thing," I added, looking hard at all of them. "No matter how innocent this place may look, we observe planet rules. No eating anything. No drinking any water. No wandering off alone. No carelessness of any kind."

"There's nothing here," said Weber. "Just the herds of critters. Just the endless plains. No trees, no hills, no nothing."

He really didn't mean it. He knew as well as I did the reason for observing planet rules. He only wanted to argue.

"All right," I said, "which is it? Do we set up camp or do we spend the night up in the ship?"

That did it.

We had the camp set up before the sun went down and by dusk we were all settled in. Carl Parsons, our ecologist, had the stove together and the supper started before the last tent peg was driven.

I dug out my diet kit and mixed up my formula and all of them kidded me about it, the way they always did.

It didn't bother me. Their jibes were automatic and I had automatic answers. It was something that had been going on for a long, long time. Maybe it was best that way, better than if they'd disregarded my enforced eating habits.

I remember Carl was grilling steaks and I had to move away so I couldn't smell them. There's never a time when I wouldn't give my good right arm for a steak or, to tell the truth, any other kind of normal chow. This diet stuff keeps a man alive all right, but that's about the only thing that can be said of it.

I know ulcers must sound silly and archaic. Ask any medic and he'll tell you they don't happen any more. But I have a riddled stomach and the diet kit to prove they sometimes do. I guess it's what you might call an occupational ailment. There's a lot of never-ending worry playing nursemaid to planet survey gangs.

After supper, we went out and dragged the critter in and had a closer look at it.

It was even worse to look at close than from a distance.

There was no fooling about that vegetation. It was the real McCoy and it was part and parcel of the critter. But it seemed that it only grew out of certain of the color blocks in the critter's body.

We found another thing that practically had Weber frothing at the mouth. One of the color blocks had holes in it—it looked almost exactly like one of those peg sets that children use as toys. When Weber took out his jack-knife and poked into one of the holes, he pried out an insect that looked something like a bee. He couldn't quite believe it, so he did some more probing and in another one of the holes he found another bee. Both of the bees were dead.

He and Oliver wanted to start dissection then and there, but the rest of us managed to talk them out of it.

We pulled straws to see who would stand first guard and, with my usual luck, I pulled the shortest straw. Actually there wasn't much real reason for standing guard, with the alarm system set to protect the camp, but it was regulation—there had to be a guard.

I got a gun and the others said good night and went to their tents, but I could hear them talking for a long time afterward. No matter how hardened you may get to this survey business, no matter how blasé, you hardly ever get much sleep the first night on any planet.

I sat on a chair at one side of the camp table, on which burned a lantern in lieu of the campfire we would have had on any other planet. But here we couldn't have a fire because there wasn't any wood.

I sat at one side of the table, with the dead critter lying on the other side of it and I did some worrying, although it wasn't time for me to start worrying yet. I'm an agricultural economist and I don't begin my worrying until at least the first reports are in.

But sitting just across the table from where it lay, I couldn't help but do some wondering about that mixed-up critter. I didn't get anywhere except go around in circles and I was sort of glad when Talbott Fullerton, the Double Eye, came out and sat down beside me.

Sort of, I said. No one cared too much for Fullerton. I have yet to see the Double Eye I or anybody else ever cared much about.

"Too excited to sleep?" I asked him.

He nodded vaguely, staring off into the darkness beyond the lantern's light.

"Wondering," he said. "Wondering if this could be the planet."

"It won't be," I told him. "You're chasing an El Dorado, hunting down a fable."

"They found it once before," Fullerton argued stubbornly. "It's all there in the records."

"So was the Gilded Man. And the Empire of Prester John. Atlantis and all the rest of it. So was the old Northwest Passage back on ancient Earth. So were the Seven Cities. But nobody ever found any of those places because they weren't there."

He sat with the lamplight in his face and he had that

wild look in his eyes and his hands were knotting into fists, then straightening out again.

"Sutter," he said unhappily, "I don't know why you do this—this mocking of yours. Somewhere in this universe there is immortality. Somewhere, somehow, it has been accomplished. And the human race must find it. We have the space for it now—all the space there is—millions of planets and eventually other galaxies. We don't have to keep making room for new generations, the way we would if we were stuck on a single world or a single solar system. Immortality, I tell you, is the next step for humanity!"

"Forget it," I said curtly, but once a Double Eye gets going, you can't shut him up.

"Look at this planet," he said. "An almost perfect Earth-type planet. Main-sequence sun. Good soil, good climate, plenty of water—an ideal place for a colony. How many years, do you think, before Man will settle here?"

"A thousand. Five thousand. Maybe more."

"That's right. And there are countless other planets like it, planets crying to be settled. But we won't settle them, because we keep dying off. And that's not all of it . . ."

Patiently, I listened to all the rest—the terrible waste of dying—and I knew every bit of it by heart. Before Fullerton, we'd been saddled by one Double Eye fanatic and, before him, yet another. It was regulation. Every planet-checking team, no matter what its purpose or its destination, was required to carry as supercargo an agent of Immortality Institute.

But this kid seemed just a little worse than the usual run of them. It was his first trip out and he was all steamed up with idealism. In all of them, though, burned the same intense dedication to the proposition that Man must live forever and an equally unyielding belief that immortality could and would be found. For had not a lost spaceship found the answer centuries before—an unnamed spaceship on an unknown planet in a long-forgotten year!

It was a myth, of course. It had all the hallmarks of one and all the fierce loyalty that a myth can muster. It was kept alive by Immortality Institute, operating under a government grant and billions of bequests and gifts from hopeful rich and poor—all of whom, of course, had died or would die in spite of their generosity.

"What are you looking for?" I asked Fullerton, just a

little wearily, for I was bored with it. "A plant? An animal? A people?"

And he replied, solemn as a judge: "That's something I can't tell you."

As if I gave a damn!

But I went on needling him. Maybe it was just something to while away my time. That and the fact that I disliked the fellow. Fanatics annoy me. They won't get off your ear.

"Would you know it if you found it?"

He didn't answer that one, but he turned haunted eyes on me.

I cut out the needling. Any more of it and I'd have had him bawling.

We sat around a while longer, but we did no talking.

He fished a toothpick out of his pocket and put it in his mouth and rolled it around, chewing at it moodily. I would have liked to reach out and slug him, for he chewed toothpicks all the time and it was an irritating habit that set me unreasonably on edge. I guess I was jumpy, too.

Finally he spit out the mangled toothpick and slouched off to bed.

I sat alone, looking up at the ship, and the lantern light was just bright enough for me to make out the legend lettered on it: *Caph VII—Ag Survey* 286, which was enough to identify us anywhere in the Galaxy.

For everyone knew Caph VII, the agricultural experimental planet, just as they would have known Alderbaran XII, the medical research planet, or Capella IX, the university planet, or any of the other special departmental planets.

Caph VII is a massive operation and the hundreds of survey teams like us were just a part of it. But we were the spearheads who went out to new worlds, some of them uncharted, some just barely charted, looking for plants and animals that might be developed on the experimental tracts.

Not that our team had found a great deal. We had discovered some grasses that did well on one of the Eltanian worlds, but by and large we hadn't done anything that could be called distinguished. Our luck just seemed to run bad—like that Hamal poison ivy business. We worked as hard as any of the rest of them, but a lot of good that did.

Sometimes it was tough to take—when all the other teams brought in stuff that got them written up and earned them bonuses, while we came creeping in with a few piddling grasses or maybe not a thing at all.

It's a tough life and don't let anyone tell you different. Some of the planets turn out to be a fairly rugged business. At times, the boys come back pretty much the worse for wear and there are times when they don't come back at all.

But right now it looked as though we'd hit it lucky—a peaceful planet, good climate, easy terrain, no hostile inhabitants and no dangerous fauna.

Weber took his time relieving me at guard, but finally he showed up.

I could see he still was goggle-eyed about the critter. He walked around it several times, looking it over.

"That's the most fantastic case of symbiosis I have ever seen," he said. "If it weren't lying over there, I'd say it was impossible. Usually you associate symbiosis with the lower, more simple forms of life."

"You mean that brush growing out of it?"

He nodded.

"And the bees?"

He gagged over the bees.

"How are you so sure it's symbiosis?"

He almost wrung his hands. "I *don't* know," he admitted.

I gave him the rifle and went to the tent I shared with Kemper. The bacteriologist was awake when I came in.

"That you, Bob?"

"It's me. Everything's all right."

"I've been lying here and thinking," he said. "This is a screwy place."

"The critters?"

"No, not the critters. The planet itself. Never saw one like it. It's positively naked. No trees. No flowers. Nothing. It's just a sea of grass."

"Why not?" I asked. "Where does it say you can't find a pasture planet?"

"It's too simple," he protested. "Too simplified. Too neat and packaged. Almost as if someone had said let's make a simple planet, let's cut out all the frills, let's skip all the biological experiments and get right down to basics. Just one form of life and the grass for it to eat."

"You're way out on a limb," I told him. "How do you know all this? There may be other life-forms. There may be complexities we can't suspect. Sure, all we've seen are the critters, but maybe that's because there are so many of them."

"To hell with you," he said and turned over on his cot.

Now there's a guy I liked. We'd been tent partners ever since he'd joined the team better than ten years before and we got along fine.

Often I had wished the rest could get along as well. But it was too much to expect.

The fighting started right after breakfast, when Oliver and Weber insisted on using the camp table for dissecting. Parsons, who doubled as cook, jumped straight down their throats. Why he did it, I don't know. He knew before he said a word that he was licked, hands down. The same thing had happened many times before and he knew, no matter what he did or said, they would use the table.

But he put up a good battle. "You guys go and find some other place to do your butchering! Who wants to eat on a table that's all slopped up?"

"But, Carl, where can we do it? We'll use only one end of the table."

Which was a laugh, because in half an hour they'd be sprawled all over it.

"Spread out a canvas," Parsons snapped back.

"You can't dissect on a canvas. You got to have—"

"Another thing. How long do you figure it will take? In a day or two, that critter is going to get ripe."

It went on like that for quite a while, but by the time I started up the ladder to get the animals, Oliver and Weber had flung the critter on the table and were at work on it.

Unshipping the animals is something not exactly in my line of duty, but over the years I'd taken on the job of getting them unloaded, so they'd be there and waiting when Weber or some of the others needed them to run off a batch of tests.

I went down into the compartment where we kept them in their cages. The rats started squeaking at me and the zartyls from Centauri started screeching at me and the punkins from Polaris made an unholy racket, because the punkins are hungry all the time. You just can't give them enough to eat. Turn them loose with food and they'd eat themselves to death.

It was quite a job to get them all lugged up to the port and to rig up a sling and lower them to the ground, but I finally finished it without busting a single cage. That was an accomplishment. Usually I smashed a cage or two and some of the animals escaped and then Weber would froth around for days about my carelessness.

I had the cages all set out in rows and was puttering with canvas flies to protect them from the weather when Kemper came along and stood watching me.

"I have been wandering around," he announced. From the way he said it, I could see he had the wind up.

But I didn't ask him, for then he'd never have told me. You had to wait for Kemper to make up his mind to talk.

"Peaceful place," I said and it was all of that. It was a bright, clear day and the sun was not too warm. There was a little breeze and you could see a long way off. And it was quiet. Really quiet. There wasn't any noise at all.

"It's a lonesome place," said Kemper.

"I don't get you," I answered patiently.

"Remember what I said last night? About this planet being too simplified?"

He stood watching me put up the canvas, as if he might be considering how much more to tell me. I waited.

Finally, he blurted it. "Bob, there are no insects!"

"What have insects—"

"You know what I mean," he said. "You go out on Earth or any Earthlike planet and lie down in the grass and watch. You'll see the insects. Some of them on the ground and others on the grass. There'll be all kinds of them."

"And there aren't any here?"

He shook his head. "None that I could see. I wandered around and lay down and looked in a dozen different places. Stands to reason a man should find some insects if he looked all morning. It isn't natural, Bob."

I kept on with my canvas and I don't know why it was, but I got a little chilled about there not being any insects. Not that I care a hoot for insects, but as Kemper said, it was unnatural, although you come to expect the so-called unnatural in this planet-checking business.

"There are the bees," I said.

"What bees?"

"The ones that are in the critters. Didn't you see any?"

"None," he said. "I didn't get close to any critter herds. Maybe the bees don't travel very far."

"Any birds?"

"I didn't see a one," he said. "But I was wrong about the flowers. The grass has tiny flowers."

"For the bees to work on."

Kemper's face went stony. "That's right. Don't you see the pattern of it, the planned—"

"I see it," I told him.

He helped me with the canvas and we didn't say much more. When we had it done, we walked into camp.

Parsons was cooking lunch and grumbling at Oliver and Weber, but they weren't paying much attention to him. They had the table littered with different parts they'd carved out of the critter and they were looking slightly numb.

"No brain," Weber said to us accusingly, as if we might have made off with it when he wasn't looking. "We can't find a brain and there's no nervous system."

"It's impossible," declared Oliver. "How can a highly organized, complex animal exist without a brain or nervous system?"

"Look at that butcher shop!" Parsons yelled wrathfully from the stove. "You guys will have to eat standing up!"

"Butcher shop is right," Weber agreed. "As near as we can figure out, there are at least a dozen different kinds of flesh—some fish, some fowl, some good red meat. Maybe a little lizard, even."

"An all-purpose animal," said Kemper. "Maybe we found something finally."

"If it's edible," Oliver added. "If it doesn't poison you. If it doesn't grow hair all over you."

"That's up to you," I told him. "I got the cages down and all lined up. You can start killing off the little cusses to your heart's content."

Weber looked ruefully at the mess on the table.

"We did just a rough exploratory job," he explained. "We ought to start another one from scratch. You'll have to get in on that next one, Kemper."

Kemper nodded glumly.

Weber looked at me. "Think you can get us one?"

"Sure," I said. "No trouble."

It wasn't.

Right after lunch, a lone critter came walking up, as if to visit us. It stopped about six feet from where we sat, gazed at us soulfully, then obligingly dropped dead.

During the next few days, Oliver and Weber barely took time out to eat and sleep. They sliced and probed. They couldn't believe half the things they found. They argued. They waved their scalpels in the air to emphasize their anguish. They almost broke down and wept. Kemper filled box after box with slides and sat hunched, half petrified, above his microscope.

Parsons and I wandered around while the others worked. He dug up some soil samples and tried to classify the grasses and failed, because there weren't any grasses—there was just one type of grass. He made notes on the weather and ran an analysis of the air and tried to pull together an ecological report without a lot to go on.

I looked for insects and I didn't find any except the bees and I never saw those unless I was near a critter herd. I watched for birds and there were none. I spent two days investigating a creek, lying on my belly and staring down into the water, and there were no signs of life. I hunted up a sugar sack and put a hoop in the mouth of it and spent another two days seining. I didn't catch a thing—not a fish, not even a crawdad, not a single thing.

By that time, I was ready to admit that Kemper had guessed right.

Fullerton walked around, too, but we paid no attention to him. All the Double Eyes, every one of them, always were looking for something no one else could see. After a while, you got pretty tired of them. I'd spent twenty years getting tired of them.

The last day I went seining, Fullerton stumbled onto me late in the afternoon. He stood up on the bank and watched me working in a pool. When I looked up, I had the feeling he'd been watching me for quite a little while.

"There's nothing there," he said.

The way he said it, he made it sound as if he'd known all along there was nothing there and that I was a fool for looking.

But that wasn't the only reason I got sore.

Sticking out of his face, instead of the usual toothpick,

was a stem of grass and he was rolling it around in his
lips and chewing it the way he chewed the toothpicks.

"Spit out that grass!" I shouted at him. "You fool, spit
it out!"

His eyes grew startled and he spit out the grass.

"It's hard to remember," he mumbled. "You see, it's my
first trip out and—"

"It could be your last one, too," I told him brutally.
"Ask Weber sometime, when you have a moment, what
happened to the guy who pulled a leaf and chewed it.
Absent-minded, sure. Habit, certainly. He was just as dead
as if he'd committed suicide."

Fullerton stiffened up.

"I'll keep it in mind," he said.

I stood there, looking up at him, feeling a little sorry
that I'd been so tough with him.

But I had to be. There were so many absent-minded,
well-intentioned ways a man could kill himself.

"You find anything?" I asked.

"I've been watching the critters," he said. "There was
something funny that I couldn't quite make out at first . . ."

"I can list you a hundred funny things."

"That's not what I mean, Sutter. Not the patchwork
color or the bushes growing out of them. There was something else. I finally got it figured out. *There aren't any
young.*"

Fullerton was right, of course. I realized it now, after he
had told me. There weren't any calves or whatever you
might call them. All we'd seen were adults. And yet that
didn't necessarily mean there *weren't* any calves. It just
meant we hadn't seen them. And the same, I knew, applied as well to insects, birds and fish. They all might be
on the planet, but we just hadn't managed to find them
yet.

And then, belatedly, I got it—the inference, the hope,
the half-crazy fantasy behind this thing that Fullerton had
found, or imagined he'd found.

"You're downright loopy," I said flatly.

He stared back at me and his eyes were shining like a
kid's at Christmas.

He said: "It had to happen sometime, Sutter, somewhere."

I climbed up the bank and stood beside him. I looked

at the net I still held in my hands and threw it back into the creek and watched it sink.

"Be sensible," I warned him. "You have no evidence. Immortality wouldn't work that way. It couldn't. That way, it would be nothing but a dead end. Don't mention it to anyone. They'd ride you without mercy all the way back home."

I don't know why I wasted time on him. He stared back at me stubbornly, but still with that awful light of hope and triumph on his face.

"I'll keep my mouth shut," I told him curtly. "I won't say a word."

"Thanks, Sutter," he answered. "I appreciate it a lot."

I knew from the way he said it that he could murder me with gusto.

We trudged back to camp.

The camp was all slicked up.

The dissecting mess had been cleared away and the table had been scrubbed so hard that it gleamed. Parsons was cooking supper and singing one of his obscene ditties. The other three sat around in their camp chairs and they had broken out some liquor and were human once again.

"All buttoned up?" I asked, but Oliver shook his head.

They poured a drink for Fullerton and he accepted it, a bit ungraciously, but he did take it. That was some improvement on the usual Double Eye.

They didn't offer me any. They knew I couldn't drink it.

"What have we got?" I asked.

"It could be something good," said Oliver. "It's a walking menu. It's an all-purpose animal, for sure. It lays eggs, gives milk, makes honey. It has six different kinds of red meat, two of fowl, one of fish and a couple of others we can't identify."

"Lays eggs," I said. "Gives milk. Then it reproduces."

"Certainly," said Weber. "What did you think?"

"There aren't any young."

Weber grunted. "Could be they have nursery areas. Certain places instinctively set aside in which to rear their young."

"Or they might have instinctive birth control," suggested Oliver. "That would fit in with the perfectly balanced ecology Kemper talks about."

Weber snorted. "Ridiculous!"

"Not so ridiculous," Kemper retorted. "Not half so ridiculous as some other things we found. Not one-tenth as ridiculous as no brain or nervous system. Not any more ridiculous than my bacteria."

"Your bacteria!" Weber said. He drank down half a glass of liquor in a single gulp to make his disdain emphatic.

"The critters swarm with them," Kemper went on. "You find them everywhere throughout the entire animal. Not just in the bloodstream, not in restricted areas, but in the entire organism. And all of them the same. Normally it takes a hundred different kinds of bacteria to make a metabolism work, but here there's only one. And that one, by definition, must be general purpose—it must do all the work that the hundred other species do."

He grinned at Weber. "I wouldn't doubt but right there are your brains and nervous systems—the bacteria doubling in brass for both systems."

Parsons came over from the stove and stood with his fists planted on his hips, a steak fork grasped in one hand and sticking out at a tangent from his body.

"If you ask me," he announced, "there ain't no such animal. The critters are all wrong. They can't be made that way."

"But they are," said Kemper.

"It doesn't make sense! One kind of life. One kind of grass for it to eat. I'll bet that if we could make a census, we'd find the critter population is at exact capacity—just so many of them to the acre, figured down precisely to the last mouthful of grass. Just enough for them to eat and no more. Just enough so the grass won't be overgrazed. Or undergrazed, for that matter."

"What's wrong with that?" I asked, just to needle him. I thought for a minute he'd take the steak fork to me.

"What's *wrong* with it?" he thundered. "Nature's never static, never standing still. But here it's standing still. Where's the competition? Where's the evolution?"

"That's not the point," said Kemper quietly. "The fact is that that's the way it is. The point is *why*? How did it happen? How was it planned? *Why* was it planned?"

"Nothing's planned," Weber told him sourly. "You know better than to talk like that."

Parsons went back to his cooking. Fullerton had wandered off somewhere. Maybe he was discouraged from hearing about the eggs and milk.

For a time, the four of us just sat.

Finally Weber said: "The first night we were here, I came out to relieve Bob at guard and I said to him . . ."

He looked at me. "You remember, Bob?"

"Sure. You said symbiosis."

"And now?" asked Kemper.

"I don't know. It simply couldn't happen. But if it did—if it *could*—this critter would be the most beautifully logical example of symbiosis you could dream up. Symbiosis carried to its logical conclusion. Like, long ago, all the life-forms said let's quit this feuding, let's get together, let's cooperate. All the plants and animals and fish and bacteria got together—"

"It's far-fetched, of course," said Kemper. "But, by and large, it's not anything unheard of, merely carried further, that's all. Symbiosis is a recognized way of life and there's nothing—"

Parsons let out a bellow for them to come and get it, and I went to my tent and broke out my diet kit and mixed up a mess of goo. It was a relief to eat in private, without the others making cracks about the stuff I had to choke down.

I found a thin sheaf of working notes on the small wooden crate I'd set up for a desk. I thumbed through them while I ate. They were fairly sketchy and sometimes hard to read, being smeared with blood and other gook from the dissecting table. But I was used to that. I worked with notes like that all the blessed time. So I was able to decipher them.

The whole picture wasn't there, of course, but there was enough to bear out what they'd told me and a good deal more as well.

For examples, the color squares that gave the critters their crazy-quiltish look were separate kinds of meat or fish or fowl or unknown food, whatever it might be. Almost as if each square was the present-day survivor of each ancient symbiont—if, in fact, there was any basis to this talk of symbiosis.

The egg-laying apparatus was described in some biologic detail, but there seemed to be no evidence of recent egg production. The same was true of the lactation system.

There were, the notes said in Oliver's crabbed writing, five kinds of fruit and three kinds of vegetables to be derived from the plants growing from the critters.

I shoved the notes to one side and sat back on my chair, gloating just a little.

Here was diversified farming with a vengeance! You had meat and dairy herds, fish pond, aviary, poultry yard, orchard and garden rolled into one, all in the body of a single animal that was a complete farm in itself!

I went through the notes hurriedly again and found what I was looking for. The food product seemed high in relation to the gross weight of the animal. Very little would be lost in dressing out.

That is the kind of thing an ag economist has to consider. But that isn't all of it, by any means. What if a man couldn't eat the critter? Suppose the critters couldn't be moved off the planet because they died if you took them from their range?

I recalled how they'd just walked up and died; that in itself was another headache to be filed for future worry.

What if they could only eat the grass that grew on this one planet? And if so, could the grass be grown elsewhere? What kind of tolerance would the critter show to different kinds of climate? What was the rate of reproduction? If it was slow, as was indicated, could it be stepped up? What was the rate of growth?

I got up and walked out of the tent and stood for a while, outside. The little breeze that had been blowing had died down at sunset and the place was quiet. Quiet because there was nothing but the critters to make any noise and we had yet to hear them make a single sound. The stars blazed overhead and there were so many of them that they lighted up the countryside as if there were a moon.

I walked over to where the rest of the men were sitting.

"It looks like we'll be here for a while," I said. "Tomorrow we might as well get the ship unloaded."

No one answered me, but in the silence I could sense the half-hidden satisfaction and the triumph. At last we'd hit the jackpot! We'd be going home with something that would make those other teams look pallid. *We'd* be the ones who got the notices and bonuses.

Oliver finally broke the silence. "Some of our animals aren't in good shape. I went down this afternoon to have a look at them. A couple of the pigs and several of the rats."

He looked at me accusingly.

I flared up at him. "Don't look at me! I'm not their keeper. I just take care of them until you're ready to use them."

Kemper butted in to head off an argument. "Before we do any feeding, we'll need another critter."

"I'll lay you a bet," said Weber.

Kemper didn't take him up.

It was just as well he didn't, for a critter came in, right after breakfast, and died with a *savoir faire* that was positively marvelous. They went to work on it immediately.

Parsons and I started unloading the supplies. We put in a busy day. We moved all the food except the emergency rations we left in the ship. We slung down a refrigerating unit Weber had been yelling for, to keep the critter products fresh. We unloaded a lot of equipment and some silly odds and ends that I knew we'd have no use for, but that some of the others wanted broken out. We put up tents and we lugged and pushed and hauled all day. Late in the afternoon, we had it all stacked up and under canvas and were completely bushed.

Kemper went back to his bacteria. Weber spent hours with the animals. Oliver dug up a bunch of grass and gave the grass the works. Parsons went out on field trips, mumbling and fretting.

Of all of us, Parsons had the job that was most infuriating. Ordinarily the ecology of even the simplest of planets is a complicated business and there's a lot of work to do. But here was almost nothing. There was no competition for survival. There was no dog eat dog. There were just critters cropping grass.

I started to pull my report together, knowing that it would have to be revised and rewritten again and again. But I was anxious to get going. I fairly itched to see the pieces fall together—although I knew from the very start some of them wouldn't fit. They almost never do.

Things went well. Too well, it sometimes seemed to me.

There were incidents, of course, like when the punkins somehow chewed their way out of their cage and disappeared.

Weber was almost beside himself.

"They'll come back," said Kemper. "With that appetite of theirs, they won't stay away for long."

And he was right about that part of it. The punkins were the hungriest creatures in the Galaxy. You could never feed them enough to satisfy them. And they'd eat anything. It made no difference to them, just so there was a lot of it.

And it was that very factor in their metabolism that made them invaluable as research animals.

The other animals thrived on the critter diet. The carnivorous ones ate the critter-meat and the vegetarians chomped on critter-fruit and critter vegetables. They all grew sleek and sassy. They seemed in better health than the control animals, which continued their regular diet. Even the pigs and rats that had been sick got well again and as fat and happy as any of the others.

Kemper told us, "This critter stuff is more than just a food. It's a medicine. I can see the signs: 'Eat Critter and Keep Well!'"

Weber grunted at him. He was never one for joking and I think he was a worried man. A thorough man, he'd found too many things that violated all the tenets he'd accepted as the truth. No brain or nervous system. The ability to die at will. The lingering hint of wholesale symbiosis. And the bacteria.

The bacteria, I think, must have seemed to him the worst of all.

There was, it now appeared, only one type involved. Kemper had hunted frantically and had discovered no others. Oliver found it in the grass. Parsons found it in the soil and water. The air, strangely enough, seemed to be free of it.

But Weber wasn't the only one who worried. Kemper worried, too. He unloaded most of it just before our bedtime, sitting on the edge of his cot and trying to talk the worry out of himself while I worked on my reports.

And he'd picked the craziest point imaginable to pin his worry on.

"You can explain it all," he said, "if you are only willing to concede on certain points. You can explain the critters if you're willing to believe in a symbiotic arrangement carried out on a planetary basis. You can believe in the utter simplicity of the ecology if you're willing to assume that, given space and time enough, anything can happen within the bounds of logic.

"You can visualize how the bacteria might take the place of brains and nervous systems if you're ready to say this is a bacterial world and not a critter world. And you can even envision the bacteria—all of them, every single one of them—as forming one gigantic linked intelligence. And if you accept that theory, then the voluntary deaths become understandable, because there's no actual death involved—it's just like you or me trimming off a hangnail. And if this is true, then Fullerton has found immortality, although it's not the kind he was looking for and it won't do him or us a single bit of good.

"But the thing that worries me," he went on, his face all knotted up with worry, "is the seeming lack of anything resembling a defense mechanism. Even assuming that the critters are no more than fronting for a bacterial world, the mechanism should be there as a simple matter of precaution. Every living thing we know of has some sort of way to defend itself or to escape potential enemies. It either fights or runs and hides to preserve its life."

He was right, of course. Not only did the critters have no defense, they even saved one the trouble of going out to kill them.

"Maybe we are wrong," Kemper concluded. "Maybe life, after all, is not as valuable as we think it is. Maybe it's not a thing to cling to. Maybe it's not worth fighting for. Maybe the critters, in their dying, are closer to the truth than we."

It would go on like that, night after night, with Kemper talking around in circles and never getting anywhere. I think most of the time he wasn't talking to me, but talking to himself, trying by the very process of putting it in words to work out some final answer.

And long after we had turned out the lights and gone to bed, I'd lie on my cot and think about all that Kemper said and I thought in circles, too. I wondered why all the critters that came in and died were in the prime of life. Was the dying a privilege that was accorded only to the fit? Or were all the critters in the prime of life? Was there really some cause to believe they might be immortal?

I asked a lot of questions, but there weren't any answers.

We continued with our work. Weber killed some of his animals and examined them and there were no signs of ill effect from the critter diet. There were traces of critter bacteria in their blood, but no sickness, reaction or antibody formation. Kemper kept on with his bacterial work. Oliver started a whole series of experiments with the grass. Parsons just gave up.

The punkins didn't come back and Parsons and Fullerton went out and hunted for them, but without success.

I worked on my report and the pieces fell together better than I had hoped they would.

It began to look as though we had the situation well nailed down.

We all were feeling pretty good. We could almost taste that bonus.

But I think that, in the back of our minds, all of us were wondering if we could get away scot free. I know I had mental fingers crossed. It just didn't seem quite possible that something wouldn't happen.

And, of course, it did.

We were sitting around after supper, with the lantern lighted, when we heard the sound. I realized afterward that we had been hearing it for some time before we paid attention to it. It started so soft and so far away that it crept upon us without alarming us. At first, it sounded like a sighing, as if a gentle wind were blowing through a little tree, and then it changed into a rumble, but a far-off rumble that had no menace in it. I was just getting ready to say something about thunder and wondering if our stretch of weather was about to break when Kemper jumped up and yelled.

I don't know what he yelled. Maybe it wasn't a word at all. But the way he yelled brought us to our feet and sent us at a dead run for the safety of the ship. Even before we got there, in the few seconds it took to reach the ladder, the character of the sound had changed and there was no mistaking what it was—the drumming of hoofs heading straight for camp.

They were almost on top of us when we reached the ladder and there wasn't time or room for all of us to use it. I was the last in line and I saw I'd never make it and a dozen possible escape plans flickered through my mind. But I knew they wouldn't work fast enough. Then I saw the rope, hanging where I'd left it after the unloading job, and I made a jump for it. I'm no rope-climbing expert, but I shinnied up it with plenty of speed. And right behind me came Weber, who was no rope-climber, either, but who was doing rather well.

I thought of how lucky it had been that I hadn't found the time to take down the rig and how Weber had ridden me unmercifully about not doing it. I wanted to shout down and point it out to him, but I didn't have the breath.

We reached the port and tumbled into it. Below us, the stampeding critters went grinding through the camp. There seemed to be millions of them. One of the terrifying things about it was how silently they ran. They made no outcry of any kind; all you could hear was the sound of their hoofs pounding on the ground. It seemed almost as if they ran in some blind fury that was too deep for outcry.

They spread for miles, as far as one could see on the starlit plains, but the spaceship divided them and they flowed to either side of it and then flowed back again, and beyond the spaceship there was a little sector that they never touched. I thought how we could have been safe staying on the ground and huddling in that sector, but that's one of the things a man never can foresee.

The stampede lasted for almost an hour. When it was all over, we came down and surveyed the damage. The animals in their cages, lined up between the ship and the camp, were safe. All but one of the sleeping tents were standing. The lantern still burned brightly on the table. But everything else was gone. Our food supply was trampled in the ground. Much of the equipment was lost and wrecked. On either side of the camp, the ground was churned up like a half-plowed field. The whole thing was a mess.

It looked as if we were licked.

The tent Kemper and I used for sleeping still stood, so our notes were safe. The animals were all right. But that was all we had—the notes and animals.

"I need three more weeks," said Weber. "Give me just three weeks to complete the tests."

"We haven't got three weeks," I answered. "All our food is gone."

"The emergency rations in the ship?"

"That's for going home."

"We can go a little hungry."

He glared at us—at each of us in turn—challenging us to do a little starving.

"I can go three weeks," he said, "without any food at all."

"We could eat critter," suggested Parsons. "We could take a chance."

Weber shook his head. "Not yet. In three weeks, when the tests are finished, then maybe we will know. Maybe we won't need those rations for going home. Maybe we can stock up on critters and eat our heads off all the way to Caph."

I looked around at the rest of them, but I knew, before I looked, the answer I would get.

"All right," I said. "We'll try it."

"It's all right for you," Fullerton retorted hastily. "You have your diet kit."

Parsons reached out and grabbed him and shook him so hard that he went cross-eyed. "We don't talk like that about those diet kits."

Then Parsons let him go.

We set up double guards, for the stampede had wrecked our warning system, but none of us got much sleep. We were too upset.

Personally, I did some worrying about why the critters had stampeded. There was nothing on the planet that could scare them. There were no other animals. There was no thunder or lightning—as a matter of fact, it appeared that the planet might have no boisterous weather ever. And there seemed to be nothing in the critter makeup, from our observation of them, that would set them off emotionally.

But there must be a reason and a purpose, I told myself. And there must be, too, in their dropping dead for us. But was the purpose intelligence or instinct?

That was what bothered me most. It kept me awake all night long.

At daybreak, a critter walked in and died for us happily.

We went without our breakfast and, when noon came, no one said anything about lunch, so we skipped that, too.

Late in the afternoon, I climbed the ladder to get some food for supper. There wasn't any. Instead, I found five of the fattest punkins you ever laid your eyes on. They had chewed holes through the packing boxes and the food was cleaned out. The sacks were limp and empty. They'd even managed to get the lid off the coffee can somehow and had eaten every bean.

The five or them sat contentedly in a corner, blinking smugly at me. They didn't make a racket, as they usually did. Maybe they knew they were in the wrong or maybe they were just too full. For once, perhaps, they'd gotten all they could eat.

I just stood there and looked at them and I knew how they'd gotten on the ship. I blamed myself, not them. If only I'd found the time to take down the unloading rig, they'd never gotten in. But then I remembered how that dangling rope had saved my life and Weber's and I couldn't decide whether I'd done right or wrong.

I went over to the corner and picked the punkins up. I stuffed three of them in my pockets and carried the other two. I climbed down from the ship and walked up to camp. I put the punkins on the table.

"Here they are," I said. "They were in the ship. That's why we couldn't find them. They climbed up the rope."

Weber took one look at them. "They look well fed. Did they leave anything?"

"Not a scrap. They cleaned us out entirely."

The punkins were quite happy. It was apparent they were glad to be back with us again. After all, they'd eaten everything in reach and there was no further reason for their staying in the ship.

Parsons picked up a knife and walked over to the critter that had died that morning.

"Tie on your bibs," he said.

He carved out big steaks and threw them on the table and then he lit his stove. I retreated to my tent as soon as he started cooking, for never in my life have I smelled anything as good as those critter steaks.

I broke out the kit and mixed me up some goo and sat there eating it, feeling sorry for myself.

Kemper came in after a while and sat down on his cot.

"Do you want to hear?" he asked me.

"Go ahead," I invited him resignedly.

"It's wonderful. It's got everything you've ever eaten backed clear off the table. We had three different kinds of red meat and a slab of fish and something that resembled lobster, only better. And there's one kind of fruit growing out of that bush in the middle of the back . . ."

"And tomorrow you drop dead."

"I don't think so," Kemper said. "The animals have been thriving on it. There's nothing wrong with them."

It seemed that Kemper was right. Between the animals and men, it took a critter a day. The critters didn't seem to mind. They were johnny-on-the-spot. They walked in promptly, one at a time, and keeled over every morning.

The way the men and animals ate was positively indecent. Parsons cooked great platters of different kinds of meat and fish and fowl and what-not. He prepared huge bowls of vegetables. He heaped other bowls with fruit. He racked up combs of honey and the men licked the platters clean. They sat around with belts unloosened and patted their bulging bellies and were disgustingly contented.

I waited for them to break out in a rash or to start turning green with purple spots or grow scales or something of the sort. But nothing happened. They thrived, just as the animals were thriving. They felt better than they ever had.

Then, one morning, Fullerton turned up sick. He lay on his cot flushed with fever. It looked like Centaurian virus, although we'd been inoculated against that. In fact, we'd been inoculated and immunized against almost everything. Each time, before we blasted off on another survey, they jabbed us full of booster shots.

I didn't think much of it. I was fairly well convinced, for a time at least, that all that was wrong with him was over-eating.

Oliver, who knew a little about medicine, but not much, got the medicine chest out of the ship and pumped Fullerton full of some new antibiotic that came highly recommended for almost everything.

We went on with our work, expecting he'd be on his feet in a day or two.

But he wasn't. If anything, he got worse.

Oliver went through the medicine chest, reading all the labels carefully, but didn't find anything that seemed to be the proper medication. He read the first-aid booklet. It didn't tell him anything except how to set broken legs or apply artificial respiration and simple things like that.

Kemper had been doing a lot of worrying, so he had

Oliver take a sample of Fullerton's blood and then prepared a slide. When he looked at the blood through the microscope, he found that it swarmed with bacteria from the critters. Oliver took some more blood samples and Kemper prepared more slides, just to doublecheck, and there was no doubt about it.

By this time, all of us were standing around the table watching Kemper and waiting for the verdict. I know the same thing must have been in the mind of each of us.

It was Oliver who put it into words. "Who is next?" he asked.

Parsons stepped up and Oliver took the sample.

We waited anxiously.

Finally Kemper straightened.

"You have them, too," he said to Parsons. "Not as high a count as Fullerton."

Man after man stepped up. All of us had the bacteria, but in my case the count was low.

"It's the critter," Parsons said. "Bob hasn't been eating any."

"But cooking kills—" Oliver started to say.

"You can't be sure. These bacteria would have to be highly adaptable. They do the work of thousands of other micro-organisms. They're a sort of handy-man, a jack-of-all-trades. They can acclimatize. They can meet new situations. They haven't weakened the strain by becoming specialized."

"Besides," said Parsons, "we don't cook all of it. We don't cook the fruit and most of you guys raise hell if a steak is more than singed."

"What I can't figure out is why it should be Fullerton," Weber said. "Why should his count be higher? He started on the critter the same time as the rest of us."

I remembered that day down by the creek.

"He got a head start on the rest of you," I explained. "He ran out of toothpicks and took to chewing grass stems. I caught him at it."

I know it wasn't very comforting. It meant that in another week or two, all of them would have as high a count as Fullerton. But there was no sense not telling them. It would have been criminal not to. There was no place for wishful thinking in a situation like that.

"We can't stop eating critter," said Weber. "It's all the food we have. There's nothing we can do."

"I have a hunch," Kemper replied, it's too late anyhow."

"If we started home right now," I said, "there's my diet kit . . ."

They didn't let me finish making my offer. They slapped me on the back and pounded one another and laughed like mad.

It wasn't funny. They just needed something they could laugh at.

"It wouldn't do any good," said Kemper. "We've already had it. Anyhow, your diet kit wouldn't last us all the way back home."

"We could have a try at it," I argued.

"It may be just a transitory thing," Parsons said. "Just a bit of fever. A little upset from a change of diet."

We all hoped that, of course.

But Fullerton got no better.

Weber took blood samples of the animals and they had a bacterial count almost as high as Fullerton's—much higher than when he'd taken it before.

Weber blamed himself. "I should have kept closer check. I should have taken tests every day or so."

"What difference would it have made?" demanded Parsons. "Even if you had, even if you'd found a lot of bacteria in the blood, we'd still have eaten critter. There was no other choice."

"Maybe it's not the bacteria," said Oliver. "We may be jumping at conclusions. It may be something else that Fullerton picked up."

Weber brightened up a bit. "That's right. The animals still seem to be okay."

They were bright and chipper, in the best of health.

We waited. Fullerton got neither worse nor better.

Then, one night, he disappeared.

Oliver, who had been sitting with him, had dozed off for a moment. Parsons, on guard, had heard nothing.

We hunted for him for three full days. He couldn't have gone far, we figured. He had wandered off in a delirium and he didn't have the strength to cover any distance.

But we didn't find him.

We did find one queer thing, however. It was a ball of some strange substance, white and fresh-appearing. It was about four feet in diameter. It lay at the bottom of a little gully, hidden out of sight, as if someone or something might have brought it there and hidden it away.

We did some cautious poking at it and we rolled it back and forth a little and wondered what it was, but we were hunting Fullerton and we didn't have the time to do much investigating. Later on, we agreed, we would come back and get it and find out what it was.

Then the animals came down with the fever, one after another—all except the controls, which had been eating regular food until the stampede had destroyed the supply. After that, of course, all of them ate critter.

By the end of two days, most of the animals were down.

Weber worked with them, scarcely taking time to rest. We all helped as best we could.

Blood samples showed a greater concentration of bacteria. Weber started a dissection, but never finished it. Once he got the animal open, he took a quick look at it and scraped the whole thing off the table into a pail. I saw him, but I don't think any of the others did. We were pretty busy.

I asked him about it later in the day, when we were alone for a moment. He briskly brushed me off.

I went to bed early that night because I had the second guard. It seemed I had no more than shut my eyes when I was brought upright by a racket that raised goose pimples on every inch of me.

I tumbled out of bed and scrabbled around to find my shoes and get them on. By that time, Kemper had dashed out of the tent.

There was trouble with the animals. They were fighting to break out, chewing the bars of their cages and throwing themselves against them in a blind and terrible frenzy. And all the time they were squealing and screaming. To listen to them set your teeth on edge.

Weber dashed around with a hypodermic. After what seemed hours, we had them full of sedative. A few of them broke loose and got away, but the rest were sleeping peacefully.

I got a gun and took over guard duty while the other men went back to bed.

I stayed down near the cages, walking back and forth because I was too tense to do much sitting down. It seemed to me that between the animals' frenzy to escape and Fullerton's disappearance, there was a parallel that was too similar for comfort.

I tried to review all that had happened on the planet and I got bogged down time after time as I tried to make the picture dovetail. The trail of thought I followed kept turning back to Kemper's worry about the critters' lack of a defense mechanism.

Maybe, I told myself, they had a defense mechanism, after all—the slickest, smoothest, trickiest one Man ever had encountered.

As soon as the camp awoke, I went to our tent to stretch out for a moment, perhaps to catch a catnap. Worn out, I slept for hours.

Kemper woke me.

"Get up, Bob!" he said. "For the love of God, get up!"

It was late afternoon and the last rays of the sun were streaming through the tent flap. Kemper's face was haggard. It was as if he'd suddenly grown old since I'd seen him less than twelve hours before.

"They're encysting," he gasped. "They're turning into cocoons or chrysalises or . . ."

I sat up quickly. "That one we found out there in the field!"

He nodded.

"Fullerton?" I asked.

"We'll go out and see, all five of us, leaving the camp and animals alone."

We had some trouble finding it because the land was so flat and featureless that there were no landmarks.

But finally we located it, just as dusk was setting in.

The ball had split in two—not in a clean break, in a jagged one. It looked like an egg after a chicken has been hatched.

And the halves lay there in the gathering darkness, in the silence underneath the sudden glitter of the stars—a last farewell and a new beginning and a terrible alien fact.

I tried to say something, but my brain was so numb that I was not entirely sure just what I should say. Anyhow, the words died in the dryness of my mouth and the thickness of my tongue before I could get them out.

For it was not only the two halves of the cocoon—it was the marks within that hollow, the impression of what had been there, blurred and distorted by the marks of what it had become.

We fled back to camp.

Someone, I think it was Oliver, got the lantern lighted. We stood uneasily, unable to look at one another, knowing that the time was past for all dissembling, that there was no use of glossing over or denying what we'd seen in the dim light in the gully.

"Bob is the only one who has a chance," Kemper finally said, speaking more concisely than seemed possible. "I think he should leave right now. Someone must get back to Caph. Someone has to tell them."

He looked across the circle of lantern light at me.

"Well," he said sharply, "get going! What's the matter with you?"

"You were right," I said, not much more than whispering. "Remember how you wondered about a defense mechanism?"

"They have it," Weber agreed. "The best you can find. There's no beating them. They don't fight you. They absorb you. They make you into them. No wonder there are just the critters here. No wonder the planet's ecology is simple. They have you pegged and measured from the instant you set foot on the planet. Take one drink of water. Chew a single grass stem. Take one bite of critter. Do any one of these things and they have you cold."

Oliver came out of the dark and walked across the lantern-lighted circle. He stopped in front of me.

"Here are your diet kit and notes," he said.

"But I can't run out on you!"

"Forget us!" Parsons barked at me. "We aren't human any more. In a few more days . . ."

He grabbed the lantern and strode down the cages and held the lantern high, so that we could see.

"Look," he said.

There were no animals. There were just the cocoons and the little critters and the cocoons that had split in half.

I saw Kemper looking at me and there was, of all things, compassion on his face.

"You don't want to stay," he told me. "If you do, in a day or two, a critter will come in and drop dead for you. And you'll go crazy all the way back home—wondering which one of us it was."

He turned away then. They all turned away from me and suddenly it seemed I was all alone.

Weber had found an axe somewhere and he started walking down the row of cages, knocking off the bars to let the little critters out.

I walked slowly over to the ship and stood at the foot of the ladder, holding the notes and the diet kit tight against my chest.

When I got there, I turned around and looked back at them and it seemed I couldn't leave them.

I thought of all we'd been through together and when I tried to think of specific things, the only thing I could think about was how they always kidded me about the diet kit.

And I thought of the times I had to leave and go off somewhere and eat alone so that I couldn't smell the food. I thought of almost ten years of eating that damn goo and that I could never eat like a normal human because of my ulcerated stomach.

Maybe *they* were the lucky ones, I told myself. If a man got turned into a critter, he'd probably come out with a whole stomach and never have to worry about how much or what he ate. The critters never ate anything except the grass, but maybe, I thought, that grass tasted just as good to them as a steak or a pumpkin pie would taste to me.

So I stood there for a while and I thought about it. Then I took the diet kit and flung it out into the darkness as far as I could throw it and I dropped the notes to the ground.

I walked back into the camp and the first man I saw was Parsons.

"What have you got for supper?" I asked him.

NO LIFE OF THEIR OWN

MA and PA were fighting again, not really mad at one another, but arguing pretty loud. They had been at it, off and on, for weeks.

"We just can't up and *leave!*" said Ma. "We have to think it out. We can't pull up and leave a place we've lived in all our lives without *some* thinking on it!"

"I *have* thought on it!" Pa said. "I've thought on it a *lot!* All these aliens moving in. There was a brood of new ones moved onto the Pierce place just a day or two ago."

"How do you know," asked Ma, "that you'll like one of the Homestead Planets once you settle on it? It might be worse than Earth."

"We can't be any more unlucky there than we been right here! There ain't *anything* gone right. I don't mind telling you I am plumb discouraged."

And Pa sure-God was right about how unlucky we had been. The tomato crop had failed and two of the cows had died and a bear had robbed the bees and busted up the hives and the tractor had broken down and cost $78.90 to get fixed.

"Everyone has some bad luck," Ma argued. "You'd have it no matter where you go."

"Andy Carter doesn't have bad luck!" yelled Pa. "I don't know how he does it, but everything he does, it turns out to a hair. He could fall down in a puddle and come up dripping diamonds!"

"I don't know," said Ma philosophically. "We got enough to eat and clothes to cover us and a roof above our head. Maybe that's as much as anyone can expect these days."

"It ain't enough," Pa said. "A man shouldn't be content

93

to just scrape along. I lay awake at night to figure out how I can manage better. I've laid out plans that should by rights have worked. But they never did. Like the time we tried that new adapted pea from Mars down on the bottom forty. It was sandy soil and they should have grown there. They ain't worth a damn on any land that will grow another thing. And that land was worthless; it should have been just right for those Martian peas. But I ask you, did they grow there?"

"No," said Ma, "now that I recollect, they didn't."

"And the next year, what happens? Andy Carter plants the same kind of peas just across the fence from where I tried to grow them. Same kind of land and all. And Andy gets bowlegged hauling those peas home."

What Pa said was true. He was a better farmer than Andy Carter could ever hope to be. And he was smarter, too. But let Pa try a thing and bad luck would beat him out. Let Andy try the same and it always went right.

And it wasn't Pa alone. It was the entire neighborhood. Everybody was just plain unlucky, except Andy Carter.

"I tell you," Pa swore, "just one more piece of bad luck and we'll throw in our hand and start over somewhere fresh. And the Homestead Planets seem the best to me. Why, you take . . ."

I didn't wait to hear any more. I knew it would go on the way it always had. So I snuck out without their seeing me and went down the road, and as I walked along, I worried that maybe one of these days they might make up their mind to move to one of the Homestead Planets. There had been an awful lot of our old neighbors who'd done exactly that.

It might be all right to emigrate, of course, but whenever I thought about it, I got a funny feeling at the thought of leaving Earth. Those other planets were so awful far away, one wouldn't have much chance of getting back again if he didn't like them. And all my friends were right in the neighborhood, and they were pretty good friends even if they were all aliens.

I got a little start when I thought of that. It was the first time it had occurred to me that they all were aliens. I had so much fun with them, I'd never thought of it.

It seemed a little queer to me that Ma and Pa should be talking about leaving Earth when all the farms that had been sold in our neighborhood had been bought up by aliens. The Homestead Planets weren't open to the aliens and that might be the reason they came to Earth. If they'd had a choice, maybe they would have gone to one of the Homesteads instead of settling down on Earth.

I walked past the Carter place and saw that the trees in the orchard were loaded down with fruit and I figured that some of us could sneak in and steal some of it when it got ripe. But we'd have to be careful, because Andy Carter was a stinker, and his hired man, Ozzie Burns, wasn't one bit better. I remembered the time we had been stealing watermelons and Andy had found us at it and I'd got caught in a barbed-wire fence when we ran away. Andy had walloped me, which was all right. But there'd been no call for him going to Pa and collecting seven dollars for the few melons we had stolen. Pa had paid up and then he'd walloped me again, worse than Andy did.

And after it was over, Pa had said bitterly that Andy was no great shakes of a neighbor. And Pa was right. He wasn't.

I got down to the old Adams place and Fancy Pants was out in the yard, just floating there and bouncing that old basketball of his.

We call him Fancy Pants because we can't pronounce his name. Some of these alien people have very funny names.

Fancy Pants was all dressed up as usual. He always is dressed up because he never gets the least bit dirty when he plays. Ma is always asking me why I can't keep neat and clean like Fancy Pants. I tell her it would be easy if I could float along like him and never had to walk, and if I could throw mud-balls like him without touching them.

This Sunday morning he was dressed up in a sky-blue shirt that looked like silk, and red britches that looked as if they might be velvet, and he had a green bow tied around his yellow curls that floated in the breeze. At first glance, Fancy Pants looked something like a girl—but you better never say so, because he'd mop up the road with you. He did with me the first time I saw him. He didn't even lay a hand on me while he was doing it, but sat up there, cross-legged, about three feet off the ground, smiling that sweet smile of his on his ugly face, and with his yellow curls floating in the breeze. And the worst of it was that I couldn't get back at him.

But that was long ago and we were good friends now.

We played catch for a while, but it wasn't too much fun. Then Fancy Pants' Pa came out of the house and he was glad to see me, too. He asked about the folks and wanted to know if the tractor was all right, now that we'd got it fixed. I answered him politely because I'm a little scared of Fancy Pants' Pa.

He is sort of spooky—not the way he looks, the way he does things. From the looks of him, he wasn't meant to be a farmer, but he does all right at it. He doesn't use a plow to plow a field. He just sits cross-legged in the air and floats up and down the field, and when he passes over a strip of ground, that strip of ground is plowed—and not only plowed, but raked and harrowed until it is as fine as face powder. He does all his work that way. There aren't any weeds in any of his crops, for he just sails up and down the rows and the weeds come out slick and clean, with the roots intact, to lie on the ground and wither.

It doesn't take too much imagination to see what a guy like that could do if he ever caught a kid in any sort of mischief, so all of us are thoughtful and polite whenever he's around.

So I told him how we'd got the tractor all fixed up and about the bear busting up the bee hives. Then I asked him about his time machine and he shook his head real sad.

"I don't know what's the matter, Steve," he said. "I put things into it and they disappear, and I should find them later, but I never have. If I'm moving them in time, I'm perhaps pushing them too far."

He would have told me more about his time machine, but there was an interruption.

While we had been talking, Fancy Pants' Pa and me, the Fancy Pants dog had run a cat up a maple tree. That is the normal situation for any cat and dog—unless Fancy Pants is around.

For Fancy Pants wasn't one to leave a situation normal. He reached up into the tree—well, he didn't reach up with his hands, of course, but with whatever he reaches with— and he nailed this cat and sort of bundled it up so it couldn't move and brought it down to the ground.

Then he held the dog so the dog couldn't do more than

twitch and he put that bundled-up cat down in front of the twitching dog, then let them loose with split-second timing.

The two of them exploded into a blur of motion, with the weirdest uproar you ever heard. The cat made it to the tree in the fastest time and nearly took off the bark swarming up the trunk. And the dog miscalculated and failed to put on his brakes in time and banged smack into the tree spread-eagled.

The cat by this time was up in the highest branches, hanging on and screaming, while the dog walked around in circles, acting kind of stunned.

Fancy Pants' Pa broke off what he was saying to me and he looked at Fancy Pants. He didn't do or say a thing, but when he looked at Fancy Pants, Fancy Pants grew terribly pale and sort of wilted down.

"Let that teach you," said Fancy Pants' Pa, "to leave those animals alone. You don't see Steve here or Nature Boy mistreating them that way, do you?"

"No, sir," mumbled Fancy Pants.

"And now get along, the two of you. You have things to do."

I got this to say for Fancy Pants' Pa: he gives Fancy Pants his lickings, or whatever they may be, and then he forgets about it. He doesn't keep on harping at it for the rest of the day.

So Fancy Pants and me went down the road, me shuffling along, kicking up the dust, and Fancy Pants floating along beside me.

We got down to Nature Boy's place and he was waiting out in front. I knew he had been hoping someone would come along. There were a couple of sparrows sitting on his shoulder and a rabbit hopping all around him and a chipmunk in the pocket of his pants, looking out at us with bright and beady eyes.

Nature Boy and I sat down underneath a tree and Fancy Pants came as close as he ever does to sitting down— floating about three inches off the ground—and we talked about what we ought to do. Trouble was, there wasn't really anything that needed any doing. So we sat there and talked and tossed pebbles and pulled stems of grass and put them in our mouths and chewed them, while Nature Boy's pet wild things gamboled all around us and didn't seem to be afraid at all. Except that they were a little leery of Fancy Pants. He is, when you come right down to it, a sort of sneaky rascal. Me they are fast friends with when I'm with Nature Boy, but let me meet them when I am alone and they keep their distance.

I can see how wild things might take to Nature Boy. He is fur all over, real sleek, glossy fur, and he wears nothing but that little pair of pants. Turn him loose without those pants and someone would be bound to take a shot at him.

So we sat there wondering what to do. Then I remembered that Pa had said a new family had moved onto the Pierce place and we decided to go down and see if they had any kids.

We went down the road to the old Pierce place and it turned out there was one just about our age. He was a sort of runty little kid, with a peaked face and big round eyes and a kind of eager look about him, like a stunted hoot owl.

He told us his name and it was even worse than Nature Boy's and Fancy Pants' names, so we had a vote on it and decided we would call him Butch. That suited him just fine.

Then he called out his family and they stood in a row, like a bunch of solemn, runty owls roosting on a limb, while he introduced them. There was his Ma and Pa and a little brother and a kid sister almost as big as he was. The rest of them went back into the house, but Butch's Pa squatted down and began to talk with us.

You could see from the way he talked that he was a little scared of this farming business. He admitted he really was no farmer, but an optical worker, and explained to us that an optical worker designed lenses and ground them. But, he said, there was no future in a job like that back on his old home planet. He told us how glad he was to be on Earth and how he wanted to be a good citizen and a good neighbor, and a lot of other things like that.

When he started to run down, we got away from him. There ain't anything more embarrassing than a crazy adult who likes to talk with kids.

We decided that maybe we should show Butch around a bit and let him in on some of the things we had been doing.

So we struck off down Dark Hollow and we didn't make much time because all of these friends of Nature Boy were popping out to join him. Before very long, we were a sort of traveling menagerie—rabbits and chipmunks and a gopher or two and a couple of raccoons.

I like Nature Boy, of course, and I've had some good times with him, but he has spoiled a lot of fun as well. Before he showed up in the neighborhood, I did a lot of fishing and hunting, but that is all spoiled now. I can't shoot a squirrel or catch a fish without wondering if it is a friend of Nature Boy's.

After a while, we got down to the creek bed where we were digging out a lizard. We'd been at it all summer long and we hadn't uncovered very much of him, but we still figured that some day we might get him all dug out.

You understand that it wasn't a live lizard we were digging out, but a lizard that had turned to stone a zillion years ago.

There is a place where the stream runs down a limestone ledge and the limestone lies in layers. The lizard was between two of those layers. We'd got four or five feet of his tail uncovered. But the digging was getting harder, for we were working back into the limestone ledge and there was more of it to move.

Fancy Pants floated up above the limestone ledge and got himself set as solid as he could. Sitting there, he hit that limestone ledge a tremendous whack, being very careful not to crack the lizard. It was one of his better whacks, busting up a lot of stone, and while Fancy Pants rested up to take another one, the three of us piled in and threw out the busted rock.

But there was one big piece he had loosened up that we couldn't move.

"Hit it just a tap," I told him. "Break it up a little and we can get it out."

"I got it loose," he said. "It's up to you to get it out."

There was no sense arguing with him. So the three of us wrestled at the rock, but we couldn't budge it and Fancy Pants sat up there, fat and sassy, taking it easy and enjoying himself.

"You ought to have a crowbar," he told us. "If you had a crowbar, you could pry that rock out."

I was getting sick and tired of Fancy Pants, and so, just

to get away from him for a while, I said I'd go and fetch a crowbar. And this new kid, this Butch, said he'd go along with me.

So we left Nature Boy and Fancy Pants and climbed up to the road and started out for my place. We didn't hurry any. It would serve Fancy Pants right if he had to wait, and Nature Boy as well, for all his showing off with his animals.

We walked along the road and talked. Butch told me about the planet he had come from and it sure was a poor-mouth place, and I told him about the neighborhood, and we were getting to be friends.

We reached the Carter place and were walking past the orchard when Butch stopped dead in the middle of the road and went sort of stiff, like a hunting dog will go when he scents a bird.

I was walking right behind him and I bumped into him, but he just stood there with those eager eyes agleam and his entire body tense—so tense it seemed to quiver when it really didn't.

"What's going on?" I asked.

He kept on looking at something in the orchard. I took a look where he was looking and I couldn't see a thing.

Then he turned around like a flash and jumped the fence on the downhill side of the road and went lickety-split down across the field opposite the orchard. I jumped the fence and ran after him and caught him just before he reached the woods. I grabbed him by the shoulder and spun him around to face me. It wasn't hard to do, he was such a spindly kid.

"What's the matter with you?" I hollered. "Where do you think you're going?"

"Home to get my gun!"

"Your *gun?* What for?"

"There's a whole bunch of them up there! We have to clean them out!"

He must have seen I didn't understand.

"Don't tell me," he said, "that you didn't see them?"

I shook my head. "There wasn't anything there."

"They're there, all right," he said. "Maybe you can't see them. Maybe you're like old folks."

There's no one who can accuse me of a thing like that.

I doubled up my fist and poked it underneath his nose. He hurried up to explain.

"They're things that only kids can see. And they bring bad luck. You can't leave them around or you'll have bad luck all the time."

I didn't believe it right away. But after all the things I'd seen done by Nature Boy and Fancy Pants, you don't ever catch me saying straight out that a thing's impossible.

And after I'd thought it over for a minute, it made a silly sort of sense. For the folks certainly had been plagued by hard luck for a long time now and it didn't stand to reason that luck should be all bad and never any good unless there was something making it that way.

And it wasn't the folks alone, but all the other neighbors—all of them, of course, except Andy Carter, and Andy Carter was too mean to be bothered by bad luck.

We were, I thought, sure a hard-luck neighborhood.

"All right," I said to Butch. "Let's go and get that gun."

And I was thinking even as I said it that it must be a funny kind of gun that would shoot a thing one couldn't even see.

We made it back to the old Pierce place in almost no time at all. Butch's Pa was sitting out underneath a tree, feeling sorry for himself. Butch came up to him and started jabbering and I couldn't understand a word.

His Pa listened to him for a while and then broke in. "You should talk this planet's language, son. It is most impolite to do otherwise. And you want to become a good citizen of this great and glorious planet, I am sure, and there's no better way to do it than to talk its language and observe its customs and try to live the way its people do."

I'll say this much for him: Butch's Pa sure knew how to fling around the words.

"Is it true, mister," I asked him, "that these things can bring bad luck?"

"Most assuredly," said Butch's Pa. "Back on our old home planet, we know them well."

"Pa," asked Butch, "should I get my gun?"

"Now I don't know," said his Pa. "It's something we have to give some study. Back on our home planet, there would be no question of it. But this is a different planet and it may have different ways. It may be that the man who has these creatures would object to your shooting them."

"But there isn't anyone really got them," I declared. "How can you have a thing when you can't even see it?"

"I was thinking about the gentleman in whose orchard they appeared."

"You mean Andy Carter. He doesn't know anything about them."

"That does not matter," said Butch's Pa, with a great deal of righteousness. "It becomes, it would seem to me, a quite deep problem in ethics. On our home planet, no man would want these things; he'd be ashamed to have them. But here it might be different. They bring good luck, you see, to the ones that they adopt."

"You mean they bring good luck to Andy?" I asked him. "But I thought you said that they brought bad luck."

"So they do," said Butch's Pa, "except to the ones that they adopt. To them they bring good luck, but bad luck to all the others. For it is an axiom that fortune for one man is misfortune for the rest. That is why we do not let them adopt any of us on our home planet."

"You think they have adopted Andy and that's why he has good luck?"

"You are most correct," said Butch's Pa. "You have admirably grasped the concept."

"Well, gee, why don't we just go in and shoot them?"

"This Carter gentleman would not object to your doing so?"

"Of course he would, but that's what you would expect of him. He'd probably run us off the place before we got the job half done, but we could sneak back again . . ."

"No," Butch's Pa said flat out.

He was an awful stickler for doing the right thing, Butch's Pa was—bound and determined he wasn't going to get caught off base doing something wrong.

"That is not the way to do," he said. "It is most unethical. You think that if this Carter knew he had these things, he would want to keep them?"

"I am sure he would. He doesn't care for anybody but himself."

Butch's Pa heaved a big sigh and crawled to his feet. "Young man, would your father be at home?"

"He most likely would."

"We'll go and talk with him," he said. "He is a native of this planet and an honest man and he will tell us what is right."

"Mister," I asked him, "what do you call these things?"

"We have a name for them, but it does not translate into your tongue with anything like ease. We call them something that is neither here nor there, something that is halfway between. Halfling would be the word for it, if there is such a word."

"I don't know if there is or not," I said, "but it sounds right."

"Then," decided Butch's Pa, "for sheer convenience we shall call them that."

At first, Pa was as flabbergasted as I was, but the more he listened to Butch's Pa and the more he thought about it, the more he seemed to become convinced there might be something to it.

"There sure-God has been something causing all this hard luck of ours," he declared. "A man can't turn his hand to a thing but it goes wrong on him. And I must admit that it makes a man sore to have all these things happen to him and then look at Carter and see all the good luck he has."

"I am profoundly sorry," said Butch's Pa, "to discover halflings exist on this planet. There were many on our old home planet and on some of the neighboring worlds, but I had no idea they had spread this far."

"What I don't rightly understand," said Pa, lighting up his pipe and settling down to hash the matter over, "is how they can be here and a man not see them."

"There is a most precise scientific explanation, but I have not the language to translate it. You might say that they are off-phase of this existence, but still not quite into it. The child eye is undulled, the mind unclosed, so that they can see somewhat, a fraction, just a little, beyond reality. And that is why they can be seen by children but are invisible to adults. I, in my time, when I was a child, saw and killed my share of them. You understand, sir, that on my planet, it is an accepted childish chore to be eternally on watch for them and vigilantly keep their numbers down."

Pa asked me: "You didn't see these things?"

"No, Pa," I said. "I didn't."

"And you didn't see them, either?" Pa asked Butch's Pa.

"I lost my ability to see them many years ago," said Butch's Pa. "So far as your boy is concerned, it may be that only the children of certain races—"

"But they must see us," Pa insisted. "Otherwise, how could they be able to bring good luck or bad?"

"They do see us. In that, all are agreed. I assure you that the scientists of my planet have devoted many long and arduous years to the study of these beings."

"And another thing. What is their purpose in adopting people? What do they get out of it? Why should they show all this favoritism?"

"We are not sure," said Butch's Pa. "There are several theories. One is that they have no life of their own, but must have a pattern in order to live. If they did not have a pattern, they would have no form or senses and probably no perception. They are, it would seem, like parasites in many ways."

But Pa interrupted him. Pa was all wound up and had a lot of thinking that he had to do out loud.

"I don't suppose," he said, "that they are doing it just for the hell of it. There must be a solid reason—there is to everything. It seems reasonable to me that everything is planned, that there's nothing without purpose. There's nothing, when you get right down to it, that basically is bad. Maybe these things, with the bad luck that they bring, are part of a plan to make folks face up to adversity and develop character."

I swear it was the first time I had ever heard Pa sound like a preacher, but he sure did then.

"You may be right," said Butch's Pa. "There is no agreement entirely on the reason for their being."

"They might," suggested Pa, "be a sort of gypsy tribe, just wandering around. They might up and move away."

Butch's Pa sadly shook his head. "It almost never happens, sir, that they move away."

"When I was a kid, I once went to the city with my Ma. I don't remember much about it, but I do remember standing in front of a great big window that was filled with toys and knowing that I never could have any of them, and wishing hard that some day I might have just one of them. Maybe that's the way it is with these folks. Maybe they're just outside the window looking in on us."

"Your analogy is exceedingly picturesque," said Butch's Pa with forthright admiration.

"But here I am running on," Pa said, "as if I took for gospel every word of it. I don't wish for the world to doubt you or what you've told us . . ."

"But you do and I cannot find it in my breast to blame you. Would you, perhaps, believe more readily if your son could tell you that he saw them?"

"Why, yes," Pa said thoughtfully. "I surely would."

"Before I came to Earth, I was a worker in the field of optics, and it may be possible that I can grind a set of lenses that would allow your son to see halflings. I am not sure he could, of course, but it is a chance worth taking. He is of the age to have still that ability to peer beyond reality. It may be that all his vision needs is a slight correction."

"If you could do that, if Steve here could really see these things, then I would believe you without the slightest question."

"I'll get on with it immediately," said Butch's Pa. "Later on, we can discuss the ethics of the situation."

Pa sat watching Butch and his Pa going down the road, and he sort of shuddered. "Some of these aliens sure-God come up with queer ideas. A man has got to watch himself or he might swallow some of them."

"These ones are all right," I told him.

Pa sat there thinking and I could almost see the wheels whirling in his brain. "I don't know too much about it, but the more one thinks about it, the more sense it makes. It seems reasonable to me that there might be just so much good luck and so much bad luck, and ordinarily both the good and the bad would be handed out in somewhat equal parts. But suppose something came along and corralled all the good luck for one particular man, then there ain't anything but bad luck left for the rest."

I wished that I could see it as clear as Pa. But the more I thought, the more like Greek it seemed.

"Maybe," said Pa, "when you get to the root of it, it's nothing more than simple competition. What is good luck for one man is bad luck for another. Say there is a job that everybody wants. One man gets it and that's good luck for him, but bad luck for the others. And say that this bear back in the woods just had to raid a hive. It would be bad luck for the man whose hive was raided, but good luck—or at least not bad luck—for the man whose hive the bear passed up. And say again that someone's tractor had to get busted . . ."

Pa went on like that for quite a while, but I don't think he even fooled himself. Both of us knew, I guess, that there would have to be more to it than that.

Fancy Pants and Nature Boy were sore at me for not coming back with the crowbar. They said I stood them up and I had to explain to them I hadn't and I had to tell them exactly what had happened before they would believe me. I suppose it might have been better if I had kept my mouth shut, but in the end I don't believe it made much difference.

Anyhow, we got to be friends again and we all liked Butch, so we had good times together. The other two kidded Butch a lot about the halflings at first, but Butch didn't seem to mind, so they gave it up.

We certainly had a good time that summer. There was the lizard and a lot of other things as well, including the family of skunks that fell in love with Nature Boy and followed him around. And there was the time Fancy Pants hauled all of Carter's machinery out into the back forty, with Andy hunting for it like lost cows and madder by the minute.

At home, and elsewhere in the neighborhood, there was still bad luck. The day the barn caved in, Pa was ready to admit flat out that there was something to what Butch's Pa had said. It was all Ma could do to keep him from going up the road to see Andy Carter and talk to him by hand.

I had another birthday and the folks gave me a live-it set and that was something I had not expected. I had wanted one, of course, but I knew they cost a lot and with all the bad luck they had been having, the folks were short of money.

You know what a live-it is, of course. It's something like TV, only better. TV you only watch and with a live-it set you live it.

It's a viewer that you clamp onto your head and you look into it and you pick your channel and turn it on, then settle back and live the things you see.

It doesn't take any imagination to live it, because it all

is there—the action and the sound and smell and even, to some extent, the actual feel of it.

My set was just a kid's set and I could only get the kid channels. But that was all right with me. I wouldn't have wanted to live through all that mushy stuff.

All morning I spent with my live-it. There was one thing called "Survey Incident" and it was all about what happened when a human survey team put down on an alien planet. Another one was about a hunting trip on a jungle world and a third was "Robin Hood." I think, of the three of them, I liked "Robin Hood" the best.

I was all puffed up with pleasure and pride and I wanted to show the kids what the folks had given me. So I took the live-it and went down to Fancy Pants' place. But I never got a chance to show the live-it to him.

Just before I got to the gate, I saw Fancy Pants floating along, silent and sneaky—and floating beside him, not more than a yard away, was that poor, beat-up, bedraggled cat that Fancy Pants was always pestering. He had the cat all wrapped up in a tight bundle and it couldn't move a muscle, but I could see its eyes were wide with fright. If you ask me, that cat had a right to be afraid. There was scarcely anything in the book Fancy Pants hadn't done to it.

"Hi, Fancy Pants!" I yelled.

He put a finger to his lips and crooked another finger to let me know I could join him in whatever he was doing. So I jumped the fence and Fancy Pants floated lower until he was about my level.

"What's going on?" I asked him.

"He went away and forgot to close the padlock," whispered Fancy Pants.

"Who went away?"

"My Pa. He forgot to lock the door to the old machine shed."

"But that's where—"

"Sure," said Fancy Pants. "That's where he's got the time machine."

"Fancy Pants, you don't intend to put that cat in there!"

"Why not? Pa ain't ever tried a living thing in it and I want to see what happens."

I didn't like it and yet I wanted awful bad to see that

time machine. I wondered what one looked like. No one had seen the time machine except Fancy Pants' Pa.

"What's the matter with you?" asked Fancy Pants. "Are you going chicken on me?"

"But the cat!"

"For the love of Mike, it's nothing but a cat."

And that was right, of course. It was nothing but a cat.

So I went along with him and we sneaked into the shed and pulled the door behind us. And there was the time machine in the middle of the floor.

It didn't look like much. It was a kind of hopper, and a bunch of things like coils ran around the throat where the hopper narrowed down, and that was all except for a crude control board that was nailed onto a post and hooked up to the hopper with a lot of wires.

The hopper came up to my chest and I put my live-it down on the edge of it and craned my neck to look into the throat to see what I could see.

At just that moment, Fancy Pants threw the switch that turned it on. I jerked away. For it was a scary business when you turned that hopper on.

When I sneaked back to have another look, it looked for all the world as if it were a whirlpool of cream, sort of thick and rich and shiny—and it was alive. You could see the liveness in it. And there was a feeling in it that maybe you should just jump in head first and I had to grip the edges of the hopper hard not to.

I *might* have dived in, if the cat at that very moment hadn't somehow wiggled free from Fancy Pants.

I don't know how that cat did it. Fancy Pants had it all rolled into a ball and really buttoned up. Maybe Fancy Pants got careless or maybe the cat had finally figured out an angle. But, anyhow, Fancy Pants had the cat poised above the hopper and was about to let it fall. The cat didn't get loose in part—it got loose entirely—and there it was, yowling and screaming, tail fluffed out, clawing at thin air to keep from falling down into the hopper. It managed to throw itself to one side as it fell and the claws of one paw hooked onto the hopper's edge while the other hooked into my live-it set.

I let out a yell and made a grab to try to save the live-it, but I was too late. The cat dragged it off balance and it slid down into that creamy whirlpool and was gone.

The cat shinnied up a post and up into the rafters and hung there, screaming and wailing.

Just then the door came open and there floated Fancy Pants' Pa and we were caught red-handed.

I figured Fancy Pants' Pa would give me the works right then and there.

But he didn't do a thing. He just floated there for a moment looking at the two of us.

Then he looked at me alone and said: "Steve, please leave."

I went out that door as fast as I could go, with just a fast glance back over my shoulder at Fancy Pants. He was pale and already beginning to appear a little shriveled. He knew what he had coming to him, and even while I realized that he deserved every bit of it, I still felt sorry for him.

But staying wouldn't help him and I was glad enough to get off scot-free.

Except that it wasn't scot-free.

I don't know what was the matter with me—just scared stiff, I guess. Anyhow, I went straight home and told Pa right out about it and he took down the strap from behind the door and let me have a few.

But it seemed to me that he didn't have his heart in it. He was getting a little uneasy about all these alien goings-on.

For several days, I didn't go off the place. To have gone anywhere, I would have had to walk past Fancy Pants' house and I didn't want to see him—not for a while, at least.

Then one day Butch and his Pa showed up and they had the glasses.

"I don't know if they'll fit," said Butch's Pa. "I had to guess the fitting."

They looked just like any other glasses except that the lenses had funny lines running every which way, as if someone had taken the glass and twisted it until it was all crinkled out of shape.

I put them on and they were a bit loose and things looked different through them, but not a great deal different. I was looking at the barnyard when I put them on. The barnyard was still there, but it appeared strange and a little weird, although it was hard to put a finger on what was wrong with it. It was a bright, hot August day and the sun was shining hard, but when I put the glasses on, it seemed suddenly to get cloudy and a little cold. And that was some of the difference, but not all of it.

There was a feeling of strangeness that sent a shiver through me, and the light was wrong, and worst of all was the sense that I didn't belong. But there was nothing you could say flat out was absolutely wrong.

"Is it any different, son?" asked Pa.

"Some different," I answered.

"Let me see."

He took the glasses off me and put them on himself.

"I can't see a thing," he said. "Just a lot of color."

"I told you," said Butch's Pa, "that only the young can see. You and I are too fixed in reality."

Pa took the glasses off and let them dangle in his hand.

"Did you see any halflings?" he asked me.

I shook my head.

"There are no halflings here," said Butch.

"To see the halflings," Butch's Pa put in, "we must journey to the Carter place."

"Well, then," said Pa, "what are we waiting for?"

So the four of us went up the road to the Carter place.

There didn't seem to be anyone at home and that was rather queer, for either Carter himself or Mrs. Carter or Ozzie Burns, the hired man, always stayed at home if the others had to go to town or anywhere.

We stood in the road and Butch had himself a good look. There weren't any halflings around the buildings and there weren't any in the orchard or in any of the fields, so far as Butch could see. Pa was getting impatient. I knew what he was thinking—that he had been made a fool of by a bunch of aliens.

Then Butch said excitedly that he thought he saw a halfling down in one corner of the pasture, just at the edge of the big Dark Hollow woods, where Andy had a hay barn, but it was so far away that he could not be sure.

"Give your boy the glasses," said Butch's Pa, "and let him have a look."

Pa handed me the glasses and I put them on. I had a hard time getting familiar landmarks sorted out, but finally I did, and sure enough, down in the corner of the pasture, there were things moving around that looked like human beings, but mighty funny human beings. They had a sort of smoky look about them, as if you could blow them away.

"Well, what do you see?" asked Pa.

I told him what I saw and he stood there considering, rubbing his hand back and forth across his chin, with the whiskers grating.

"There doesn't seem to be a soul around," he said. "I don't suppose it would hurt if we went down there. If the things are there, I want Steve to have a good, hard look at them."

"You think it is all right?" asked Butch's Pa, worried. "It's not unethical?"

"Well, sure," said Pa, "I suppose it is. But if we are quick about it and get out right away, Andy never needs to know."

So we crawled underneath the fence and went over the pasture and crossed into the woods so we could sneak up on the place where we had seen halflings.

The going was a little rough, for in places the brush was rather heavy, and there were thick blackberry patches with the bushes loaded with black and shiny fruit.

But we sneaked along as quietly as we could and we finally reached a point opposite the place where we had seen the halflings.

Butch nudged me and whispered fiercely: "There they are!"

I put the glasses on and there they were, by golly.

Up at the edge of the hayfield, just beyond the woods, stood Andy's hay barn, really just a roof set on poles to cover the hay that Andy didn't have the room to get into his regular barn.

It was a rundown, dilapidated thing, and there was Andy standing up there on the roof, and some packs of shingles sat on the roof beside him, while climbing up a ladder with a bunch of shingles on his shoulder was Ozzie Burns, the hired man. Andy was reaching down to get the shingles that Ozzie was carrying up the ladder and at the foot of the ladder, hanging onto it so it wouldn't tip, was Mrs. Burns. And that was the reason none of them had been around—they were all down here, fixing to patch up the shingles on the barn.

And there were the halflings, a good two dozen of them.

A bunch of them were up on the roof with Andy and a couple on the ladder with the hired man and a couple more of them helping to hold up the ladder. They looked busy and energetic and efficient, and every single one of them was the spitting image of Andy Carter.

Not that they really resembled Andy, for they didn't. They were actually wraithlike things that seemed to have but little substance to them. They were little more than a smoky outline, but those smoky outlines—every single one of them—was the squat, bulldog outline of Andy Carter. And they walked like him, with a belligerent swagger, and all their motions were like his, and you could sense the meanness in them.

In the time that I was gaping at them, Ozzie Burns had handed the shingles up to Andy and clambered up on the roof beside him and Mrs. Burns had stepped away from the ladder, not needing to hold it any longer, since Ozzie was safe up on the roof. I saw the ladder was standing on uneven ground and that was why she'd had to hold it.

Andy had been crouched down to lay the pack of shingles on the roof. Now he straightened up and looked toward the woods and he saw us standing there.

"What are you doing here?" he roared at us, and started down the ladder.

And now comes the funny part of it. I'll have to take it slow and try to tell it straight.

To me, it seemed the ladder separated and became two ladders. One was standing there against the hay barn and the other left it, and the top of this second ladder began to slide along the roof and was about to fall and carry Andy with it to the ground, just as sure as shooting.

I was about to shout for Andy to look out, although I don't know why I should have. If he fell and broke his neck, it'd have been all right with me.

But just as I was about to yell, two halflings moved fast and this second ladder disappeared. It had been sliding along the roof and was about to fall, with a second Andy clinging to it and beginning to look scared—and then suddenly there was just one ladder and one Andy instead of two.

I stood there, shaking, and I knew what I had seen, but at that moment I wouldn't admit it, not even to myself.

It was, I told myself, as if I had been looking at two

separate times—at a time when the ladder should have fallen and at another time when it had not fallen because the halflings hadn't let it. I had seen good luck in actual operation. Or the averting of bad luck. Whichever it might be, it all came out the same.

And now Andy was almost at the ladder's foot and the halflings were coming down from off the roof in a helter-skelter fashion—some of them jumping off and others dropping off, and if they had been human instead of what they were, there would have been a flock of broken legs and necks.

Pa stepped out of the woods into the field and I stepped along with him. We knew we were walking into trouble, but we weren't ones to run. And trailing along behind us were Butch and his Pa, but both of them looked scared and you could see they had no heart for it.

Then Andy was down off the ladder and walking straight toward us and he sure was on the warpath. And walking along beside him, in a line on either side of him, were all those halflings, and they kept in step with him and swung their arms like him and looked as mean as he did.

"Now, Andy," said Pa, trying to be conciliatory, "let us be reasonable." But it was quite an effort, I can tell you, for Pa to speak that way. He hated Andy Carter clear up from the ground and he sure-God had his reasons. Andy had been a rotten neighbor for an awful lot of years.

"Don't you tell me to be reasonable!" yelled Andy. "I been hearing all this talk about how you are blaming me for what you call hard luck. And I tell you to your face it ain't hard luck at all. It's plain downright shiftlessness and bad management. And if you think you're going to get anywhere with all this talk of yours, you are just plain crazy. You been taken in by a lot of alien nonsense. If I had my way, I'd run all those stinking aliens right off the planet."

Pa took a quick step forward and I thought he was about to clobber Andy. But Butch's Pa jumped forward and grabbed him by the arm.

"No! No!" he shouted. "There's no need to fight him! Let us go away!"

Pa stood there with Butch's Pa hanging to his arm, and I wondered for a minute which one he would clobber, Butch's Pa or Andy.

"I never liked you," Andy said to Pa, "from the first day

I saw you. I had you figured for a bum and that is what you are. And this taking up with aliens is the lowest thing any human ever did. You ain't no better than they are. Now get off this place and don't you ever dare set foot on it again."

Pa jerked his arm and sent Butch's Pa staggering to one side. Then he brought it up and back. I saw Andy's head start moving to one side, dropping over toward his shoulder, and for a second it looked like he had the beginning of two heads. And I knew that I was watching another accident beginning to unhappen, although it was no accident, for Pa sure meant to paste him.

But they weren't fast enough to get Andy's head tilted out of danger. They weren't dealing this time with a slowly sliding ladder.

There was a solid crack like someone had hit a tree with an axe on a frosty morning, and Andy's head jerked back and his feet came off the ground and he went tincup over teakettle, flat on his back.

And there were all those silly halflings standing in a row, with shocked looks upon their faces, as if they couldn't quite believe it. You could have bought the lot of them for no more than half a buck.

Pa turned around and held out his hand to me and said: "Come on, Steve. Let's go."

He said it in a quiet voice that was clear and level, and there was, I thought, a note of pride in it. And we turned around, the two of us, and we walked away from there, not hurrying any and not even looking back.

"I swear to God," said Pa, "I've meant to do that ever since I laid eyes on him fifteen years ago."

I hadn't noticed what had happened to Butch or to his Pa and I wondered where they might have gone to, for there wasn't hide nor hair of them. But I didn't say anything to Pa about it, for I had a hunch he might not be harboring exactly friendly feelings toward Butch's Pa.

But I needn't have worried about them, for when we got out to the road they were waiting for us, breathing kind of hard and considerably scratched up. The way they'd gone through that brush and all those blackberry patches must have been a caution.

"I am glad to see," said Butch's Pa, "that you got back safely."

"Don't mention it," Pa told him coldly, and went on down the road, hanging tight onto my hand so that I had to trot along.

We got back home and went into the kitchen to get a drink of water.

Pa said to me, "Steve, have you got those glasses?"

I dug them out of my pocket and handed them to him. He put them on the shelf above the washstand.

"Leave them there," he said. "Don't touch them again—not ever. Do you understand me?"

"Yes, sir," I replied.

To tell the truth, I would have liked it better if he'd gone ranting up and down. I was afraid that what had happened out there in the woods had made him decide to go to one of the Homestead Planets. I told myself he maybe already had made up his mind and didn't need to rant.

But he never said a word about the fight with Andy nor about the Homestead Planets and he wasn't sore at me. He kept on being quiet and I knew that he still was mad clean through and I figured that he was mostly sore at Butch and Butch's Pa for their having made a complete fool of him.

I did a lot of wondering about what I'd seen down there in Andy's hayfield. And the more I thought about it, the more I was convinced that I had grasped the secret of how the halflings operated.

For I must have been seeing in two different times when I'd been looking at the ladder. I must have looked into the future and seen the ladder slip. Except it never slipped, for the halflings, seeing that it would slip, had made one leg of it settle in the ground. And then, with the ladder sitting solid, it never slipped, of course. The halflings had done no more than look ahead a bit and then righted something that was about to happen before it had a chance to happen.

And that, I told myself, was the basis of good luck and bad. The halflings could spot disaster coming and try to head it off. Except they couldn't always make it. They had tried to protect Andy when Pa took a lick at him and they had failed. So I figured that they weren't infallible and that made me feel some better.

For if they could make good luck for Andy, it stood to reason they could make bad luck for the rest of us. All they had to do, if they had a mind to, was to see good luck heading for us and change it into bad.

It might even be possible, I told myself, that the half-lings lived ahead of us, by a few seconds or so, and that the only thing which separated us from them was this matter of a different time.

But there was something else that troubled me a lot. Why had I been able to see two different times? It was clear to me that Butch and his people couldn't, for if they could, they'd have more answers to the halfling situation. They'd been studying it for years, and so far as I could figure, they didn't know for certain about this two-time business.

It seemed to me, when I thought about it, that Butch's Pa might have ground better than he knew when he made my glasses. He might have put in something or taken out something or done something he didn't know about at all.

Or it might be that the human race had a different kind of vision, or maybe just a little different, and when you added the correction for Butch's kind of vision to our kind of vision, you brought out a thing you couldn't even guess at.

I tried and tried to get it clear within my mind, but I couldn't do it. I just went around in circles.

I stayed close to home for several days because I had a feeling that I should be ignoring Butch to uphold the family honor and that is how I missed the big hassle between Fancy Pants and Nature Boy.

It seems that Nature Boy got sick and tired of how Fancy Pants was mistreating that poor, bedraggled cat. So he took one member of the skunk family that had fallen in love with him and he clipped and dyed that skunk to look exactly like the cat. And one day he sneaked over to Fancy Pants' place and switched the skunk for the cat without anyone seeing him.

The skunk didn't want to be Fancy Pants' skunk; he belonged to Nature Boy. So he started beating it back home as fast as he could go, which wasn't very fast.

Just then Fancy Pants floated out of the door and he saw the skunk going through the gate. He thought the cat was trying to sneak away from him, so he reached out and grabbed it up and rolled it into a ball and tossed it pretty high into the air, sort of careless like, to teach that cat a lesson.

It went up in the air and came down smack-dab on top of Fancy Pants, who was floating out there in the yard a few feet off the ground.

The skunk was scared witless. As soon as it got its claws fastened into Fancy Pants and had some leverage, it retaliated with enthusiasm. And for the first time in his life, Fancy Pants thumped down to the ground and, among other things, he got his clothes as dirty as any other kid.

I would give a zillion dollars to have seen it.

For a while, they figured that they might have to take Fancy Pants out somewhere and bury him for a week or two to make him presentable again. But they finally got him to a point where one could come near him.

Fancy Pants' Pa went storming down to talk with Nature Boy's Pa and the two of them put on a ruckus that had the neighborhood chuckling for a week.

And now I was really strapped for playmates. I was still cold-shouldering Butch and I knew better than to take up again with either Nature Boy or Fancy Pants. They both were mean cusses when they set their mind to it. I was sure we hadn't heard the last of this feud of theirs and I didn't want to get tangled up in it by being friends with either one of them.

It was plenty tough, let me tell you. Here I was with vacation almost ended and no one to pal around with and my live-it gone. I watched the days slip past and regretted every minute of it.

Then one day the sheriff drove up to the house.

Pa and I were out in the barnyard trying to tinker up a corn binder that was all tied together with haywire and other makeshift odds and ends. Pa had been threatening to buy one for a long time now, but with all the tough luck we'd been having, there wasn't any money.

"Good morning, Henry," the sheriff said to Pa.

Pa said good morning back.

"I hear you been having a little trouble with your neighbors," said the sheriff.

"Not what you would call real trouble," Pa told him. "I busted one in the snoot the other day is all."

"Right on his own farm, too."

Pa quit working on the binder and squatted back on his

heels to look up at the sheriff. "Andy been around complaining?"

"He was in the other day. Said you had swallowed some fool story that this new alien family started. About some kind of badluck critters he'd been harboring on his farm."

"And you talked him out of it?"

"Well, now," said the sheriff, "I am a peaceable man and I hate to see two neighbors fighting. Andy wanted to put you under peace bond, but I said I'd come over and have a talk with you."

"All right," invited Pa. "Go ahead and talk."

"Now look here, Henry. You know the story about them hardluck critters is so much poppycock. I'm surprised you took any stock in it."

Pa got up slowly. He had a hard look on his face and I thought for a minute he was about to bust the sheriff. I was scared, I tell you, for that is something no one should ever do—up and bust a sheriff.

I don't know what he might have done or what he might have said, for at that moment Nature Boy's Pa came tearing down the road in his old jalopy and pulled in behind the sheriff's car, intending to park there. But he miscalculated some and he smacked into the sheriff's car hard enough to skid it ahead six feet or so with the brakes all set.

The sheriff broke into a run. "By God!" he said. "It isn't even safe to drive out into this corner of the county!"

The two of us ran along behind him. I was running just because there was some excitement, but I figure maybe Pa was running so he could help Nature Boy's Pa if the sheriff should take it into his head to get feisty with him.

And the funny thing about it was that Nature Boy's Pa, instead of sitting there and waiting for the sheriff, had jumped out of his car and was running up the slope to meet us.

"They told me I'd find you here," he panted to the sheriff.

"You found me, all right," said the sheriff, practically breathing fire. "Now I'm going to—"

"My boy is gone!" yelled Nature Boy's Pa. "He wasn't home last night . . ."

The sheriff grabbed him and said to him: "Now let's take this easy. Tell me exactly what happened."

"He went off yesterday, early in the morning, and he didn't show up for meals, but we didn't think too much of it—he often goes off for an entire day. He has a lot of friends out there in the woods."

"And he didn't come home last night?"

Nature Boy's Pa shook his head. "Along about dusk, we got worried. I went out and hunted for him and I didn't find him. I hunted all night long, but there wasn't any sign of him. I thought maybe he'd just holed up for the night with one of his friends in the woods. I thought maybe he'd show up when it got light, but he never did."

"Well, all right," said the sheriff, "you leave it to me. We'll rouse out all the neighbors and organize a hunt. We'll find him." He said to me: "You know the lad? You did some playing with him?"

"All the time," I answered.

"Lead us to all the places where you played. We'll look there first."

Pa said: "I'll start phoning the neighbors. I'll get them here right away."

He ran up the hill toward the house.

In an hour or less, there were a hundred people gathered and the sheriff took them all in hand. He divided them into posses and appointed captains for each posse and told them where to hunt.

It was the most excitement we've ever had in the neighborhood.

The sheriff took me with the posse he headed up and we went down Dark Hollow. I took them to the place where we were digging out the lizard and the place where we had started to dig ourselves a cave and the hole in the creek where Nature Boy had made friends with some whopping trout, and some other places, too. We found some old tracks of Nature Boy's, but there was no fresh sign, although we hunted up and down the hollow clear to where it flowed into the river, and we trailed back come night, and I was tuckered out.

And a little scared as well.

For an awful suspicion had come to me.

And no matter how hard I tried to keep from thinking of it, I couldn't help myself, for all the time I was trying to remember if the hopper in that time machine had been big enough to take a kid the size of Nature Boy.

Ma fed me and sent me up to bed and later she came up and tucked me in and kissed me. She hadn't done that in years. She knew I was too big to be tucked in and kissed, but she did it anyhow.

And then she went downstairs and I lay there listening to some men who still were out there in the yard, talking among themselves. Some of the others still were hunting and I knew that I should be out there hunting with them, but I knew Ma wouldn't let me go and I was glad of it. For I was tired all through and the woods at night can be a scary place.

I should by rights have gone straight to sleep. Any other night I would have. But I lay there thinking about that hopper in the time machine and I wondered how long it would take before someone told the sheriff about the ruckus between Fancy Pants and Nature Boy, and I thought perhaps they had already. And if so, the sheriff probably was looking into it right now, for the sheriff was nobody's fool.

I wondered if I should tell him myself if no one else had. But that was one fight I didn't have any hankering to get tangled up in.

Finally I went to sleep and it seemed to me I hadn't been asleep any time at all when something woke me up. It still was dark, but there was a red glow shining through the window. I sat up quick, with my hair standing half on end.

I thought at first it might be our barn or the machine shed, but then I saw it wasn't that close. I skinned out of bed and over to the window. That fire was a big one and it wasn't too far up the road.

It looked as if it was on the Carter place, but I knew that must be wrong, for if bad luck like that struck anyone, it wouldn't be Andy Carter. Unless, of course, he was loaded with insurance.

I went downstairs in my bare feet and Ma was standing at the door, looking up the road toward the blaze.

"What is it, Ma?" I asked.

"It's the barn on the Carter place," she said. "They phoned the neighborhood for help, but all the men are out hunting Nature Boy."

We stood there, Ma and me, and watched until the blaze almost died out, and then Ma hiked me off to bed.

I crawled underneath the covers, weak with this new excitement. I wondered why we should tag along for months with nothing happening, and then all at once have it busting out all over.

I lay there and thought about Andy Carter's barn and there was something wrong about it. Andy had been the luckiest man in seven counties and now, without any warning, he was having bad luck just like the rest of us.

I wondered if the halflings might have gone off and left him, and if that was the case, I wondered why they had. Maybe, I told myself, they had gotten plain disgusted with Andy's meanness.

It was broad daylight when I woke again and I jumped straight out of bed and climbed into my clothes. I rushed downstairs to see if there was any word of Nature Boy.

Ma said there wasn't, that the men were still out hunting. She had breakfast ready for me and insisted I eat it and warned me about wandering off or trying to join one of the searching parties. She said it wasn't safe for me to be out in the woods with so many bears about. And that was funny, for she had never worried about the bears before.

But she made me promise I wouldn't.

As soon as I got out, I zipped down the road as fast as I could go. I had to see the place where the Carter barn had burned down and I just had to talk with someone. And Butch was the only one left that I could talk to.

There wasn't much to see at the Carter place, just burned and blackened timbers that still were smoking some. I stood out in the road a while and then I saw Andy come out of the house and he stood there for a minute looking straight at me. So I got out of there.

I went past Fancy Pants' place real fast, hoping I wouldn't see him. At the moment, I didn't want a thing to do with Fancy Pants.

When I got to Butch's place, his Ma told me he was sick in bed. She didn't think it was catching, she said, so I went up to see him.

Butch sure looked terrible lying there—more like a runty hoot owl than he ever had before—but he was glad to see me. I asked him how he was and he said he felt better. He made me promise I wouldn't tell his Ma, then told me that he'd got sick from eating some green apples he'd pinched off the Carter orchard.

He'd heard about Nature Boy and I told him in a whisper the suspicions I had.

He lay there looking at me solemnly and finally he said: "Steve, I should have told you this before. That is no time machine."

"No time machine? How do you know?"

"Because I saw the stuff that Fancy Pants' Pa put through it. It didn't go anywhere. It still is lying there."

"You saw . . ." And then I had it. "You mean it went to where the halflings are?"

"That's what I mean," said Butch.

Sitting there on the edge of the bed, I tried to think it through, but there were so many questions bubbling up in me that I couldn't do it.

"Butch," I asked, "where is this place that the halflings are?"

"I don't know," said Butch. "It's close to us, almost in this world, but not really."

And I remembered something Pa had said several weeks before. "You mean it's like a place behind a plate-glass window that's between our world and theirs?"

"Something like that."

"And if Nature Boy is there, what would happen to him?"

Butch shuddered. "I don't know."

"Would he be all right? Could he breathe in there?"

"I suppose he could," said Butch. "I think the halflings do."

I got up from the bed and started for the door. Then I turned back again.

"Butch, what are the halflings doing? What are they hanging around for?"

"No one's sure," said Butch. "There are a lot of ideas about what they are after. One is that they have to be near something that is living before they can live themselves. They can't live a life themselves; they've got to have a life to—well, like imitate, only that's not the word."

"They need a pattern," I said, remembering what Butch's Pa had said that day, before Pa choked him off with his own rambling about what the halflings might be after.

"I guess you could call it that," said Butch.

And I stood there thinking what a lousy life the halflings must have led, using Andy Carter as their pattern.

But that wasn't so, for the halflings, that time I had seen them, had sure-God been happy. They'd been running around up there on the roof and keeping themselves busy and enjoying themselves.

And they had, every one of them, looked like Andy Carter. And of course they would, with Andy as their pattern.

Thinking about it, I could see how someone like Andy, with his kind of disposition, might enjoy being mean as dirt and ornery with his neighbors. He'd have a sense of independence and the feel of every hand being raised against him and him standing there like a mighty warrior, defying all of them. And from that he'd get a sense of strength and domination. All in all, I supposed, Andy, for a man like him, might be living a pretty darned satisfactory life.

I started for the door, and Butch called after me, "Where are you going, Steve?"

"I'm going to find Nature Boy," I said.

"I'll go with you."

"No, you stay in bed. Your Ma will skin both of us if you don't."

I got out of the house and headed fast for home, and as I ran, I kept on thinking about how the halflings had no life of their own, but had to find another life and pattern themselves on it.

Sometimes they'd be mighty lucky and fasten onto someone who'd give them a good and exciting life, or maybe a good and contented life, but other times they'd get a mighty poor one. But you had to say this for them—they gave all the help they could to the one they'd picked out as a pattern, and they kept working at it.

And I wondered how many persons who had been great successes might have been watched over by the halflings. What an awful letdown it would be if they were to learn that they had not become great or rich or famous through any particular effort or brilliance of their own, but by the grace of a bunch of things that helped them from outside.

I got home and went into the kitchen and over to the sink.

"Is that you, Steve?" Ma called from the living room.

"I'm getting a drink," I told her.

"Where you been?"

"Just around."

"Now don't you go running off," she warned.

"No, ma'am, I won't."

And all the time I was talking to her, I was climbing on a chair so I could reach those glasses where Pa had put them on the shelf and told me not to touch them again—not ever.

Then I had them in my pocket and was climbing off the chair.

I heard Ma heading for the kitchen and I hurried out as quickly as I could.

I didn't put the glasses on until I got to where the Carter farm cornered on the road. I went along the road, watching carefully, and finally I found a bunch of halflings down in a fence corner just beyond the orchard. They were standing there and squabbling over something and they didn't seem to notice me until I got real close.

Then they all swung around and stood facing me. They seemed to be talking among themselves and pointed at me.

And there on the head of one of them, pushed up on his forehead, was the live-it set I had lost down the time machine.

When I saw that, I realized Butch actually had seen the stuff that Fancy Pants' Pa had put through the time machine.

At first I don't think they realized that I could see them, but after I stood there for a while, staring at them, they began to move up closer to me.

I could feel the hair rearing right up on my head. There was nothing I wanted to do more than turn around and run. But I told myself they couldn't reach me and there was nothing to be scared of, so I stood my ground.

They reminded me of a bunch of crows. They must have seen I didn't have a gun, or maybe this particular bunch didn't know about the guns Butch's people had. And they crowded up real close to me, like a flock of crows is not afraid of an empty-handed man, but will keep their distance when he has a gun.

I could see their mouths moving at me, but naturally I couldn't hear a thing, and they kept pointing at the one that had my live-it on his head.

To tell the honest truth, I didn't pay too close attention to what they might have been doing at the start of it. I was too busy looking at them and trying to figure out what might have happened to them. There was one thing certain —this either was a different bunch than I had seen down in Andy Carter's hayfield or they had changed a lot. There was still some of Andy in them, although not as much of him as someone else, as if Andy and someone else had gotten sort of scrambled together.

Finally I made out that they were pointing at the one with the live-it on his head and then tapping their own heads, and I figured out that each of them was asking for a live-it, too.

I don't know what I would have said to them or how I would have said it, if I had had the chance, only I never had the chance. They suddenly parted, as if someone from behind had pushed them to one side, and there was Nature Boy, standing face to face with me.

We stood there and looked at one another for a good long time, not saying anything, not making any motion. Then he stepped forward and I stepped forward until we were almost nose to nose. I was afraid there, for a moment, we'd walk right through each other. What would have hapened then? Probably nothing much.

"You O.K.?" I asked him, thinking maybe he could read my lips even if he couldn't hear me, but he shook his head. So I asked him once again, talking slowly and forming my words as distinctly as I could. But he shook his head again.

Then I thought of something else.

I lifted up my hand and stuck out my finger and pretended I was writing on the imaginary window that separated us.

"YOU O.K.?" I wrote, taking it slow, because he'd have to read it backwards.

He didn't get it right away and I did it once again and this time he understood.

"O.K.," he wrote. And then he wrote real slow: "GET ME OUT!"

I stood there looking at him and it was horrible, for there he was and here I was, and so far as I could see, there was no way to get him out.

He must have sensed what I was thinking, because all at once his mouth trembled and that was the first time I'd ever seen Nature Boy even close to crying. Not even that time when we were digging out the lizard and a big rock fell on his toe.

I thought how bad it must have been for him, trapped in that place and able to see out, but knowing that no one could see in. He might even have followed some of the searching parties, hoping that someone might accidentally glimpse him, but knowing they couldn't. Maybe he had trailed along behind his Pa, as close as he could get to him, and his Pa not knowing it. And maybe he'd gone back home and watched his family and been all the lonelier for their not knowing he was there. And undoubtedly he'd hunted around for Butch, who he knew could see him, only Butch had been sick in bed.

And while I was thinking all of this, I got a faint idea. I told myself that it probably wouldn't work, but the more I thought about it, the more it seemed it might.

So I reached up with my finger and I wrote: "MEET ME AT FANCY PANTS'."

I pocketed my glasses and hurried along home. I circled around the house because I didn't want to take the chance of Ma seeing me and not letting me go. I went into the machine shed and found a length of rope and hunted up a hacksaw.

Lugging these, I made my way back to Fancy Pants' place. The machine shed was back of the barn, so no one from the house could see me, and anyhow no one seemed to be around. I knew that Fancy Pants' Pa, and maybe Fancy Pants himself, would be out with the searchers, floating around over places where it would be impossible for the men on foot to go.

I laid down the rope and hacksaw and put on my glasses and Nature Boy was there, right beside the machine shed door. He had some of the halflings with him, including the one who still had the live-it perched up on his forehead. And scattered all around the place, just like Butch had said, were tea cups and pie plates and children's blocks and a lot of other junk—the stuff that Fancy Pants' Pa had fed into the time machine.

I looked at the halflings again and all at once I knew what was different about them. They were still some of Andy, but they were Nature Boy as well. And then I knew why Andy's barn had burned. These halflings of his had been so busy tagging around after Nature Boy that they had not been able to give Andy their attention.

It seemed only natural, of course. A halfling would get a lot more good out of a real live human inside that world of theirs than they would someone they could only see from behind a plate-glass window.

I took the glasses off and put them in my pocket and got to work. It was no easy job to saw through that padlock. The steel was awfully hard and the blade was dull and I was afraid it might break before I got through the steel. I cussed myself for not thinking to bring along an extra blade or two.

The sawing made an awful racket because I had forgotten to bring along some oil to squirt into the cut. But nobody heard the sawing.

Finally I got through.

I opened the door and stepped into the shed and the time machine was there, just the way I remembered it. I laid down the rope and went over to the control board and studied it, but it wasn't very complicated.

I got it turned on and the creamy whirlpool was sliding in the hopper's throat.

I picked up the rope and put my glasses on and got an awful fright. The machine shed was built on a gentle slope and the floor I was standing on was four or five feet above the ground and there I was, standing in the air, or so it seemed to me.

I had a sense, not of falling, but that by rights I should be falling, that any minute now I would begin to fall. I knew I wouldn't, naturally—I was standing on a transparent but solid floor. But knowing that didn't help much. That horrible, dreamlike feeling that I was about to tumble to the ground still kept hold of me.

And to make it even worse, there was Nature Boy, standing underneath me, with his head about level with my feet, looking up at me. His face was hopeful and he was motioning me to get busy with the rope.

Moving cautiously, even if there was no need of caution, I took one end of the rope and tossed it down the hopper and felt the suck and tug of the creamy whirlpool pulling down the rope. Down underneath the hopper, I could see the rope coming out, dangling into that place where Nature Boy was trapped. He moved over quickly and grabbed hold of the rope and I could feel the weight of the pull he put on it.

Nature Boy was about my size, perhaps a little smaller, and I knew I'd have to pull as hard as ever I could to get him out of there. I even wound a hitch around my hand to make sure it wouldn't slip. I pulled with all my might. And that rope didn't budge. It felt as if I were pulling against a house. I couldn't gain an inch.

So I quit pulling and knelt down, still hanging to the rope, peerng at the base of the time machine.

It was a funny thing. The rope went to the bottom of the hopper's throat and then it skipped a foot or two. There was a foot or so of sidewise space where there wasn't any rope, and then the rope took up again, dangling down into that other place where Nature Boy had hold of it.

It didn't make sense. That rope should have gone into that other world in a straight and simple line. But the fact was that it didn't. It went off somewhere else before it fell into the other world.

And that, I figured, was the reason I couldn't pull it out.

You could put a thing through the time machine, but you couldn't pull it back.

I looked down at Nature Boy and he looked back at me. I knew he'd seen it and knew as well as I did exactly what it meant. He looked pretty pitiful and I don't suppose I looked any better.

Just then the machine shed door screeched open.

I jumped up, still hanging to the rope, and there was Fancy Pants' Pa.

He was all burned up and I couldn't blame him. Not after seeing how I had sawed the padlock to break into the place.

"Steve," he said, and you could hear him fighting to keep his voice level, "I thought I told you to keep out of here."

"Yes, sir," I said, "but Nature Boy's in there."

"Nature Boy!" he shouted. Then his voice dropped. "You don't know what you're talking about. How could he get in?"

"I don't know," I said, though I could have told him.

"Those glasses you are wearing," asked Fancy Pants' Pa. "Are those the ones that were made for you by Butch's father?"

I nodded.

"Then you can see?"

"I can see Nature Boy," I said. "Just as plain as day."

I let go of the rope to take my glasses off and the rope slid down that hopper slicker than a whistle.

"It's all right, I guess," I said. "I couldn't pull him out."

"Steve," said Fancy Pants' Pa, "I want you to tell me the truth. You're not just thinking up a story? You are not pretending?"

He was awful pale and I saw what he was thinking—if Nature Boy had gone down that hopper, the entire neighborhood would be down on him like a ton of bricks.

I crossed my heart. "And hope to die," I added.

That seemed good enough for him.

He shut off the time machine, then went outdoors. I followed him.

"Now," he said, "you stay right here. I'll be back immediately."

He floated off in somewhat of a hurry, zooming away above the pasture woods. He was out of sight in no time.

I sat down with my back against the machine shed and I was feeling pretty low. I knew I should put on my glasses, but I kept them in my pocket. I couldn't have stood the sight of Nature Boy looking out at me.

It was done and over with, I knew. There was no way in the world for me or anyone to rescue Nature Boy. He was gone for good and all. He was worse than gone.

And sitting there, I thought up some pretty dreadful things to do to Fancy Pants. For there was no doubt in my mind that Fancy Pants had got into the shed and had grabbed Nature Boy, just like he did the cat, and dumped him down the hopper.

He was pretty sore, I knew, about the trick that Nature Boy had played on him with that skunk disguised as a cat. There was nothing he would have stopped at to get even.

I was sitting there and thinking when Fancy Pants' Pa came floating up the road, and panting along behind him were Pa and the sheriff and Butch's Pa and Nature Boy's Pa and some other neighbors.

The sheriff came straight for me and he grabbed me by the shoulders and gave me a good, sharp shake.

"Now," he bellowed, "what is all this foolishness? I

warn you, boy, it will go hard with you if you've been pulling our leg."

I tried to break away from him, but he wouldn't let me go. Then Pa stepped up and flung out his arm so that it caught the sheriff straight across the chest and sent him staggering back.

"You keep your hands off him," Pa said to the sheriff.

"But that story," blustered the sheriff. "You surely don't believe—"

"I do," said Pa. "I believe every word of it. My boy doesn't lie."

I'll say this for Pa: He may storm around and yell and he may take the strap to you for a lot of trifling things, but when it comes down to the pinch, he's standing there beside you.

"I'll remind you, Henry," said the sheriff, bristling, "that you're not entirely in the clear yourself. There's that business of the breach of peace I talked Andy Carter out of."

"Andy Carter," said Pa, speaking more slowly than one would expect him to. "He's the man who lives just down the road, if I recall correctly. Has there been any of you who have seen him lately?"

He looked around the crowd and it seemed that no one had.

"Last time I talked to Andy," said Pa, "was when I called him on the phone and told him we needed help. He said he was too busy to go hunting any alien whelp. He said it would be good riddance if all of them got lost."

He looked around the crowd and no one spoke a word. I don't suppose it was quite polite of Pa to say what he had, with Nature Boy's Pa and Butch's Pa and all the rest of those alien people standing there before us. But it sure-God was the truth, and they needed it right then, and Pa was the one who was not afraid to give it to them right between the eyes.

Then someone spoke up from the crowd and there were so many of them I couldn't be sure exactly who it was. But whoever it was said: "I tell you, folks, it was nothing but plain justice when Andy's barn burned down."

The sheriff bristled up. "If I thought one of you had a hand in that, I would—"

"You wouldn't do a thing," said Pa. He turned to me. "All right, Steve, tell us what you have to tell. I promise

you that everyone will listen and there won't be any inter-
ruptions."

He looked straight at the sheriff when he was saying it.

"Just a second, sir," said Butch's Pa. "I want to voice
one important point. I know this boy can see the halflings,
for I myself am the one who made the glasses for him. I
know it is immodest of me to say a thing like this, but if I
am nothing else, I am one fine optician."

"Thank you, sir," Pa said. "And now, Steve, go ahead."

But I never got a chance to say a single word, for Butch
came stumbling around the barn and he had the gun with
him. Or at least I took it for the gun, although it didn't
look like one. It was a sticklike thing and it glittered in the
sunlight from all sorts of prisms and mirrors set into it at
all kinds of crazy angles.

"Pa," yelled Butch, "I heard about it and I brought the
gun. I hope I'm not too late."

He ran up to his Pa and his Pa took the gun away from
him and held it with everyone looking at him.

"Thank you, son," said Butch's Pa. "It was good of you,
but we won't need a gun. We aren't shooting anything
today."

Then Butch cried out: "There he is, Pa! There's Nature
Boy!"

I am not too sure that all of them believed I had found
Nature Boy. Some might have had their reservations, and
kept quiet about it because they didn't want to tangle with
my Pa. But Butch was a different matter. He could see
these things without any silly glasses. And he was an alien,
and everyone expected aliens to do these sort of crazy
things.

"All right," admitted the sheriff, "so I guess he must be
there. Now what do we do?"

"There doesn't seem to be much to go on," said Pa, "but
we can't leave the boy in there." He looked at Nature
Boy's Pa. "Don't you worry. We'll figure a way to get him
out."

But he spoke with so much confidence that I knew he
was only talking so that Nature Boy's Pa would know we
weren't giving up.

Personally, I could see no hope. If you couldn't get him
out the way he had gotten in, there didn't seem to be any
other way. There were no doors into that other place.

"Gentlemen," said Butch's Pa, "I have a small idea."

We all turned and waited.

"This gun," he said, "is used to keep down the number of halflings. It ruptures the wall between the two worlds sufficiently to let a bullet through. There might be an adaptation made of it, and we can do that later, or have someone do it for us, if that be necessary. But it seems possible to me we could use the gun itself."

"But we don't want to shoot the boy," the sheriff protested. "What we want to do is get him out."

"I have no intention, sir, of shooting him. There will be no bullet in the gun. All we'll use is the device to rupture the curtain or whatever it may be that lies between the worlds. And I can—what is the word?—tinker, I believe. I can tinker up the gun so that rupture will be greater."

He sat down on the ground and began working on the gun, shifting prisms here and there and adjusting tiny mirrors.

"There is just one thing," he said. "The rupture will last for but a moment. The boy must be immediate to take advantage of it. He must leap outward instantly the rupture should appear."

He turned to me. "Steve, can you communicate with him?"

"Communicate?"

"Talk to him. With signs, perhaps? Or the reading of the lips? Or some other way?"

"Sure, I can do that."

"Please, would you do it then?"

So I put on my glasses and looked around until I found Nature Boy. I had quite a time making him understand what we planned to do. It wasn't any easier to talk with him with all those crazy halflings standing all around him and making motions at me and pointing at the live-it, then tapping their own heads.

I was sweating plenty, for I was afraid that I had not got it all across to him, but I knew that any more of it would do no more than confuse him.

So I told Butch's Pa that we were all set, and Butch's Pa handed Butch the gun, and the rest stepped back a ways, and there was Butch with the gun and me standing right behind him. And there was Nature Boy standing in that other place, and a bunch of those silly halflings clustered all about him, and they sure didn't know about the alien gun or they'd not have been standing there. And Nature Boy looked like someone who'd been stood against a wall and was being executed without even any blindfold.

Out of the tail of my eye, I saw Fancy Pants floating off to one side of us, and he was the saddest-looking sack you ever saw.

Suddenly there was a strange white flash of brilliance as all the prisms and the mirrors moved on the gun that Butch was holding. He had pulled a trigger, or whatever it was.

For a second, straight in front of us, a funny sort of hole seemed to open up in the place that should not have been there at all—a jagged, ragged hole that appeared in nothingness. And I caught sight of Nature Boy jumping through the hole the second it stayed open.

And there he was, staggering a bit from the jump that he had made—only he was not alone. He had one of the halflings with him!

He had him by the wrist in a good tight grip and it was plain to see that he had jerked him through with him, for the halfling did not seem at all happy about what had happened to him. I saw at once that it was the halfling who had the live-it on his head.

Butch pushed the halfling toward me and he said: "Here, Steve. It was the only way I could get your live-it back."

I saw that Butch was letting go of the halfling and I grabbed him quick by the other wrist and was somewhat surprised to find that he was solid. I would not have been astonished if my hand had gone right through him, for he still had that swirly-smoky look about him, although it seemed to me he might be hardening up a bit and becoming more substantial.

Pa moved over close beside me, saying, "You be careful, Steve!"

"Aw, he's all right," I said. "He's not even trying to get away from me."

Someone raised a shout and I whirled around and stared.

A half-dozen of the halflings had grabbed hold of the edges of that door into the other world, and they were tugging for dear life so it would stay open, and pouring out of it was that entire herd of halflings! They were shoving and pushing and scrambling to get through, and there were a lot more of them, it seemed to me, than I had thought there were.

We just stood there and watched them until they all were through. We didn't do a thing because there was not a thing we could do. And they stood there in a bunch, packed tight together, staring back at us.

The sheriff came alongside Pa. He pushed back his hat until it roosted on his neck. You could see that the sheriff was flabbergasted and I enjoyed it, for it had been apparent from the very first that the sheriff hadn't believed a word he'd heard about the halflings.

I don't know, maybe he still was thinking that it might be nothing but some sort of alien joke. You could see, without half trying, that the sheriff didn't cotton to any aliens.

"How come," he asked suspiciously, "that this one here has got a live-it on?"

So I told him and he blinked at me, dazed and dumbfounded, but he said nothing back. I sure had shut him up.

Fancy Pants' Pa had floated up while I was telling it and he said I told the truth, for he'd been there and seen it.

Everyone began to talk at once, but Fancy Pants' Pa floated up a little higher and held up his hand to command attention.

"Just a moment, if you please," he said. "Before we get down to more serious business, I have something you must hear. As you may suspect, knowing the episode of the skunk, my family undoubtedly has a great deal to answer for in this incident."

A human saying things like that would sound silly and pompous, but Fancy Pants' Pa could get away with it.

"So," said Fancy Pants' Pa, "I now announce to you that my malefactor son, for the forthcoming thirty days, must walk upon his feet. He must not float an inch. If the punishment does not seem sufficient—"

"It's enough," Pa cut in. "The boy has to learn his lesson, but there is no use being harsh with him."

"Now, sir," said Nature Boy's Pa, being very formal, "it is not necessary—"

"I insist," Fancy Pant's Pa said. "I really must insist. It can be no other way."

"Say," bawled the sheriff, "will someone explain to me what this is all about?"

"Sheriff," Pa said to him, "your understanding of this matter is of no great importance and it would take too long to explain. We have more important business we should be attending to." He turned around a bit so he faced the crowd. "Well, gentlemen, what do we do next? It appears to me that we have some guests. And remembering that these critters are bearers of good luck, it would seem to me we should treat them as kindly as we can."

"Pa," I said, tugging at his coat sleeve, "I know how we can get them over on our side. Every one of them wants a live-it set."

"That's right," spoke up Nature Boy. "All the time I was in there, they pestered me and pestered me about how to get the sets. All the time they squabbled over who would get to use Steve's set next."

"You mean," the sheriff asked, in a weak voice, "that these things can talk?"

"Why, sure they can," said Nature Boy. "They learn a lot more back in that world of theirs than you could ever guess."

"Well, now," Pa said with a lot of satisfaction, "if that is all they want, it's not too great a price for us to pay to get us some good luck. We'll just buy a lot of live-it sets. We can probably get them wholesale—"

"But if we get the live-its," objected Butch's Pa, "they'll just lie around and use them and be of no help to us at all. They won't need us any more. They'll have all these patterns they need from the live-it sets."

"Well, anyhow," said Pa, "even if that should be true, we'll get them off our necks. They won't pester us with this bad luck they commit."

"It won't do us any good however you look at it," declared Butch's Pa, who had a mighty low opinion of the halflings. "They all live together. That's the way it's always been. They never helped an entire neighborhood, but just one man or family in the neighborhood. A whole tribe of them comes in and they give one family all the benefit. You couldn't get them to split up and work for all of us."

"If you jerks would listen," said the halfling with the live-it on his head, "I can get you straightened out."

It was a shock, I tell you, to hear him speak at all. He

was the kind of thing you'd figure shouldn't speak at all—just a sort of dummy. And the way he spoke and the tone he used made it even worse. It was the way Andy Carter always talked—either wild and blustering, or out of the corner of his mouth, sarcastic. After listening to Andy all these years, that poor halfling didn't know any different.

Everyone just stood there, staring at the halfling who had spoken, while all the other halflings were nodding their heads in such mad agreement with him that I thought they'd snap their necks.

Pa was the first one to get his feet back under him.

"Go ahead," he said to the halfling. "We all are listening."

"We'll make a deal with you," said the halfling, using ornery words but speaking most respectful, "but you'll have to level with us, see? We'll work hard for you and guard against mishap, but we got to have the live-its and no mistake about it. One for each of us—and if I was you, mister, I wouldn't try to chisel."

"Well, now," said Pa, "that sounds fair enough. But you mean all of us?"

"All of you," the live-it halfling said.

"You mean you will split up?" asked Pa. "Each of us will have at least one of you? You won't all live together any more?"

"I think, sir," said Fancy Pants' Pa, "that we can depend on that. I believe I understand what this gentleman is thinking. It is something that happened with the human race on Earth."

"What happened here on Earth?" asked Pa, sort of flabbergasted.

"Why," said Fancy Pants' Pa, "the elimination of the need for social clustering. There was a time when the human race found it necessary to congregate in families and tribes for companionship and entertainment. Then the race got the record player and the radio and TV and there was less need for get-togethers. A man had entertainment of his own in his home. He need not move beyond his living room to be entertained. So the spectator and group sports simply petered out."

"And you think," asked Pa, "that the same thing will happen with the halflings if we gave them live-its?"

"Certainly," said Fancy Pants' Pa. "We supply them, as

it were, entertainment for the home, personal entertainment. There will be no further need for tribal living."

"You said it, pal!" the halfling said enthusiastically.

All the rest of them were nodding in agreement.

"But it's still no good," yelped Butch's Pa, getting real riled up. "They're in this world now, and how do you get them back? And while they're here, can they do anything for us?"

"You can stop shooting off your mouth right now," the halfling said to Butch's Pa with utmost respect. "We can't do anything here for you, that's sure. In this world of yours, we can't see ahead. And to do you any good, we have to see ahead."

"You mean that if we give you live-its, you'll go back home again?" asked Pa.

"Sure," said the halfling. "Back there is our home. Just try to keep us from it."

"We won't even try," Pa said. "We might even push you back. We'll give you the live-its and you get back there and start to work for us."

"We'll work for you hard," said the halfling, "but not all the time. We take out some time for looking at the live-it. That all right with you?"

"Sure," Pa agreed. "Sure, that's O.K. with us."

"All right," said the halfling, "get us back where we belong."

I turned around and walked out of the crowd, out to the edge of it. For it was all settled now and I had a belly full of it. It would be all right with me if we never had any more excitement in the neighborhood.

Up by the barn, I saw Fancy Pants limping along on the ground. He was having a tough time walking. But I didn't feel the least bit sorry for him. He had it coming.

I figured in just a little while I'd go up around the barn and clobber him for that time he mopped up the road with me.

It should be an easy job, I told myself, with him grounded by his Pa for thirty days.

THE SITTERS

THE first week of school was finished. Johnson Dean, superintendent of Millville High, sat at his desk, enjoying the quiet and the satisfaction of late Friday afternoon.

The quiet was massacred by Coach Jerry Higgins. He clomped into the office and threw his muscular blond frame heavily in a chair.

"Well, you can call off football for the year," he said angrily. "We can drop out of the conference."

Dean pushed away the papers on which he had been working and leaned back in his chair. The sunlight from the western windows turned his silver thatch into a seeming halo. His pale, blue-veined, wrinkled hands smoothed out, painstakingly, the fading crease in his fading trousers.

"What has happened now?" he asked.

"It's King and Martin, Mr. Dean. They aren't coming out this year."

Dean clucked sympathetically, but somewhat hollowly, as if his heart was not quite in it. "Let me see," he said. "If I remember rightly, those two were very good last year. King was in the line and Martin quarterback."

Higgins exploded in righteous indignation. "Who ever heard of a quarterback deciding he wouldn't play no more? And not just an ordinary boy, but one of the very best. He made all-conference last year."

"You've talked to them, of course?"

"I got down on my knees to them," said the coach. "I asked them did they want that I should lose my job. I asked is there anything you got against me. I told them they were letting down the school. I told them we wouldn't have a team without them. They didn't laugh at me, but—"

138

"They wouldn't laugh at you," said Dean. "Those boys are gentlemen. In fact, all the youngsters in school—"

"They're a pack of sissies!" stormed the coach.

Dean said gently, "That is a matter of opinion. There have been moments when I also wasn't able to attach as much importance to football as it seemed to me I should."

"But that's different," argued the coach. "When a man grows up, naturally he will lose some interest. But these are kids. This just isn't healthy. These young fellows should be out there pawing up the earth. All kids should have a strong sense of competition. And even if they don't, there's the financial angle. Any outstanding football man has a chance, when he goes to college—"

"Our kids don't need athletic subsidies," said Dean, a little sharply. "They're getting more than their share of scholastic scholarships."

"If we had a lot more material," moaned Higgins, "King and Martin wouldn't mean so much. We wouldn't win too often, but we still would have a team. But as it is —do you realize, Mr. Dean, that there have been fewer coming out each year? Right now, I haven't more than enough—"

"You've talked to King and Martin. You're sure they won't reconsider?"

"You know what they told me? They said football interfered with studies!"

The way Higgins said it, it was rank heresy.

"I guess, then," Dean said cheerfully, "that we'll just have to face it."

"But it isn't normal," the coach protested. "There aren't any kids who think more of studies than they do of football. There aren't any kids so wrapped up in books—"

"There are," said Dean. "There are a lot, right here at Millville. You should take a look at the grade averages over the past ten years, if you don't believe it."

"What gets me is that they don't act like kids. They act like a bunch of adults." The coach shook his head, as if to say it was all beyond him. "It's a dirty shame. If only some of those big bruisers would turn out, we'd have the makings of a team."

"Here, also," Dean reminded him, "we have the makings of men and women that Millville in the future may very well be proud of."

The coach got up angrily. "We won't win a game," he warned. "Even Bagley will beat us."

"That is something," Dean observed philosophically, "that shan't worry me too much."

He sat quietly at his desk and listened to the hollow ringing of the coach's footsteps going down the corridor, dimming out with distance.

And he heard the swish and rumble of a janitorial servo-mechanism wiping down the stairs. He wondered where Stuffy was. Fiddling around somewhere, no doubt. With all the scrubbers and the washers and wipers and other mechanical contraptions, there wasn't too much to take up Stuffy's time. Although Stuffy, in his day, had done a lot of work—he'd been on the go from dark to dark, a top-notch janitor.

If it weren't for the labor shortage, Stuffy would have been retired several years ago. But they didn't retire men any more the way they had at one time. With Man going to the stars, there now was more than the human race could do. If they had been retiring men, Dean thought, he himself would be without a job.

And there was nothing he would have hated more than that. For Millville High was his. He had made it his. For more than fifty years, he'd lived for Millville High, first as a young and eager teacher, then as principal, and now, the last fifteen years or so, as its superintendent.

He had given everything he had. And it had given back. It had been wife and child and family, a beginning and an end. And he was satisfied, he told himself—satisfied on this Friday of a new school year, with Stuffy puttering somewhere in the building and no football team—or, at least, next to none.

He rose from the desk and stood looking out the window. A student, late in going home, was walking across the lawn. Dean thought he knew her, although of late his eyes had not been so good for distance.

He squinted at her harder, almost certain it was Judy Charleson. He'd known her grandfather back in the early days and the girl, he thought, had old Henry Charleson's gait. He chuckled, thinking back. Old Charleson, he recalled, had been a slippery one in a business deal. There had been that time he had gotten tangled up in the deal for tube-liners to be used by a starship outfit . . .

He jerked his mind away, tried to wipe out his thinking of the old days. It was a sign of advancing age, the dawn of second childhood.

But however that might be, old Henry Charleson was the only man in Millville who had ever had a thing to do with starships—except Lamont Stiles.

Dean grinned a little, remembering Lamont Stiles and the grimness in him and how he'd amounted to something after many years, to the horrified exasperation of many people who had confidently prophesied he'd come to no good end.

And there was no one now, of course, who knew, or perhaps would ever know, what kind of end Lamont Stiles had finally come to. Or if, in fact, he'd come to an end as yet.

Lamont Stiles, Dean thought, might this very moment be striding down the street of some fantastic city on some distant world.

And if that were so, and if he came home again, what would he bring this time?

The last time he'd come home—the only time he ever had come home—he had brought the Sitters, and they were a funny lot.

Dean turned from the window and walked back to the desk. He sat down and pulled the papers back in front of him. But he couldn't get down to work. That was the way it often was. He'd start thinking of the old days, when there were many friends and many things to do, and get so involved in thinking that he couldn't settle down to work.

He heard the shuffle coming along the hall and shoved the papers to one side. He could tell that it was Stuffy, from the familiar shuffle, coming by to pass the time of day.

Dean wondered at the quiet anticipation he felt within himself. Although it was not so strange, once one considered it. There weren't many left like Stuffy, not many he could talk with.

It was odd with the old, he thought. Age dissolved or loosened the ties of other days. The old died or moved away or were bound by infirmities. Or they drew within themselves, into a world of their own, where they sought a comfort they could find no longer in the outer world.

Stuffy shuffled to the doorway, stopped and leaned

against the jamb. He wiped his drooping yellow mustaches with a greasy hand.

"What's ailing the coach?" he asked. "He went busting out of here like he was turpentined."

"He has no football team," said Dean. "Or he tells me that he hasn't any."

"He cries early every season," Stuffy said. "It's just an act."

"I'm not so sure this time. King and Martin aren't coming out."

Stuffy shuffled a few more paces into the room and dropped into a chair.

"It's them Sitters," Stuffy declared. "They're the cause of it."

Dean sat upright. "What is that you said!"

"I been watching it for years. You can spot the kids that the Sitters sat with or that went to their nursery school. They done something to them kids."

"Fairy tale," said Dean.

"It ain't a fairy tale," Stuffy declared stubbornly. "You know I don't take no stock in superstition. Just because them Sitters are from some other planet . . . Say, did you ever find out what planet they were from?"

Dean shook his head. "I don't know that Lamont ever said. He might have, but I never heard it."

"They're weird critters," said Stuffy, stroking his mustaches slowly to lend an air of deliberation to his words, "but I never held their strangeness against them. After all, they ain't the only aliens on the Earth. The only ones we have in Millville, of course, but there are thousands of other critters from the stars scattered round the Earth."

Dean nodded in agreement, scarcely knowing what he was agreeing with. He said nothing, however, for there was no need of that. Once Stuffy got off to a running start, he'd go on and on.

"They seem right honest beings," Stuffy said. "They never played on no one's sympathy. They just settled in, after Lamont went away and left them, and never asked no one to intercede for them. They made an honest living all these years and that is all one could expect of them."

"And yet," said Dean, "you think they've done something to the kids."

"They changed them. Ain't you noticed it?"

Dean shook his head. "I never thought to notice. I've known these youngsters for years. I knew their folks before them. How do you think they were changed?"

"They grew them up too fast," Stuffy said.

"Talk sense," snapped Dean. "Who grew what too fast?"

"The Sitters grew the kids too fast. That's what's wrong with them. Here they are in high school and they're already grown up."

From somewhere on one of the floors below came the dismal hooting of a servo-mechanism in distress.

Stuffy sprang to his feet. "That's the mopper-upper. I'll bet you it got caught in a door again."

He swung around and galloped off at a rapid shuffle.

"Stupid machine!" he yelped as he went out the door.

Dean pulled the papers back in front of him again and picked up a pencil. It was getting late and he had to finish.

But he didn't see the papers. He saw many little faces staring up at him from where the papers lay—solemn, big-eyed little faces with an elusive look about them.

And he knew that elusive look—the look of dawning adulthood staring out of childish faces.

They grew them up too fast!

"No," said Dean to himself. "No, it couldn't be!"

And yet there was corroborative evidence: The high averages, the unusual number of scholarships, the disdain for athletics. And, as well, the general attitude. And the lack of juvenile delinquency—for years, Millville had been proud that its juvenile delinquency had been a minor problem. He remembered that several years ago he had been asked to write an article about it for a parent-teacher magazine.

He tried to remember what he had written in that article and slowly bits of it came back to him—the realization of parents that their children were a part of the family and not mere appendages; the role played by the churches of the town; the emphasis placed on the social sciences by the schools.

"And was I wrong?" he asked himself. "Was it none of these, but something else entirely—someone else entirely?"

He tried to work and couldn't. He was too upset. He could not erase the smiling little faces that were staring up at him.

Finally he shoved the papers in a drawer and got up from the desk. He put on his worn topcoat and sat the battered old black felt hat atop his silver head.

On the ground floor, he found Stuffy herding the last of the servo-mechanisms into their cubby for the night. Stuffy was infuriated.

"It got itself caught in a heating grill," he raged. "If I hadn't gotten there in the nick of time, it would have wrecked the works." He shook his head dolefully. "Them machines are fine when everything goes well. But just let something happen and they panic. It was best the old way, John."

Stuffy slammed the door on the last of the waddling machines and locked it savagely.

"Stuffy, how well did you know Lamont Stiles?" asked Dean.

Stuffy rubbed his mustaches in fine deliberation. "Knew him well. Lamont and me, we were kids together. You were a little older. You were in the crowd ahead."

Dean nodded his head slowly. "Yes, I remember, Stuffy. Odd that you and I stayed on in the old home town. So many of the others left."

"Lamont ran away when he was seventeen. There wasn't much to stay for. His old lady was dead and his old man was drinking himself to death and Lamont had been in a scrape or two. Everyone was agreed Lamont never would amount to nothing."

"It's hard for a boy when a whole town turns against him."

"That's a fact," said the janitor. "There was no one on his side. He told me when he left that someday he'd come back and show them. But I just thought he was talking big. Like a kid will do, you know, to bolster himself."

"You were wrong," said Dean.

"Never wronger, John."

For Lamont Stiles had come back, more than thirty years after he had run away, back to the old weather-beaten house on Maple Street that had waited empty for him all the lonely years; had come back, an old man when he still was scarcely fifty, big and tough despite the snow-white hair and the skin turned cordovan with the burn of many alien suns; back from far wandering among the distant stars.

But he was a stranger. The town remembered him; he

had forgotten it. Years in alien lands had taken the town and twisted it in his brain, and what he remembered of it was more fantasy than truth—the fantasy spawned by years of thinking back and of yearning and of hate.

"I must go," Dean said. "Carrie will have supper ready. She doesn't like to have it getting cold."

"Good night, John," said the janitor.

The sun was almost down when Dean came out the door and started down the walk. It was later than he'd thought. Carrie would be sore at him and she would bawl him out.

Dean chuckled to himself. There was no one quite like Carrie.

Not wife, for he'd never had a wife. Not mother or sister, for both of those were dead. But housekeeper, faithful all the years—and a bit of wife and sister, and sometimes even mother.

A man's loyalties are queer, he thought. They blind him and they bind him and they shape the man he is. And, through them, he serves and achieves a kind of greatness, although at times the greatness may be gray and pallid and very, very quiet.

Not like the swaggering and the bitter greatness of Lamont Stiles, who came striding from the stars, bringing with him those three queer creatures who became the Sitters. Bringing them and installing them in his house on Maple Street and then, in a year or two, going off to the stars again and leaving them in Millville.

Queer, Dean thought, that so provincial a town as this should accept so quietly these exotic beings. Queerer still that the mothers of the town, in time, should entrust their children to the aliens' care.

As Dean turned the corner into Lincoln Street, he met a woman walking with a knee-high boy.

It was Mildred Anderson, he saw—or had been Mildred Anderson, but she was married now and for the life of him he could not recall the name. Funny, he thought, how fast the young ones grew up. Not more than a couple of years ago, it seemed, that Mildred was in school—although he knew he must be wrong on that; it would be more like ten.

He tipped his hat. "Good evening, Mildred. My, how the boy is growing."

"I doe to cool," the child lisped.

His mother interpreted. "He means he goes to school. He is so proud of it."

"Nursery school, of course."

"Yes, Mr. Dean. The Sitters. They are such lovely things. And so good with children. And there's the cost. Or, rather, the lack of it. You just give them a bouquet of flowers or a little bottle of perfume or a pretty picture and they are satisfied. They positively refuse to take any money. I can't understand that. Can you, Mr. Dean?"

"No," said Dean. "I can't."

He'd forgotten what a talker Mildred was. There had been a period in school, he recalled, when she had been appropriately nicknamed Gabby.

"I sometimes think," she said, hurrying on so she'd miss no time for talk, "that we people here on Earth attach too much importance to money. The Sitters don't seem to know what money is, or if they do, they pay no attention to it. As if it were something that was not important. But I understand there are other races like that. It makes one think, doesn't it, Mr. Dean?"

And he remembered now another infuriating trait of Mildred's—how she inevitably ended any string of sentences with a dangling question.

He didn't try to answer. He knew an answer was not expected of him.

"I must be getting on," he said. "I am late already."

"It was nice to see you, Mr. Dean," said Mildred. "I so often think of my days in school and sometimes it seems like just positively ages and there are other times when it seems no more than just yesterday and . . ."

"Very nice, indeed," said Dean, lifting his hat to her, then almost scurrying off.

It was undignified, he grumbled to himself, being routed in broad daylight on a public street by a talkative woman.

As he went up the walk to the house, he heard Carrie bustling angrily about.

"Johnson Dean," she cried the instant he came in the door, "you sit right down and eat. Your food's already cold. And it's my circle night. Don't you even stop to wash."

Dean calmly hung up his hat and coat.

"For that matter," he said, "I guess I don't need to wash. My kind of job, a man doesn't get too dirty."

She was bustling about in the dining area, pouring his cup of coffee and straightening up the bouquet of mums that served for the centerpiece.

"Since it's my circle night," she said, laying deliberate stress upon the words to shame him for being late, "I won't stay to wash the dishes. You just leave them on the table. I will do them later."

He sat down meekly to eat.

Somehow, for some reason he could not understand, fulfilling a need of which he was not aware, he suddenly felt safe. Safe and secure against a nagging worry and a half-formed fear that had been building up within him without his knowing it.

Carrie came through the living room, settling a determined hat upon her determined head. She had the very air of a woman who was late for her circle meeting through no fault of her own. She halted at the door.

"You got everything you need?" she asked, her eyes making a swift inventory of the table.

"Everything." He chuckled. "Have a good time at the circle. Pick up a lot of gossip."

It was his favorite quip and he knew it irked her—and it was childish, too. But he could not resist it.

She flounced out of the door and he heard her putting down her heels with unnecessary firmness as she went down the walk.

With her going, a hard silence gripped the house and the deeper dusk moved in as he sat at the table eating.

Safe, he thought—old Johnson Dean, school man, safe inside the house his grandfather had built—how many years ago? Old-fashioned now, with its split-level floor plan and its high-bricked fireplace, with its double, attached garage and the planter out in front.

Safe and lonely.

And safe against what threat, against what creeping disturbance, so subtle that it failed of recognition?

He shook his head at that.

But lonely—that was different. That could be explained. The middle-young, he thought, and the very old are lonely. The middle-young because full communication had not been established, and the very old because communication had broken down.

Society was stratified, he told himself, stratified and sectored and partitioned off by many different factors—by age, by occupation, by education, by financial status. And the list did not end there. One could go on and on. It would be interesting, if a man could only find the time, to chart the stratification of humanity. Finished, if it ever could be finished, that chart would be a weird affair.

He finished the meal and wiped his mouth carefully with the napkin. He pushed back from the table and prowled the darkening living area.

He knew that he should at least pick up the dishes and tidy up the table. By rights, he should even wash them. He had caused Carrie a lot of fuss because he had been late. But he couldn't bring himself to do it. He couldn't settle down. Safe, he still was not at peace.

There was no use in putting this business off any longer, he realized, no use to duck the fear that was nagging at him. He knew what it was he faced, if he only would admit it.

Stuffy was crazy, of course. He could not possibly be right. He'd been thinking too much—imagining, rather.

The kids were no different now than they'd ever been.

Except that the grade averages had improved noticeably in the last ten years or so.

Except that there was, as one might expect of such grade averages, an increase in scholarships.

Except that the glitter of competitive sports was beginning to wear off.

Except that there was, in Millville, almost no delinquency.

And those solemn childish faces, with the big, bright eyes, staring up at him from the papers on his desk.

He paced slowly up and down the carpeting before the big brick fireplace, and the dead, black maw beneath the chimney throat, with the bitter smell of old wood ashes in it, seemed to be a mouth making sport of him.

He cracked one feebly clenched old fist into a shaky palm.

"It can't be right," he said fiercely to himself.

And yet, on the face of all evidence, it was.

The children in Millville were maturing faster; they

were growing up, intellectually, much faster than they should.

And perhaps even more than that.

Growing in a new dimension, he wondered. Receding farther from the savage that still lingered in humanity. For sports, organized sports on whatever basis, still remained a refined product of the cave—some antagonism that Man had carried forward under many different guises and which broke forth at least partially in the open in the field of sports.

If he could only talk with the students, he thought, if he could somehow find out what they thought, then there might be a chance of running this thing to the ground.

But that was impossible. The barriers were too high and intricate, the lines of communication much too cluttered. For he was old and they were young; he was authority and they were the regimented. Once again the stratifications would keep them apart. There was no way in which he could approach them.

It was all right to say there was something happening, ridiculous as it might sound. But the important matter, if such should be the case, was to discover the cause and to plot the trend.

And Stuffy must be wrong. For it was fantastic to suggest the Sitters were engineering it.

Peculiarly enough, the Sitters, alien as they were, had established themselves as solid citizens of Millville. They would, he was sure, do nothing to jeopardize the position they had won—the position of being accepted and generally let alone and little talked about.

They would do nothing to attract attention to themselves. Through the years, too many other aliens had gotten into trouble through attempts to meddle and by exhibitionism. Although, come to think of it, what might have seemed to be exhibitionism, from the human viewpoint, possibly had been no more than normal alien conduct.

It had been the good fortune of the Sitters that their natural mother-disposition had enabled them to fit into the human pattern. They had proven ideal baby-sitters and in this they had an economic value and were the more readily accepted.

For many years, they had taken care of the Millville

babies and they were everything that a sitter ought to be. And now they ran a nursery school, although, he remembered, there had been some ruckus over that, since they quite understandably did not hold formal education credits.

He turned on a light and went to the shelves to find something he could read. But there was nothing there that held any interest for him. He ran a finger along the backs of the rows of volumes and his eyes flicked down the titles, but he found absolutely nothing.

He left the shelves and paced over to the large front window and stared out at the street. The street lamps had not come on yet, but there were lights here and there in windows and occasionally a bubble-shaped car moved silently down the pavement, the fanning headlights catching a scurrying bunch of leaves or a crouching cat.

It was one of the older streets in town; at one time, he had known everyone who had lived upon it. He could call out without hesitation the names of the one-time owners—Wilson, Becket, Johnson, Random—but none of them lived here any longer. The names had changed and the faces were faces that he did not know; the stratification had shifted and he knew almost no one on the street.

The middle-young and the very old, he thought, they are the lonely ones.

He went back to the chair beside the lamp he'd lighted and sat down rather stiffly in it. He fidgeted, drumming his fingers on the arms. He wanted to get up, but there was nothing to get up for, unless it was to wash the dishes, and he didn't want to wash them.

He could take a walk, he told himself. That might be a good idea. There was a lot of comfort in an evening walk.

He got his coat and hat and went out the door and down the walk and turned west at the gate.

He was more than halfway there, skirting the business section, before he admitted to himself that he was heading for the Stiles house and the Sitters—that he had, in fact, never intended doing otherwise.

What he might do there, what he might learn there, he had no idea. There was no actual purpose in his mind. It was almost as if he were on an unknown mission, as if he were being pushed by some unseen force into a situation of no-choice.

He came to the Stiles house and stood on the walk outside, looking at it.

It was an old house, surrounded by shade trees that had been planted many years before, and the front yard was a wilderness of shrubs. Every once in a while, someone would come and cut the lawn and maybe trim the hedges and fix up the flower beds to pay the Sitters for all the baby-minding they had done, since the Sitters took no money.

And that was a funny thing, Dean thought, their not taking any money—just as if they didn't need it, as if they might not know what to do with it even if they had any. Perhaps they didn't need it, for they bought no food and still they kept on living and never had been sick enough for anyone to know about it. There must have been times when they were cold, although no one ever mentioned it, but they bought no fuel, and Lamont Stiles had left a fund to pay the taxes—so maybe it was true that they had no need of money.

There had been a time, Dean recalled, when there had been a lot of speculation in the town about their not eating—or at least not buying any food. But after a time the speculation dwindled down and all anyone would say was that you could never figure a lot of things about alien people and there was no use in trying.

And that was right, of course.

The Stiles house, Dean realized with something of a start, was even older than his house. It was a rambler and they had been popular many years before the split-level had come in.

Heavy drapes were drawn at the windows, but there was light behind the drapes and he knew the Sitters were at home. They were usually home, of course. Except on baby-sitting jobs, they never left the house, and in recent years they had gone out but little, for people had gotten in the habit of dropping off the kids at the Sitters' house. The kids never made a fuss, not even the tiny ones. They all liked going to the Sitters.

He went up the walk and climbed the stoop to ring the bell.

He waited and heard movement in the house.

The door came open and one of the Sitters stood there,

with the light behind it, and he had forgotten—it had been many years since he'd seen one of the Sitters.

Shortly after Lamont Stiles had come home, Dean remembered, he had met all three of them, and in the years between, he had seen one of them from time to time a distance on the street. But the memory and the wonder had faded from his mind and now it struck him once again with all the olden force—the faery grace, the sense of suddenly standing face to face with a gentle flower.

The face, if it might be called a face, was sweet—too sweet, so sweet that it had no character and hardly an individuality. A baffling skin arrangement, like the petals of a flower, rose above the face, and the body of the Sitter was sender beyond all belief and yet so full of grace and poise that one forgot the slimness. And about the entire creature hung an air of such sweet simplicity and such a scent of innocence that it blotted out all else.

No wonder, Dean found himself thinking, that the children liked them so.

"Mr. Dean," the Sitter said, "won't you please come in? We are very honored."

"Thank you," he said, taking off his hat.

He stepped inside and heard the closing of the door and then the Sitter was at his side again.

"This chair right here," it said. "We reserve this one for our special visitors."

And it was all very sweet and friendly, and yet there was an alien, frightening touch.

Somewhere there were children laughing in the house. He twisted his head around to find where the laughter came from.

"They're in the nursery," said the Sitter. "I will close the door."

Dean sank into the chair and perched his battered old soft hat on one bony knee, fondling it with his bony fingers.

The Sitter came back and sat down on the floor in front of him, sat down with a single, effortless motion and he had the distinct impression of the swirl of flaring skirts, although the Sitter wore none.

"Now," the Sitter said by way of announcing that Dean commanded its entire attention.

But he did not speak, for the laughter still was in the

room. Even with the door to the nursery shut, there still was childish laughter. It came from everywhere all about the room and it was an utterly happy laughter, the gay and abandoned, the unthinking, the spontaneous laughter of children hard at play.

Nor was that all.

Childish sparkle glittered in the air and there was the long forgotten sense of timelessness—of the day that never ended, that was never meant to end. A breeze was blowing out of some never-never land and it carried with it the scent of brook water bearing on its tide flotillas of fallen autumn leaves, and there was, as well, the hint of clover and of marigolds and the smell of fuzzy, new-washed blankets such as are used in cribs.

"Mr. Dean," the Sitter said.

He roused himself guiltily.

"I'm sorry," he told the Sitter. "I was listening to the children."

"But the door is closed."

"The children in this room," he said.

"There are no children in this room."

"Quite right," he said. "Quite right."

But there were. He could hear their laughter and the patter of their feet.

There were children, or at least the sense of them, and there was also the sense of many flowers, long since died and shriveled in actuality, but with the feel of them still caged inside the room. And the sense of beauty—the beauty of many different things, of flowers and gee-gaw jewelry and little painted pictures and of gaily colored scarves, of all the things that through the years had been given to the Sitters in lieu of money.

"This room," he said haltingly, half-confused. "It is such a pleasant room. I'd just like to sit here."

He felt himself sink into the room, into the youngness and the gayety. If he let go, he thought, if he only could let go, he might join the running and be the same as they.

"Mr. Dean," the Sitter said, "you are very sensitive."

"I am very old," said Dean. "Maybe that's the reason."

The room was both ancient and antique. It was a cry across almost two centuries, with its small brick fireplace paneled in white wood, its arched doorways and the windows that stretched from floor to ceiling, covered by heavy drapes of black and green, etched with golden thread. And it had a solid comfort and a deep security that the present architecture of aluminum and glass never could achieve. It was dusty and moldy and cluttered and perhaps unsanitary, but it had the feel of home.

"I am old-fashioned," said Dean, "and, I suspect, very close to senile, and I am afraid that the time has come again to believe in fairy tales and magic."

"It is not magic," the Sitter replied. "It is the way we live, the only way we can live. You will agree that even Sitters must somehow stay alive."

"Yes, I agree," said Dean.

He lifted the battered hat from off his knee and rose slowly to his feet.

The laughter seemed to be fainter now and the patter not so loud. But the sense of youth—of youngness, of vitality and of happiness—still lay within the room. It lent a sheen to the ancient shabbiness and it made his heart begin to ache with a sudden gladness.

The Sitter still sat upon the floor. "There was something you wanted, Mr. Dean?"

Dean fumbled with his hat. "Not any more. I think I've found my answer."

And even as he said it, he knew it was unbelievable, that once he stood outside the door, he'd know with certainty there could be no truth in what he'd found.

The Sitter rose. "You will come again? We would love to have you."

"Perhaps," said Dean, and turned toward the door.

Suddenly there was a top spinning on the floor, a golden top with flashing jewels set in it that caught the light and scattered it in a million flashing colors, and as it spun, it played a whistling tune—the kind of music that got inside and melted down one's soul.

Dean felt himself go—as, sitting in the chair, he had thought it was impossible for him to do. And the laughter came again and the world outside withdrew and the room suddenly was filled with the marvelous light of Christmas.

He took a quick step forward and he dropped his hat. He didn't know his name, nor where he was, nor how he might have come there, and he didn't care. He felt a gurgling happiness welling up in him and he stooped to reach out for the top.

He missed it by an inch or two and he shuffled forward, stooping, reaching, and his toe caught in a hole in the ancient carpeting and he crashed down on his knees.

The top was gone and the Christmas light snapped out and the world rushed in upon him. The gurgling happiness had gone and he was an old man in a beauty-haunted house, struggling from his knees to face an alien creature.

"I am sorry," said the Sitter. "You almost had it. Perhaps some other time."

He shook his head. "No! Not another time!"

The Sitter answered kindly, "It's the best we have to offer."

Dean fumbled his hat back on his head and turned shakily to the door. The Sitter opened it and he staggered out.

"Come again," the Sitter said, most sweetly. "Any time you wish."

On the street outside, Dean stopped and leaned against a tree. He took off his hat and mopped his brow.

Now, where he had felt only shock before, the horror began creeping in—the horror of a kind of life that did not eat as human beings ate, but in another way, who sucked their nourishment from beauty and from youth, who drained a bouquet dry and who nibbled from the happy hours of a laughing child, and even munched the laughter.

It was no wonder that the children of this village matured beyond their years. For they had their childishness stripped from them by a hungry form of life that looked on them as fodder. There might be, he thought, only so much of happy running and of childish laughter dealt out to any human. And while some might not use their quota, there still might be a limit on it, and once one had used it all, then it was gone and a person became an adult without too much of wonder or of laughter left within him.

The Sitters took no money. There was no reason that they should, for they had no need of it. Their house was filled with all the provender they had stowed away for years.

And in all those years, he was the first to know, the first to sense the nature of those aliens brought home by Lamont Stiles. It was a sobering thought—that he should be the first to find it out. He had said that he was old and

that might be the reason. But that had been no more than
words, rising to his lips almost automatically as a part of
his professional self-pity. Yet there might be something
in it even so.

Could it be possible that, for the old, there might be
certain compensations for the loss of other faculties? As
the body slowed and the mind began to dim, might some
magical ability, a sort of psychic bloodhound sense, rise
out of the embers of a life that was nearly spent?

He was always pothering around about how old he was,
he told himself, as if the mere fact of getting old might
be a virtue. He was forgetful of the present and his pre-
occupation with the past was growing to the danger point.
He was close to second childhood and he was the one who
knew it—and might that be the answer? Might that be
why he'd seen the top and known the Christmas lights?

He wondered what might have happened if he could
have grabbed the top.

He put his hat back on and stepped out from the tree
and went slowly up the walk, heading back for home.

What could he do about it, he wondered, now that he'd
unearthed the Sitters' secret? He could run and tattle,
surely, but there'd be no one to believe him. They would
listen to him and they would be polite so as not to hurt
his feelings, yet there was no one in the village but would
take it for an old man's imaginings, and there'd be nothing
that he could do about it. For beyond his own sure knowledge, he had not a shred of proof.

He might call attention to the maturity of the young
people, as Stuffy had called his attention to it this very
afternoon. But even there he would find no proof, for in
the final reckoning, all the villagers would retreat to rationalization. Parental pride, if nothing else, might require they
should. Not a single one of them would find much cause
for wonder in the fact that a boy or girl of theirs was
singularly well-mannered and above the average in intelligence.

One might say that the parents should have noticed, that
they should have known that an entire village full of children could not possibly be so well-behaved or so level-
headed or so anything else as were these Millville children.
And yet they had not noticed. It had crept along so slowly,

had insinuated itself so smoothly, that the change was not apparent.

For that matter, he himself had not noticed it, he who most of his life had been intimately associated with these very children in which he found so much wonder now. And if he had not noticed, then why expect that someone else should? It had remained for a gossipy old busybody like the janitor to put a finger on it.

His throat was dry and his belly weak and sick and what he needed most of all, Dean told himself, was a cup of coffee.

He turned off on a street that would take him to the downtown section and he plodded along with his head bent against the dark.

What would be the end of it, he asked himself. What would be the gain for this lost childhood? For this pilfering of children? What the value that growing boys and girls should cease to play a little sooner, that they take up the attitude of adults before the chosen time?

There was some gain already seen. The children of Millville were obedient and polite; they were constructive in their play; they'd ceased to be little savages or snobs.

The trouble was, now that one thought of it, they'd almost ceased being children, too.

And in the days to come? Would Millville supply Earth with great statesmen, with canny diplomats, with top-notch educators and able scientists? Perhaps, but that was not the point at all. The question of robbing childhood of its heritage to achieve these qualities was the basic question.

Dean came into the business district, not quite three blocks long, and walked slowly down the street, heading for the only drugstore in the town.

There were only a few people in the store and he walked over to the lunch counter and sat down. He perched on the stool forlornly, with the battered hat pulled down above his eyes, and he gripped the counter's edge to keep his hands from shaking.

"Coffee," he said to the girl who came to take his order, and she brought it to him.

He sipped at it, for it was too hot to drink. He was sorry he had come.

He felt all alone and strange, with all the bright light

and the chrome, as if he were something that had shuffled from the past into a place reserved for the present.

He almost never came downtown any more and that must be the reason for the way he felt. Especially he almost never came down in the evening, although there had been a time he had.

He smiled, remembering how the old crowd used to get together and talk around in circles, about inconsequential things, their talk not getting anywhere and never meaning to.

But that was all ended now. The crowd had disappeared. Some of them were dead and some had moved away and the few of them still left seldom ventured out.

He sat there, thinking, knowing he was maudlin and not caring if he was, too tired and shaken to flinch away from it.

A hand fell on his shoulder and he swung around, surprised.

Young Bob Martin stood there, and although he smiled, he still had the look of someone who had done a thing that he was unsure of.

"Sir, there are some of us down here at a table," said young Martin, gulping a little at his own boldness.

Dean nodded. "That's very nice," he mumbled.

"We wondered if maybe—that is, Mr. Dean, we'd be pleased if you would care to join us."

"Well, that is very nice of you, indeed."

"We didn't mean, sir—that is—"

"Why, certainly," said Dean. "I'd be very glad to."

"Here, sir, let me take your coffee. I won't spill a drop of it."

"I'll trust you, Bob," said Dean, getting to his feet. "You almost never fumble."

"I can explain that, Mr. Dean. It's not that I don't want to play. It's just that . . ."

Dean tapped him on the shoulder lightly. "I understand. There is no need to explain."

He paused a second, trying to decide if it were wise to say what was in his mind.

He decided to: "If you don't tell the coach, I might even say I agree with you. There comes a time in life when football begins to seem a little silly."

Martin grinned, relieved. "You've hit it on the head. Exactly."

He led the way to the table.

There were four of them—Ronald King, George Woods, Judy Charleson and Donna Thompson. All good kids, thought Dean, every one of them. He saw they had been dawdling away at sodas, making them stretch out as long as possible.

They all looked up at him and smiled, and George Woods pulled back a chair in invitation. Dean sat down carefully and placed his hat on the floor beside him. Bob set down the coffee.

"It was good of you to think of me," said Dean and wondered why he found himself embarrassed. After all, these were his kids—the kids he saw every day in school, the ones he pushed and coddled into an education, the kids he'd never had himself.

"You're just the man we need," said Ronald King. "We've been talking about Lamont Stiles. He is the only Millville man who ever went to space and . . ."

"You must have known him, Mr. Dean," said Judy.

"Yes," Dean said slowly, "I did know him, but not as well as Stuffy did. Stuffy and he were kids together. I was a little older."

"What kind of man is he?" asked Donna.

Dean chuckled. "Lamont Stiles? He was the town's delinquent. He was poor in school and he had no home life and he just mostly ran wild. If there was trouble, you could bet your life that Lamont had had a hand in it. Everyone said that Lamont never would amount to anything and when it had been said often enough and long enough, Lamont must have take it to heart . . ."

He talked on and on, and they asked him questions, and Ronald King went to the counter and came back with another cup of coffee for him.

The talk switched from Stiles to football. King and Martin told him what they had told the coach. Then the talk went on to problems in student government and from that to the new theories in ionic drive, announced just recently.

Dean did not do all the talking; he did a lot of listening, too, and he asked questions of his own and time flowed on unnoticed.

Suddenly the lights blinked and Dean looked up, startled.

Judy laughed at him. "That means the place is closing. It's the signal that we have to leave."

"I see," said Dean. "Do you folks do this often—staying until closing time, I mean?"

"Not often," Bob Martin told him. "On weekdays, there is too much studying."

"I remember many years ago—" Dean began, then left the words hanging in the air.

Yes, indeed, he thought, many years ago. And again tonight!

He looked at them, the five faces around the table. Courtesy, he thought, and kindness and respect. But something more than that.

Talking with them, he had forgotten he was old. They had accepted him as another human being, not as an aged human being, not as a symbol of authority. They had moved over for him and made him one of them and themselves one of him; they had broken down the barrier not only of pupil and teacher, but of age and youth as well.

"I have my car," Bob Martin said. "Can I drive you home?"

Dean picked his hat from off the floor and rose slowly to his feet.

"No, thanks," he said. "I think I'd like to walk. I have an idea or two I'd like to mull a bit. Walking helps one think."

"Come again," said Judy Charleson. "Some other Friday night, perhaps."

"Why, thanks," said Dean. "I do believe I will."

Great kids, he told himself with a certain pride. Full of a kindness and a courtesy beyond even normal adult courtesy and kindness. Not brash, not condescending, not like kids at all, and yet with the shine of youthfulness and the idealism and ambition that walked hand in hand with youth.

Premature adults, lacking cynicism. And that was an important thing, the lack of cynicism.

Surely there could be nothing wrong in a humanity like that. Perhaps this was the very coin which the Sitters paid for the childhood they had stolen.

If they had stolen it. For they might not have stolen it; they might merely have captured it and stored it.

And in such a case, then they had given free this new maturity and this new equality. And they had taken something which would have been lost in any event—something for which the human race had no use at all, but which was the stuff of life for the Sitter people.

They had taken youth and beauty and they had stored it in the house; they had preserved something that a human could not preserve in memory. They had caught a fleeting thing and held it and it was there—the harvest of many years; the house was bulging with it.

Lamont Stiles, he wondered, talking in his mind to that man so long ago, so far away, how much did you know? What purpose was in your mind?

Perhaps a rebuke to the smugness of the town that had driven him to greatness. Perhaps a hope, maybe a certainty, that no one in Millville could ever say again, as they had said of Lamont Stiles, that this or that boy or girl would amount to nothing.

That much, perhaps, but surely not any more than that.

Donna had put her hand upon his arm, was tugging at his sleeve.

"Come on, Mr. Dean," she urged. "You can't stay standing here."

They walked with him to the door and said good night and he went up the street at a little faster gait, it seemed to him, than he ordinarily traveled.

But that, he told himself quite seriously, was because now he was just slightly younger than he had been a couple of hours before.

Dean went on even faster and he didn't hobble and he wasn't tired at all, but he wouldn't admit it to himself—for it was a dream, a hope, a seeking after that one never must admit. Until one said it aloud, there was no commitment to the hope, but once the word was spoken, then bitter disappointment lurked behind a tree.

He was walking in the wrong direction. He should be heading back for home. It was getting late and he should be in bed.

And he mustn't speak the word. He must not breathe the thought.

He went up the walk, past the shrub-choked lawn, and he saw that the light still filtered through the drawn drapes.

He stopped on the stoop and the thought flashed through his mind: *There are Stuffy and myself and old Abe Hawkins. There are a lot of us . . .*

The door came open and the Sitter stood there, poised and beautiful and not the least surprised. It was, he thought, almost as if it had been expecting him.

And the other two of them, he saw, were sitting by the fireplace.

"Won't you please come in?" the Sitter said. "We are so glad you decided to come back. The children all are gone. We can have a cozy chat."

He came in and sat down in the chair again and perched the hat carefully on one knee.

Once again the children were running in the room and there was the sense of timelessness and the sound of laughter.

He sat and nodded, thinking, while the Sitters waited.

It was hard, he thought. Hard to make the words come right.

He felt again as he had felt many years ago, when the teacher had called upon him to recite in the second grade.

They were waiting, but they were patient; they would give him time.

He had to say it right. He must make them understand. He couldn't blurt it out. It must be made to sound natural, and logical as well.

And how, he asked himself, could he make it logical?

There was nothing logical at all in men as old as he and Stuffy needing baby-sitters.

CRYING JAG

It was Saturday evening and I was sitting on the stoop, working up a jag. I had my jug beside me, handy, and I was feeling good and fixing to feel better, when this alien and his robot came tramping up the driveway.

I knew right off it was an alien. It looked something like a man, but there weren't any humans got robots trailing at their heels.

If I had been stone sober, I might have gagged a bit at the idea there was an alien coming up the driveway and done some arguing with myself. But I wasn't sober—not entirely, that is.

So I said good evening and asked him to sit down and he thanked me and sat.

"You, too," I said to the robot, moving over to make room.

"Let him stand," the alien said. "He cannot sit. He is a mere machine."

The robot clanked a gear at him, but that was all it said.

"Have a snort," I said, picking up the jug, but the alien shook his head.

"I wouldn't dare," he said. "My metabolism."

That was one of the double-jointed words I had acquaintance with. From working at Doc Abel's sanatorium, I had picked up some of the medic lingo.

"That's a dirty shame," I said. "You don't mind if I do?"

"Not at all," the alien said.

So I had a long one. I felt the need of it.

I put down the jug and wiped my mouth and asked him if there was something I could get him. It seemed plain inhospitable for me to be sitting there, lapping up that liquor, and him not having any.

"You can tell me about this town," the alien said. "I think you call it Millville."

"That's the name, all right. What you want to know about it?"

"All the sad stories," said the robot, finally speaking up.

"He is correct," the alien said, settling down in an attitude of pleasurable anticipation. "Tell me about the troubles and the tribulations."

"Starting where?" I asked.

"How about yourself?"

"Me? I never have no troubles. I janitor all week at the sanatorium and I get drunk on Saturday. Then I sober up on Sunday so I can janitor another week. Believe me, mister," I told him, "I haven't got no troubles. I am sitting pretty. I have got it made."

"But there must be people . . ."

"Oh, there are. You never saw so much complaining as there is in Millville. There ain't nobody here except myself but has got a load of trouble. And it wouldn't be so bad if they didn't talk about it."

"Tell me," said the alien.

So I had another snort and then I told him about the Widow Frye, who lives just up the street. I told him how her life had been just one long suffering, with her husband running out on her when their boy was only three years old, and how she took in washing and worked her fingers to the bone to support the two of them, and the kid ain't more than thirteen or fourteen when he steals this car and gets sent up for two years to the boys' school over at Glen Lake.

"And that is all of it?" asked the alien.

"Well, in rough outline," I said. "I didn't put in none of the flourishes nor the grimy details, the way the widow would. You should hear her tell it."

"Could you arrange it?"

"Arrange what?"

"To have her tell it to me."

"I wouldn't promise you," I told him honestly. "The widow has a low opinion of me. She never speaks to me."

"But I can't understand."

"She is a decent, church-going woman," I explained, "and I am just a crummy bum. And I drink."

"She doesn't like drinking?"

"She thinks it is a sin."

The alien sort of shivered. "I know. I guess all places are pretty much alike."

"You have people like the Widow Frye?"

"Not exactly but the attitude's the same."

"Well," I said, after another snort, "I figure there is nothing else to do but bear up under it."

"Would it be too much bother," asked the alien, "to tell me another one?"

"None at all," I said.

So I told him about Elmer Trotter, who worked his way through law school up at Madison, doing all kinds of odd jobs to earn his way, since he had no folks, and how he finally got through and passed the bar examination, then came back to Millville to set up an office.

I couldn't tell him how it happened or why, although I had always figured that Elmer had got a bellyful of poverty and grabbed this chance to earn a lot of money fast. No one should have known better than he did that it was dishonest, being he was a lawyer. But he went ahead and did it and he got caught.

"And what happened then?" asked the alien breathlessly. "Was he punished?"

I told him how Elmer got disbarred and how Eliza Jenkins gave him back his ring and how Elmer went into insurance and just scraped along in a hand-to-mouth existence, eating out his heart to be a lawyer once again, but he never could.

"You got all this down?" the alien asked the robot.

"All down," the robot said.

"What fine nuances!" exclaimed the alien, who seemed to be much pleased. "What stark, overpowering reality!"

I didn't know what he was talking about, so I had another drink instead.

Then I went ahead, without being asked, and I told him about Amanda Robinson and her unhappy love affair and how she turned into Millville's most genteel and sorriest old maid. And about Abner Jones and his endless disappointments, but his refusal to give up the idea that he was a great inventor, and how his family went in rags and hungry while he spent all his time inventing.

"Such sadness!" said the alien. "What a lovely planet!"

"You better taper off," the robot warned him. "You know what happens to you."

"Just one more," the alien begged. "I'm all right. Just one more."

"Now, look here," I told him, "I don't mind telling them, if that is what you want. But maybe first you better tell me a bit about yourself. I take it you're an alien."

"Naturally," said the alien.

"And you came here in a spaceship."

"Well, not exactly a spaceship."

"Then, if you're an alien, how come you talk so good?"

"Now, that," the alien said, "is something that still is tender to me."

The robot said scornfully: "They took him good and proper."

"You mean you paid for it."

"Too much," the robot said. "They saw that he was eager, so they hiked the price on him."

"But I'll get even with them," the alien cut in. "If I don't turn a profit on it, my name isn't ———." And he said a word that was long and twisted and didn't make no sense.

"That your name?" I asked.

"Yeah, sure. But you can call me Wilbur. And the robot, you may call him Lester."

"Well, boys," I said, "I'm mighty glad to know you. You can call me Sam."

And I had another drink.

We sat there on the stoop and the moon was coming up and the fireflies were flickering in the lilac hedge and the world had an edge on it. I'd never felt so good.

"Just one more," said Wilbur pleadingly.

So I told him about some of the mental cases up at the sanatorium and I picked the bad ones and alongside of me Wilbur started blubbering and the robot said: "Now see what you've done. He's got a crying jag."

But Wilbur wiped his eyes and said it was all right and that if I'd just keep on he'd do the best he could to get a grip on himself.

"What is going on here?" I asked in some astonishment. "You sound like you get drunk from hearing these sad stories."

"That's what he does," said Lester, the robot. "Why else do you think he'd sit and listen to your blabber."

"And you?" I asked of Lester.

"Of course not," Wilbur said. "He has no emotions. He is a mere machine."

I had another drink and I thought it over and it was as clear as day. So I told Wilbur my philosophy: "This is Saturday night and that's the time to howl. So let's you and I together—"

"I am with you," Wilbur cried, "as long as you can talk."

Lester clanked a gear in what must have been disgust, but that was all he did.

"Get down every word of it," Wilbur told the robot. "We'll make ourselves a million. We'll need it to get back all overpayment for our indoctrination." He sighed. "Not that it wasn't worth it. What a lovely, melancholy planet."

So I got cranked up and kept myself well lubricated and the night kept getting better every blessed minute.

Along about midnight, I got falling-down drunk and Wilbur maudlin drunk and we gave up by a sort of mutual consent. We got up off the stoop and by bracing one another we got inside the door and I lost Wilbur somewhere, but made it to my bed and that was the last I knew.

When I woke up, I knew it was Sunday morning. The sun was streaming through the window and it was bright and sanctimonious, like Sunday always is around here.

Sundays usually are quiet, and that's one thing wrong with them. But this one wasn't quiet. There was an awful din going on outside. It sounded like someone was throwing rocks and hitting a tin can.

I rolled out of bed and my mouth tasted as bad as I knew it would. I rubbed some of the sand out of my eyes and started for the living room and just outside the bedroom door I almost stepped on Wilbur.

He gave me quite a start and then I remembered who he was and I stood there looking at him, not quite believing it. I thought at first that he might be dead, but I saw he wasn't. He was lying flat upon his back and his catfish mouth was open and every time he breathed the feathery whiskers on his lips stood straight out and fluttered.

I stepped over him and went to the door to find out what all the racket was. And there stood Lester, the robot, exactly where we'd left him the night before, and out in the driveway a bunch of kids were pegging rocks at him.

Those kids were pretty good. They hit Lester almost every time.

I yelled at them and they scattered down the road. They knew I'd tan their hides.

I was just turning around to go back into the house when a car swung into the drive. Joe Fletcher, our constable, jumped out and came striding toward me and I could see that he was in his best fire-eating mood.

Joe stopped in front of the stoop and put both hands on his hips and stared first at Lester and then at me.

"Sam," he asked with a nasty leer, "what is going on here? Some of your pink elephants move in to live with you?"

"Joe," I said solemn, passing up the insult, "I'd like you to meet Lester."

Joe had opened up his mouth to yell at me when Wilbur showed up at the door.

"And this is Wilbur," I said. "Wilbur is an alien and Lester is a . . ."

"Wilbur is a *what!*" roared Joe.

Wilbur stepped out on the stoop and said: "What a sorrowful face. And so noble, too!"

"He means you," I said to Joe.

"If you guys keep this up," Joe bellowed, "I'll run in the bunch of you."

"I meant no harm," said Wilbur. "I apologize if I have bruised your sensitivities."

That was a hot one—Joe's sensitivities!

"I can see at a glance," said Wilbur, "that life's not been easy for you."

"I'll tell the world it ain't," Joe said.

"Nor for me," said Wilbur, sitting down upon the stoop. "It seems that there are days a man can't lay away a dime."

"Mister, you are right," said Joe. "Just like I was telling the missus this morning when she up and told me that the kids needed some new shoes . . ."

"It does beat hell how a man can't get ahead."

"Listen, you ain't heard nothing yet . . ."

And so help me Hannah, Joe sat down beside him and before you could count to three started telling his life story.

"Lester," Wilbur said, "be sure you get this down."

I beat it back into the house and had a quick one to settle my stomach before I tackled breakfast.

I didn't feel like eating, but I knew I had to. I got out some eggs and bacon and wondered what I would feed Wilbur. For I suddenly remembered how his metabolism couldn't stand liquor, and if it couldn't take good whisky, there seemed very little chance that it would take eggs and bacon.

As I was finishing my breakfast, Higman Morris came busting through the back door and straight into the kitchen. Higgy is our mayor, a pillar of the church, a member of the school board and a director of the bank, and he is a big stuffed shirt.

"Sam," he yelled at me, "this town has taken a lot from you. We have put up with your drinking and your general shiftlessness and your lack of public spirit. But this is too much!"

I wiped some egg off my chin. "What is too much?"

Higgy almost strangled, he was so irritated. "This public exhibition. This three-ring circus! This nuisance! And on a Sunday, too!"

"Oh," I said, "you mean Wilbur and his robot."

"There's a crowd collecting out in front and I've had a dozen calls, and Joe is sitting out there with this—this—"

"Alien," I supplied.

"And they're bawling on one another's shoulders like a pair of three-year-olds and . . . *Alien!*"

"Sure," I said. "What did you think he was?"

Higgy reached out a shaky hand and pulled out a chair and fell weakly into it. "Samuel," he said slowly, "give it to me once again. I don't think I heard you right."

"Wilbur is an alien," I told him, "from some other world. He and his robot came here to listen to sad stories."

"Sad stories?"

"Sure. He likes sad stories. Some people like them happy and others like them dirty. He just likes them sad."

"If he is an alien," said Higgy, talking to himself.

"He's one, sure enough," I said.

"Sam, you're sure of this?"

"I am."

Higgy got excited. "Don't you appreciate what this means to Millville? This little town of ours—the first place on all of Earth that an alien visited!"

I wished he would shut up and get out so I could have an after-breakfast drink. Higgy didn't drink, especially on Sundays. He'd have been horrified.

"The world will beat a pathway to our door!" he shouted. He got out of the chair and started for the living room. "I must extend my official welcome."

I trailed along behind him, for this was one I didn't want to miss.

Joe had left and Wilbur was sitting alone on the stoop and I could see that he already had on a sort of edge.

Higgy stood in front of him and thrust out his chest and held out his hand and said, in his best official manner: "I am the mayor of Millville and I take great pleasure in extending to you our sincerest welcome."

Wilbur shook hands with him and then he said: "Being the mayor of a city must be something of a burden and a great responsibility. I wonder that you bear up under it."

"Well, there are times . . ." said Higgy.

"But I can see that you are the kind of man whose main concern is the welfare of his fellow creatures and as such, quite naturally, you become the unfortunate target of outrageous and ungrateful actions."

Higgy sat down ponderously on the stoop. "Sir," he said to Wilbur, "you would not believe all I must put up with."

"Lester," said Wilbur, "see that you get this down."

I went back into the house. I couldn't stomach it.

There was quite a crowd standing out there in the road —Jake Ellis, the junkman, and Don Myers, who ran the Jolly Miller, and a lot of others. And there, shoved into the background and sort of peering out, was the Widow Frye. People were on their way to church and they'd stop and look and then go on again, but others would come and take their place, and the crowd was getting bigger instead of thinning out.

I went out to the kitchen and had my after-breakfast drink and did the dishes and wondered once again what I would feed Wilbur. Although, at the moment, he didn't seem to be too interested in food.

Then I went into the living room and sat down in the rocking chair and kicked off my shoes. I sat there wiggling my toes and thinking about what a screwy thing it was that Wilbur should get drunk on sadness instead of good red liquor.

The day was warm and I was wore out and the rocking must have helped to put me fast asleep, for suddenly I woke up and there was someone in the room. I didn't see who it was right off, but I knew someone was there.

It was the Widow Frye. She was all dressed up for Sunday, and after all those years of passing my house on the opposite side of the street and never looking at it, as if the sight of it or me might contaminate her—after all these years, there she was all dressed up and smiling. And me sitting there with all my whiskers on and my shoes off.

"Samuel," said the Widow Frye, "I couldn't help but tell you. I think your Mr. Wilbur is simply wonderful."

"He's an alien," I said. I had just woke up and was considerable befuddled.

"I don't care what he is," said the Widow Frye. "He is such a gentleman and so sympathetic. Not in the least like a lot of people in this horrid town."

I got to my feet and I didn't know exactly what to do. She'd caught me off my guard and at a terrible disadvantage. Of all people in the world, she was the last I would have expected to come into my house.

I almost offered her a drink, but caught myself just in time.

"You been talking to him?" I asked lamely.

"Me and everybody else," said the Widow Frye. "And he has a way with him. You tell him your troubles and they seem to go away. There's a lot of people waiting for their turn."

"Well," I told her, "I am glad to hear you say that. How's he standing up under all this?"

The Widow Frye moved closer and dropped her voice to a whisper. "I think he's getting tired. I would say—well, I'd say he was intoxicated if I didn't know better."

I took a quick look at the clock.

"Holy smoke!" I yelled.

It was almost four o'clock. Wilbur had been out there six or seven hours, lapping up all the sadness this village could dish out. By now he should be stiff clear up to his eyebrows.

I busted out the door and he was sitting on the stoop and tears were running down his face and he was listening to Jack Ritter—and Old Jack was the biggest liar in all of seven counties. He was just making up this stuff he was telling Wilbur.

"Sorry, Jack," I said, pulling Wilbur to his feet.

"But I was just telling him . . ."

"Go on home," I hollered, "you and the others. You got him all tired out."

"Mr. Sam," said Lester, "I am glad you came. He wouldn't listen to me."

The Widow Frye held the door open and I got Wilbur in and put him in my bed, where he could sleep it off.

When I came back, the Widow Frye was waiting. "I was just thinking, Samuel," she said. "I am having chicken for supper and there is more than I can eat. I wonder if you'd like to come on over."

I couldn't say nothing for a moment. Then I shook my head.

"Thanks just the same," I said, "but I have to stay and watch over Wilbur. He won't pay attention to the robot."

The Widow Frye was disappointed. "Some other time?"

"Yeah, some other time."

I went out after she was gone and invited Lester in.

"Can you sit down," I asked, "or do you have to stand?"

"I have to stand," said Lester.

So I left him standing there and sat down in the rocker.

"What does Wilbur eat?" I asked. "He must be getting hungry."

The robot opened a door in the middle of his chest and took out a funny-looking bottle. He shook it and I could hear something rattling around inside of it.

"This is his nourishment," said Lester. "He takes one every day."

He went to put the bottle back and a big fat roll fell out. He stooped and picked it up.

"Money," he explained.

"You folks have money, too?"

"We got this when we were indoctrinated. Hundred-dollar bills."

"Hundred-dollar bills!"

"Too bulky otherwise," said Lester blandly. He put the money and the bottle back into his chest and slapped shut the door.

I sat there in a fog. Hundred-dollar bills!

"Lester," I suggested, "maybe you hadn't ought to show

anyone else that money. They might try to take it from you."

"I know," said Lester. "I keep it next to me." And he slapped his chest. His slap would take the head right off a man.

I sat rocking in the chair and there was so much to think about that my mind went rocking back and forth with the chair. There was Wilbur first of all and the crazy way he got drunk, and the way the Widow Frye had acted, and all those hundred-dollar bills.

Especially those hundred-dollar bills.

"This indoctrination business?" I asked. "You said it was bootleg."

"It is, most definitely," said Lester. "Acquired by some misguided individual who sneaked in and taped it to sell to addicts."

"But why sneak in?"

"Off limits," Lester said. "Outside the reservation. Beyond the pale. Is the meaning clear?"

"And this misguided adventurer figured he could sell the information he had taped, the—the—"

"The culture pattern," said Lester. "Your logic trends in the correct direction, but it is not as simple as you make it sound."

"I suppose not," I said. "And this same misguided adventurer picked up the money, too."

"Yes, he did. Quite a lot of it."

I sat there for a while longer, then went in for a look at Wilbur. He was fast asleep, his catfish mouth blowing the whiskers in and out. So I went into the kitchen and got myself some supper.

I had just finished eating when a knock came at the door.

It was old Doc Abel from the sanatorium.

"Good evening, Doc," I said. "I'll rustle up a drink."

"Skip the drink," said Doc. "Just trot out your alien."

He stepped into the living room and stopped short at the sight of Lester.

Lester must have seen that he was astonished for he tried immediately to put him at ease. "I am the so-called alien's robot. Yet despite the fact that I am a mere machine, I am a faithful servant. If you wish to tell your sadness, you may relate it to me with perfect confidence. I shall relay it to my master."

Doc sort of rocked back on his heels, but it didn't floor him.

"Just any kind of sadness?" he asked, "or do you hanker for a special kind?"

"The master," Lester said, "prefers the deep-down sadness, although he will not pass up any other kind."

"Wilbur gets drunk on it," I said. "He's in the bedroom now sleeping off a jag."

"Likewise," Lester said, "confidentially, we can sell the stuff. There are people back home with their tongues hanging to their knees for this planet's brand of sadness."

Doc looked at me and his eyebrows were so high that they almost hit his hairline.

"It's on the level, Doc," I assured him. "It isn't any joke. You want to have a look at Wilbur?"

Doc nodded and I led the way into the bedroom and we stood there looking down at Wilbur. Sleeping all stretched out, he was a most unlovely sight.

Doc put his hand up to his forehead and dragged it down across his face, pulling down his chops so he looked like a bloodhound. His big, thick, loose lips made a blubbering sound as he pulled his palm across them.

"I'll be damned!" said Doc.

Then he turned around and walked out of the bedroom and I trailed along behind him. He walked straight to the door and went out. He walked a ways down the driveway, then stopped and waited for me. Then he reached out and grabbed me by the shirt front and pulled it tight around me.

"Sam," he said, "you've been working for me for a long time now and you are getting sort of old. Most other men would fire a man as old as you are and get a younger one. I could fire you any time I want to."

"I suppose you could," I said, and it was an awful feeling, for I had never thought of being fired. I did a good job of janitoring up at the sanatorium and I didn't mind the work. And I thought how terrible it would be if a Saturday came and I had no drinking money.

"You been a loyal and faithful worker," said old Doc, still hanging onto my shirt, "and I been a good employer.

I always give you a Christmas bottle and another one at Easter."

"Right," I said. "True, every word of it."

"So you wouldn't fool old Doc," said Doc. "Maybe the rest of the people in this stupid town, but not your old friend Doc."

"But, Doc," I protested, "I ain't fooling no one."

Doc let loose of my shirt. "By God, I don't believe you are. It's like the way they tell me? He sits and listens to their troubles, and they feel better once they're through?"

"That's what the Widow Frye said. She said she told him her troubles and they seemed to go away."

"That's the honest truth, Sam?"

"The honest truth," I swore.

Doc Abel got excited. He grabbed me by the shirt again. "Don't you see what we have?" he almost shouted at me.

"*We?*" I asked.

But he paid no attention. "The greatest psychiatrist," said Doc, "this world has ever known. The greatest aid to psychiatry anyone ever has dredged up. You get what I am aiming at?"

"I guess I do," I said, not having the least idea.

"The most urgent need of the human race," said Doc, "is someone or something they can shift their troubles to— someone who by seeming magic can banish their anxieties. Confession is the core of it, of course—a symbolic shifting of one's burden to someone else's shoulders. The principle is operative in the church confessional, in the profession of psychiatry, in those deep, abiding friendships offering a shoulder that one can cry upon."

"Doc, you're right," I said, beginning to catch on.

"The trouble always is that the agent of confession must be human, too. He has certain human limitations of which the confessor is aware. He can give no certain promise that he can assume the trouble and anxiety. But here we have something different. Here we have an alien—a being from the stars—unhampered by human limitations. By very definition, he can take anxieties and smother them in the depths of his own nonhumanity . . ."

"Doc," I yelled, "if you could only get Wilbur up at the sanatorium!"

Doc rubbed mental hands together. "The very thing that I had been thinking."

I could have kicked myself for my enthusiasm. I did the best I could to gain back the ground I'd lost.

"I don't know, Doc. Wilbur might be hard to handle."

"Well, let's go back in and have a talk with him."

"I don't know," I stalled.

"We got to get him fast. By tomorrow, the word will be out and the place will be overrun with newspapermen and TV trucks and God knows what. The scientific boys will be swarming in, and the government, and we'll lose control."

"I'd better talk to him alone," I said. "He might freeze up solid if you were around. He knows me and he might listen to me."

Doc hemmed and hawed, but finally he agreed.

"I'll wait in the car," he said. "You call me if you need me."

He went crunching on down the driveway to where he had the car parked, and I went inside the house.

"Lester," I said to the robot, "I've got to talk to Wilbur. It's important."

"No more sad stories," Lester warned. "He's had enough today."

"No. I got a proposition."

"Proposition?"

"A deal. A business arrangement."

"All right," said Lester. "I will get him up."

It took quite a bit of getting up, but finally we had him fought awake and sitting on the bed.

"Wilbur, listen carefully," I told him. "I have something right down your alley. A place where all the people have big and terrible troubles and an awful sadness. Not just some of them, but every one of them. They are so sad and troubled they can't live with other people . . ."

Wilbur struggled off the bed, stood swaying on his feet.

"Lead me to 'em, pal," he said.

I pushed him down on the bed again. "It isn't as easy as all that. It's a hard place to get into."

"I thought you said—"

"Look, I have a friend who can arrange it for you. But it might take some money—"

"Pal," said Wilbur, "we got a roll of cash. How much would you need?"

"It's hard to say."

"Lester, hand it over to him so he can make this deal."

"Boss," protested Lester, "I don't know if we should."

"We can trust Sam," said Wilbur. "He is not the grasping sort. He won't spend a cent more than is necessary."

"Not a cent," I promised.

Lester opened the door in his chest and handed me the roll of hundred-dollar bills and I stuffed it in my pocket.

"Now you will wait right here," I told them, "and I'll see this friend of mine. I'll be back soon."

And I was doing some fast arithmetic, wondering how much I could dare gouge out of Doc. It wouldn't hurt to start a little high so I could come down when Doc would roar and howl and scream and say what good friends we were and how he always had given me a bottle at Christmas and Easter.

I turned to go out into the living room and stopped dead in my tracks.

For standing in the doorway was another Wilbur, although when I looked at him more closely I saw the differences. And before he said a single word or did a single thing, I had a sinking feeling that something had gone wrong.

"Good evening, sir," I said. "It's nice of you to drop in."

He never turned a hair. "I see you have guests. It shall desolate me to tear them away from you."

Behind me, Lester was making noises as if his gears were stripping, and out of the corner of my eye I saw that Wilbur sat stiff and stricken and whiter than a fish.

"But you can't do that," I said. "They only just showed up."

"You do not comprehend," said the alien in the doorway. "They are breakers of the law. I have come to get them."

"Pal," said Wilbur, speaking to me, "I am truly sorry. I knew all along it would not work out."

"By this time," the other alien said to Wilbur, "you should be convinced of it and give up trying."

And it was plain as paint, once you came to think of it, and I wondered why I hadn't thought of it before. For if Earth was closed to the adventurers who'd gathered the indoctrination data. . . .

"Mister," I said to the alien in the doorway, "there are factors here of which I know you ain't aware. Couldn't you and me talk the whole thing over alone?"

"I should be happy," said the alien, so polite it hurt, "but please understand that I must carry out a duty."

"Why, certainly," I said.

The alien stepped out of the doorway and made a sign behind him and two robots that had been standing in the living room just out of my line of vision came in.

"Now all is secure," said the alien, "and we can depart to talk. I will listen most attentively."

So I went out into the kitchen and he followed me. I sat down at the table and he sat across from me.

"I must apologize," he told me gravely. "This miscreant imposes upon you and your planet."

"Mister," I told him back, "you have got it all wrong. I like this renegade of yours."

"Like him?" he asked, horrified. "That is impossible He is a drunken lout and furthermore than that—"

"And furthermore than that," I said, grabbing the words right from his mouth, "he is doing us an awful lot of good."

The alien looked flabbergasted. "You do not know that which you say! He drags from you your anxieties and feasts upon them most disgustingly, and he puts them down on record so he can pull them forth again and yet again to your eternal shame, and furthermore than that—"

"It's not that way at all," I shouted. "It does us a lot of good to pull out our anxieties and show them—"

"Disgusting! More than that, indecent!" He stopped. "What was that?"

"Telling our anxieties does us good," I said as solemnly as I could. "It's a matter of confession."

The alien banged an open palm against his forehead and the feathers on his catfish mouth stood straight out and quivered.

"It could be true," he said in horror. "Given a culture so primitive and so besodden and so shameless . . ."

"Ain't we, though?" I agreed.

"In our world," said the alien, "there are no anxieties—well, not many. We are most perfectly adjusted."

"Except for folks like Wilbur?"

"Wilbur?"

"Your pal in there," I said. "I couldn't say his name, so I call him Wilbur. By the way . . ."

He rubbed his hand across his face, and no matter what

he said, it was plain to see that at that moment he was loaded with anxiety. "Call me Jake. Call me anything. Just so we get this mess resolved."

"Nothing easier," I said. "Let's just keep Wilbur here. You don't really want him, do you?"

"*Want* him?" wailed Jake. "He and all the others like him are nothing but a headache. But they are our problem and our responsibility. We can't saddle you."

"You mean there are more like Wilbur?"

Jake nodded sadly.

"We'll take them all," I said. "We would love to have them. Every one of them."

"You're crazy!"

"Sure we are," I said. "That is why we need them."

"You are certain, without any shadow of your doubt?"

"Absolutely certain."

"Pal," said Jake, "you have made a deal."

I stuck out my hand to shake on it, but I don't think he even saw my hand. He rose out of the chair and you could see a vast relief lighting up his face.

Then he turned and stalked out of the kitchen.

"Hey, wait a minute!" I yelled. For there were details that I felt we should work out. But he didn't seem to hear me.

I jumped out of the chair and raced for the living room, but by the time I got there, there was no sign of Jake. I ran into the bedroom and the two robots were gone, too. Wilbur and Lester were in there all alone.

"I told you," Lester said to Wilbur, "that Mr. Sam would fix it."

"I don't believe it, pal," said Wilbur. "Have they really gone? Have they gone for good? Is there any chance they will be coming back?"

I raised my arm and wiped off my forehead with my sleeve. "They won't bother you again. You are finally shut of them."

"That is excellent," said Wilbur. "And now about this deal."

"Sure," I said. "Give me just a minute. I'll go out and see the man."

I stepped out on the stoop and stood there for a while to get over shaking. Jake and his two robots had come very close to spoiling everything. I needed a drink worse than I had ever needed one, but I didn't dare take the time. I had to get Doc on the dotted line before something else turned up.

I went out to the car.

"It took you long enough," Doc said irritably.

"It took a lot of talking for Wilbur to agree," I said.

"But he did agree?"

"Yeah, he agreed."

"Well, then," said Doc, "what are we waiting for?"

"Ten thousand bucks," I said.

"Ten thousand . . ."

"That's the price for Wilbur. I'm selling you my alien."

"*Your* alien! He is not your alien!"

"Maybe not," I said, "but he's the next best thing. All I have to do is say the word and he won't go with you."

"Two thousand," declared Doc. "That's every cent I'll pay."

We got down to haggling and we wound up at seven thousand dollars. If I'd been willing to spend all night at it, I would have got eighty-five hundred. But I was all fagged out and I needed a drink much worse than I needed fifteen hundred extra dollars. So we settled on the seven.

We went back into the house and Doc wrote out a check.

"You know you're fired, of course," he said, handing it to me.

"I hadn't thought about it," I told him, and I hadn't. The check for seven thousand in my hand and that roll of hundred-dollar bills bulging out my pocket added up to a lot of drinking money.

I went to the bedroom door and called out Wilbur and Lester and I said to them: "Old Doc here has made up his mind to take you."

And Wilbur said, "I am so happy and so thankful. Was it hard, perhaps, to get him to agree to take us?"

"Not too hard," I said. "He was reasonable."

"Hey," yelled Doc, with murder in his eyes, "what is going on here?"

"Not a thing," I said.

"Well, it sounds to me . . ."

"There's your boy," I said. "Take him if you want him. If it should happen you don't want him, I'll be glad to keep him. There'll be someone else along."

And I held out the check to give it back to him. It was a risky thing to do, but I was in a spot where I had to bluff.

Doc waved the check away, but he was still suspicious that he was being taken, although he wasn't sure exactly how. But he couldn't take the chance of losing out on Wilbur. I could see that he had it all figured out—how he'd become world famous with the only alien psychiatrist in captivity.

Except there was one thing that he didn't know. He had no idea that in just a little while there would be other Wilburs. And I stood there, laughing at him without showing it, while he herded Wilbur and Lester out the door.

Before he left, he turned back to me.

"There is something going on," he said, "and when I find out about it, I am going to come back and take you apart for it."

I never said a word, but just stood there listening to the three of them crunching down the driveway. When I heard the car leave, I went out into the kitchen and took down the bottle.

I had a half a dozen fast ones. Then I sat down in a chair at the kitchen table and practiced some restraint. I had a half a dozen slow ones.

I got to wondering about the other Wilburs that Jake had agreed to send to Earth and I wished I'd been able to pin him down a bit. But I had had no chance, for he had jumped up and disappeared just when I was ready to get down to business.

All I could do was hope he'd deliver them to me—either in the front yard or out in the driveway—but he'd never said he would. A far lot of good it would do me if he just dropped them anywhere.

And I wondered when he would deliver them and how many there might be. It might take a bit of time, for more than likely he would indoctrinate them before they were dropped on Earth, and as to number, I had not the least idea. From the way he talked, there might even be a couple of dozen of them. With that many, a man could make a roll of cash if he handled the situation right.

Although, it seemed to me, I had a right smart amount of money now.

I dug the roll of hundred-dollar bills out of my pocket

and made a stab at counting them, but for the life of me I couldn't keep the figures straight.

Here I was drunk and it wasn't even Saturday, but Sunday. I didn't have a job and now I could get drunk any time I wanted.

So I sat there working on the jug and finally passed out.

There was an awful racket and I came awake and wondered where I was. In a little while I got it figured out that I'd been sleeping at the kitchen table and I had a terrible crick in my neck and a hangover that was even worse.

I stumbled to my feet and looked at the clock. It was ten minutes after nine.

The racket kept right on.

I made it out to the living room and opened the front door. The Widow Frye almost fell into the room, she had been hammering on the door so hard.

"Samuel," she gasped, "have you heard about it?"

"I ain't heard a thing," I told her, "except you pounding on the door."

"It's on the radio."

"You know darn well I ain't got no radio nor no telephone nor no TV set. I ain't got no time for modern trash like that."

"It's about the aliens," she said. "Like the one you have. The nice, kind, understanding alien people. They are everywhere. Everywhere on Earth. There are a lot of them all over. Thousands of them. Maybe millions . . ."

I pushed past her out the door.

They were sitting on front steps all up and down the street, and they were walking up and down the road, and there were a bunch of them playing, chasing one another, in a vacant lot.

"It's like that everywhere!" cried the Widow Frye. "The radio just said so. There are enough of them so that everyone on Earth can have one of their very own. Isn't it wonderful?"

That dirty, doublecrossing Jake, I told myself. Talking like there weren't many of them, pretending that his culture was so civilized and so well adjusted that there were almost no psychopaths.

Although, to be fair about it, he hadn't said how many there might be of them—not in numbers, that is. And even all he had dumped on Earth might be a few in relation to the total population of his particular culture.

And then, suddenly, I thought of something else.

I hauled out my watch and looked at it. It was only a quarter after nine.

"Widow Frye," I said, "excuse me. I got an errand to run."

I legged it down the street as fast as I could.

One of the Wilburs detached himself from a group of them and loped along with me.

"Mister," he said, "have you got some troubles to tell me?"

"Naw," I said. "I never have no troubles."

"Not even any worries?"

"No worries, either."

Then it occurred to me that there was a worry—not for me alone, but for the entire world.

For with all the Wilburs that Jake had dumped on Earth, there would in a little while be no human psychopaths. There wouldn't be a human with a worry or a trouble. God, would it be dull!

But I didn't worry none.

I just loped along as fast as I could go.

I had to get to the bank before Doc had time to stop payment on that check for seven thousand dollars.

INSTALLMENT PLAN

I

THE mishap came at dusk, as the last floater was settling down above the cargo dump, the eight small motors flickering bluely in the twilight.

One instant it was floating level, a thousand feet above the ground, descending gently, with its cargo stacked upon it and the riding robots perched atop the cargo. The next instant it tilted as first one motor failed and then a second one. The load of cargo spilled and the riding robots with it. The floater, unbalanced, became a screaming wheel, spinning crazily, that whipped in a tightening, raging spiral down upon the base.

Steve Sheridan tumbled from the pile of crates stacked outside his tent. A hundred yards away, the cargo hit with a thundering crash that could be heard and felt above the screaming of the floater. The crates and boxes came apart and the crushed and twisted merchandise spread into a broken mound.

Sheridan dived for the open tent flaps and, as he did, the floater hit, slicing into the radio shack, which had been set up less than an hour before. It tore a massive hole into the ground, half burying itself, throwing up a barrage of sand and gravel that bulleted across the area, drumming like a storm of sleet against the tent.

A pebble grazed Sheridan's forehead and he felt the blast of sand against his cheek. Then he was inside the tent and scrambling for the transmog chest that stood beside the desk.

"Hezekiah!" he bawled. "Hezekiah, where are you!"

He fumbled his ring of keys and found the right one and

184

got it in the lock. He twisted and the lid of the chest snapped open.

Outside, he could hear the pounding of running robot feet.

He thrust back the cover of the chest and began lifting out the compartments in which the transmogs were racked.

"Hezekiah!" he shouted.

For Hezekiah was the one who knew where all the transmogs were; he could lay his hands upon any one of them that might be needed without having to hunt for it.

Behind Sheridan, the canvas rustled and Hezekiah came in with a rush. He brushed Sheridan to one side.

"Here, let me, sir," he said.

"We'll need some roboticists," said Sheridan. "Those boys must be smashed up fairly bad."

"Here they are. You better handle them, sir. You do it better than any one of us."

Sheridan took the three transmogs and dropped them in the pocket of his jacket.

"I'm sorry there are no more, sir," Hezekiah said. "That is all we have."

"These will have to do," said Sheridan. "How about the radio shack? Was anyone in there?"

"I understand that it was quite empty. Silas had just stepped out of it. He was very lucky, sir."

"Yes, indeed," agreed Sheridan.

He ducked out of the tent and ran toward the mound of broken crates and boxes. Robots were swarming over it, digging frantically. As he ran, he saw them stoop and lift free a mass of tangled metal. They hauled it from the pile and carried it out and laid it on the ground and stood there looking at it.

Sheridan came up to the group that stood around the mass of metal.

"Abe," he panted, "did you get out both of them?"

Abraham turned around. "Not yet, Steve. Max is still in there."

Sheridan pushed his way through the crowd and dropped on his knees beside the mangled robot. The midsection, he saw, was so deeply dented that the front almost touched the back. The legs were limp and the arms were canted and locked at a crazy angle. The head was twisted and the crystal eyes were vacant.

"Lem," he whispered. "Lemuel, can you hear me?"

"No, he can't," said Abraham. "He's really busted up."

"I have roboticists in my pocket." Sheridan got to his feet. "Three of them. Who wants a go at it? It'll have to be fast work."

"Count me in," Abraham said, "and Ebenezer there and . . ."

"Me, too," volunteered Joshua.

"We'll need tools," said Abraham. "We can't do a thing unless we have some tools."

"Here are the tools," Hezekiah called out, coming on the trot. "I knew you would need them."

"And light," said Joshua. "It's getting pretty dark, and from the looks of it, we'll be tinkering with his brain."

"We'll have to get him up someplace," declared Abraham, "so we can work on him. We can't with him lying on the ground."

"You can use the conference table," Sheridan suggested.

"Hey, some of you guys," yelled Abraham, "get Lem over there on the conference table."

"We're digging here for Max," Gideon yelled back. "Do it yourself."

"We can't," bawled Abraham. "Steve is fixing to get our transmogs changed . . ."

"Sit down," ordered Sheridan. "I can't reach you standing up. And has someone got a light?"

"I have one, sir," said Hezekiah, at his elbow. He held out a flash.

"Turn it on those guys so I can get the transmogs in."

Three robots came stamping over and picked up the damaged Lemuel. They lugged him off toward the conference table.

In the light of the flash, Sheridan got out his keys, shuffled swiftly through them and found the one he wanted.

"Hold that light steady. I can't do this in the dark."

"Once you did," said Ebenezer. "Don't you remember, Steve? Out on Galanova. Except you couldn't see the labels and you got a missionary one into Ulysses when you thought you had a woodsman and he started preaching. Boy, was that a night!"

"Shut up," said Sheridan, "and hold still. How do you expect me to get these into you if you keep wiggling?"

He opened the almost invisible plate in the back of Ebenezer's skull and slid it quickly down, reached inside and found the spacehand transmog. With a quick twist, he jerked it out and dropped it in his pocket, then popped in the roboticist transmog, clicked it into place and drove it home. Then he shoved up the brain plate and heard it lock with a tiny click.

Swiftly he moved along. He had switched the transmog in the other two almost as soon as Ebenezer had regained his feet and picked up the kit of tools.

"Come on, men," said Ebenezer. "We have work to do on Lem."

The three went striding off.

Sheridan looked around. Hezekiah and his light had disappeared, galloping off somewhere, more than likely, to see to something else.

The robots still were digging into the heap of merchandise. He ran around the pile to help them. He began pulling stuff from the pile and throwing it aside.

Beside him, Gideon asked: "What did you run into, Steve?"

"Huh?"

"Your face is bloody."

Sheridan put up his hand. His face was wet and sticky. "A piece of gravel must have hit me."

"Better have Hezekiah fix it."

"After Max is out," said Sheridan, going back to work.

They found Maximilian fifteen minutes later, at the bottom of the heap. His body was a total wreck, but he still could talk.

"It sure took you guys long enough," he said.

"Ah, dry up," Reuben said. "I think you engineered this so you could get a new body."

They hauled him out and skidded him along the ground. Bits of broken arms and legs kept dropping off him. They plunked him on the ground and ran toward the radio shack.

Maximilian squalled after them: "Hey, come back! You can't just dump me here!"

Sheridan squatted down beside him. "Take it easy, Max. The floater hit the radio shack and there's trouble over there."

"Lemuel? How is Lemuel?"

"Not too good. The boys are working on him."

"I don't know what happened, Steve. We were going all right and all at once the floater bucked us off."

"Two of the motors failed," said Sheridan. "Just why, we'll probably never know, now that the floater's smashed. You sure you feel all right?"

"Positive. But don't let the fellows fool around. It would be just like them to hold out on a body. Just for laughs. Don't let them."

"You'll have one as soon as we can manage. I imagine Hezekiah is out running down spare bodies."

"It does beat all," said Maximilian. "Here we had all the cargo down—a billion dollars' worth of cargo and we hadn't broken—"

"That's the way it is, Max. You can't beat the averages."

Maximilian chuckled. "You human guys," he said. "You always figure averages and have hunches and . . ."

Gideon came running out of the darkness. "Steve, we got to get those floater motors stopped. They're running wild. One of them might blow."

"But I thought you fellows—"

"Steve, it's more than a spacehand job. It needs a nuclear technician."

"Come with me."

"Hey!" yelled Maximilian.

"I'll be back," said Sheridan.

At the tent, there was no sign of Hezekiah. Sheridan dug wildly through the transmog chest. He finally located a nuclear technician transmog.

"I guess you're elected," he said to Gideon.

"Okay," the robot said. "But make it fast. One of those motors can blow and soak the entire area with radiation. It wouldn't bother us much, but it would be tough on you."

Sheridan clicked out the spacehand transmog, shoved the other in.

"Be seeing you," said Gideon, dashing from the tent.

Sheridan stood staring at the scattered transmogs.

Hezekiah will give me hell, he thought.

Napoleon walked into the tent. He had his white apron tucked into the belt. His white cook's hat was canted on his head.

"Steve," he asked, "how would you like a cold supper for tonight?"

"I guess it would be all right."

"That floater didn't only hit the shack. It also flattened the stove."

"A cold supper is fine. Will you do something for me?"

"What is it?"

"Max is out there, scared and busted up and lonely. He'll feel better in the tent."

Napoleon went out, grumbling: "Me, a chef, lugging a guy . . ."

Sheridan began picking up the transmogs, trying to get them racked back in order once again.

Hezekiah returned. He helped pick up the transmogs, began rearranging them.

"Lemuel will be all right, sir," he assured Sheridan. "His nervous system was all tangled up and short-circuiting. They had to cut out great hunks of wiring. About all they have at the moment, sir, is a naked brain. It will take a while to get him back into a body and all hooked up correctly."

"We came out lucky, Hezekiah."

"I suppose you are right, sir. I imagine Napoleon told you about the stove."

Napoleon came in, dragging the wreckage that was Maximilian, and propped it against the desk.

"Anything else?" he asked with withering sarcasm.

"No, thank you, Nappy. That is all."

"Well," demanded Maximilian, "how about my body?"

"It will take a while," Sheridan told him. "The boys have their hands full with Lemuel. But he's going to be all right."

"That's fine," said Maximilian. "Lem is a damn good robot. It would be a shame to lose him."

"We don't lose many of you," Sheridan observed.

"No," said Maximilian. "We're plenty tough. It takes a lot to destroy us."

"Sir," Hezekiah said, "you seem to be somewhat injured. Perhaps I should call in someone and put a medic transmog in him . . ."

"It's all right," said Sheridan. "Just a scratch. If you could find some water, so I could wash my face?"

"Certainly, sir. If it is only minor damage, perhaps I can patch you up."

He went to find the water.

"That Hezekiah is a good guy, too," said Maximilian, in an expansive mood. "Some of the boys think at times that he's a sort of sissy, but he comes through in an emergency."

"I couldn't get along without Hezekiah," Sheridan answered evenly. "We humans aren't rough and tough like you. We need someone to look after us. Hezekiah's job is in the very best tradition."

"Well, what's eating you?" asked Maximilian. "I *said* he was a good guy."

Hezekiah came back with a can of water and a towel. "Here's the water, sir. Gideon said to tell you the motors are okay. They have them all shut off."

"I guess that just about buttons it all up—if they're sure of Lemuel," Sheridan said.

"Sir, they seemed very sure."

"Well, fine," said Maximilian, with robotic confidence. "Tomorrow morning we can start on the selling job."

"I imagine so," Sheridan said, standing over the can of water and taking off his jacket.

"This will be an easy one. We'll be all cleaned up and out of here in ninety days or less."

Sheridan shook his head. "No, Max. There's no such thing as an easy one."

He bent above the can and sloshed water on his face and head.

And that was true, he insisted to himself. An alien planet was an alien planet, no matter how you approached it. No matter how thorough the preliminary survey, no matter how astute the planning, there still would always be that lurking factor one could not foresee.

Maybe if a crew could stick to just one sort of job, he thought, it eventually might be possible to work out what amounted to a foolproof routine. But that was not the way it went when one worked for Central Trading.

Central Trading's interests ran to many different things. Garson IV was sales. Next time it could just as well be a diplomatic mission or a health-engineering job. A man never knew what he and his crew of robots might be in for until he was handed his assignment.

He reached for the towel.

"You remember Carver VII?" he asked Maximilian.

"Sure, Steve. But that was just hard luck. It wasn't Ebenezer's fault he made that small mistake."

"Moving the wrong mountain is not a small mistake," Sheridan observed with pointed patience.

"That one goes right back to Central," Maximilian declared, with a show of outrage. "They had the blueprints labeled wrong . . ."

"Now let's hold it down," Sheridan advised. "It is past and done with. There's no sense in getting all riled up."

"Maybe so," said Maximilian, "but it burns me. Here we go and make ourselves a record no other team can touch. Then Central pulls this boner and pins the blame on us. I tell you, Central's got too big and clumsy."

And smug as well, thought Sheridan, but he didn't say it.

Too big and too complacent in a lot of ways. Take this very planet, for example. Central should have sent a trading team out here many years ago, but instead had fumed and fussed around, had connived and schemed; they had appointed committees to delve into the situation and there had been occasional mention of it at the meetings of the board, but there had been nothing done until the matter had ground its way through the full and awesome maze of very proper channels.

A little competition, Sheridan told himself, was the very thing that Central needed most. Maybe, if there were another outfit out to get the business, Central Trading might finally rouse itself off its big, fat dignity.

Napoleon came clumping in and banged a plate and glass and bottle down upon the table. The plate was piled with cold cuts and sliced vegetables; the bottle contained beer.

Sheridan looked surprised. "I didn't know we had beer."

"Neither did I," said Napoleon, "but I looked and there it was. Steve, it's getting so you never know what is going on."

Sheridan tossed away the towel and sat down at the desk. He poured a glass of beer.

"I'd offer you some of this," he told Maximilian, "except I know it would rust your guts."

Napoleon guffawed.

"Right as of this moment," Maximilian said, "I haven't any guts to speak of. Most of them dropped out."

Abraham came tramping briskly in. "I hear you have Max hidden out some place."

"Right here, Abe," called Maximilian eagerly.

"You certainly are a mess," said Abraham. "Here we were going fine until you two clowns gummed up the works."

"How is Lemuel?" asked Sheridan.

"He's all right," said Abraham. "The other two are working on him and they don't really need me. So I came hunting Max." He said to Napoleon, "Here, grab hold and help me get him to the table. We have good light out there."

Grumbling, Napoleon lent a hand. "I've lugged him around half the night," he complained. "Let's not bother with him. Let's just toss him on the scrap heap."

"It would serve him right," Abraham agreed, with pretended wrath.

The two went out, carrying Maximilian between them. He still was dropping parts.

Hezekiah finished with the transmog chest, arranging all the transmogs neatly in their place. He closed the lid with some satisfaction.

"Now that we're alone," he said, "let me see your face."

Sheridan grunted at him through a mouth stuffed full of food.

Hezekiah looked him over. "Just a scratch on the forehead, but the left side of your face, sir, looks as if someone had sandpapered it. You are sure you don't want to transmog someone? A doctor should have a look at it."

"Just leave it as it is," said Sheridan. "It will be all right."

Gideon stuck his head between the tent flaps. "Hezekiah, Abe is raising hell about the body you found for Max. He says it's an old, rebuilt job. Have you got another one?"

"I can look and see," said Hezekiah. "It was sort of dark. There are several more. We can look them over."

He left with Gideon, and Sheridan was alone.

He went on eating, mentally checking through the happenings of the evening.

It had been hard luck, of course, but it could have been far worse. One had to expect accidents and headaches every now and then. After all, they had been downright lucky. Except for some lost time and a floater load of cargo, they had come out unscathed.

All in all, he assured himself, they'd made a good beginning. The cargo sled and ship were swinging in tight orbits, the cargo had been ferried down and on this small peninsula, jutting out into the lake, they had as much security as one might reasonably expect on any alien planet.

The Garsonians, of course, were not belligerent, but even so one could never afford to skip security.

He finished eating and pushed the plate aside. He pulled a portfolio out of a stack of maps and paper work lying on the desk. Slowly he untied the tapes and slid the contents out. For the hundredth time, at least, he started going through the summary of reports brought back to Central Trading by the first two expeditions.

Man first had come to the planet more than twenty years ago to make a preliminary check, bringing back field notes, photographs and samples. It had been mere routine; there had been no thorough or extensive survey. There had been no great hope nor expectation; it had been simply another job to do. Many planets were similarly spot-checked, and in nineteen out of twenty of them, nothing every came of it.

But something very definite had come of it in the case of Garson IV.

The something was a tuber that appeared quite ordinary, pretty much, in fact, like an undersize, shriveled-up potato. Brought back by the survey among other odds and ends picked up on the planet, it had in its own good time been given routine examination and analysis by the products laboratory—with startling results.

From the *podar*, the tuber's native designation, had been derived a drug which had been given a long and agonizing name and had turned out to be the almost perfect tranquilizer. It appeared to have no untoward side-effects; it was not lethal if taken in too enthusiastic dosage; it was slightly habit-forming, a most attractive feature for all who might be concerned with the sale of it.

To a race vitally concerned with an increasing array of disorders traceable to tension, such a drug was a boon, indeed. For years, a search for such a tranquilizer had been carried on in the laboratories and here it suddenly was, a gift from a new-found planet.

Within an astonishingly short time, considering the deliberation with which Central Trading usually operated, a second expedition had been sent out to Garson IV, with the robotic team heavily transmogged as trade experts, psychologists and diplomatic functionaries. For two years the team had worked, with generally satisfactory results. When they had blasted off for Earth, they carried a cargo of the *podars,* a mass of meticulously gathered data and a trade agreement under which the Garsonians agreed to produce and store the *podars* against the day when another team should arrive to barter for them.

And that, thought Sheridan, is us.

And it was all right, of course, except that they were late by fifteen years.

For Central Trading, after many conferences, had decided to grow the *podars* on Earth. This, the economists had pointed out, would be far cheaper than making the long and expensive trips that would be necessary to import them from a distant planet. That it might leave the Garsonians holding the bag insofar as the trade agreement was concerned seemed not to have occurred to anyone at all. Although, considering the nature of the Garsonians, they probably had not been put out too greatly.

For the Garsonians were a shiftless tribe at best and it had been with some initial difficulty that the second team had been able to explain to them the mechanics and desirability of interstellar trade. Although, in fairness, it might be said of them that, once they understood it, they had been able to develop a creditable amount of eagerness to do business.

Podars had taken to the soil of Earth with commendable adaptiveness. They had grown bigger and better than they'd ever grown on their native planet. This was not surprising when one took into account the slap-dash brand of agriculture practiced by the Garsonians.

Using the tubers brought back by the second expedition for the initial crop, it required several years of growing before a sufficient supply of seed *podars* were harvested to justify commercial growing.

But finally that had come about and the first limited supply of the wonder drug had been processed and put on sale with wide advertising fanfare and an accompanying high price.

And all seemed well, indeed.

Once again the farmers of the Earth had gained a new cash crop from an alien planet. Finally, Man had the tranquilizer which he'd sought for years.

But as the years went by, some of the enthusiasm dimmed. For the drug made from the *podars* appeared to lose its potency. Either it had not been as good as first believed or there was some factor lacking in its cultivation on Earth.

The laboratories worked feverishly on the problem. The *podars* were planted in experimental plots on other planets in the hope that the soil or air or general characteristics there might supply the needed element—if missing element it were.

And Central Trading, in its ponderous, bureaucratic fashion, began preliminary plans for importation of the tubers, remembering belatedly, perhaps, the trade agreement signed many years before. But the plans were not pushed too rapidly, for any day, it was believed, the answer might be found that would save the crop for Earth.

But when the answer came, it ruled out Earth entirely; it ruled out, in fact, every place but the *podar's* native planet. For, the laboratories found, the continued potency of the drug relied to a large extent upon the chemical reaction of a protozoan which the *podar* plants nourished in their roots. And the protozoan flourished, apparently, on Garson IV alone.

So finally, after more than fifteen years, the third expedition had started out for Garson IV. And had landed and brought the cargo down and now was ready, in the morning, to start trading for the *podars*.

Sheridan flipped idly through the sheets from the portfolio. There was, he thought, actually no need to look at all the data once again. He knew it all by heart.

The canvas rustled and Hezekiah stepped into the tent.

Sheridan looked up. "Good," he said, "you're back. Did you get Max fixed up?"

"We found a body, sir, that proved acceptable."

Sheridan pushed the pile of reports aside. "Hezekiah, what are your impressions?"

"Of the planet, sir?"

"Precisely."

"Well, it's those barns, sir. You saw them, sir, when we were coming down. I believe I mentioned them to you."

Sheridan nodded. "The second expedition taught the natives how to build them. To store the *podars* in."

"All of them painted red," the robot said. "Just like the barns we have on Christmas cards."

"And what's wrong with that?"

"They look a little weird, sir."

Sheridan laughed. "Weird or not, those barns will be the making of us. They must be crammed with *podars*. For fifteen years, the natives have been piling up their *podars*, more than likely wondering when we'd come to trade . . ."

"There were all those tiny villages," Hezekiah said, "and those big red barns in the village square. It looked, if you will pardon the observation, sir, like a combination of New England and Lower Slobbovia."

"Well, not quite Lower Slobbovia. Our Garsonian friends are not as bad as that. They may be somewhat shiftless and considerably scatterbrained, but they keep their villages neat and their houses spic and span."

He pulled a photograph from a pile of data records. "Here, take a look at this."

The photograph showed a village street, neat and orderly and quiet, with its rows of well-kept houses huddled underneath the shade trees. There were rows of gay flowers running along the roadway and there were people—little, gnomelike people—walking in the road.

Hezekiah picked it up. "I will admit, sir, that they look fairly happy. Although, perhaps, not very smart."

Sheridan got to his feet. "I think I'll go out and check around and see how things are going."

"Everything is all right, sir," said Hezekiah. "The boys have the wreckage cleared up. I'm sorry to have to tell you, sir, that not much of the cargo could be saved."

"From the looks of it, I'm surprised we could salvage any of it."

"Don't stay out too long," Hezekiah warned him. "You'll need a good night's sleep. Tomorrow will be a busy day and you'll be out at the crack of dawn."

"I'll be right back," Sheridan promised and ducked out of the tent.

Batteries of camp lights had been erected and now held back the blackness of the night. The sound of hammering came from the chewed-up area where the floater had come down. There was no sign of the floater now and a gang of spacehand robots was busily going about the building of another radio shack. Another gang was erecting a pavilion tent above the conference table, where Abraham and his fellow roboticists still worked on Lemuel and Maximilian. And in front of the cook shack, Napoleon and Gideon squatted down, busily shooting craps.

Sheridan saw that Napoleon had set up his outdoors stove again.

He walked over to them and they turned their heads and greeted him, then went back to their game.

Sheridan watched them for a while and then walked slowly on.

He shook his head in some bewilderment—a continuing bewilderment over this robotic fascination with all the games of chance. It was, he supposed, just one of the many things that a human being—any human being—would never understand.

For gambling seemed entirely pointless from a robotic point of view. They had no property, no money, no possessions. They had no need of any and they had no wish for any—and yet they gambled madly.

It might be, he told himself, no more than an aping of their fellow humans. By his very nature, a robot was barred effectively from participating in most of the human vices. But gambling was something that he could do as easily and perhaps more efficiently than any human could.

But what in the world, he wondered, did they get out of it? No gain, no profit, for there were no such things as gain or profit so far as a robot was concerned. Excitement, perhaps? An outlet for aggressiveness?

Or did they keep a phantom score within their mind—mentally chalking up their gains and loss—and did a heavy winner at a game of chance win a certain prestige that was not visible to Man, that might, in fact, be carefully hidden from a man?

A man, he thought, could never know his robots in their entirety and that might be as well—it would be an unfair act to strip the final shreds of individuality from a robot.

For if the robots owed much to Man—their conception and their manufacture and their life—by the same token Man owed as much, or even more, to robots.

Without the robots, Man could not have gone as far or fast, or as effectively, out into the Galaxy. Sheer lack of transportation for skilled manpower alone would have held his progress to a crawl.

But with the robots there was no shipping problem.

And with the transmogs there was likewise no shortage of the kind of brains and skills and techniques—as there would otherwise have been—necessary to cope with the many problems found on the far-flung planets.

He came to the edge of the camp area and stood, with the lights behind him, facing out into the dark from which came the sound of running waves and the faint moaning of the wind.

He tilted back his head and stared up at the sky and marveled once again, as he had marveled many other times on many other planets, at the sheer, devastating loneliness and alienness of unfamiliar stars.

Man pinned his orientation to such fragile things, he thought—to the way the stars were grouped, to how a flower might smell, to the color of a sunset.

But this, of course, was not entirely unfamiliar ground. Two human expeditions already had touched down.

And now the third had come, bringing with it a cargo sled piled high with merchandise.

He swung around, away from the lake, and squinted at the area just beyond the camp and there the cargo was, piled in heaps and snugged down with tough plastic covers from which the starlight glinted. It lay upon the alien soil like a herd of humpbacked monsters bedded for the night.

There was no ship built that could handle that much cargo—no ship that could carry more than a dribble of the merchandise needed for interstellar trade.

For that purpose, there was the cargo sled.

The sled, set in an orbit around the planet of its origin, was loaded by a fleet of floaters, shuttling back and forth. Loaded, the sled was manned by robots and given the star on its long journey by the expedition ship. By the dint of the engines on the sled itself and the power of the expedition ship, the speed built up and up.

There was a tricky point when one reached the speed of light, but after that it became somewhat easier—although for interstellar travel, there was need of speed many times in excess of the speed of light.

And so the sled sped on, following close behind the expedition ship, which served as a pilot craft through tha strange gray area where space and time were twisted into something other than normal space and time.

Without robots, the cargo sleds would have been impossible; no human crew could ride a cargo ship and maintain the continuous routine of inspection that was necessary.

Sheridan swung back toward the lake again and wondered if he could actually see the curling whiteness of the waves or if it were sheer imagination. The wind was moaning softly and the stranger stars were there, and out beyond the waters the natives huddled in their villages with the big red barns looming in the starlit village squares.

II

IN the morning, the robots gathered around the conference table beneath the gay pavilion tent and Sheridan and Hezekiah lugged out the metal transmog boxes labeled SPECIAL—GARSON IV.

"Now I think," said Sheridan, "that we can get down to business, if you gentlemen will pay attention to me." He opened one of the transmog boxes. "In here, we have some transmogs tailor-made for the job that we're to do. Because we had prior knowledge of this planet, it was possible to fabricate this special set. So on this job we won't start from scratch, as we are often forced to do . . ."

"Cut out the speeches, Steve," yelled Reuben, "and let's get started with this business."

"Let him talk," said Abraham. "He certainly has the right to, just like any one of us."

"Thank you, Abe," Sheridan said.

"Go ahead," said Gideon. "Rube's just discharging excess voltage."

"These transmogs are basically sales transmogs, of course. They will provide you with the personality and all the techniques of a salesman. But, in addition to that, they contain as well all the data pertaining to the situation here and the language of the natives, plus a mass of planetary facts."

He unlocked another of the boxes and flipped back the lid.

"Shall we get on with it?" he asked.

"Let's get going," demanded Reuben. "I'm tired of this spacehand transmog."

Sheridan made the rounds, with Hezekiah carrying the boxes for him.

Back at his starting point, he shoved aside the boxes, filled now with spacehand and other assorted transmogs. He faced the crew of salesmen.

"How do they feel?" he asked.

"They feel okay," said Lemuel. "You know, Steve, I never realized until now how dumb a spacehand is."

"Pay no attention to him," Abraham said, disgusted. "He always makes that crack."

Maximilian said soberly: "It shouldn't be too bad. These people have been acclimated to the idea of doing business with us. There should be no initial sales resistance. In fact, they may be anxious to start trading."

"Another thing," Douglas pointed out. "We have the kind of merchandise they've evinced interest in. We won't have to waste our time in extensive surveys to find out what they want."

"The market pattern seems to be a simple one," said Abraham judiciously. "There should be no complications. The principal thing, it would appear, is the setting of a proper rate of exchange—how many *podars* they must expect to pay for a shovel or a hoe or other items that we have."

"That will have to come," said Sheridan, "by a process of trial and error."

"We'll have to bargain hard," Lemuel said, "in order to establish a fictitious retail price, then let them have it wholesale. There are many times when that works effectively."

Abraham rose from his chair. "Let's get on with it. I suppose, Steve, that you will stay in camp."

Sheridan nodded. "I'll stay by the radio. I'll expect reports as soon as you can send them."

The robots got on with it. They scrubbed and polished one another until they fairly glittered. They brought out fancy dress hardware and secured it to themselves with magnetic clamps. There were colorful sashes and glistening rows of metals and large chunks of jewelry not entirely in the best of taste, but designed to impress the natives.

They got out their floaters and loaded up with samples

from the cargo dump. Sheridan spread out a map and assigned each one a village. They checked their radios. They made sure they had their order boards.

By noon, they all were off.

Sheridan went back to the tent and sat down in his camp chair. He stared down the shelving beach to the lake, sparkling in the light of the noon-high sun.

Napoleon brought his lunch and hunkered down to talk, gathering his white cook's apron carefully in his lap so it would not touch the ground. He pushed his tall white cap to a rakish angle.

"How you got it figured, Steve?"

"You can never figure one beforehand," Sheridan told him. "The boys are all set for an easy time and I hope they have it. But this is an alien planet and I never bet on aliens."

"You look for any trouble?"

"I don't look for anything. I just sit and wait and hope feebly for the best. Once the reports start coming in . . ."

"If you worry so much, why not go out yourself?"

Sheridan shook his head. "Look at it this way, Nappy. I am not a salesman and this crew is. There'd be no sense in my going out. I'm not trained for it."

And, he thought, the fact of the matter was that he was not trained for anything. He was not a salesman and he was not a spacehand; he was not any of the things that the robots were or could be.

He was just a human, period, a necessary cog in a team of robots.

There was a law that said no robot or no group of robots could be assigned a task without human supervision, but that was not the whole of it. It was, rather, something innate in the robot makeup, not built into them, but something that was there and always might be there—the ever-present link between the robot and his human.

Sent out alone, a robot team would blunder and bog down, would in the end become unstuck entirely—would wind up worse than useless. With a human accompanying them, there was almost no end to their initiative and their capability.

It might, he thought, be their need of leadership, although in very truth the human member of the team sometimes showed little of that. It might be the necessity for some symbol of authority and yet, aside from their respect and consideration for their human, the robots actually bowed to no authority.

It was something deeper, Sheridan told himself, than mere leadership or mere authority. It was comparable to the affection and rapport which existed as an undying bond between a man and dog and yet it had no tinge of the god-worship associated with the dog.

He said to Napoleon: "How about yourself? Don't you ever hanker to go out? If you'd just say the word, you could."

"I like to cook," Napoleon stated. He dug at the ground with a metal finger. "I guess, Steve, you could say I'm pretty much an old retainer."

"A transmog would take care of that in a hurry."

"And then who'd cook for you? You know you're a lousy cook."

Sheridan ate his lunch and sat in his chair, staring at the lake, waiting for the first reports on the radio.

The job at last was started. All that had gone before—the loading of the cargo, the long haul out through space, the establishing of the orbits and the unshipping of the cargo—had been no more than preliminary to this very moment.

The job was finally started, but it was far from done. There would be months of work. There would be many problems and a thousand headaches. But they'd get it done, he told himself with a sure pride. There was nothing, absolutely nothing, that could stump this gang of his.

Late in the afternoon, Hezekiah came with the word: "Abraham is calling, sir. It seems that there is trouble."

Sheridan leaped to his feet and ran to the shack. He pulled up a chair and reached for the headset. "That you, Abe? How is it going, boy?"

"Badly, Steve," said Abraham. "They aren't interested in doing business. They want the stuff, all right. You can see the way they look at it. But they aren't buying. You know what I think? I don't believe they have anything to trade."

"That's ridiculous, Abe! They've been growing *podars* all these years. The barns are crammed with them."

"Their barn is all nailed up," said Abraham. "They have bars across the doors and the windows boarded. When I tried to walk up to it, they acted sort of ugly."

"I'll be right out," decided Sheridan. "I want to look this over." He stood up and walked out of the shack. "Hezekiah, get the flier started. We're going out and have a talk with Abe. Nappy, you mind the radio. Call me at Abe's village if anything goes wrong."

"I'll stay right here beside it," Napoleon promised him.

Hezekiah brought the flier down in the village square, landing it beside the floater, still loaded with its merchandise.

Abraham strode over to them as soon as they were down. "I'm glad you came, Steve. They want me out of here. They don't want us around."

Sheridan climbed from the flier and stood stiffly in the square. There was a sense of wrongness—a wrongness with the village and the people—something wrong and different.

There were a lot of natives standing around the square, lounging in the doorways and leaning against the trees. There was a group of them before the barred door of the massive barn that stood in the center of the square, as if they might be a guard assigned to protect the barn.

"When I first came down," said Abraham, "they crowded around the floater and stood looking at the stuff and you could see they could hardly keep their hands off it. I tried to talk to them, but they wouldn't talk too much, except to say that they were poor. Now all they do is just stand off and glare."

The barn was a monumental structure when gauged against the tiny houses of the village. It stood up four-square and solid and entirely without ornament and it was an alien thing—alien of Earth. For, Sheridan realized, it was the same kind of barn that he had seen on the backwoods farms of Earth—the great hip-roof, the huge barn door, the ramp up to the door, and even the louvered cupola that rode astride the ridge-pole.

The man and the two robots stood in a pool of hostile silence and the lounging natives kept on staring at them and there was something decidedly wrong.

Sheridan turned slowly and glanced around the square and suddenly he knew what the wrongness was.

The place was shabby; it approached the downright squalid. The houses were neglected and no longer neat and the streets were littered. And the people were a piece with all the rest of it.

"Sir," said Hezekiah, "they are a sorry lot."

And they were all of that.

There was something in their faces that had a look of haunting and their shoulders stooped and there was fatigue upon them.

"I can't understand it," said the puzzled Abraham. "The data says they were a happy-go-lucky bunch, but look at them out there. Could the data have been wrong?"

"No, Abe. It's the people who have changed."

For there was no chance that the data could be wrong. It had been compiled by a competent team, one of the very best, and headed by a human who had long years of experience on many alien planets. The team had spent two years on Garson IV and had made it very much its business to know this race inside out.

Something had happened to the people. They had somehow lost their gaiety and pride. They had let the houses go uncared for. They had allowed themselves to become a race of ragamuffins.

"You guys stay here," Sheridan said.

"You can't do it, sir," said Hezekiah in alarm.

"Watch yourself," warned Abraham.

Sheridan walked toward the barn. The group before it did not stir. He stopped six feet away.

Close up, they looked more gnomelike than they had appeared in the pictures brought back by the survey team. Little wizened gnomes, they were, but not happy gnomes at all. They were seedy-looking and there was resentment in them and perhaps a dash of hatred. They had a hangdog look and there were some among them who shuffled in discomfiture.

"I see you don't remember us," said Sheridan conversationally. "We were away too long, much longer than we had thought to be."

He was having, he feared, some trouble with the language. It was, in fact, not the easiest language in the Galaxy to handle. For a fleeting moment, he wished that there were some sort of transmog that could be slipped into the human brain. It would make moments like this so much easier.

"We remember you," said one of them in a sullen voice.

"That's wonderful," said Sheridan with forced enthusiasm. "Are you speaker for this village?"

Speaker because there was no leader, no chief—no government at all beyond a loose, haphazard talking over what daily problems they had, around the local equivalent of the general store, and occasional formless town meetings to decide what to do in their rare crises, but no officials to enforce the decisions.

"I can speak for them," the native said somewhat evasively. He shuffled slowly forward. "There were others like you who came many years ago."

"You were friends to them."

"We are friends to all."

"But special friends to them. To them you made the promise that you would keep the *podars*."

"Too long to keep the *podars*. The *podars* rot away."

"You had the barn to store them in."

"One *podar* rots. Soon there are two *podars* rotten. And then a hundred *podars* rotten. The barn is no good to keep them. No place is any good to keep them."

"But we—those others showed you what to do. You go through the *podars* and throw away the rotten ones. That way you keep the other *podars* good."

The native shrugged. "Too hard to do. Takes too long."

"But not all the *podars* rotted. Surely you have some left."

The creature spread his hands. "We have bad seasons, friend. Too little rain, too much. It never comes out right. Our crop is always bad."

"But we have brought things to trade you for the *podars*. Many things you need. We had great trouble bringing them. We came from far away. It took us long to come."

"Too bad," the native said. "No *podars*. As you can see, we are very poor."

"But where have all the *podars* gone?"

"We," the man said stubbornly, "don't grow *podars* any more. We changed the *podars* into another crop. Too much bad luck with *podars*."

"But those plants out in the fields?"

"We do not call them *podars*."

"It doesn't matter what you call them. Are they *podars* or are they not?"

"We do not grow the *podars*."

Sheridan turned on his heel and walked back to the robots.

"No soap," he said. "Something's happened here. They gave me a poor-mouth story and finally, as a clincher, said they don't grow *podars* any more."

"But there are fields of *podars*," declared Abraham. "If the data's right, they've actually increased their acreage. I checked as I was coming in. They're growing more right now than they ever grew before."

"I know," said Sheridan. "It makes no sense at all. Hezekiah, maybe you should give base a call and find what's going on."

"One thing," Abraham pointed out. "What about this trade agreement that we have with them? Has it any force?"

Sheridan shook his head. "I don't know. Maybe we can wave it in their faces, just to see what happens. It might serve as a sort of psychological wedge a little later on, once we get them softened up a bit."

"*If* we get them softened up."

"This is our first day and this is only one village."

"You don't think we could use the agreement as a club?"

"Look, Abe, I'm not a lawyer, and we don't have a lawyer transmog along with us for a damned good reason —there isn't any legal setup whatever on this planet. But let's say we could haul them into a galactic court. Who signed for the planet? Some natives *we* picked as its representatives, not the natives themselves; their signing couldn't bind anything or anybody. The whole business of drawing up a contract was nothing but an impressive ceremony without any legal basis—it was just meant to awe the natives into doing business with us."

"But the second expedition must have figured it would work."

"Well, sure. The Garsonians have a considerable sense of morality—individually and as families. Can we make that sense of morality extend to bigger groups? That's our problem."

"That means we have to figure out an angle," said Abraham. "At least for this one village."

"If it's just this village," declared Sheridan, "we can let them sit and wait. We can get along without it."

But it wasn't just one village. It was all the rest of them, as well.

Hezekiah brought the news.

"Napoleon says everyone is having trouble," he announced. "No one sold a thing. From what he said, it's just like this all over."

"We better call in all the boys," said Sheridan. "This is a situation that needs some talking over. We'll have to plan a course of action. We can't go flying off at a dozen different angles."

"And we'd better pull up a hill of *podars,*" Abraham suggested, "and see if they are *podars* or something else."

III

SHERIDAN inserted a chemist transmog into Ebenezer's brain case and Ebenezer ran off an analysis.

He reported to the sales conference seated around the table.

"There's just one difference," he said. "The *podars* that I analyzed ran a higher percentage of calenthropodensia—that's the drug used as a tranquilizer—than the *podars* that were brought in by the first and second expeditions. The factor is roughly ten per cent, although that might vary from one field to another, depending upon weather and soil conditions—I would suspect especially soil conditions."

"Then they lied," said Abraham, "when they said they weren't growing *podars.*"

"By their own standards," observed Silas, "they might not have lied to us. You can't always spell out alien ethics —satisfactorily, that is—from the purely human viewpoint. Ebenezer says that the composition of the tuber has changed to some extent. Perhaps due to better cultivation, perhaps to better seed or to an abundance of rainfall or a heavier concentration of the protozoan in the soil—or maybe because of something the natives did deliberately to make it shift . . ."

"Si," said Gideon, "I don't see what you are getting at."

"Simply this. If they knew of the shift or change, it might have given them an excuse to change the *podar* name. Or their language or their rules of grammar might have demanded that they change it. Or they may have applied some verbal mumbo-jumbo so they would have an out. And it might even have been a matter of superstition. The native told Steve at the village that they'd had bad luck with *podars*. So perhaps they operated under the premise that if they changed the name, they likewise changed the luck."

"And this is ethical?"

"To them, it might be. You fellows have been around enough to know that the rest of the Galaxy seldom operates on what we view as logic or ethics."

"But I don't see," said Gideon, "why they'd want to change the name unless it was for the specific purpose of not trading with us—so they could tell us they weren't growing *podars*."

"I think that is exactly why they changed the name," Maximilian said. "It's all a piece with those nailed-up barns. They knew we had arrived. They could hardly have escaped knowing. We had clouds of floaters going up and down and they must have seen them."

"Back at that village," said Sheridan, "I had the distinct impression that they had some reluctance telling us they weren't growing *podars*. They had left it to the last, as if it were a final clincher they'd hoped they wouldn't have to use, a desperate, last-ditch argument when all the other excuses failed to do the trick and—"

"They're just trying to jack up the price," Lemuel interrupted in a flat tone.

Maximilian shook his head. "I don't think so. There was no price set to start with. How can you jack it up when you don't know what it is?"

"Whether there was a price or not," said Lemuel testily, "they still could create a situation where they could hold us up."

"There is another factor that might be to our advantage," Maximilian said. "If they changed the name so they'd have an excuse not to trade with us, that argues that the whole village feels a moral obligation and has to justify its refusal."

"You mean by that," said Sheridan, "that we can reason with them. Well, perhaps we can. I think at least we'll try."

"There's too much wrong," Douglas put in. "Too many things have changed. The new name for the *podars* and the nailed-up barns and the shabbiness of the villages and the people. The whole planet's gone to pot. It seems to me our job—the first job we do—is to find what happened here. Once we find that out, maybe we'd have a chance of selling."

"I'd like to see the inside of those barns," said Joshua. "What have they got in there? Do you think there's any chance we might somehow get a look?"

"Nothing short of force," Abraham told him. "I have a hunch that while we're around, they'll guard them night and day."

"Force is out," said Sheridan. "All of you know what would happen to us if we used force short of self-defense against an alien people. The entire team would have its license taken away. You guys would spend the rest of your lives scrubbing out headquarters."

"Maybe we could just sneak around. Do some slick detective work."

"That's an idea, Josh," Sheridan said. "Hezekiah, do you know if we have some detective transmogs?"

"Not that I know of, sir. I have never heard of any team using them."

"Just as well," Abraham observed. "We'd have a hard time disguising ourselves."

"If we had a volunteer," Lemuel said with some enthusiasm, "we could redesign him . . ."

"It would seem to me," said Silas, "that what we have to do is figure out all the different approaches that are possible. Then we can try each appproach on a separate village till we latch onto one that works."

"Which presupposes," Maximilian pointed out, "that each village will react the same."

Silas said: "I would assume they would. After all, the culture is the same and their communications must be primitive. No village would know what was happening in another village until some little time had passed, which makes each village a perfectly isolated guinea pig for our little tests."

"Si, I think you're right," said Sheridan. "Somehow or other we have to find a way to break their sales resistance. I don't care what kind of prices we have to pay for the *podars* at the moment. I'd be willing to let them skin us alive to start with. Once we have them buying, we can squeeze down the price and come out even in the end. After all, the main thing is to get that cargo sled of ours loaded down with all the *podars* it can carry."

"All right," said Abraham. "Let's get to work."

They got to work. They spent the whole day at it. They mapped out the various sales approaches. They picked the villages where each one would be tried. Sheridan divided the robots into teams and assigned a team to each project. They worked out every detail. They left not a thing to chance.

Sheridan sat down to his supper table with the feeling that they had it made—if one of the approaches didn't work, another surely would. The trouble was that, as he saw it, they had done no planning. They had been so sure that this was an easy one that they had plunged ahead into straight selling without any thought upon the matter.

In the morning, the robots went out, full of confidence.

Abraham's crew had been assigned to a house-to-house campaign and they worked hard and conscientiously. They didn't miss a single house in the entire village. At every house, the answer had been no. Sometimes it was a firm but simple no; sometimes it was a door slammed in the face; at other times, it was a plea of poverty.

One thing was plain: Individual Garsonians could be cracked no more readily than Garsonians en masse.

Gideon and his crew tried the sample racket—handing out gift samples door to door with the understanding they would be back again to display their wares. The Garsonian householders weren't having any. They refused to take the samples.

Lemuel headed up the lottery project. A lottery, its proponents argued, appealed to basic greed. And this lottery had been rigged to carry maximum appeal. The price was as low as it could be set—one *podar* for a ticket. The list of prizes offered was just this side of fabulous. But the Garsonians, as it appeared, were not a greedy people. Not a ticket was sold.

And the funny thing about it—the unreasonable, maddening, impossible thing about it—was that the Garsonians seemed tempted.

"You could see them fighting it," Abraham reported at the conference that night. "You could see they wanted something we had for sale, but they'd steel themselves against it and they never weakened."

"We may have them on the very edge," said Lemuel. "Maybe just a little push is all it will take. Do you suppose we could start a whispering campaign? Maybe we could get it rumored that some other villages are buying right and left. That should weaken the resistance."

But Ebenezer was doubtful. "We have to dig down to causes. We have to find out what is behind this buyers' strike. It may be a very simple thing. If we only knew . . ."

Ebenezer took out a team to a distant village. They hauled along with them a pre-fabricated supermarket, which they set up in the village square. They racked their wares attractively. They loaded the place with glamor and excitement. They installed loud-speakers all over town to bellow out their bargains.

Abraham and Gideon headed up two talking-billboard crews. They ranged far and wide, setting up their billboards, splashed with attractive color, and installing propaganda tapes.

Sheridan had transmogged Oliver and Silas into semantics experts and they had engineered the tapes—a careful, skillful job. They did not bear down too blatantly on the commercial angle, although it certainly was there. The tapes were cuddly in spots and candid in others. At all times, they rang with deep sincerity. They sang the praises of the Garsonians for the decent, upstanding folks they were; they preached pithy homilies on honesty and fairness and the keeping of contracts; they presented the visitors as a sort of cross between public benefactors and addle-pated nitwits who could easily be outsmarted.

The tapes ran day and night. They pelted the defenseless Garsonians with a smooth, sleek advertising—and the effects should have been devastating, since the Garsonians were entirely unfamiliar with any kind of advertising.

Lemuel stayed behind at base and tramped up and down the beach, with his hands clenched behind his back, thinking furiously. At times he stopped his pacing long enough to scribble frantic notes, jotting down ideas.

Lemuel was trying to arrive at some adaptation of an old sales gag that he felt sure would work if he could only get it fiigured out—the ancient I-am-working-my-way-through-college wheeze.

Joshua and Thaddeus came to Sheridan for a pair of playwright transmogs. Sheridan said they had none, but Hezekiah, forever optimistic, ferreted into the bottom of the transmog chest. He came up with one transmog labeled auctioneer and another public speaker. They were the closest he could find.

Disgusted, the two rejected them and retired into seclusion, working desperately and as best they could on a medicine show routine.

For example, how did one write jokes for an alien people? What would they regard as funny? The off-color joke —oh, very fine, except that one would have to know in some detail the sexual life of the people it was aimed at. The mother-in-law joke—once again one would have to know; there were a lot of places where mothers-in-law were held in high regard, and other places where it was bad taste to even mention them. The dialect routine, of course, was strictly out, as it well deserved to be. Also, so far as the Garsonians were concerned, was the business slicker joke. The Garsonians were no commercial people; such a joke would sail clear above their heads.

But Joshua and Thaddeus, for all of that, were relatively undaunted. They requisitioned the files of data from Sheridan and spent hours poring over them, analyzing the various aspects of Garsonian life that might be safely written into their material. They made piles of notes. They drafted intricate charts showing relationships of Garsonian words and the maze of native social life. They wrote and rewrote and revised and polished. Eventually, they hammered out their script.

"There's nothing like a show," Joshua told Sheridan with conviction, "to loosen up a people. You get them feeling good and they lose their inhibitions. Besides, you have made them become somewhat indebted to you. You have entertained them and naturally they must feel the need to reciprocate."

"I hope it works," said Sheridan, somewhat doubtful and discouraged.

For nothing else was working.

In the distant village, the Garsonians had unbent sufficiently to visit the supermarket—to visit, not to buy. It almost seemed as if to them the market was some great museum or showplace. They would file down the aisles and goggle at the merchandise and at times reach out and touch it, but they didn't buy. They were, in fact, insulted if one suggested perhaps they'd like to buy.

In the other villages, the billboards had at first attracted wide attention. Crowds had gathered around them and had listened by the hour. But the novelty had worn off by now and they paid the tapes very little attention. And they still continued to ignore the robots. Even more pointedly, they ignored or rebuffed all attempts to sell.

It was disheartening.

Lemuel gave up his pacing and threw away his notes. He admitted he was licked. There was no way, on Garson IV, to adapt the idea of the college salesman.

Baldwin headed up a team that tried to get the whisper campaign started. The natives flatly disbelieved that any other village would go out and buy.

There remained the medicine show and Joshua and Thaddeus had a troupe rehearsing. The project was somewhat hampered by the fact that even Hezekiah could not dig up any actor transmogs, but, even so, they were doing well.

Despite the failure of everything they had tried, the robots kept going out to the villages, kept plugging away, kept on trying to sell, hoping that one day they would get a clue, a hint, an indication that might help them break the shell of reserve and obstinacy set up by the natives.

One day Gideon, out alone, radioed to base.

"There's something out here underneath a tree that you should take a look at," he told Sheridan.

"Something?"

"A different kind of being. It looks intelligent."

"A Garsonian?"

"Humanoid, all right, but it's no Garsonian."

"I'll be right out," said Sheridan. "You stay there so you can point it out to me."

"It has probably seen me," Gideon said, "but I did not approach it. I thought you might like first whack at it yourself."

As Gideon had said, the creature was sitting underneath a tree. It had a glittering cloth spread out and an ornate jug set out and was taking things out of a receptacle that probably was a hamper.

It was more attractively humanoid than the Garsonians. Its features were finely chiseled and its body had a look of lithe ranginess. It was dresed in the richest fabrics and was all decked out with jewels. It had a decided social air about it.

"Hello, friend," Sheridan said in Garsonian.

The creature seemed to understand him, but it smiled in a superior manner and seemed not to be too happy at Sheridan's intrusion.

"Perhaps," it finally said, "you have the time to sit down for a while."

Which, the way that it was put, was a plain and simple invitation for Sheridan to say no, he was sorry, but he hadn't and he must be getting on.

"Why, certainly," said Sheridan. "Thank you very much."

He sat down and watched the creature continue to extract things from the hamper.

"It's slightly difficult," the creature told him, "for us to communicate in this barbaric language. But I suppose it's the best we can do. You do not happen to know Ballic, do you?"

"I'm sorry," said Sheridan. "I've never heard of it."

"I had thought you might. It is widely used."

"We can get along," said Sheridan quietly, "with the language native to this planet."

"Oh, certainly," agreed the creature. "I presume I'm not trespassing. If I am, of course—"

"Not at all. I'm glad to find you here."

"I would offer you some food, but I hesitate to do so. Your metabolism undoubtedly is not the same as mine. It should pain me to poison you."

Sheridan nodded to indicate his gratitude. The food indeed was tempting. All of it was packaged attractively and some of it looked so delectable that it set the mouth to watering.

"I often come here for . . ." The creature hunted for the Garsonian word and there wasn't any.

Sheridan tried to help him out. "I think in my language I would call it picnic."

"An eating-out-of-doors," the stranger said. "That is the nearest I can come in the language of our host."

"We have the same idea."

The creature brightened up considerably at this evidence of mutual understanding. "I think, my friend, that we have much in common. Perhaps I could leave some of this food with you and you could analyze it. Then the next time I come, you could join me."

Sheridan shook his head. "I doubt I'll stay much longer."

"Oh," the stranger said, and he seemed pleased at it. "So you're a transitory being, too. Wings passing in the night. One hears a rustle and then the sound is gone forever."

"A most poetic thought," said Sheridan, "and a most descriptive one."

"Although," the creature said, "I come here fairly often. I've grown to love this planet. It is such a fine spot for an eating-out-of-doors. So restful and simple and unhurried. It is not cluttered up with activity and the people are so genuine, albeit somewhat dirty and very, very stupid. But I find it in my heart to love them for their lack of sophistication and their closeness to the soil and the clear-eyed view of life and their uncomplicated living of that life."

He halted his talk and cocked an eye at Sheridan.

"Don't you find it so, my friend?"

"Yes, of course I do," agreed Sheridan, rather hurriedly.

"There are so few places in the Galaxy," mourned the stranger, "where one can be alone in comfort. Oh, I do not mean alone entirely, or even physically. But an aloneness in the sense that there is space to live, that one is not pushed about by boundless, blind ambitions or smothered by the impact of other personalities. There are, of course, the lonely planets which are lonely only by the virtue of their being impossible for one to exist upon. These we must rule out."

He ate a little, daintily, and in a mincing manner. But he took a healthy snort from the ornate jug.

"This is excellent," said the creature, holding out the jug. "You are sure you do not want to chance it?"

"I think I'd better not."

"I suppose it's wise of you," the stranger admitted. "Life is not a thing that a person parts from without due consideration."

He had another drink, then put the jug down in his lap and sat there fondling it.

"Not that I am one," he said, "to extoll the virtue of living above all other things. Surely there must be other facets of the universal pattern that have as much to offer . . ."

They spent a pleasant afternoon together.

When Sheridan went back to the flier, the creature had

finished off the jug and was sprawled, happily pickled, among the litter of the picnic.

IV

GRASPING at straws, Sheridan tried to fit the picnicking alien into the pattern, but there was no place where he'd fit.

Perhaps, after all, he was no more than what he seemed —a flitting dilettante with a passion for a lonely eating-out-of-doors and an addiction to the bottle.

Yet he knew the native language and he had said he came here often and that in itself was more than merely strange. With apparently the entire Galaxy in which to flit around, why should he gravitate to Garson IV, which, to the human eye, at least, was a most unprepossessing planet?

And another thing—how had he gotten here?

"Gideon," asked Sheridan, "did you see, by any chance, any sort of conveyance parked nearby that our friend could have traveled in?"

Gideon shook his head. "Now that you mention it, I am sure there wasn't. I would have noticed it."

"Has it occurred to you, sir," inquired Hezekiah, "that he may have mastered the ability of teleportation? It is not impossible. There was that race out on Pilico . . ."

"That's right," said Sheridan, "but the Pilicoans were good for no more than a mile or so at a time. You remember how they went popping along, like a jack rabbit making mile-long jumps, but making them so fast that you couldn't see him jump. This gent must have covered light-years. He asked me about a language that I never heard of. Indicated that it is widely spoken in at least some parts of the Galaxy."

"You are worrying yourself unduly, sir," cautioned Hezekiah. "We have more important things than this galivanting alien to trouble ourselves about."

"You're right," said Sheridan. "If we don't get this cargo moving, it will be my neck."

But he couldn't shake entirely the memory of the afternoon.

He went back, in his mind, through the long and idle

chatter and found, to his amazement, that it had been completely idle. So far as he could recall, the creature had told him nothing of itself. For three solid hours or more, it had talked almost continuously and in all that time had somehow managed to say exactly nothing.

That evening, when he brought the supper, Napoleon squatted down beside the chair, gathering his spotless apron neatly in his lap.

"We are in a bad way, aren't we?" he asked.

"Yes, I suppose you could say we are."

"What will we do, Steve, if we can't move the stuff at all—if we can't get any *podars?*"

"Nappy," said Sheridan, "I've been trying very hard not to think of it."

But now that Napoleon had brought it up, he could well imagine the reaction of Central Trading if he should have to haul a billion-dollar cargo back intact. He could imagine, a bit more vividly, what might be said to him if he simply left it here and went back home without it.

No matter how he did it, he had to sell the cargo!

If he didn't, his career was in a sling.

Although there was more, he realized, than just his career at stake. The whole human race was involved.

There was a real and pressing need for the tranquilizer made from *podar* tubers. A search for such a drug had started centuries before and the need of it was underlined by the fact that through all those centuries the search had never faltered. It was something that Man needed badly—that Man, in fact, had needed badly since the very moment he'd become something more than animal.

And here, on this very planet, was the answer to that terrible human need—an answer denied and blocked by the stubbornness of a shiftless, dirty, backward people.

"If we only had this planet," he said, speaking more to himself than to Napoleon, "if we could only take it over, we could grow all the *podars* that we needed. We'd make it one big field and we'd grow a thousand times more *podars* than these natives ever grew."

"But we can't," Napoleon said. "It is against the law."

"Yes, Nappy, you are right. Very much against the law."

For the Garsonians were intelligent—not startlingly so, but intelligent, at least, within the meaning of the law.

And you could do nothing that even hinted of force

against an intelligent race. You couldn't even buy or lease their land, for the law would rule that in buying one would be dispossessing them of the inalienable rights of all alien intelligences.

You could work with them and teach them—that was very laudable. But the Garsonians were almost unteachable. You could barter with them if you were very careful that you did not cheat them too outrageously. But the Garsonians refused to barter.

"I don't know what we'll do," Sheridan told Napoleon. "How are we going to find a way?"

"I have a sort of suggestion. If we could introduce these natives to the intricacies of dice, we might finally get somewhere. We robots, as you probably know, are very good at it."

Sheridan choked on his coffee. He slowly and with great care set the cup down.

"Ordinarily," he told Napoleon solemnly, "I would frown upon such tactics. But with the situation as it stands, why don't you get some of the boys together and have a try at it?"

"Glad to do it, Steve."

"And . . . uh, Nappy . . ."

"Yes, Steve?"

"I presume you'd pick the best crap-shooters in the bunch."

"Naturally," said Napoleon, getting up and smoothing his apron.

Joshua and Thaddeus took their troupe to a distant village in entirely virgin territory, untouched by any of the earlier selling efforts, and put on the medicine show.

It was an unparalleled success. The natives rolled upon the ground, clutching at their bellies, helpless with laughter. They howled and gasped and wiped their streaming eyes. They pounded one another on the back in appreciation of the jokes. They'd never seen anything like it in all their lives—there had never been anything like it on all of Garson IV.

And while they were weak with merriment, while they were still well-pleased, at the exact psychological moment when all their inhibitions should be down and all stubbornness and hostility be stilled, Joshua made the sales pitch.

The laughter stopped. The merriment went away. The audience simply stood and stared.

The troupe packed up and came trailing home, deep in despondency.

Sheridan sat in his tent and faced the bleak prospect. Outside the tent, the base was still as death. There was no happy talk or singing and no passing laughter. There was no neighborly tramping back and forth.

"Six weeks," Sheridan said bitterly to Hezekiah. "Six weeks and not a sale. We've done everything we can and we've not come even close."

He clenched his fist and hit the desk. "If we could only find what the trouble is! They want our merchandise and still they refuse to buy. What is the holdup, Hezekiah? Can you think of anything?"

Hezekiah shook his head. "Nothing, sir, I'm stumped. We all are."

"They'll crucify me back at Central," Sheridan declared. "They'll nail me up and keep me as a horrible example for the next ten thousand years. There've been failures before, but none like this."

"I hesitate to say this, sir," said Hezekiah, "but we could take it on the lam. Maybe that's the answer. The boys would go along. Theoretically they're loyal to Central, but deep down at the bottom of it, it's you they're really loyal to. We could load up the cargo and that would give us capital and we'd have a good head start . . ."

"No," Sheridan said firmly. "We'll try a little longer and we may solve the situation. If not, I face the music."

He scraped his hand across his jaw.

"Maybe," he said, "Nappy and his crap-shooters can turn the trick for us. It's fantastic, sure, but stranger things have happened."

Napoleon and his pals came back, sheepish and depressed.

"They beat the pants off us," the cook told Sheridan in awe. "Those boys are really naturals. But when we tried to pay our bets, they wouldn't take our stuff!"

"We have to try to arrange a powwow," said Sheridan, "and talk it out with them, although I hold little hope for it. Do you think, Napoleon, if we came clean and told them what a spot we're in, it would make a difference?"

"No, I don't," Napoleon said.

"If they only had a government," observed Ebenezer, who had been a member of Napoleon's gambling team, "we might get somewhere with a powwow. Then you could talk with someone who represented the entire population. But this way you'll have to talk with each village separately and that will take forever."

"We can't help it, Eb," said Sheridan. "It's all we have left."

But before any powwow could be arranged, the *podar* harvest started. The natives toiled like beavers in the fields, digging up the tubers, stacking them to dry, packing them in carts and hauling them to the barns by sheer manpower, for the Garsonians had no draft animals.

They dug them up and hauled them to the barns, the very barns where they'd sworn that they had no *podars*. But that was not to wonder at when one stopped to think of it, for the natives had also sworn that they grew no *podars*.

They did not open the big barn doors, as one would have normally expected them to do. They simply opened a tiny, man-size door set into a bigger door and took the *podars* in that way. And when any of the Earth party hove in sight, they quickly stationed a heavy guard around the entire square.

"We'd better let them be," Abraham advised Sheridan. "If we try to push them, we may have trouble in our lap."

So the robots pulled back to the base and waited for the harvest to end. Finally it was finished and Sheridan counseled lying low for a few days more to give the Garsonians a chance to settle back to their normal routine.

Then they went out again and this time Sheridan rode along, on one of the floaters with Abraham and Gideon.

The first village they came to lay quiet and lazy in the sun. There was not a creature stirring.

Abraham brought the floater down into the square and the three stepped off.

The square was empty and the place was silent—a deep and deathly silence.

Sheridan felt the skin crawling up his back, for there was a stealthy, unnatural menace in the noiseless emptiness.

"They may be laying for us," suggested Gideon.

"I don't think so," said Abraham. "Basically they are peaceful."

They moved cautiously across the square and walked slowly down a street that opened from the square.

And still there was no living thing in sight.

And stranger still—the doors of some of the houses stood open to the weather and the windows seemed to watch them out of blind eyes, with the colorful crude curtains gone.

"Perhaps," Gideon suggested, "they may have gone away to some harvest festival or something of that nature."

"They wouldn't leave their doors wide open, even for a day," declared Abraham. "I've lived with them for weeks and I've studied them. I know what they would do. They'd have closed the doors very carefully and tried them to be sure that they were closed."

"But maybe the wind . . ."

"Not a chance," insisted Abraham. "One door, possibly. But I see four of them from here."

"Someone has to take a look," said Sheridan. "It might as well be me."

He turned in at a gate where one of the doors stood open and went slowly up the path. He halted at the threshold and peered in. The room beyond was empty. He stepped into the house and went from room to room and all the rooms were empty—not simply of the natives, but of everything. There was no furniture and the utensils and the tools were gone from hooks and racks. There was no scrap of clothing. There was nothing left behind. The house was dead and bare and empty, a shabby and abandoned thing discarded by its people.

He felt a sense of guilt creep into his soul. What if we drove them off? What if we hounded them until they'd rather flee than face us?

But that was ridiculous, he told himself. There must be some other reason for this incredibly complete masse exodus.

He went back down the walk. Abraham and Gideon went into other houses. All of them were empty.

"It may be this village only," suggested Gideon. "The rest may be quite normal."

But Gideon was wrong.

Back at the floater, they got in touch with base.

"I can't understand it," said Hezekiah. "I've had the same report from four other teams. I was about to call you, sir."

"You'd better get out every floater that you can," said Sheridan. "Check all the villages around. And keep a lookout for the people. They may be somewhere in the country. There's a possibility they're at a harvest festival."

"If they're at a festival, sir," asked Hezekiah, "why did they take their belongings? You don't take along your furniture when you attend a festival."

"I know," said Sheridan. "You put your finger on it. Get the boys out, will you?"

"There's just a possibility," Gideon offered, "that they are changing villages. Maybe there's a tribal law that says they have to build a new village every so often. It might have its roots in an ancient sanitation law that the camp must be moved at stated intervals."

"It could be that," Sheridan said wearily. "We'll have to wait and see."

Abraham thumbed a fist toward the barn.

Sheridan hesitated, then threw caution to the winds.

"Go ahead," he said.

Gideon stalked up the ramp and reached the door. He put out a hand and grasped one of the planks nailed across the door. He wrenched and there was an anguished shriek of tortured nails ripping from the wood and the board came free. Another plank came off and then another one and Gideon put his shoulder to the door and half of it swung open.

Inside, in the dimness of the barn, was the dull, massive shine of metal—a vast machine sitting on the driveway floor.

Sheridan stiffened with a cold, hollow sense of terror.

It was wrong, he thought. There could be no machine. The Garsonians had no business having a machine. Their culture was entirely non-mechanical. The best they had achieved so far had been the hoe and wheel, and even yet they had not been able to put the hoe and wheel together to make themselves a plow.

They had had no machine when the second expedition left some fifteen years ago, and in those fifteen years they could not have spanned the gap. In those fifteen years, from all surface indications, they had not advanced an inch.

And yet the machine stood in the driveway of the barn. It was a fair-sized cylinder, set on end and with a door in one side of it. The upper end of it terminated in a dome-shaped cap. Except for the door, it resembled very much a huge and snub-nosed bullet.

Interference, thought Sheridan. There had been some-one here between the time the second expedition left and the third one had arrived.

"Gideon," he said.

"What is it, Steve?"

"Go back to base and bring the transmog chest. Tell Hezekiah to get my tent and all the other stuff over here as soon as he is able. Call some of the boys off recon-naissance. We have work to do."

There had been someone here, he thought—and most certainly there had. A very urbane creature who sat be-neath a tree beside a spread-out picnic cloth, swigging at his jug and talking for three solid hours without saying anything at all!

V

THE messenger from Central Trading brought his small ship down to one side of the village square, not far from where Sheridan's tent was pitched. He slid back the visi-dome and climbed out of his seat.

He stood for a moment, shining in the sun, during which he straightened his SPECIAL COURIER badge, which had become askew upon his metal chest. Then he walked deliberately toward the barn, heading for Sheridan, who sat upon the ramp.

"You are Sheridan?" he asked.

Sheridan nodded, looking him over. He was a splendid thing.

"I had trouble finding you. Your base seems to be deserted."

"We ran into some difficulty," Sheridan said quietly.

"Not too serious, I trust. I see your cargo is untouched."

"Let me put it this way—we haven't been bored."

"I see," the robot said, disappointed that an explanation

was not immediately forthcoming. "My name is Tobias and I have a message for you."

"I'm listening."

Sometimes, Sheridan told himself, these headquarters robots needed taking down a peg or two.

"It is a verbal message. I can assure you that I am thoroughly briefed. I can answer any questions you may wish to ask."

"Please," said Sheridan. "The message first."

"Central Trading wishes to inform you that they have been offered the drug calenthropodensia in virtually unlimited supply by a firm which describes itself as Galactic Enterprises. We would like to know if you can shed any light upon the matter."

"Galactic Enterprises," said Sheridan. "I've never heard of them."

"Neither has Central Trading. I don't mind telling you that we're considerably upset."

"I should imagine you would be."

Tobias squared his shoulders. "I have been instructed to point out to you that you were sent to Garson IV to obtain a cargo of *podars,* from which this drug is made, and that the assignment, in view of the preliminary work already done upon the planet, should not have been so difficult that—"

"Now, now," cautioned Sheridan, "Let us keep our shirts on. If it will quiet your conscience any, you may consider for the record that I have accepted the bawling out you're supposed to give me."

"But you—"

"I assume," said Sheridan, "that Galactic Enterprises is quoting a good stiff price on this drug of theirs."

"It's highway robbery. What Central Trading has sent me to find out—"

"Is whether I am going to bring in a cargo of *podars.* At the moment, I can't tell you.".

"But I must take back my report!"

"Not right now, you aren't. I won't be able to make a report to you for several days at least. You'll have to wait."

"But my instructions are—"

"Suit yourself," Sheridan said sharply. "Wait for it or go back without it. I don't give a damn which you do."

He got up from the ramp and walked into the barn.

The robots, he saw, had finally pried or otherwise dislodged the cap from the big machine and had it on the side on the driveway floor, tilted to reveal the innards of it.

"Steve," said Abraham bitterly, "take a look at it."

Sheridan took a look. The inside of the cap was a mass of fused metal.

"There were some working parts in there," said Gideon, "but they have been destroyed."

Sheridan scratched his head. "Deliberately? A self-destruction relay?"

Abraham nodded. "They apparently were all finished with it. If we hadn't been here, I suppose they would have carted this machine and the rest of them back home, wherever that may be. But they couldn't take a chance of one of them falling in our hands. So they pressed the button or whatever they had to do and the entire works went pouf."

"But there are other machines. Apparently one in every barn."

"Probably just the same as this," said Lemuel, rising from his knees beside the cap.

"What's your guess?" asked Sheridan.

"A matter transference machine, a teleporter, whatever you want to call it," Abraham told him. "Not deduced, of course, from anything in the machine itself, but from the circumstances. Look at this barn. There's not a *podar* in it. Those *podars* went somewhere. This picknicking friends of yours—"

"They call themselves," said Sheridan, "Galactic Enterprises. A messenger just arrived. He says they offered Central Trading a deal on the *podar* drug."

"And now Central Trading," Abraham supplied "enormously embarrassed and financially outraged, will pin the blame on us because we've delivered not a *podar*."

"I have no doubt of it," said Sheridan. "It all depends upon whether or not we can locate these native friends of ours."

"I would think that most unlikely," Gideon said. "Our reconnaissance showed all the villages empty through the entire planet. Do you suppose they might have left in these machines? If they'd transport *podars*, they'd probably transport people."

"Perhaps," said Lemuel, making a feeble joke, "everything that begins with the letter *p*."

"What are the chances of finding how they work?" asked Sheridan. "This is something that Central could make a lot of use of."

Abraham shook his head. "I can't tell you, Steve. Out of all these machines on the planet, which amounts to one in every barn, there is a certain mathematical chance that we might find one that was not destroyed."

"But even if we did," said Gideon, "there is an excellent chance that it would immediately destroy itself if we tried to tamper with it."

"And if we don't find one that is not destroyed?"

"There is a chance," Lemuel admitted. "All of them would not destroy themselves to the same degree, of course. Nor would the pattern of destruction always be the same. From, say, a thousand of them, you might be able to work out a good idea of what kind of machinery there was in the cone."

"And say we could find out what kind of machinery was there?"

"That's a hard one to answer, Steve," Abraham said. "Even if we had one complete and functioning, I honestly don't know if we could ferret out the principle to the point where we could duplicate it. You must remember that at no time has the human race come even close to something of this nature."

It made a withering sort of sense to Sheridan. Seeing a totally unfamiliar device work, even having it blueprinted in exact detail, would convey nothing whatever if the theoretical basis was missing. It was, completely, and there was a great deal less available here than a blueprint or even working model.

"They used those machines to transport the *podars*," he said, "and possibly to transport the people. And if that is true, it must be the people went voluntarily—we'd have known if there was force involved. Abe, can you tell me: Why would the people go?"

"I wouldn't know," said Abraham. "All I have now is a physicist transmog. Give me one on sociology and I'll wrestle with the problem."

There was a shout outside the barn and they whirled

toward the door. Ebenezer was coming up the ramp and in his arms he carried a tiny, dangling form.

"It's one of them," gasped Gideon. "It's a native, sure enough!"

Ebenezer knelt and placed the little native tenderly on the floor. "I found him in the field. He was lying in a ditch. I'm afraid he's done for."

Sheridan stepped forward and bent above the native. It was an old man—any one of the thousands of old men he'd seen in the villages. The same leathery old face with the wind and weather wrinkles in it, the same shaggy brows shielding deep-sunk eyes, the same scraggly crop of whiskers, the same sense of forgotten shiftlessness and driven stubbornness.

"Left behind," said Ebenezer. "Left behind when all the others went. He must have fallen sick out in the field . . ."

"Get my canteen," Sheridan said. "It's hanging by the door."

The oldster opened his eyes and glanced around the circle of faces that stared down at him. He rubbed a hand across his face, leaving streaks of dirt.

"I fell," he mumbled. "I remember falling. I fell into a ditch."

"Here's the water, Steve," said Abraham.

Sheridan took it, lifted the old man and held him half upright against his chest. He tilted the canteen to the native's lips. The oldster drank unneatly, gulping at the water. Some of it spilled, splashing down his whiskers to drip onto his belly.

Sheridan took the canteen away.

"Thank you," the native said and, Sheridan reflected, that was the first civil word to come their way from any of the natives.

The native rubbed his face again with a dirty claw. "The people all are gone?"

"All gone," said Sheridan.

"Too late," the old man said. "I would have made it if I hadn't fallen down. Perhaps they hunted for me . . ." His voice trailed off into nothingness.

"If you don't mind, sir," suggested Hezekiah, "I'll get a medic transmog."

"Perhaps you should," said Sheridan. "Although I doubt

it'll do much good. He should have died days ago out there in the field."

"Steve," said Gideon, speaking softly, "a human doctor isn't too much use treating alien people. In time, if we had the time, we could find out about this fellow—something about his body chemistry and his metabolism. Then we could doctor him."

"That's right," Steve," Abraham said.

Sheridan shrugged. "All right then, Hezekiah. Forget about the transmog."

He laid the old man back on the floor again and got up off his knees. He sat on his heels and rocked slowly back and forth.

"Perhaps," he said to the native, "you'll answer one question. Where did all your people go?"

"In there," the native said, raising a feeble arm to point at the machine. "In there, and then they went away just as the harvest we gathered did."

Sheridan stayed squatting on the floor beside the stricken native.

Reuben brought in an armload of grass and wadded it beneath the native's head as a sort of pillow.

So the Garsonians had really gone away, Sheridan told himself, had up and left the planet. Had left it, using the machines that had been used to make delivery of the *podars*. And if Galactic Enterprises had machines like that, then they (whoever, wherever they might be) had a tremendous edge on Central Trading. For Central Trading's lumbering cargo sleds, snaking their laborious way across the light-years, could offer only feeble competition to machines like those.

He had thought, he remembered, the first day they had landed, that a little competition was exactly what Central Trading needed. And here was that competition—a competition that had not a hint of ethics. A competition that sneaked in behind Central Trading's back and grabbed the market that Central Trading needed—the market that Central could have cinched if it had not fooled around, if it had not been so sly and cynical about adapting the *podar* crop to Earth.

Just where and how, he wondered, had Galactic Enterprises found out about the *podars* and the importance of the drug? Under what circumstances had they learned the exact time limit during which they could operate in the *podar* market without Central interference? And had they, perhaps, been slightly optimistic in regard to that time limit and gotten caught in a situation where they had been forced to destroy all those beautiful machines?

Sheridan chuckled quietly to himself. That destruction must have hurt them!

It wasn't hard, however, to imagine a hundred or a thousand ways in which they might have learned about the *podar* situation, for they were a charming people and really quite disarming. He would not be surprised if some of them might be operating secretly inside of Central Trading.

The native stirred. He reached out a skinny hand and tugged at the sleeve of Sheridan's jacket.

"Yes, what is it, friend?"

"You will stay with me?" the native begged. "These others here, they are not the same as you and I."

"I will stay with you," Sheridan promised.

"I think we'd better go," said Gideon. "Maybe we disturb him."

The robots walked quietly from the barn and left the two alone.

Reaching out, Sheridan put a hand on the native's brow. The flesh was clammy cold.

"Old friend," he said, "I think perhaps you owe me something."

The old man shook his head, rolling it slowly back and forth upon the pillow. And the fierce light of stubbornness and a certain slyness came into his eyes.

"We don't owe you," he said. "We owed the other ones."

And that, of course, hadn't been what Sheridan had meant.

But there they lay—the words that told the story, the solution to the puzzle that was Garson IV.

"That was why you wouldn't trade with us," said Sheridan, talking to himself rather than to the old native on the floor. "You were so deep in debt to these other people that you needed all the *podars* to pay off what you owed them?"

And that must have been the way it was. Now that he thought back on it, that supplied the one logical explanation for everything that happened. The reaction of the

natives, the almost desperate sales resistance was exactly
the kind of thing one would expect from people in debt
up to their ears.

That was the reason, too, the houses had been so neglected and the clothes had been in rags. It accounted for
the change from the happy-go-lucky shiftlessness to the
beaten and defeated and driven attitude. So pushed, so
hounded, so fearful that they could not meet the payments
on the debt that they strained their every resource, drove
themselves to ever harder work, squeezing from the soil
every *podar* they could grow.

"That was it?" he demanded sharply. "That was the
way it was?"

The native nodded with reluctance.

"They came along and offered such a bargain that you
could not turn it down. For the machines, perhaps? For
the machines to send you to other places?"

The native shook his head. "No, not the machines. We
put the *podars* in the machines and the *podars* went away.
That was how we paid."

"You were paying all these years?"

"That is right," the native said. Then he added, with a
flash of pride: "But now we're all paid up."

"That is fine," said Sheridan. "It is good for a man to
pay his debts."

"They took three years off the payments," said the
native eagerly. "Was that not good of them?"

"I'm sure it was," said Sheridan, with some bitterness.

He squatted patiently on the floor, listening to the
faint whisper of a wind blowing in the loft and the rasping
breath of the dying native.

"But then your people used the machines to go away.
Can't you tell me why?"

A racking cough shook the old man and his breath came
in gasping sobs.

Sheridan felt a sense of shame in what he had to do. I
should let him die in peace, he thought. I should not badger
him. I should let him go in whatever dignity he can—not
pushed and questioned to the final breath he draws.

But there was that last answer—the one Sheridan had
to have.

Sheridan said gently: "But tell me, friend, what did you
bargain for? What was it that you bought?"

He wondered if the native heard. There was no indication that he had.

"What did you buy?" Sheridan insisted.

"A planet," said the native.

"But you had a planet!"

"This one was different," the native told him in a feeble whisper. "This was a planet of immortality. Anyone who went there would never, never die."

Sheridan squatted stiffly in shocked and outraged silence.

And from the silence came a whisper—a whisper still of faith and belief and pity that would haunt the human all his life.

"That was what I lost," the whisper said. "That was what I lost . . ."

Sheridan opened his hands and closed them, strangling the perfect throat and the winning smile, shutting off the cultured flow of words.

If I had him now, he thought, if I only had him now!

He remembered the spread-out picnic cloth and the ornate jug and the appetizing food, the smooth, slick gab and the assurance of the creature. And even the methodical business of getting very drunk so that their meeting could end without unpleasant questions of undue suspicion.

And the superior way in which he'd asked if the human might know Ballic, all the time, more than likely, being able to speak English himself.

So Central Trading finally had its competition. From this moment, Central Trading would be fighting with its back against the wall. For these jokers in Galactic Enterprises played dirty and for keeps.

The Garsonians had been naïve fools, of course, but that was no true measure of Galactic Enterprises. They undoubtedly would select different kinds of bait for different kinds of fish, but the old never-never business of immortality might be deadly bait for even the most sophisticated if appropriately presented.

An utter lack of ethics and the transference machines were the trumps Galactic held.

What had really happened, he wondered, to all the people who had lived on this planet? Where had they really gone when they followed the *podars* into those machines?

Could the Galactic boys, by chance, have ferreted out

a place where there would be a market for several million slaves?

Or had they simply planned to get the Garsonians out of the way as an effective means of cutting off the *podar* supply for Central Trading, thus insuring a ready and profitable sale for their supply of drugs?

Or had they lured the Garsonians away so they themselves could take over the planet?

And if that was the case—perhaps in *any* case—Galactic Enterprises definitely had lost this first encounter. Maybe, Sheridan told himself, they are really not so hot.

They gave us exactly what we need, he realized with a pleased jolt. They did us a favor!

Old blundering, pompous Central Trading had won the first round, after all.

He got to his feet and headed for the door.

He hesitated and turned back to the native.

"Maybe, friend," he said, "you were the lucky one."

The native did not hear him.

Gideon was waiting at the door.

"How is he?" he asked.

"He's dead," Sheridan said. "I wonder if you'd arrange for burial."

"Of course," said Gideon. "You'll let me see the data. I'll have to bone up on the proper rites."

"But first do something else for me."

"Name it, Steve."

"You know this Tobias, the messenger that Central Trading sent? Find him and see that he doesn't leave."

Gideon grinned. "You may rest assured."

"Thank you," said Sheridan.

On his way to the tent, he passed the courier's ship. It was, he noted, a job that was built for speed—little more than an instrument board and seat tacked onto a powerful engine.

In a ship like that, he thought, a pilot could really make some time.

Almost to the tent, he met Hezekiah.

"Come along with me," he said. "I have a job for you."

Inside the tent, he sat down in his chair and reached for a sheet of paper.

"Hezekiah," he said, "dig into that chest. Find the finest diplomatic transmog that we have."

"I know just where it is, sir," said Hezekiah, pawing through the chest.

He came out with the transmog and laid it on the desk.

"Hezekiah," said Sheridan, "listen to me carefully. Remember every word I say."

"Sir," replied Hezekiah, a little huffily, "I always listen carefully."

"I know you do. I have perfect faith and trust in you. That is why I'm sending you to Central."

"To Central, sir! You must be joking, surely. You know I cannot go. Sir, who would look after you? Who would see that you—"

"I can get along all right. You'll be coming back. And I'll still have Napoleon."

"But I don't want to go, sir!"

"Hezekiah, I must have someone I can trust. We'll put that transmog in you and—"

"But it will take me weeks, sir!"

"Not with the courier ship. You're going back instead of the courier. I'll write an authorization for you to represent me. It'll be as if I were there myself."

"But there is Abraham. Or Gideon. Or you could send any of the others . . ."

"It's you, Hezekiah. You are my oldest friend."

"Sir," said Hezekiah, straightening to attention, "what do you wish me to do?"

"You're to tell Central that Garson IV is now uninhabited. You're to say that such being the case, I'm possessing it formally in the name of Central Trading. Tell them I'll need reinforcements immediately because there is a possibility that Galactic Enterprises may try to take it from us. They're to send out one sled loaded with robots as an initial occupying and colonizing force, and another sledload of agricultural implements so we can start our farming. And every last *podar* that they have, for seed. And, Hezekiah . . ."

"Yes, sir?"

"That sledload of robots. They'd better be deactivated and knocked down. That way they can pile on more of them. We can assemble them here."

Hezekiah repressed a shudder. "I will tell them, sir."

"I am sorry, Hezekiah."

"It is quite all right, sir."

Sheridan finished writing out the authorization.

"Tell Central Trading," he said, "that in time we'll turn this entire planet into one vast *podar* field. But they must not waste a minute. No committee sessions, no meetings of the board, no dawdling around. Keep right on their tail every blessed second."

"I will not let them rest, sir," Hezekiah assured him.

VI

THE courier ship had disappeared from sight. Try as he might, Sheridan could catch no further glimpse of it.

Good old Hezekiah, he thought, he'll do the job. Central Trading will be wondering for weeks exactly what it was that hit them.

He tilted his head forward and rubbed his aching neck.

He said to Gideon and Ebenezer: "You can get up off him now."

The two arose, grinning, from the prostrate form of Tobias.

Tobias got up, outraged. "You'll hear of this," he said to Sheridan.

"Yes, I know," said Sheridan. "You hate my guts."

Abraham stepped forward. "What is next?" he asked.

"Well," Sheridan said, "I think we should all turn gleaners."

"Gleaners?"

"There are bound to be some *podars* that the natives missed. We'll need every one we can find for seed."

"But we're all physicists and mechanical engineers and chemists and other things like that. Surely you would not expect such distinguished specialists—"

"I think I can remedy that," said Sheridan. "I imagine we still can find those spacehand transmogs. They should serve until Central sends us some farmer units."

Tobias stepped forward and ranged himself alongside of Abraham. "As long as I must remain here, I demand to be of use. It's not in a robot's nature just to loaf around."

Sheridan slapped his hand against his jacket pocket, felt the bulge of the transmog he'd taken out of Hezekiah.

"I think," he told Tobias, "I have just the thing for you."

CONDITION OF EMPLOYMENT

He had been dreaming of home, and when he came awake, he held his eyes tight shut in a desperate effort not to lose the dream. He kept some of it, but it was blurred and faint and lacked the sharp distinction and the color of the dream. He could tell it to himself, he knew just how it was, he could recall it as a lost and far-off thing and place, but it was not there as it had been in the dream.

But even so, he held his eyes tight shut, for now that he was awake, he knew what they'd open on, and he shrank from the drabness and the coldness of the room in which he lay. It was, he thought, not alone the drabness and the cold, but also the loneliness and the sense of not belonging. So long as he did not look at it, he need not accept this harsh reality, although he felt himself on the fringe of it, and it was reaching for him, reaching through the color and the warmth and friendliness of this other place he tried to keep in mind.

At last it was impossible. The fabric of the held-onto dream became too thin and fragile to ward off the moment of reality, and he let his eyes come open.

It was every bit as bad as he remembered it. It was drab and cold and harsh, and there was the maddening alienness waiting for him, crouching in the corner. He tensed himself against it, trying to work up his courage, hardening himself to arise and face it for another day.

The plaster of the ceiling was cracked and had flaked away in great ugly blotches. The paint on the wall was peeling and dark stains ran down it from the times the rain leaked in. And there was the smell, the musty human smell that had been caged in the room too long.

Staring at the ceiling, he tried to see the sky. There had
235

been a time when he could have seen it through this or any ceiling. For the sky had belonged to him, the sky and the wild, dark space beyond it. But now he'd lost them. They were his no longer.

A few marks in a book, he thought, an entry in the record. That was all that was needed to smash a man's career, to crush his hope forever and to keep him trapped and exiled on a planet that was not his own.

He sat up and swung his feet over the edge of the bed, hunting for the trousers he'd left on the floor. He found and pulled them on and scuffed into his shoes and stood up in the room.

The room was small and mean—and cheap. There would come a day when he could not afford a room even as cheap as this. His cash was running out, and when the last of it was gone, he would have to get some job, any kind of job. Perhaps he should have gotten one before he began to run so short. But he had shied away from it. For settling down to work would be an admission that he was defeated, that he had given up his hope of going home again.

He had been a fool, he told himself, for ever going into space. Let him just get back to Mars and no one could ever get him off it. He'd go back to the ranch and stay there as his father had wanted him to do. He'd marry Ellen and settle down, and other fools could fly the death-traps around the Solar System.

Glamor, he thought—it was the glamor that sucked in the kids when they were young and starry-eyed. The glamor of the far place, of the wilderness of space, of the white eyes of the stars watching in that wilderness—the glamor of the engine-song and of the chill white metal knifing through the blackness and the loneliness of the emptiness, and the few cubic feet of courage and defiance that thumbed its nose at that emptiness.

But there was no glamor. There was brutal work and everlasting watchfulness and awful sickness, the terrible fear that listened for the stutter in the drive, for the *ping* against the metal hide, for any one of the thousand things that could happen out in space.

He picked up his wallet off the bedside table and put it in his pocket and went out into the hall and down the rickety stairs to the crumbling, lopsided porch outside.

And the greenness waited for him, the unrelenting, bilious green of Earth. It was a thing to gag at, to steel oneself against, an indecent and abhorrent color for anyone to look at. The grass was green and all the plants and every single tree. There was no place outdoors and few indoors where one could escappe from it, and when one looked at it too long, it seemed to pulse and tremble with a hidden life.

The greenness, and the brightness of the sun, and the sapping heat—these were things of Earth that it was hard to bear. The light one could get away from, and the heat one could somehow ride along with—but the green was always there.

He went down the steps, fumbling in his pocket for a cigarette. He found a crumpled package and in it one crumpled cigarette. He put it between his lips and threw the pack away and stood at the gate, trying to make up his mind.

But it was a gesture only, this hardening of his mind, for he knew what he would do. There was nothing else to do. He'd done it day after day for more weeks than he cared to count, and he'd do it again today and tomorrow and tomorrow, until his cash ran out.

And after that, he wondered, what?

Get a job and try to strike a bargain with his situation? Try to save against the day when he could buy passage back to Mars—for they'd surely let him ride the ships even if they wouldn't let him run them. But, he told himself, he'd figured that one out. It would take twenty years to save enough, and he had no twenty years.

He lit the cigarette and went tramping down the street, and even through the cigarette, he could smell the hated green.

Ten blocks later, he reached the far edge of the space-port. There was a ship. He stood for a moment looking at it before he went into the shabby restaurant to buy himself some breakfast.

There was a ship, he thought, and that was a hopeful sign. Some days there weren't any, some days three or four. But there was a ship today and it might be the one.

One day, he told himself, he'd surely find the ship out there that would take him home—a ship with a captain so desperate for an engineer that he would overlook the entry in the book.

But even as he thought it, he knew it for a lie—a lie he told himself each day. Perhaps to justify his coming here each day to check at the hiring hall, a lie to keep his hope alive, to keep his courage up. A lie that made it even barely possible to face the bleak, warm room and the green of Earth.

He went into the restaurant and sat down on a stool.

The waitress came to take his order. "Cakes again?" she asked.

He nodded. Pancakes were cheap and filling and he had to make his money last.

"You'll find a ship today," said the waitress. "I have a feeling you will."

"Perhaps I will," he said, without believing it.

"I know just how you feel," the waitress told him. "I know how awful it can be. I was homesick once myself, the first time I left home. I thought I would die."

He didn't answer, for he felt it would not have been dignified to answer. Although why he should now lay claim to dignity, he could not imagine.

But this, in any case, was more than simple homesickness. It was planetsickness, culturesickness, a cutting off of all he'd known and wanted.

Sitting, waiting for the cakes to cook, he caught the dream again—the dream of red hills rolling far into the land, of the cold, dry air soft against the skin, of the splendor of the stars at twilight and the faery yellow of the distant sandstorm. And the low house crouched against the land, with the old gray-haired man sitting stiffly in a chair upon the porch that faced toward the sunset.

The waitress brought the cakes.

The day would come, he told himself, when he could afford no longer this self-pity he carried. He knew it for what it was and he should get rid of it. And yet it was a thing he lived with—even more than that, it had become a way of life. It was his comfort and his shield, the driving force that kept him trudging on each day.

He finished the cakes and paid for them.

"Good luck," said the waitress, with a smile.

"Thank you," he said.

He tramped down the road, with the gravel crunching

underfoot and the sun like a blast upon his back, but he had left the greenness. The port lay bare and bald, scalped and cauterized.

He reached where he was going and went up to the desk.

"You again," said the union agent.

"Anything for Mars?"

"Not a thing. No, wait a minute. There was a man in here not too long ago."

The agent got up from the desk and went to the door. Then he stepped outside the door and began to shout at someone.

A few minutes later, he was back. Behind him came a lumbering and irate individual. He had a cap upon his head that said CAPTAIN in greasy, torn letters, but aside from that he was distinctly out of uniform.

"Here's the man," the agent told the captain. "Name of Anson Cooper. Engineer first class, but his record's not so good."

"Damn the record!" bawled the captain. He said to Cooper: "Do you know Morrisons?"

"I was raised with them," said Cooper. It was not the truth, but he knew he could get by.

"They're good engines," said the captain, "but cranky and demanding. You'll have to baby them. You'll have to sleep with them. And if you don't watch them close, they'll up and break your back."

"I know how to handle them," said Cooper.

"My engineer ran out on me." The captain spat on the floor to show his contempt for runaway engineers. "He wasn't man enough."

"I'm man enough," Cooper declared.

And he knew, standing there, what it would be like. But there was no other choice. If he wanted to get back to Mars, he had to take the Morrisons.

"O.K., then, come on with you," the captain said.

"Wait a minute," said the union agent. "You can't rush off a man like this. You have to give him time to pick up his duffle."

"I haven't any to pick up," Cooper said, thinking of the few pitiful belongings back in the boarding house. "Or none that matters."

"You understand," the agent said to the captain, "that

the union cannot vouch for a man with a record such as his."

"To hell with that," said the captain. "Just so he can run the engines. That's all I ask."

The ship stood far out in the field. She had not been much to start with and she had not improved with age. Just the job of riding on a craft like that would be high torture, without the worry of nursing Morrisons.

"She'll hang together, no fear," said the captain. "She's got a lot more trips left in her than you'd think. It beats all hell what a tub like that can take."

Just one more trip, thought Cooper. Just so she gets me to Mars. Then she can fall apart, for all I care.

"She's beautiful," he said, and meant it.

He walked up to one of the great landing fins and laid a hand upon it. It was solid metal, with all the paint peeled off it, with tiny pits of corrosion speckling its surface and with a hint of cold, as if it might not as yet have shed all the touch of space.

And this was it, he thought. After all the weeks of waiting, here finally was the thing of steel and engineering that would take him home again.

He walked back to where the captain stood.

"Let's get on with it," he said. "I'll want to look the engines over."

"They're all right," said the captain.

"That may be so. I still want to run a check on them."

He had expected the engines to be bad, but not as bad as they turned out to be. If the ship had not been much to look at, the Morrisons were worse.

"They'll need some work," he said. "We can't lift with them, the shape they're in."

The captain raved and swore. "We have to blast by dawn, damn it! This is a goddamn emergency."

"You'll lift by dawn," snapped Cooper. "Just leave me alone."

He drove his gang to work, and he worked himself, for fourteen solid hours, without a wink of sleep, without a bite to eat.

Then he crossed his fingers and told the captain he was ready.

They got out of atmosphere with the engines holding together. Cooper uncrossed the fingers and sighed with deep relief. Now all he had to do was keep them running.

The captain called him forward and brought out a bottle. "You did better, Mr. Cooper, than I thought you would."

Cooper shook his head. "We aren't there yet, Captain. We've a long way still to go."

"Mr. Cooper," said the captain, "you know what we are carrying? You got any idea at all?"

Cooper shook his head.

"Medicines," the captain told him. "There's an epidemic out there. We were the only ship anywhere near ready for takeoff. So we were requisitioned."

"It would have been much better if we could have overhauled the engines."

"We didn't have the time. Every minute counts."

Cooper drank the liquor, stupid with a tiredness that cut clear to the bone. "Epidemic, you say. What kind?"

"Sand fever," said the captain. "You've heard of it, perhaps."

Cooper felt the chill of deadly fear creep along his body. "I've heard of it." He finished off the whisky and stood up. "I have to get back, sir. I have to watch those engines."

"We're counting on you, Mr. Cooper. You have to get us through."

He went back to the engine room and slumped into a chair, listening to the engine-song that beat throughout the ship.

He had to keep them going. There was no question of it now, if there'd ever been a question. For now it was not the simple matter of getting home again, but of getting needed drugs to the old home planet.

"I promise you," he said, talking to himself. "I promise you we'll get there."

He drove the engine crew and he drove himself, day after dying day, while the howling of the tubes and the thunder of the haywire Morrisons racked a man almost beyond endurance.

There was no such thing as sleep—only catnaps caught as one could catch them. There were no such things as meals, only food gulped on the run. And there was work, and worse than work were the watching and the waiting, the shoulders tensed against the stutter or the sudden screech of metal that would spell disaster.

Why, he wondered dully, did a man ever go to space? Why should one deliberately choose a job like this? Here in the engine room, with its cranky motors, it might be worse than elsewhere in the ship. But that didn't mean it wasn't bad. For throughout the ship stretched tension and discomfort and, above all, the dead black fear of space itself, of what space could do to a ship and the men within it.

In some of the bigger, newer ships, conditions might be better, but not a great deal better. They still tranquilized the passengers and colonists who went out to the other planets—tranquilized them to quiet the worries, to make them more insensitive to discomfort, to prevent their breaking into panic.

But a crew you could not tranquilize. A crew must be wide-awake, with all its faculties intact. A crew had to sit and take it.

Perhaps the time would come when the ships were big enough, when the engines and the drives would be perfected, when Man had lost some of his fear of the emptiness of space—then it would be easier.

But the time might be far off. It was almost two hundred years now since his family had gone out, among the first colonists, to Mars.

If it were not that he was going home, he told himself, it would be beyond all tolerance and endurance. He could almost smell the cold, dry air of home—even in this place that reeked with other smells. He could look beyond the metal skin of the ship in which he rode and across the long dark miles and see the gentle sunset on the redness of the hills.

And in this he had an advantage over all the others. For without going home, he could not have stood it.

The days wore on and the engines held and the hope built up within him. And finally hope gave way to triumph.

And then came the day when the ship went mushing down through the thin, cold atmosphere and came in to a landing.

He reached out and pulled a switch and the engines rumbled to a halt. Silence came into the tortured steel that still was numb with noise.

He stood beside the engines, deafened by the silence, frightened by this alien thing that never made a sound.

He walked along the engines, with his hand sliding on their metal, stroking them as he would pet an animal, astonished and slightly angry at himself for finding in himself a queer, distorted quality of affection for them.

But why not? They had brought him home. He had nursed and pampered them, he had cursed them and watched over them, he had slept with them, and they had brought him home.

And that was more, he admitted to himself, than he had ever thought they would do.

He found that he was alone. The crew had gone swarming up the ladder as soon as he had pulled the switch. And now it was time that he himself was going.

But he stood there for a moment, in that silent room, as he gave the place one final visual check. Everything was all right. There was nothing to be done.

He turned and climbed the ladder slowly, heading for port.

He found the captain standing in the port, and out beyond the port stretched the redness of the land.

"All the rest have gone except the purser," said the captain. "I thought you'd soon be up. You did a fine job with the engines, Mr. Cooper. I'm glad you shipped with us."

"It's my last run," Cooper said, staring out at the redness of the hills. "Now I settle down."

"That's strange," said the captain. "I take it you're a Mars man."

"I am. And I never should have left."

The captain stared at him and said again: "That's strange."

"Nothing strange," said Cooper. "I—"

"It's my last run, too," the captain broke in. "There'll be a new commander to take her back to Earth."

"In that case," Cooper offered, "I'll stand you a drink as soon as we get down."

"I'll take you up on that. First we'll get our shots."

They climbed down the ladder and walked across the field toward the spaceport buildings. Trucks went whining past them, heading for the ship, to pick up the unloaded cargo.

And now it was all coming back to Cooper, the way he had dreamed it in that shabby room on Earth—the exhilarating taste of the thinner, colder air, the step that was springier because of the lesser gravity, the swift and clean elation of the uncluttered, brave red land beneath a weaker sun.

Inside, the doctor waited for them in his tiny office.

"Sorry, gentlemen," he said, "but you know the regulations."

"I don't like it," said the captain, "but I suppose it does make sense."

They sat down in the chairs and rolled up their sleeves.

"Hang on," the doctor told them. "It gives you quite a jolt."

It did.

And it had before thought Cooper, every time before. He should be used to it by now.

He sat weakly in the chair, waiting for the weakness and the shock to pass, and he saw the doctor, there behind his desk, watching them and waiting for them to come around to normal.

"Was it a rough trip?" the doctor finally asked.

"They all are rough," the captain replied curtly.

Cooper shook his head. "This one was the worst I've ever known. Those engines . . ."

The captain said: "I'm sorry, Cooper. This time it was the truth. We were *really* carrying medicine. There *is* an epidemic. Mine was the only ship. I'd planned an overhaul, but we couldn't wait."

Cooper nodded. "I remember now," he said.

He stood up weakly and stared out the window at the cold, the alien, the forbidding land of Mars.

"I never could have made it," he said flatly, "if I'd not been psyched."

He turned back to the doctor. "Will there ever be a time?"

The doctor nodded. "Some day, certainly. When the ships are better. When the race is more conditioned to space travel."

"But this homesickness business—it gets downright brutal."

"It's the only way," the doctor declared. "We'd not have any spacemen if they weren't always going home."

"That's right," the captain said. "No man, myself included, could face that kind of beating unless it was for something more than money."

Cooper looked out the window at the Martian sandscape and shivered. Of all the God-forsaken places he had ever seen!

He was a fool to be in space, he told himself, with a wife like Doris and two kids back home. He could hardly wait to see them.

And he knew the symptoms. He was getting homesick once again—but this time it was for Earth.

The doctor was taking a bottle out of his desk and pouring generous drinks into glasses for all three of them.

"Have a shot of this," he said, "and let's forget about it."

"As if we could remember," said Cooper, laughing suddenly.

"After all," the captain said, far too cheerfully, "we have to see it in the right perspective. It's nothing more than a condition of employment."

PROJECT MASTODON

THE chief of protocol said, "Mr. Hudson of—ah—Mastodonia."

The secretary of state held out his hand. "I'm glad to see you, Mr. Hudson. I understand you've been here several times."

"That's right," said Hudson. "I had a hard time making your people believe I was in earnest."

"And are you, Mr. Hudson?"

"Believe me, sir, I would not try to fool you."

"And this Mastodonia," said the secretary, reaching down to tap the document upon the desk. "You will pardon me, but I've never heard of it."

"It's a new nation," Hudson explained, "but quite legitimate. We have a constitution, a democratic form of government, duly elected officials, and a code of laws. We are a free, peace-loving people and we are possessed of a vast amount of natural resources and—"

"Please tell me, sir," interrupted the secretary, "just where are you located?"

"Technically, you are our nearest neighbors."

"But that is ridiculous!" exploded Protocol.

"Not at all," insisted Hudson. "If you will give me a moment, Mr. Secretary, I have considerable evidence."

He brushed the fingers of Protocol off his sleeve and stepped forward to the desk, laying down the portfolio he carried.

"Go ahead, Mr. Hudson," said the secretary. "Why don't we all sit down and be comfortable while we talk this over?"

"You have my credentials, I see. Now here is a propos—"

"I have a document signed by a certain Wesley Adams."

"He's our first president," said Hudson. "Our George Washington, you might say."

"What is the purpose of this visit, Mr. Hudson?"

"We'd like to establish diplomatic relations. We think it would be to our mutual benefit. After all, we are a sister republic in perfect sympathy with your policies and aims. We'd like to negotiate trade agreements and we'd be grateful for some Point Four aid."

The secretary smiled. "Naturally. Who doesn't?"

"We're prepared to offer something in return," Hudson told him stiffly. "For one thing, we could offer sanctuary."

"Sanctuary!"

"I understand," said Hudson, "that in the present state of international tensions, a foolproof sanctuary is not something to be sneezed at."

The secretary turned stone cold. "I'm an extremely busy man."

Protocol took Hudson firmly by the arm. "Out you go."

General Leslie Bowers put in a call to State and got the secretary.

"I don't like to bother you, Herb," he said, "but there's something I want to check. Maybe you can help me."

"Glad to help you if I can."

"There's a fellow hanging around out here at the Pentagon, trying to get in to see me. Said I was the only one he'd talk to, but you know how it is."

"I certainly do."

"Name of Huston or Hudson or something like that."

"He was here just an hour or so ago," said the secretary. "Crackpot sort of fellow."

"He's gone now?"

"Yes. I don't think he'll be back."

"Did he say where you could reach him?"

"No, I don't believe he did."

"How did he strike you? I mean what kind of impression did you get of him?"

"I told you. A crackpot."

"I suppose he is. He said something to one of the colonels that got me worrying. Can't pass up anything, you know—not in the Dirty Tricks Department. Even if it's crackpot, these days you got to have a look at it."

"He offered sanctuary," said the secretary indignantly. "Can you imagine that!"

"He's been making the rounds, I guess," the general said. "He was over at AEC. Told them some sort of tale about knowing where there were vast uranium deposits. It was the AEC that told me he was heading your way."

"We get them all the time. Usually we can ease them out. This Hudson was just a little better than the most of them. He got in to see me."

"He told the colonel something about having a plan that would enable us to establish secret bases anywhere we wished, even in the territory of potential enemies. I know it sounds crazy . . ."

"Forget it, Les."

"You're probably right," said the general, "but this idea sends me. Can you imagine the look on their Iron Curtain faces?"

The scared little government clerk, darting conspiratorial glances all about him, brought the portfolio to the FBI.

"I found it in a bar down the street," he told the man who took him in tow. "Been going there for years. And I found this portfolio laying in the booth. I saw the man who must have left it there and I tried to find him later, but I couldn't."

"How do you know he left it there?"

"I just figured he did. He left the booth just as I came in and it was sort of dark in there and it took a minute to see this thing laying there. You see, I always take the booth every day and Joe sees me come in and he brings me the usual and—"

"You saw this man leave the booth you usually sit in?"

"That's right."

"Then you saw the portfolio."

"Yes, sir."

"You tried to find the man, thinking it must have been his."

"That's exactly what I did."

"But by the time you went to look for him, he had disappeared."

"That's the way it was."

"Now tell me—why did you bring it here? Why didn't you turn it in to the management so the man could come back and claim it?"

"Well, sir, it was like this. I had a drink or two and I was wondering all the time what was in that portfolio. So finally I took a peek and—"

"And what you saw decided you to bring it here to us."

"That's right. I saw—"

"Don't tell me what you saw. Give me your name and address and don't say anything about this. You understand that we're grateful to you for thinking of us, but we'd rather you said nothing."

"Mum's the word," the little clerk assured him, full of vast importance.

The FBI phoned Dr. Ambrose Amberly, Smithsonian expert on paleontology.

"We've got something, Doctor, that we'd like you to have a look at. A lot of movie film."

"I'll be most happy to. I'll come down as soon as I get clear. End of the week, perhaps?"

"This is very urgent, Doctor. Damnedest thing you ever saw. Big, shaggy elephants and tigers with teeth down to their necks. There's a beaver the size of a bear."

"Fakes," said Amberly, disgusted. "Clever gadgets. Camera angles."

"That's what we thought first, but there are no gadgets, no camera angles. This is the real McCoy."

"I'm on my way," the paleontologist said, hanging up.

Snide item in smug, smartaleck gossip column: Saucer's are passé at the Pentagon. There's another mystery that's got the high brass very high.

II

PRESIDENT Wesley Adams and Secretary of State John Cooper sat glumly under a tree in the capital of Mastodonia and waited for the ambassador extraordinary to return.

"I tell you, Wes," said Cooper, who, under various pseudonyms, was also the secretaries of commerce, treasury and war, "this is a crazy thing we did. What if Chuck can't get back? They might throw him in jail or something might happen to the time unit or the helicopter. We should have gone along."

"We had to stay," Adams said. "You know what would

happen to this camp and our supplies if we weren't around here to guard them."

"The only thing that's given us any trouble is that old mastodon. If he comes around again, I'm going to take a skillet and bang him in the brisket."

"That isn't the only reason, either," said President Adams, "and you know it. We can't go deserting this nation now that we've created it. We have to keep possession. Just planting a flag and saying it's ours wouldn't be enough. We might be called upon for proof that we've established residence. Something like the old homestead laws, you know."

"We'll establish residence sure enough," growled Secretary Cooper, "if something happens to that time unit or the helicopter."

"You think they'll do it, Johnny?"

"Who do what?"

"The United States. Do you think they'll recognize us?"

"Not if they know who we are."

"That's what I'm afraid of."

"Chuck will talk them into it. He can talk the skin right off a cat."

"Sometimes I think we're going at this wrong. Sure, Chuck's got the long-range view and I suppose it's best. But maybe what we ought to do is grab a good, fast profit and get out of here. We could take in hunting parties at ten thousand a head or maybe we could lease it to a movie company."

"We can do all that and do it legally and with full protection," Cooper told him, "if we can get ourselves recognized as a sovereign nation. It we negotiate a mutual defense pact, no one would dare get hostile because we could squawk to Uncle Sam."

"All you say is true," Adams agreed, "but there are going to be questions. It isn't just a matter of walking into Washington and getting recognition. They'll want to know about us, such as our population. What if Chuck has to tell them it's a total of three persons?"

Cooper shook his head. "He wouldn't answer that way, Wes. He'd duck the question or give them some diplomatic double-talk. After all, how can we be *sure* there are only three of us? We took over the whole continent, remember."

"You know well enough, Johnny, there are no other humans back here in North America. The farthest back any scientist will place the migrations from Asia is 30,000 years. They haven't got here yet."

"Maybe we should have done it differently," mused Cooper. "Maybe we should have included the whole world in our proclamation, not just the continent. That way, we could claim quite a population."

"It wouldn't have held water. Even as it is, we went a little further than precedent allows. The old explorers usually laid claim to certain watersheds. They'd find a river and lay claim to all the territory drained by the river. They didn't go grabbing off whole continents."

"That's because they were never sure of exactly what they had," said Cooper. "We are. We have what you might call the advantage of hindsight."

He leaned back against the tree and stared across the land. It was a pretty place, he thought—the rolling ridges covered by vast grazing areas and small groves, the forest-covered, ten-mile river valley. And everywhere one looked, the grazing herds of mastodon, giant bison and wild horses, with the less gregarious fauna scattered hit and miss.

Old Buster, the troublesome mastodon, a lone bull which had been probably run out of a herd by a younger rival, stood at the edge of a grove a quarter-mile away. He had his head down and was curling and uncurling his trunk in an aimless sort of way while he teetered slowly in a lazy-crazy fashion by lifting first one foot and then another.

The old cuss was lonely, Cooper told himself. That was why he hung around like a homeless dog—except that he was too big and awkward to have much pet-appeal and, more than likely, his temper was unstable.

The afternoon sun was pleasantly warm and the air, it seemed to Cooper, was the freshest he had ever smelled. It was, altogether, a very pleasant place, an Indian-summer sort of land, ideal for a Sunday picnic or a camping trip.

The breeze was just enough to float out from its flag-staff before the tent the national banner of Mastodonia—a red rampant mastodon upon a field of green.

"You know, Johnny," said Adams, "there's one thing

that worries me a lot. It we're going to base our claim on precedent, we may be way off base. The old explorers always claimed their discoveries for their nations or their king, never for themselves."

"The principle was entirely different," Cooper told him. "Nobody ever did anything for himself in those days. Everyone was always under someone else's protection. The explorers either were financed by their governments or were sponsored by them or operated under a royal charter or a patent. With us, it's different. Ours is a private enterprise. You dreamed up the time unit and built it. The three of us chipped in to buy the helicopter. We've paid all of our expenses out of our own pockets. We never got a dime from anyone. What we found is ours."

"I hope you're right," said Adams uneasily.

Old Buster had moved out from the grove and was shuffling warily toward the camp. Adams picked up the rifle that lay across his knees.

"Wait," said Cooper sharply. "Maybe he's just bluffing. It would be a shame to plaster him; he's such a nice old guy."

Adams half raised the rifle.

"I'll give him three steps more," he announced. "I've had enough of him."

Suddenly a roar burst out of the air just above their heads. The two leaped to their feet.

"It's Chuck!" Cooper yelled. "He's back!"

The helicopter made a half-turn of the camp and came rapidly to Earth.

Trumpeting with terror, Old Buster was a dwindling dot far down the grassy ridge.

III

THEY built the nightly fires circling the camp to keep out the animals.

"It'll be the death of me yet," said Adams wearily, "cutting all this wood."

"We have to get to work on that stockade," Cooper said. "We've fooled around too long. Some night, fire or no fire, a herd of mastodon will come busting in here and if they ever hit the helicopter, we'll be dead ducks. It wouldn't take more than just five seconds to turn us into Robinson Crusoes of the Pleistocene."

"Well, now that this recognition thing has petered out on us," said Adams, "maybe we can get down to business."

"Trouble is," Cooper answered, "we spent about the last of our money on the chain saw to cut this wood and on Chuck's trip to Washington. To build a stockade, we need a tractor. We'd kill ourselves if we tried to rassle that many logs bare-handed."

"Maybe we could catch some of those horses running around out there."

"Have you ever broken a horse?"

"No, that's one thing I never tried."

"Me, either. How about you, Chuck?"

"Not me," said the ex-ambassador extraordinary bluntly.

Cooper squatted down beside the coals of the cooking fire and twirled the spit. Upon the spit were three grouse and half a dozen quail. The huge coffee pot was sending out a nose-tingling aroma. Biscuits were baking in the reflector.

"We've been here six weeks," he said, "and we're still living in a tent and cooking on an open fire. We better get busy and get something done."

"The stockade first," said Adams, "and that means a tractor."

"We could use the helicopter."

"Do you want to take the chance? That's our getaway. Once something happens to it . . ."

"I guess not," Cooper admitted, gulping.

"We could use some of that Point Four aid right now," commented Adams.

"They threw me out," said Hudson. "Everywhere I went, sooner or later they got around to throwing me out. They were real organized about it."

"Well, we tried," Adams said.

"And to top it off," added Hudson, "I had to go and lose all that film and now we'll have to waste our time taking more of it. Personally, I don't ever want to let another saber-tooth get that close to me while I hold the camera."

"You didn't have a thing to worry about," Adams objected. "Johnny was right there behind you with the gun."

"Yeah, with a muzzle about a foot from my head when he let go."

"I stopped him, didn't I?" demanded Cooper.

"With his head right in my lap."

"Maybe we won't have to take any more pictures," Adams suggested.

"We'll have to," Cooper said. "There are sportsmen up ahead who'd fork over ten thousand bucks easy for two weeks of hunting here. But before we could sell them on it, we'd have to show them movies. That scene with the saber-tooth would cinch it."

"If it didn't scare them off," Hudson pointed out. "The last few feet showed nothing but the inside of his throat."

Ex-ambassador Hudson looked unhappy. "I don't like the whole setup. As soon as we bring someone in, the news is sure to leak. And once the word gets out, there'll be guys lying in ambush for us—maybe even nations—scheming to steal the know-how, legally or violently. That's what scares me the most about those films I lost. Someone will find them and they may guess what it's all about, but I'm hoping they either won't believe it or can't manage to trace us."

"We could swear the hunting parties to secrecy," said Cooper.

"How could a sportsman keep still about the mounted head of a saber-tooth or a record piece of ivory? And the same thing would apply to anyone we approached. Some university could raise dough to send a team of scientists back here and a movie company would cough up plenty to use this place as a location for a caveman epic. But it wouldn't be worth a thing to either of them if they couldn't tell about it.

"Now if we could have gotten recognition as a nation, we'd have been all set. We could make our own laws and regulations and be able to enforce them. We could bring in settlers and establish trade. We could exploit our natural resources. It would all be legal and aboveboard. We could tell who we were and where we were and what we had to offer."

"We aren't licked yet," said Adams. "There's a lot that we can do. Those river hills are covered with ginseng. We can each dig a dozen pounds a day. There's good money in the root."

"Ginseng root," Cooper said, "is peanuts. We need *big* money."

"Or we could trap," offered Adams. "The place is alive with beaver."

"Have you taken a good look at those beaver? They're about the size of a St. Bernard."

"All the better. Think how much money just one pelt would bring."

"No dealer would believe that it was beaver. He'd think you were trying to pull a fast one on him. And there are only a few states that allow beaver to be trapped. To sell the pelts—even if you could—you'd have to take licenses in each of those states."

"Those mastodon carry a lot of ivory," said Cooper. "And if we wanted to go north, we'd find mammoths that would carry even more . . ."

"And get socked into the jug for ivory smuggling?"

They sat, all three of them, staring at the fire, not finding anything to say.

The moaning complaint of a giant hunting cat came from somewhere up the river.

IV

HUDSON lay in his sleeping bag, staring at the sky. It bothered him a lot. There was not one familiar constellation, not one star that he could name with any certainty. This juggling of the stars, he thought, emphasized more than anything else in this ancient land the vast gulf of years which lay between him and the Earth where he had been—or would be—born.

A hundred and fifty thousand years, Adams had said, give or take ten thousand. There just was no way to know. Later on, there might be. A measurement of the stars and a comparison with their positions in the twentieth century might be one way of doing it. But at the moment, any figure could be no more than a guess.

The time machine was not something that could be tested for calibration or performance. As a matter of fact, there *was* no way to test it. They had not been certain, he remembered, the first time they had used it, that it would really work. There had been no way to find out. When it worked, you knew it worked. And if it hadn't worked, there would have been no way of knowing beforehand that it wouldn't.

Adams had been sure, of course, but that had been because he had absolute reliance in the half-mathematical, half-philosophic concepts he had worked out—concepts that neither Hudson nor Cooper could come close to understanding.

That had always been the way it had been, even when they were kids, with Wes dreaming up the deals that he and Johnny carried out. Back in those days, too, they had used time travel in their play. Out in Johnny's back yard, they had rigged up a time machine out of a wonderful collection of salvaged junk—a wooden crate, an empty five-gallon paint pail, a battered coffee maker, a bunch of discarded copper tubing, a busted steering wheel and other odds and ends. In it, they had "traveled" back to Indian-before-the-white-man land and mammoth-land and dinosaur-land and the slaughter, he remembered, had been wonderfully appalling.

But, in reality, it had been much different. There was much more to it than gunning down the weird fauna that one found.

And they should have known there would be, for they had talked about it often.

He thought of the bull session back in university and the little, usually silent kid who sat quietly in the corner, a law-school student whose last name had been Pritchard.

And after sitting silently for some time, this Pritchard kid had spoken up: "If you guys ever do travel in time, you'll run up against more than you bargain for. I don't mean the climate or the terrain or the fauna, but the economics and the politics."

They all jeered at him, Hudson remembered, and then had gone on with their talk. And after a short while, the talk had turned to women, as it always did.

He wondered where that quiet man might be. Some day, Hudson told himself, I'll have to look him up and tell him he was right.

We did it wrong, he thought. There were so many other ways we might have done it, but we'd been so sure and greedy for the triumph and the glory—and now there was no easy way to collect.

On the verge of success, they could have sought out help, gone to some large industrial concern or an educational foundation or even to the government. Like historic explorers, they could have obtained subsidization and sponsorship. Then they would have had protection, funds to do a proper job and they need not have operated on their present shoestring—one beaten-up helicopter and one time unit. They could have had several and at least one standing by in the twentieth century as a rescue unit, should that be necessary.

But that would have meant a bargain, perhaps a very hard one, and sharing with someone who had contributed nothing but the money. And there was more than money in a thing like this—there were twenty years of dreams and a great idea and the dedication to that great idea—years of work and years of disappointment and an almost fanatical refusal to give up.

Even so, thought Hudson, they had figured well enough. There had been many chances to make blunders and they'd made relatively few. All they lacked, in the last analysis, was backing.

Take the helicopter, for example. It was the one satisfactory vehicle for time traveling. You had to get up in the air to clear whatever upheavals and subsidences there had been through geologic ages. The helicopter took you up and kept you clear and gave you a chance to pick a proper landing place. Travel without it and, granting you were lucky with land surfaces, you still might materialize in the heart of some great tree or end up in a swamp or the middle of a herd of startled, savage beasts. A plane would have done as well, but back in this world, you couldn't land a plane—or you couldn't be certain that you could. A helicopter, though, could land almost anywhere.

In the time-distance they had traveled, they almost certainly had been lucky, although one could not be entirely sure just how great a part of it was luck. Wes had felt that he had not been working as blindly as it sometimes might appear. He had calibrated the unit for jumps of 50,000 years. Finer calibration, he had said realistically, would have to wait for more developmental work.

Using the 50,000-year calibrations, they had figured it out. One jump (conceding that the calibration was correct) would have landed them at the end of the Wisconsin

glacial period; two jumps, at its beginning. The third
would set them down toward the end of the Sangamon
Interglacial and apparently it had—give or take ten thousand years or so.

They had arrived at a time when the climate did not
seem to vary greatly, either hot or cold. The flora was
modern enough to give them a homelike feeling. The fauna,
modern and Pleistocenic, overlapped. And the surface
features were little altered from the twentieth century.
The rivers ran along familiar paths, the hills and bluffs
looked much the same. In this corner of the Earth, at least,
150,000 years had not changed things greatly.

Boyhood dreams, Hudson thought, were wondrous. It
was not often that three men who had daydreamed in
their youth could follow it out to its end. But they had
and here they were.

Johnny was on watch, and it was Hudson's turn next,
and he'd better get to sleep. He closed his eyes, then
opened them again for another look at the unfamiliar stars.
The east, he saw, was flushed with silver light. Soon the
Moon would rise, which was good. A man could keep a
better watch when the Moon was up.

He woke suddenly, snatched upright and into full awareness by the marrow-chilling clamor that slashed across the
night. The very air seemed curdled by the savage racket
and, for a moment, he sat numbed by it. Then, slowly, it
seemed—his brain took the noise and separated it into
two distinct but intermingled categories, the deadly screaming of a cat and the maddened trumpeting of a mastodon.

The Moon was up and the countryside was flooded by
its light. Cooper, he saw, was out beyond the watchfires,
standing there and watching, with his rifle ready. Adams
was scrambling out of his sleeping bag, swearing softly
to himself. The cooking fire had burned down to a bed of
mottled coals, but the watchfires still were burning and the
helicopter, parked within their circle, picked up the glint
of flames.

"It's Buster," Adams told him angrily. "I'd know that
bellowing of his anywhere. He's done nothing but parade
up and down and bellow ever since we got here. And now
he seems to have gone out and found himself a saber-
tooth."

Hudson zipped down his sleeping bag, grabbed up his

rifle and jumped to his feet, following Adams in a silent rush to where Cooper stood.

Cooper motioned at them. "Don't break it up. You'll never see the like of it again."

Adams brought his rifle up.

Cooper knocked the barrel down.

"You fool!" he shouted. "You want them turning on us?"

Two hundred yards away stood the mastodon and, on his back, the screeching saber-tooth. The great beast reared into the air and came down with a jolt, bucking to unseat the cat, flailing the air with his massive trunk. And as he bucked, the cat struck and struck again with his gleaming teeth, aiming for the spine.

Then the mastodon crashed head downward, as if to turn a somersault, rolled and was on his feet again, closer to them now than he had been before. The huge cat had sprung off.

For a moment, the two stood facing one another. Then the tiger charged, a flowing streak of motion in the moonlight. Buster wheeled away and the cat, leaping, hit his shoulder, clawed wildly and slid off. The mastodon whipped to the attack, tusks slashing, huge feet stamping. The cat, caught a glancing blow by one of the tusks, screamed and leaped up, to land in spread-eagle fashion upon Buster's head.

Maddened with pain and fright, blinded by the tiger's raking claws, the old mastodon ran—straight toward the camp. And as he ran, he grasped the cat in his trunk and tore him from his hold, lifted him high and threw him.

"Look out!" yelled Cooper and brought his rifle up and fired.

For an instant, Hudson saw it all as if it were a single scene, motionless, one frame snatched from a fantastic movie epic—the charging mastodon, with the tiger lifted and the sound track one great blast of bloodthirsty bedlam.

Then the scene dissolved in a blur of motion. He felt his rifle thud against his shoulder, knowing he had fired, but not hearing the explosion. And the mastodon was almost on top of him, bearing down like some mighty and remorseless engine of blind destruction.

He flung himself to one side and the giant brushed past

him. Out of the tail of his eye, he saw the thrown saber-
tooth crash to Earth within the circle of the watchfires.

He brought his rifle up again and caught the area behind
Buster's ear within his sights. He pressed the trigger. The
mastodon staggered, then regained his stride and went
rushing on. He hit one of the watchfires dead center and
went through it, scattering coals and burning brands.

Then there was a thud and the screeching clang of
metal.

"Oh, no!" shouted Hudson.

Rushing forward, they stopped inside the circle of the
fires.

The helicopter lay tilted at a crazy angle. One of its
rotor blades was crumpled. Half across it, as if he might
have fallen as he tried to bull his mad way over it, lay
the mastodon.

Something crawled across the ground toward them, its
spitting, snarling mouth gaping in the firelight, its back
broken, hind legs trailing.

Calmly, without a word, Adams put a bullet into the
head of the saber-tooth.

V

GENERAL Leslie Bowers rose from his chair and paced
up and down the room. He stopped to bang the conference
table with a knotted fist.

"You can't do it," he bawled at them. "You can't kill
the project. I *know* there's something to it. We can't give
it up!"

"But it's been ten years, General," said the secretary of
the army. "If they were coming back, they'd be here by
now."

The general stopped his pacing, stiffened. Who did that
little civilian squirt think he was, talking to the military
in that tone of voice!

"We know how you feel about it, General," said the
chairman of the joint chiefs of staff. "I think we all recognize how deeply you're involved. You've blamed yourself
all these years and there is no need of it. After all, there
may be nothing to it."

"Sir, said the general, "I *know* there's something to it.

I thought so at the time, even when no one else did. And what we've turned up since serves to bear me out. Let's take a look at these three men of ours. We knew almost nothing of them at the time, but we know them now. I've traced out their lives from the time that they were born until they disappeared—and I might add that, on the chance it might be all a hoax, we're searched for them for years and we're found no trace at all.

"I've talked with those who knew them and I've studied their scholastic and military records. I've arrived at the conclusion that if any three men could do it, they were the ones who could. Adams was the brains and the other two were the ones who carried out the things that he dreamed up. Cooper was a bulldog sort of man who could keep them going and it would be Hudson who would figure out the angles.

"And they knew the angles, gentlemen. They had it all doped out.

"What Hudson tried here in Washington is substantial proof of that. But even back in school, they were thinking of those angles. I talked some years ago to a lawyer in New York, name of Pritchard. He told me that even back in university, they talked of the economic and political problems that they might face if they ever cracked what they were working at.

"Wesley Adams was one of our brightest young scientific men. His record at the university and his war work bears that out. After the war, there were at least a dozen jobs he could have had. But he wasn't interested. And I'll tell you why he wasn't. He had something bigger—something he wanted to work on. So he and these two others went off by themselves—"

"You think he was working on a temporal—" the army secretary cut in.

"He was working on a time machine," roared the general. "I don't know about this 'temporal' business. Just plain 'time machine' is good enough for me."

"Let's calm down, General," said the JCS chairman. "After all, there's no need to shout."

The general nodded. "I'm sorry, sir. I get all worked up about this. I've spent the last ten years with it. As you say, I'm trying to make up for what I failed to do ten years ago. I should have talked to Hudson. I was busy, sure, but not that busy. It's an official state of mind that we're too busy to see anyone and I plead guilty on that score. And now that you're talking about closing the project—"

"It's costing us money," said the army secretary.

"And we have no direct evidence," pointed out the JCS chairman.

"I don't know what you want," snapped the general. "If there was any man alive who could crack time, that man was Wesley Adams. We found where he worked. We found the workshop and we talked to neighbors who said there was something funny going on and—"

"But ten years, General!" the army secretary protested.

"Hudson came here, bringing us the greatest discovery in all history, and we kicked him out. After that, do you expect them to come crawling back to us?"

"You think they went to someone else?"

"They wouldn't do that. They know what the thing they have found would mean. They wouldn't sell us out."

"Hudson came with a preposterous proposition," said the man from the state department.

"They had to protect themselves!" yelled the general. "If you had discovered a virgin planet with its natural resources intact, what would you do about it? Come trotting down here and hand it over to a government that's too 'busy' to recognize—"

"General!"

"Yes, sir," apologized the general tiredly. "I wish you gentlemen could see my view of it, how it all fits together. First there were the films and we have the word of a dozen competent paleontologists that it's impossible to fake anything as perfect as those films. But even granting that they could be, there are certain differences that no one would ever think of faking, because no one ever knew. Who, as an example, would put lynx tassels on the ears of a saber-tooth? Who would know that young mastodon were black?

"And the location. I wonder if you've forgotten that we tracked down the location of Adams' workshop from those films alone: They gave us clues so positive that we didn't even hesitate—we drove straight to the old deserted farm where Adams and his friends had worked. Don't you see how it all fits together?"

"I presume," the man from the state department said

nastily, "that you even have an explanation as to why they chose that particular location."

"You thought you had me there," said the general, "but I have an answer. A good one. The southwestern corner of Wisconsin is a geologic curiosity. It was missed by all the glaciations. Why, we do not know. Whatever the reason, the glaciers came down on both sides of it and far to the south of it and left it standing there, a little island in a sea of ice.

"And another thing: Except for a time in the Triassic, that same area of Wisconsin has always been dry land. That and a few other spots are the only areas in North America which have not, time and time again, been covered by water. I don't think it necessary to point out the comfort it would be to an experimental traveler in time to be certain that, in almost any era he might hit, he'd have dry land beneath him."

The economics expert spoke up: "We've given this matter a lot of study and, while we do not feel ourselves competent to rule upon the possibility or impossibility of time travel, there are some observations I should like, at some time, to make."

"Go ahead right now," said the JCS chairman.

"We see one objection to the entire matter. One of the reasons, naturally, that we had some interest in it is that, if true, it would give us an entire new planet to exploit, perhaps more wisely than we've done in the past. But the thought occurs that any planet has only a certain grand total of natural resources. If we go into the past and exploit them, what effect will that have upon what is left of those resources for use in the present? Wouldn't we, in doing this, be robbing ourselves of our own heritage?"

"That contention," said the AEC chairman, "wouldn't hold true in every case. Quite the reverse, in fact. We know that there was, in some geologic ages in the past, a great deal more uranium than we have today. Go back far enough and you'd catch that uranium before it turned into lead. In southwestern Wisconsin, there is a lot of lead. Hudson told us he knew the location of vast uranium deposits and we thought he was a crackpot talking through his hat. If we'd known—let's be fair about this—if we had known and believed him about going back in time, we'd have snapped him up at once and all this would not have happened."

"It wouldn't hold true with forests, either," said the chairman of the JCS. "Or with pastures or with crops."

The economics expert was slightly flushed. "There is another thing," he said. "If we go back in time and colonize the land we find there, what would happen when that—well, let's call it retroactive—when that retroactive civilization reaches the beginning of our historic period? What will result from that cultural collision? Will our history change? Is what has happened false? Is all—"

"That's all poppycock!" the general shouted. "That and this other talk about using up resources. Whatever we did in the past—or are about to do—has been done already. I've lain awake nights, mister, thinking about all these things and there is no answer, believe me, except the one I give you. The question which faces us here is an immediate one. Do we give all this up or do we keep on watching that Wisconsin farm, waiting for them to come back? Do we keep on trying to find, independently, the process or formula or method that Adams found for traveling in time?"

"We've had no luck in our research so far, General," said the quiet physicist who sat at the table's end. "If you were not so sure and if the evidence were not so convincing that it had been done by Adams, I'd say flatly that it is impossible. We have no approach which holds any hope at all. What we've done so far, you might best describe as flounder. But if Adams turned the trick, it must be possible. There may be, as a matter of fact, more ways than one. We'd like to keep on trying."

"Not one word of blame has been put on you for your failure," the chairman told the physicist. "That you could do it seems to be more than can be humanly expected. If Adams did it—if he did, I say—it must have been simply that he blundered on an avenue of research no other man has thought of."

"You will recall," said the general, "that the research program, even from the first, was thought of strictly as a gamble. Our one hope was, and must remain, that they will return."

"It would have been so much simpler all around," the

state department man said, "if Adams had patented his method."

The general raged at him. "And had it published, all neat and orderly, in the patent office records so that anyone who wanted it could look it up and have it?"

"We can be most sincerely thankful," said the chairman, "that he did not patent it."

VI

THE helicopter would never fly again, but the time unit was intact.

Which didn't mean that it would work.

They held a powwow at their camp site. It had been, they decided, simpler to move the camp than to remove the body of Old Buster. So they had shifted at dawn, leaving the old mastodon still sprawled across the helicopter.

In a day or two, they knew, the great bones would be cleanly picked by the carrion birds, the lesser cats, the wolves and foxes and the little skulkers.

Getting the time unit out of the helicopter had been quite a chore, but they finally had managed and now Adams sat with it cradled in his lap.

"The worst of it," he told them, "is that I can't test it. There's no way to. You turn it on and it works or it doesn't work. You can't know till you try."

"That's something we can't help," Cooper replied. "The problem, seems to me, is how we're going to use it without the whirlybird."

"We have to figure out some way to get up in the air," said Adams. "We don't want to take the chance of going up into the twentieth century and arriving there about six feet underground."

"Common sense says that we should be higher here than up ahead," Hudson pointed out. "These hills have stood here since Jurassic times. They probably were a good deal higher then and have weathered down. That weathering still should be going on. So we should be higher here than in the twentieth century—not much, perhaps, but higher."

"Did anyone ever notice what the altimeter read?" asked Cooper.

"I don't believe I did," Adams admitted.

"It wouldn't tell you, anyhow," Hudson declared. "It would just give our height then and now—and we were moving, remember—and what about air pockets and relative atmosphere density and all the rest?"

Cooper looked as discouraged as Hudson felt.

"How does this sound?" asked Adams. "We'll build a platform twelve feet high. That certainly should be enough to clear us and yet small enough to stay within the range of the unit's force-field."

"And what if we're two feet higher here?" Hudson pointed out.

"A fall of fourteen feet wouldn't kill a man unless he's plain unlucky."

"It might break some bones."

"So it might break some bones. You want to stay here or take a chance on a broken leg?"

"All right, if you put it that way. A platform, you say. A platform out of what?"

"Timber. There's a lot of it. We just go out and cut some logs."

"A twelve-foot log is heavy. And how are we going to get that big a log uphill?"

"We drag it."

"We try to, you mean."

"Maybe we could fix up a cart," said Adams, after thinking a moment.

"Out of what?" Cooper asked.

"Rollers, maybe. We could cut some and roll the logs up here."

"That would work on level ground," Hudson said. "It wouldn't work to roll a log uphill. It would get away from us. Someone might get killed."

"The logs would have to be longer than twelve feet, anyhow," Cooper put in. "You'd have to set them in a hole and that takes away some footage."

"Why not the tripod principle?" Hudson offered "Fasten three logs at the top and raise them."

"That's a gin-pole, a primitive derrick. It'd still have t‍ be longer than twelve feet. Fifteen, sixteen, maybe. An‍

how are we going to hoist three sixteen-foot logs? We'd
need a block and tackle."

"There's another thing," said Cooper. "Part of those
logs might just be beyond the effective range of the force-
field. Part of them would have to—*have to*, mind you—
move in time and part couldn't. That would set up a
stress . . ."

"Another thing about it," added Hudson, "is that we'd
travel with the logs. I don't want to come out in another
time with a bunch of logs flying all around me."

"Cheer up," Adams told them. "Maybe the unit won't
work, anyhow."

VII

THE general sat alone in his office and held his head between his hands. The fools, he thought, the goddam
knuckle-headed fools! Why couldn't they see it as clearly
as he did?

For fifteen years now, as head of Project Mastodon, he
had lived with it night and day and he could see all the
possibilies as clearly as if they had been actual fact. Not
military possibilities alone, although as a military man, he
naturally would think of those first.

The hidden bases, for example, located within the very
strongholds of potential enemies—within, yet centuries removed in time. Many centuries removed and only seconds
distant.

He could see it all: The materialization of the fleets;
the swift, devastating blow, then the instantaneous retreat
into the fastnesses of the past. Terrific destruction, but not
a ship lost nor a man.

Except that if you had the bases, you need never strike
the blow. If you had the bases and let the enemy know
you had them, there would never be the provocation.

And on the home front, you'd have air-raid shelters that
would be effective. You'd evacuate your population not in
space, but time. You'd have the sure and absolute defense
against any kind of bombing—fission, fusion, bacterio-
logical or whatever else the labs had in stock.

And if the worst should come—which it never would
with a setup like that—you'd have a place to which the

entire nation could retreat, leaving to the enemy the empty, blasted cities and the lethally dusted countryside.

Sanctuary—that had been what Hudson had offered the then-secretary of state fifteen years ago—and the idiot had frozen up with the insult of it and had Hudson thrown out.

And if war did not come, think of the living space and the vast new opportunities—not the least of which would be the opportunity to achieve peaceful living in a virgin world, where the old hatreds would slough off and new concepts have a chance to grow.

He wondered where they were, those three who had gone back in time. Dead, perhaps. Run down by a mastodon. Or stalked by tigers. Or maybe done in by warlike tribesmen. No, he kept forgetting there weren't any in that era. Or trapped in time, unable to get back, condemned to exile in an alien time. Or maybe, he thought, just plain disgusted. And he couldn't blame them if they were.

Or maybe—let's be fantastic about this—sneaking in colonists from some place other than the watched Wisconsin farm, building up in actuality the nation they had claimed to be.

They had to get back to the present soon or Project Mastodon would be killed entirely. Already the research program had been halted and if something didn't happen quickly, the watch that was kept on the Wisconsin farm would be called off.

"And if they do that," said the general, "I know just what I'll do."

He got up and strode around the room.

"By God," he said, "I'll show 'em!"

VIII

IT had taken ten full days of back-breaking work to build the pyramid. They'd hauled the rocks from the creek bed half a mile away and had piled them, stone by rolling stone, to the height of a full twelve feet. It took a lot of rocks and a lot of patience, for as the pyramid went up, the base naturally kept broadening out.

But now all was finally ready.

Hudson sat before the burned-out campfire and held his blistered hands before him.

It should work, he thought, better than the logs—and less dangerous.

Grab a handful of sand. Some trickled back between your fingers, but most stayed in your grasp. That was the principle of the pyramid of stones. When—and if—the time machine should work, most of the rocks would go along.

Those that didn't go would simply trickle out and do no harm. There'd be no stress or strain to upset the working of the force-field.

And if the time unit didn't work?

Or if it did?

This was the end of the dream, thought Hudson, no matter how you looked at it.

For even if they did get back to the twentieth century, there would be no money and with the film lost and no other taken to replace it, they'd have no proof they had traveled back beyond the dawn of history—back almost to the dawn of Man.

Although how far you traveled would have no significance. An hour or a million years would be all the same; if you could span the hour, you could span the million years. And if you could go back the million years, it was within your power to go back to the first tick of eternity, the first stir of time across the face of emptiness and nothingness—back to that initial instant when nothing as yet had happened or been planned or thought, when all the vastness of the Universe was a new slate waiting the first chalk stroke of destiny.

Another helicopter would cost thirty thousand dollars—and they didn't even have the money to buy the tractor that they needed to build the stockade.

There was no way to borrow. You couldn't walk into a bank and say you wanted thirty thousand to take a trip back to the Old Stone Age.

You still could go to some industry or some university or the government and if you could persuade them you had something on the ball—why, then, they might put up the cash after cutting themselves in on just about all of the profits. And, naturally, they'd run the show because it was their money and all you had done was the sweating and the bleeding.

"There's one thing that still bothers me," said Cooper, breaking the silence. "We spent a lot of time picking our spot so we'd miss the barn and house and all the other buildings . . ."

"Don't tell me the windmill!" Hudson cried.

"No. I'm pretty sure we're clear of that. But the way I figure, we're right astraddle that barbed-wire fence at the south end of the orchard."

"If you want, we could move the pyramid over twenty feet or so."

Cooper groaned. "I'll take my chances with the fence." Adams got to his feet, the time unit tucked underneath his arm. "Come on, you guys. It's time to go."

They climbed the pyramid gingerly and stood unsteadily at its top.

Adams shifted the unit around, clasped it to his chest.

"Stand around close," he said, "and bend your knees a little. It may be quite a drop."

"Go ahead," said Cooper. "Press the button."

Adams pressed the button.

Nothing happened.

The unit didn't work.

IX

THE chief of Central Intelligence was white-lipped when he finished talking.

"You're sure of your information?" asked the President.

"Mr. President," said the CIA chief, "I've never been more sure of anything in my entire life."

The President looked at the other two who were in the room, a question in his eyes.

The JCS chairman said, "It checks, sir, with everything we know."

"But it's incredible!" the President said.

"They're afraid," said the CIA chief. "They lie awake nights. They've become convinced that we're on the verge of traveling in time. They've tried and failed, but they think we're near success. To their way of thinking, they've got to hit us now or never, because once we actually get time travel, they know their number's up."

"But we dropped Project Mastodon entirely almost three years ago. It's been all of ten years since we stopped the research. It was twenty-five years ago that Hudson——"

"That makes no difference, sir. They're convinced we dropped the project publicly, but went underground with it. That would be the kind of strategy they could understand."

The President picked up a pencil and doodled on a pad.

"Who was that old general," he asked, "the one who raised so much fuss when we dropped the project? I remember I was in the Senate then. He came around to see me."

"Bowers, sir," said the JCS chairman.

"That's right. What became of him?"

"Retired."

"Well, I guess it doesn't make any difference now." He doodled some more and finally said, "Gentlemen, it looks like this is it. How much time did you say we had?"

"Not more than ninety days, sir. Maybe as little as thirty."

The President looked up at the JCS chairman.

"We're as ready," said the chairman, "as we will ever be. We can handle them—I think. There will, of course, be some——"

"I know," said the President.

"Could we bluff?" asked the secretary of state, speaking quietly. "I know it wouldn't stick, but at least we might buy some time."

"You mean hint that we have time travel?"

The secretary nodded.

"It wouldn't work," said the CIA chief tiredly. "If we really had it, there'd be no question then. They'd become exceedingly well-mannered, even neighborly, if they were sure we had it."

"But we haven't got it," said the President gloomily.

X

THE two hunters trudged homeward late in the afternoon, with a deer slung from a pole they carried on their shoulders. Their breath hung visibly in the air as they walked along, for the frost had come and any day now, they knew, there would be snow.

"I'm worried about Wes," said Cooper, breathing heavily. "He's taking this too hard. We got to keep an eye on him."

"Let's take a rest," panted Hudson.

They halted and lowered the deer to the ground.

"He blames himself too much," said Cooper. He wiped his sweaty forehead. "There isn't any need to. All of us walked into this with our eyes wide open."

"He's kidding himself and he knows it, but it gives him something to go on. As long as he can keep busy with all his puttering around, he'll be all right."

"He isn't going to repair the time unit, Chuck."

"I know he isn't. And he knows it, too. He hasn't got the tools or the materials. Back in the workshop, he might have a chance, but here he hasn't."

"It's rough on him."

"It's rough on all of us."

"Yes, but we didn't get a brainstorm that marooned two old friends in this tail end of nowhere. And we can't make him swallow it when we say that it's okay, we don't mind at all."

"That's a lot to swallow, Johnny."

"What's going to happen to us, Chuck?"

"We've got ourselves a place to live and there's lots to eat. Save our ammo for the big game—a lot of eating for each bullet—and trap the smaller animals."

"I'm wondering what will happen when the flour and all the other stuff is gone. We don't have too much of it because we always figured we could bring in more."

"We'll live on meat," said Hudson. "We got bison by the million. The plains Indians lived on them alone. And in the spring, we'll find roots and in the summer berries. And in the fall, we'll harvest a half-dozen kinds of nuts."

"Some day our ammo will be gone, no matter how careful we are with it."

"Bows and arrows. Slingshots. Spears."

"There's a lot of beasts here I wouldn't want to stand up to with nothing but a spear."

"We won't stand up to them. We'll duck when we can and run when we can't duck. Without our guns, we're no lords of creation—not in this place. If we're going to live, we'll have to recognize that fact."

"And if one of us gets sick or breaks a leg or—"

"We'll do the best we can. Nobody lives forever."

But they were talking around the thing that really bothered them, Hudson told himself—each of them afraid to speak the thought aloud.

They'd live, all right, so far as food, shelter and clothing were concerned. And they'd live most of the time in plenty, for this was a fat and open-handed land and a man could make an easy living.

But the big problem—the one they were afraid to talk about—was their emptiness of purpose. To live, they had to find some meaning in a world without society.

A man cast away on a desert isle could always live for hope, but here there was no hope. A Robinson Crusoe was separated from his fellow-humans by, at the most, a few thousand miles. Here they were separated by a hundred and fifty thousand years.

Wes Adams was the lucky one so far. Even playing his thousand-to-one shot, he still held tightly to a purpose, feeble as it might be—the hope that he could repair the time machine.

We don't need to watch him now, thought Hudson. The time we'll have to watch is when he is forced to admit he can't fix the machine.

And both Hudson and Cooper had been kept sane enough, for there had been the cabin to be built and the winter's supply of wood to cut and the hunting to be done.

But then there would come a time when all the chores were finished and there was nothing left to do.

"You ready to go?" asked Cooper.

"Sure. All rested now," said Hudson.

They hoisted the pole to their shoulders and started off again.

Hudson had lain awake nights thinking of it and all the thoughts had been dead ends.

One could write a natural history of the Pleistocene, complete with photographs and sketches, and it would be a pointless thing to do, because no future scientist would ever have a chance to read it.

Or they might labor to build a memorial, a vast pyramid, perhaps, which would carry a message forward across fifteen hundred centuries, snatching with bare hands at a semblance of immortality. But if they did, they would be working against the sure and certain knowledge that it all would come to naught, for they knew in advance that no such pyramid existed in historic time.

Or they might set out to seek contemporary Man, hiking across four thousand miles of wilderness to Bering Strait and over into Asia. And having found contemporary Man cowering in his caves, they might be able to help him immeasurably along the road to his great inheritance. Except that they'd never make it and even if they did, contemporary Man undoubtedly would find some way to do them in and might eat them in the bargain.

They came out of the woods and there was the cabin, just a hundred yards away. It crouched against the hillside above the spring, with the sweep of grassland billowing beyond it to the slate-gray skyline. A trickle of smoke came up from the chimney and they saw the door was open.

"Wes oughtn't to leave it open that way," said Cooper. "No telling when a bear might decide to come visiting."

"Hey, Wes!" yelled Hudson.

But there was no sign of him.

Inside the cabin, a white sheet of paper lay on the table top. Hudson snatched it up and read it, with Cooper at his shoulder.

Dear guys—I don't want to get your hopes up again and have you disappointed. But I think I may have found the trouble. I'm going to try it out. If it doesn't work, I'll come back and burn this note and never say a word. But if you find the note, you'll know it worked and I'll be back to get you. Wes.

Hudson crumpled the note in his hand. "The crazy fool!"

"He's gone off his rocker," Cooper said. "He just thought . . ."

The same thought struck them both and they bolted for the door. At the corner of the cabin, they skidded to a halt and stood there, staring at the ridge above them.

The pyramid of rocks they'd built two months ago was gone!

XI

The crash brought Gen. Leslie Bowers (ret.) up out of bed—about two feet out of bed—old muscles tense, white mustache bristling.

Even at his age, the general was a man of action. He flipped the covers back, swung his feet out to the floor and grabbed the shotgun leaning against the wall.

Muttering, he blundered out of the bedroom, marched across the dining room and charged into the kitchen. There, beside the door, he snapped on the switch that turned on the floodlights. He practically took the door off its hinges getting to the stoop and he stood there bare feet gripping the planks, nightshirt billowing in the wind, the shotgun poised and ready.

"What's going on out there?" he bellowed.

There was a tremendous pile of rocks resting where he'd parked his car. One crumpled fender and a drunken headlight peeped out of the rubble.

A man was clambering carefully down the jumbled stones, making a detour to dodge the battered fender.

The general pulled back the hammer of the gun and fought to control himself.

The man reached the bottom of the pile and turned round to face him. The general saw that he was hugging something tightly to his chest.

"Mister," the general told him, "your explanation better a good one. That was a brand-new car. And this was the first time I was set for a night of sleep since my tooth quit aching."

The man just stood and looked at him.

"Who in thunder are you?" roared the general.

The man walked slowly forward. He stopped at the bottom of the stoop.

"My name is Wesley Adams," he said. "I'm—"

"Wesley Adams!" howled the general. "My God, man, where have you been all these years?"

"Well, I don't imagine you'll believe me, but the fact is . . ."

"We've been waiting for you. For twenty-five long years! Or rather, *I've* been waiting for you. Those other idiots gave up. I've waited right here for you, Adams, for the last three years, ever since they called off the guard."

Adams gulped. "I'm sorry about the car. You see, it was this way . . ."

The general, he saw, was beaming at him fondly.

"I had faith in you," the general said.

He waved the shotgun by way of invitation. "Come on in. I have a call to make."

Adams stumbled up the stairs.

"Move!" the general ordered, shivering. "On the double! You want me to catch my death of cold out here?"

Inside, he fumbled for the lights and turned them on. He laid the shotgun across the kitchen table and picked up the telephone.

"Give me the White House at Washington," he said. "Yes, I said the White House . . . The President? Naturally he's the one I want to talk to . . . Yes, it's all right. He won't mind my calling him."

"Sir," said Adams tentatively.

The general looked up. "What is it, Adams? Go ahead and say it."

"Did you say *twenty-five years?*"

"That's what I said. What were you doing all that time?"

Adams grasped the table and hung on. "But it wasn't . . ."

"Yes," said the general to the operator. "Yes, I'll wa

He held his hand over the receiver and looked in ingly at Adams. "I imagine you'll want the same term before."

"Terms?"

"Sure. Recognition. Point Four Aid. Defense pact."

"I suppose so," Adams said.

"You got these saps across the barrel," the general told him happily. "You can get anything you want. You rate it, too, after what you've done and the bonehead treatment you got—but especially for not selling out."

XII

THE night editor read the bulletin just off the teletype.

"Well, what do you know!" he said. "We just recognized Mastodonia."

He looked at the copy chief.

"Where the hell is Mastodonia?" he asked.

The copy chief shrugged. "Don't ask me. You're the brains in this joint."

"Well, let's get a map for the next edition," said the night editor.

XIII

TABBY, the saber-tooth, dabbed playfully at Cooper with his mighty paw.

Cooper kicked him in the ribs—an equally playful gesture.

Tabby snarled at him.

"Show your teeth at me, will you!" said Cooper. "Raised you from a kitten and that's the gratitude you show. Do it just once more and I'll belt you in the chops."

Tabby lay down blissfully and began to wash his face.

"Some day," warned Hudson, "that cat will miss a meal and that's the day you're it."

"Gentle as a dove," Cooper assured him. "Wouldn't hurt a fly."

"Well, one thing about it, nothing dares to bother us h that monstrosity around."

Best watchdog there ever was. Got to have something uard all this stuff we've got. When Wes gets back, be millionaires. All those furs and ginseng and the y."

"If he gets back."

"He'll be back. Quit your worrying."

"But it's been five years," Hudson protested.

"He'll be back. Something happened, that's all. He's probably working on it right now. Could be that he messed up the time setting when he repaired the unit or it might have been knocked out of kilter when Buster hit the helicopter. That would take a while to fix. I don't worry that he won't come back. What I can't figure out is why did he go and leave us?"

"I've told you," Hudson said. "He was afraid it wouldn't work."

"There wasn't any need to be scared of that. We never would have laughed at him."

"No. Of course we wouldn't."

"Then what *was* he scared of?" Cooper asked.

"If the unit failed and we knew it failed, Wes was afraid we'd try to make him see how hopeless and insane it was. And he knew we'd probably convince him and then all his hope would be gone. And he wanted to hang onto that, Johnny. He wanted to hang onto his hope even when there wasn't any left."

"That doesn't matter now," said Cooper. "What counts is that he'll come back. I can feel it in my bones."

And here's another case, thought Hudson, of hope begging to be allowed to go on living.

God, he thought, I wish I could be that blind!

"Wes is working on it right now," said Cooper confidently.

XIV

HE was. Not he alone, but a thousand others, working desperately, knowing that the time was short, working not alone for two men trapped in time, but for the peace they all had dreamed about—that the whole world had yearned for through the ages.

For to be of any use, it was imperative that they co zero in the time machines they meant to build as an leryman would zero in a battery of guns, that each machine would take its occupants to the same insta the past, that their operation would extend over the s period of time, to the exact second.

It was a problem of control and calibration—starting with a prototype that was calibrated, as its finest adjustment, for jumps of 50,000 years.

Project Mastodon was finally under way.

SCIENCE FICTION AND FANTASY
FROM AVON BOOKS

- [ ] **All My Sins Remembered**   Joe Haldeman 39321 $1.95
- [ ] **All Flesh Is Grass**   Clifford D. Simak   39933 $1.75
- [ ] **Behold the Man**   Michael Moorcock   39982 $1.50
- [ ] **Cities In Flight**   James Blish   41616 $2.50
- [ ] **Cryptozoic**   Brian Aldiss   33415 $1.25
- [ ] **Forgotten Beasts of Eld**   Patricia McKillip 42523 $1.75
- [ ] **The Investigation**   Stanislaw Lem   29314 $1.50
- [ ] **The Lathe of Heaven**   Ursula K. LeGuin   38299 $1.50
- [ ] **Lord of Light**   Roger Zelazny   33985 $1.75
- [ ] **Macroscope**   Piers Anthony   45690 $2.25
- [ ] **Memoirs Found In A Bathtub**
      Stanislaw Lem   29959 $1.50
- [ ] **Mindbridge**   Joe Haldeman   33605 $1.95
- [ ] **Mind of My Mind**   Octavia E. Butler   40972 $1.75
- [ ] **Moon Pool**   A. Merritt   39370 $1.75
- [ ] **Omnivere**   Piers Anthony   40527 $1.75
- [ ] **Orn**   Piers Anthony   40964 $1.7
- [ ] **Ox**   Piers Anthony   41392 $1.7
- [ ] **Pilgrimage**   Zenna Henderson   36681 $1
- [ ] **Rogue Moon**   Algis Budrys   38950
- [ ] **Song for Lya and Other Stories**
      George R. Martin   27581
- [ ] **Starship**   Brian W. Aldiss   22588
- [ ] **Sword of the Demon**   Richard A. Lupoff   37911 $1.7
- [ ] **334**   Thomas M. Disch   42630 $2.25

Available at better bookstores everywhere, or order direct from the publisher.